THE MYSTIC ROSE

THE MYSTIC ROSE

THE CELTIC CRUSADES: BOOK III

Stephen R. Lawhead

An Imprint of HarperCollins Publishers

ZONDERVAN

EOS

EOS
An Imprint of HarperCollins *Publishers*
10 East 53rd Street
New York, New York 10022-5299

Copyright © 2001 by Stephen R. Lawhead
ISBN: 0-06-105031-8

Library of Congress Cataloging-in-Publication Data

Lawhead, Stephen R.
The mystic rose / Stephen R. Lawhead.
p. cm.—(The Celtic crusades ; bk. 3)
ISBN 0-06-105031-8
1. Scotland—History—1057-1603—Fiction. 2. Scots—Spain, Northern—Fiction.
3. Christian antiquities—Fiction. 4. Spain, Northern—Fiction. 5. Young women—Fiction.
6. Grail—Fiction. I. Title.
PS3562.A865 M97 2001
813'.54—dc21
2001033523

First Eos hardcover printing: October 2001
First U.S. edition co-published by Eos and ZondervanPublishingHouse

Printed in the U.S.A.

FIRST EDITION

10 9 8 7 6 5 4 3 2 1

www.eosbooks.com

For
Jeff and Susie and Hailey

THE MYSTIC ROSE

PART I

August 27, 1916: Edinburgh, Scotland

A young woman of my acquaintance saw a ghost. Ordinarily, I would not have given such a melodramatic triviality even passing notice, save for two pertinent facts. One: the ghost appeared in broad daylight at the same country house where my wife and I had been staying that very weekend, and two: the ghost was Pemberton.

What made this eerie curiosity more peculiar still was the fact that the specter materialized in the room we would have occupied if my wife had not come down with a cold earlier that day, thus necessitating our premature departure. We returned to the city so she might rest more comfortably in her own bed that night. Otherwise, we would surely have witnessed the apparition ourselves, and spared Miss Euphemia Gillespie, a young lady of twenty, and the daughter of one of the other guests who was staying that weekend, with whom my wife and I were reasonably well acquainted.

Rumor had it that Miss Gillespie was woken from her nap by a strange sound to find a tall, gaunt figure standing at the foot of her bed. Dressed in a dark suit of clothes, and holding his hat in his hands, he was, she reported, soaking wet, ". . . as if he had been caught in a fearsome shower without his brolly." The young lady took fright and issued a cry of surprise, whereupon the apparition introduced himself, apologized, and promptly vanished with a bewildered expression on his face.

Be that as it may, the full significance of this event did not truly strike home until word of Pemberton's death reached us two days later, along with news of the loss of RMS *Lusitania* in the early afternoon of May 7, 1915, roughly the time when his ghost was seen by Miss Gillespie.

This ghostly manifestation might have made a greater stir if it had not been so completely overshadowed by the sinking of the *Lusitania*. The daily broadsheets were full of venomous outrage at this latest atrocity: a luxury liner torpedoed without warning by a German U-boat, taking almost twelve hundred civilian souls to a watery grave. The *Edinburgh Evening Herald* published a list of the missing drawn from the ship's manifest. Among those who had embarked on the trip to Liverpool from New York were a few score Americans; the rest were Europeans of several nationalities. Pemberton's name was on the list. Thus, while the rest of the world contemplated the fact that the war had taken a sinister turn, I mourned the death of a very dear and close friend.

I pondered the meaning of the spectral portent and, no doubt, would have given the matter its due consideration, but I was very soon distracted by the precipitous and worrying decline in my wife's health. The chill which she contracted that day in the country had grown steadily worse, and by the time the doctor diagnosed influenza, it was too late. My dearest, beloved helpmate and partner of forty-four years passed away two days later.

Within the space of a week, I had lost the two most important people in my life. I was bereft and broken. Where I might have expected to rely upon one to help me through the death of the other, I had neither. Both were gone, and I was left behind to struggle on as best I could. The children were some comfort, it is true; but they had busy lives of their own, and were soon called back to their affairs, leaving me to flounder in quiet misery.

Following my dear Caitlin's funeral, I attempted to resume my work at the firm, but quickly found that there was no joy or solace to be had in the to-ing and fro-ing of the legal trade. In truth, I had for some time been deriving little pleasure from the practice of my profession. Now, however, I found the whole enterprise so grindingly tedious that it was all I could do to maintain civil relations with my younger colleagues. I endured the daily agony for three months and then retired.

All through this time, I had been wondering over the future of the Brotherhood. I daily expected the summons, but it never came. I suppose I began to feel as if the death of our leader had dealt a killing blow to our clandestine organization—in my sorry state of mind it would not have surprised me greatly, I confess. However, the wheels of our Order may grind slowly, but they grind exceedingly fine.

Owing to the unfortunate circumstances surrounding Pemberton's death, we of the Inner Circle could not officially recognize our leader's demise until certain protocols had been observed. I understand that now; I didn't then.

Also, owing to the war, Evans—our esteemed Second Principal—adopted a cautious and conservative policy. It would not have been the first time a passenger listed as missing at sea later turned up alive and well. So, we waited until there could be no doubt, and prepared to mourn the death of our inestimable leader in our own way.

Meanwhile, I became a man of enforced leisure. With plenty of idle hours on my hands, I filled my time with little tasks and such chores as I deemed needful or pleasing, and kept an increasingly anxious eye out for the daily post—waiting for the summons I knew must come at some point.

Spring passed into summer, and the days lengthened. News of the war in Europe—the Great War, the newspapers were calling it—grew more and more dismal by degrees. I forced myself to read the accounts, and was sickened by them; the more so, I suppose, because my own life was sliding into a season of desperate unhappiness. I naturally found myself pondering the recent tragic events.

Time and again, I wrapped myself in melancholy, recalling some happy time I had shared with my wife, and brooding ruefully on the cruelty of time and the manifold weaknesses of the human frame. Still, I did not descend entirely into the Slough of Despond. I reviewed often Pemberton's attempt to communicate with me on the threshold of Eternity, as it were. That was how I came to see it. That fateful weekend in the country had been planned for some time—part of a confirmation celebration for the young son of a mutual acquaintance—and Pemberton knew about it. Indeed, I had been surprised that he was acquainted with the family in question, and we discussed it. If Caitlin had not become ill, we would have been in that room to see him. Thus, he had appeared in the place he reckoned I was to be found.

But why me? Why not Genotti, De Cardou, Zaccaria, or Kutch? Why not Evans, our number two? What had he been trying to tell *me*?

The question gnawed at me until I decided one day to go and interview Miss Gillespie in the hope of finding an answer. I wrote to her and established a place and time to meet: Kerwood's Tea House on Castle

Street, a quiet place where we could discuss the matter discreetly. My guest turned out to be one of those modern emancipated young women for whom conventions of dress and manner are dictated by personal taste and not by tradition or propriety or, indeed, modesty. She appeared wearing one of those shimmery sheaths with little rows of tassels up and down its short, shapeless length, complete with spangled yellow hat and gloves. Confident, educated, and indifferent to matters domestic, she proudly disclosed that she was soon to take up training as a nurse in order to assist in the war effort.

Despite her deliberately provocative ways, I soon discovered in Miss Gillespie a competent, capable, level-headed young person, not at all given to flights of fancy. She also had a fine sense of humor—as I quickly learned, once the tea had come and we had settled into the discussion which was the purpose of my visit. "To tell the truth, Mr. Murray, I do not know which of us was the more frightened. If you could have seen the startled look he gave me. The poor chap—if he had been a haddock plucked from the sea and tossed into the middle of Waverley Station, he could not have looked more surprised. He was the most polite ghost you could imagine."

"Oh, I can well imagine."

She looked at me over the rim of her cup. "Daddy told me you knew the gentleman in question."

"I knew him quite well, and I can tell you that finding himself in a lady's bedroom would certainly have given him cause for alarm."

She smiled, her pleasant round face lighting the dullness of a rainy Saturday afternoon. "I really didn't mean to startle him. But waking up and seeing him standing there at the foot of the bed, all tall and rumpled, and dripping like a drainpipe—well, I'm afraid I shouted at him terribly."

"You were frightened, I expect."

"I was at first. But that passed in an instant for I could see he was perplexed."

"Perplexed?"

"Yes," she said, nodding thoughtfully, "that is the word. He didn't seem to know what he was about. You know how it is—you'll be going on about your business, absorbed in your thoughts, and then you look up and . . . where am I?" She laughed. "Happens to me all the time—don't tell me it's never happened to you."

"It has been known," I confessed, enjoying the pleasure of her lively company. "I once found myself in the Royal Museum with no recollection of how I'd got there."

"Well, that's how he looked to me—like he didn't quite know where he was or how he got there."

"Did you know he was aboard the ship that was sunk by the German torpedo?"

"So Daddy told me." She shook her head gravely, and was silent for a moment, then said, "That would explain the dripping water."

"Did he say anything? Did he make any sound at all?"

"He did indeed. He said he was sorry for disturbing me; he told me his name and begged my pardon. Then he wished me a good day—as least that's what I thought he said. I can't be at all certain."

"Why is that?"

"He was already vanishing by then, you see. He didn't go all of a snap!" She clicked her fingers. "He began to fade away—like when a cloud passes over the sun and the day goes dim."

"I see. Well . . ." I regarded the young woman. As much as I appreciated the information, it carried me no closer to the solution of the mystery which so exercised my mind.

A frown of concentration appeared on Miss Gillespie's face. "There was one more thing."

"Yes?" I leaned forward, eager to pounce on the smallest scrap of information.

"I had quite forgotten until just now," she said slowly, as if trying to remember precisely. "Just before he faded away completely, he looked at me and said—if I recall it correctly—something like: 'The pain is swallowed in peace, and grief in glory.' "

The message was obscure. It made no sense to me, and of all the things he might have wished to say, I could not think this had any importance whatsoever. "Forgive me, Miss Gillespie, but you're certain that is what he said?"

She shook her head vehemently. "No, Mr. Murray, I'm not at all sure. It was very faint and by then he had mostly vanished. Nevertheless, that's what it sounded like to me." She regarded me with a hopeful expression. "Does it mean anything to you?"

"I fear not," I sighed. "But perhaps something will yet come of it." We finished our tea then, and made our farewells. "I thank you, my

7

dear, for taking the time to speak to an old busybody," I said as we parted. "Please, give my kind regards to your parents."

The rain had stopped and so I walked with her to the corner, whereupon we went our separate ways. As the day had come clear and bright, and I had nothing pressing for my attention, I decided to take a turn or two around the park. I walked to the little square just down the street, and entered by the iron gate. A few children had come out to play; their voices jiggled as they skipped and ran to the accompaniment of a barking terrier. A young mother pushed her baby in a large black pram, stopping every now and then to tuck up the blankets, all the while doting on the face of her infant.

I strolled awhile along the fresh rain-washed gravel paths, taking the air and watching the clouds as they broke apart and drifted eastward toward the North Sea. After a time, I sat down on a bench and dozed—only a moment, it seemed to me—but I awoke to find the lowering sun had disappeared and a wind was blowing stiff and chill out of the west where darker, more ominous clouds had gathered.

They were, it seemed to me, clouds of war, shadows of the great evil rushing eastward to feed and strengthen the darkness already rampant there. The political quagmire of the European noble houses was inexorably sucking one government and power after another deeper and deeper into the ruinous morass. The fighting, which had now spread on many fronts, grew continually sharper, more brutal and vicious by the day. As yet there was no end in sight.

The splendor of the summer day was, I reflected, like our own lives upon the earth: short-lived, and bounded by darkness on every side.

It was in this somber mood that I turned my steps toward home. By the time I reached the house, the weather had turned foul. I unlocked the front door just as the first drops of rain spattered onto the pavement behind me.

I quickly stepped inside and, as I turned to close the door behind me, my eye fell upon a small, buff-colored envelope lying on the mat. I turned it over and saw my name neatly lettered in black ink. My heart began beating faster as I opened the envelope and saw the single word: *Tonight.*

ONE

At the pronouncement of the Patriarch of Constantinople, the bride was carried from the cathedral on a silver bed draped with cloth of gold. Alone on that wide and glittering expanse, she looked frightened, cowed, and far younger than her thirteen years. Before her went a hundred black-robed monks chanting the *Gloria*, followed by the stiffly dignified metropolitan in his high-crowned, ruby and ivory-beaded red satin hat; the imposing prelate carried a large silver frame containing the Sacred Mandelion: the cloth bearing the indelible image of Christ, one of Byzantium's most highly valued treasures.

Veiled in delicate silver netting from the top of her golden wedding crown to the tips of her white-stockinged toes, the young woman's slender form shimmered in the light of ten thousand candles as she passed through the standing congregation, borne aloft on the shoulders of eight black Ethiopians in yellow tunics. The noble groom followed his new bride on a white horse, leading a dove-gray mare; both animals were caparisoned in scarlet edged with silver, and both wore white ostrich plumes attached to their silver headpieces.

From her place in the gallery high above the floor, Caitríona, mute with amazement, gazed upon the dazzling spectacle and knew she had never seen anything half so magnificent, and probably never would again. Everything, from the golden crowns to the purple clouds of incense drifting like the mists of Heaven, worked an enchantment of wealth and power that left her breathless.

When the wedding procession passed beneath the upper gallery of Aÿia Sophia, all the onlookers rushed to the opposite side and leaned over the marble balustrade to see the towering iron-clad doors of the great church flung open wide and the newly married couple depart on billows of pink rose petals. The crowds which had been waiting outside the church since dawn roared with delight to see the royal party as it began the parade through the city to the Triconchos Palace where the official marriage banquet would be held amidst the marble columns of the Hall of Pearl.

"Well, dear heart," said Duncan to his daughter, "what did you think of that?"

"You were very brave to bring me here," Caitríona replied. "I have always admired that in you, Papa."

"Indulgent, perhaps. But why do you say brave?"

"Because," she said, her lips curving with sardonic glee, "now that I have seen how a lowly niece of the emperor is fêted on her wedding day, I shall accept nothing less on mine."

Duncan clucked his tongue, and said, "If I thought there was even the slightest chance you would deign to marry, I swear this cathedral would witness a ceremony far more grand than that which just took place."

"Bring on the king and golden bed," snipped Cait. "Let us get it done here and now."

"Is it too much for a father to hope the treasure of his life might find a little happiness in wedlock?"

"And ensure the continuance of the noble line, yes." She frowned dangerously. "Look at me, Papa, and tell me the truth: who in their right mind would want to marry me?"

"Any number of men, dear heart, given half a chance."

"Papa!"

"There are fairer women perhaps," allowed Duncan delicately. "But the beauty of the soul far outlasts the charms of the flesh."

"Show me a man enraptured with the beauty of the soul, and I will show you a eunuch."

Duncan sighed. His daughter's refusal to consider a suitable marriage had long been a thorn in his flesh. While Cait herself imagined it was her lack of loveliness which kept acceptable men at a distance, her father strongly suspected it was the quick, dagger-like edge of her tongue. Why, oh why, did she have to be so hardheaded and immovable? It was, he realized, the family curse.

"Poor, poor Papa," she cooed, sliding her arm through his. "Lumbered with a thankless wench of a daughter who makes his life a dreary cavalcade of suffering from dawn to dusk. Oh, will this unendurable misery never cease?"

Leaving their places at the marble rail, they began following the other nobles from the gallery. Once in the outer corridor, they entered the slow-moving stream of people shuffling toward the wide staircase leading down to the main floor of the cathedral. "I suppose," mused Duncan philosophically, "there are worse things than having a daughter who thinks she is King of Caithness."

Cait laughed. The sound delighted her father, who heard in it the echo of her mother's voice. Alas, that was all she had inherited from her mother; Caitríona's green eyes and long black hair were hers alone. Tall and long-limbed like her forefathers—her stature made the vaunted Grecian beauties seem scrawny and underfed—she was a fully fleshed woman whose imposing presence easily dominated the more demure members of her sex.

Few men could match his wilful daughter for strength of resolve and cold, clear-eyed reckoning, he admitted to himself; fewer still were keen to try. The ancestral blood which flowed through her veins contained too much wild Celt, and too little refined nobility. It was, he knew, often remarked that she was more at ease with a spear in her hand than a spindle—but what of that? When Cait passed by, one caught the scent of sea air and rain-misted heather; the bracing, blustery wind off the highland moors was in her hair and in her impetuous, exuberant nature.

Cait herself was not unaware of what people thought of her. But if other women were more comfortable in costly silks and satins than rough boots and riding trews, more content to sit moon-eyed beside the hearthfire with their needlework than hunt with the hounds, so be it. To Cait's way of thinking, these shrinking, swooning sisters had no one to blame for their drab and insipid lives but themselves.

"Papa, were you and Sydoni married here?" she asked, gazing up at a glittering mosaic of the holy family, resplendent in purple robes and gilded halos.

"Here—in Ayia Sophia?" Duncan glanced at her to see if she were teasing him, but saw that she was in earnest. "No, not here. Such splendor was far beyond our scanty means." He paused, remembering. "Also, I seem to remember that to be married in the cathedral required a ten-month delay. I fear neither one of us would have survived the wait—the fires of passion would have consumed us to cinders."

Cait pretended shock. "Presented with such a lackluster jewel of virtue as yourself, dear Papa, I am amazed they allowed you to be married at all. So, where *did* you find a priest to proclaim the banns?"

"We were married at the Church of Christ Pantocrator. Padraig knew of it, but then he knows everything. As it happens, it is not far from here. We might go there this evening, if you would like to see it."

"If *I* would like . . ." she chided. "It is the sole and entire purpose of this journey to drag your dutiful daughters over every last footprint of your great pilgrimage, and well you know it."

Duncan took her hand from his arm and kissed it. "You are a very treasure, my light."

"I wish Sydoni were here," Cait said. "Padraig, too. I am certain they would have a few tales to tell."

"Oh, indeed," agreed Duncan somewhat wistfully, remembering the day more than twenty years ago when he and Sydoni had been married in this city, and that night had celebrated their union. "Well," he continued after a moment, pressing his daughter's hand, "we must enjoy our brief stay all the more for their sake, and hear what they have to say when we get home."

They reached the staircase and started down, following the crowds, and eventually joined the throng in the huge hall-like vestibule just as the royal family emerged from the sanctuary. Imperial Varangian guards moved with silent efficiency into the crowd and swiftly formed a double rank stretching from the sanctuary entrance to the outer doors, whereupon they turned and stood shoulder-to-shoulder behind their gold-trimmed shields, ceremonial lances upraised; the blades of their spears were gold, and dressed with scarlet pennons, but sharp nonetheless. Once this protective corridor was established, other guardsmen marched through it, clearing the crowds before them.

"The emperor and empress!" said Cait. In spite of herself, she was enjoying the imperial display.

"Go, my dear," he said, urging her forward. "I will wait here."

Cait released his arm and darted forward. She threaded her way through the gathered horde and peered over the shoulders of the Varangians to catch a glimpse of Emperor Manuel and Empress Irene, and their sallow-faced daughter, as they swept from the church. They were followed by the Patriarch and the Archbishop, and a long triple row of priests holding lanterns and chanting, their voices rising and falling in rhythmic waves.

As soon as the priests passed, the twin ranks of imperial bodyguards took three paces toward one another, turned, and marched from the church. Instantly, there was a rush behind them as the congregation surged for the door to see the emperor flinging handfuls of gold coins to the crowds. Caitríona was momentarily caught up in the flow and quickly found herself outside the church. The royal party moved on, the clamoring populace with them, and Cait turned against the stream to make her way back inside the church to rejoin her father.

Darting and sliding between close-packed clumps and clusters of people hurrying to follow the procession, she made for the place where she had left him—but he was no longer in the vestibule. She paused and looked around, but could not see Duncan anywhere, and was at the point of going back outside to look for him when she caught sight of him in the dimly lit sanctuary. Lord Duncan was standing next to one of the gigantic porphyry columns so as to be out of the way of the departing masses.

Cait forced her way through the streaming multitude at the door, and struggled to reach her father. As she came nearer, she saw that he was talking to someone; she could not see who it might be, for the stranger was hidden behind the column; but from the expression on her father's face the conversation was far from cordial.

Duncan's brow was lowered and his jaw was tight, his chin thrust forward defiantly. His eyes glinted cold fire which, although fearsome, was not easily kindled.

Indeed, Caitríona had seen him this way but once in her life: when an uninvited party of Danes, after setting up camp on the beach below the stronghold, had stolen, butchered, and roasted three good breeding cows. When Duncan found out about it, he marched down and confronted them in their camp. The roistering Danes got off lightly, she thought, with an apology and double payment for the cows. He was not facing marauding Danes now, but the expression was the same—his noble features were alight with righteous wrath.

The sudden strangeness of the situation sent a thrill of alarm through her. Cait felt her scalp tingle with dread anticipation and her stomach tighten into a hard knot. She put her head down and forced her way through the oncoming stream of people. Drawing near, she called her father's name. He heard and turned his head. At that instant another man's face moved out from the shadow of the pillar and Cait saw it clearly: he was bearded, the beard gray but neatly trimmed—in contrast to the stark white hair of his head, which was long and brushed into an untidy nimbus around his high-domed forehead. A long, thin scar puckered the flesh above his left eye, lifting the eyebrow into an expression of scorn which, married to the ferocity glaring from his dark eyes, gave him an aspect of ruthless malice that chilled Cait to the bone.

Then, as if having seen the young woman hastening toward them, the bearded man moved behind the pillar again. She saw the glint of his bared teeth as he slid back into the shadows. Duncan turned toward him and the two continued their conversation.

Cait sidestepped one group of noisy celebrants, and shoved her way through another, reaching her father at last. By the time she rejoined him, the bearded man was gone. She looked where he had been standing and caught the fleeting glimmer of a long white surcoat with a red cross on the back as it disappeared into the crowd.

"Papa, who was that?" she asked, stepping in beside him.

Duncan, staring fixedly ahead, seemed to be concentrating most intently on her question. He strained for the words, which caught in his throat.

"Papa?" Her voice became urgent.

Duncan turned toward his daughter and forced a sickly smile, his face suddenly gray. He lost his balance and stretched his hand to the polished column to steady himself.

Instinctively, Cait stepped in to bear him up. "What is wrong?" Even as she spoke the words, she glanced down at his other hand, clutched at his side just below the ribs where a ribbon of blood seeped between his fingers.

"Papa!"

"Cait . . ." he replied absently. "He . . . he . . ." Duncan looked down at his wound and shuddered. "Ah! For the love of God!" he said, his teeth clenched against the pain. "Ah!"

"Here—" She slid her arm under his and took his weight onto herself. "Sit down and rest." Looking up she cried out, "Help me! Someone, please! He is wounded!"

But Cait's cry was swallowed in the general crush and confusion, and the nearer passersby, if they heard, paid no attention. She eased him to the floor, and sat him down on the plinth which formed a step at the base of the column. He slumped back, resting his shoulders against the purple stone. "Do not move," she told him. "I will get help."

She made to dart away, but he seized her wrist and held tight. "No, Cait," he said, his voice shaking. "Stay."

"I will be back before you know it." She stood, but he held her tight in his grasp.

"No time, my light. Stay with me."

"Father, please," she said. "Let me find help." She removed his hand and started off once more.

"Caitríona, no!" he said, his voice recovering something of its former strength. "There is only one who can help me now, and I will soon stand before him. Stay and pray with me."

She turned and knelt beside him, slipping her arm behind his head, fighting down the panic clawing at her heart and blurring her vision.

"Listen, Cait. I love you very much."

"Oh, Papa, I love you, too."

"Then promise me you will not seek to avenge me," he said, cold sweat beading on his ashen face. "Let it end here."

"I do not understand. Who was that man? Why did he do this?"

"Promise me!" he insisted, raising himself up again. The effort brought a spasm of pain which made him cough. Blood trickled from the corner of his mouth. "I know you, Cait. Promise you will not avenge me."

"Very well, I promise." She dabbed away the blood with the hem of her blue satin mantle. "Now, lie back and rest a little."

Having received her promise, Duncan slumped against the base of the column. "Good," he sighed, settling back against the cool stone. "Good."

Cait put her hand to her father's cheek. "Please, Papa," she persisted, "I need to understand."

"Pray for me, Caitríona." He closed his eyes.

"I will—every day. But I need to understand."

"Renaud . . ." He coughed again; more blood came up, staining his teeth and chin. She wiped it away.

At first the name meant nothing. Then the memory surfaced. "Re-

15

naud de Bracineaux? The Templar?" She searched her father's face for a clue to the meaning of this mystery. "Why?"

He opened his eyes and tried to smile. "Poor Alethea . . . I am glad she is not here. She is not as strong as you . . ." he coughed, and slumped further down, ". . . take care of her, Cait."

"Hush." She put her cheek next to his and held him tight, as if to hold off death through the strength of her embrace. "I will watch over her."

He raised his hand and cupped his palm to her chin, holding her face so that he could see her. His eyes were hazy, and his voice wavered. "Take my heart . . ." He gulped air, his voice tight with pain, and forced out the words. "Take it home. Tell Padraig . . . bury it in the church. He will know what to do."

Unable to speak, Caitríona simply nodded.

"Sydoni," he rasped. "Tell Sydoni . . . my last thought was of her." His voice had grown suddenly soft and tenuous as spider-silk. "Tell her I . . . thanking God . . ."

"I will tell her." The tears spilled freely down her cheeks and onto her father's hand.

Duncan raised his hand and kissed the tear with blood-stained lips; Caitríona clutched his hand and pressed it to her cheek. "Dear heart," he said, his voice a fading whisper. "I go."

He slumped back against the column base with a sigh. In that last exhalation, Cait thought she saw a light flicker briefly in his eyes and heard him say her mother's name . . . "Ah, Rhona . . ."—the most delicate ghost of an utterance, a word spoken from the threshold of another world, and he was gone.

TWO

The dull iron glow of a new day was staining the dark waters of the Bosphorus by the time Cait finally returned to the ship. She stood at the rail and stared with red-rimmed eyes at the dirty yellow gleam burning through the gray cloudwrack like a hot poker singeing through sackcloth. After a time, she turned her unblinking gaze to the famed seven hills of Byzantium, all hung in purple mist and smoke, as if in mourning for her murdered father.

She heard a footfall on the deck behind her, but did not turn.

"Good morrow, my lady." The voice was that of Haemur, their aged Orkneyjar pilot, a loyal and trusted servant, and the one person in the world Duncan would allow to captain *Persephone* to the Holy Land. A skilled but uneducated man, Haemur spoke only Norse, peppered with a smattering of Gaelic. "When you did not return last night, I was worried that—"

She turned and he saw the look on her face. His hands fluttered like distracted birds. "Lady Caitríona," he gasped, "what has happened?" Then, as if realizing for the first time that she was alone, he said, "But where is my lord Duncan?"

"He is gone, Haemur," she replied in a voice as brittle and empty as a dry husk.

The seaman gazed uncomprehendingly at the young woman. "He is coming later perhaps?"

"No." She shook her head. "He is dead, Haemur."

The elderly sailor rubbed his red face with a rough hand. Tears came to his pale blue eyes. "I see." He turned away abruptly, and started toward his bench at the stern, dabbing at his eyes. She called him back.

"I am sorry, Haemur." She moved to him and, taking one of his thick-calloused hands in both her own, explained what had taken place at the cathedral. It was quickly and simply told, and then she said, "The body will be buried later today, and we will attend the rites. Right now, I want you to wake your men and move the ship."

He regarded her without understanding. "Dead? Are you certain?"

"Yes," she confirmed. "We must move the ship at once. I have arranged for a berth in the Bucoleon Harbor—the one below the light-house."

"The Greek harbor—where the grain ships call."

"The same. They will not think to look for us there."

"Who?" he asked.

But she was already moving away. "I am going to my quarters now to wash and change my clothes."

She descended the wooden steps into the hold, which was divided into three sections. The first, near the bow, was shared by the two crew-men who helped Haemur; the middle, and largest section, was the hold proper where all the supplies, provisions, and dry goods for the voyage were kept; the third section, in the stern, was divided into two small compartments for the passengers. Cait and Alethea shared one, and the other belonged to Duncan.

Cait put her hand to the wooden latch and quietly opened the door. Pale dawnlight showed in the small round window over the boxed pallet where Alethea lay sleeping. Cait sat down on the edge of the bed and regarded the young woman. Fifteen years old—although she looked, and often behaved, as one younger than her years—she had Sydoni's thick, dark lustrous hair, and smooth tawny skin. Nor did the similarity between the young lady and her mother end there. Alethea was slender and lanky, with a high smooth brow and large dark eyes.

Cait was nearly twelve years old when Alethea was born; and though at first she thought a baby sister a fine and wonderful thing, the joy quickly palled. Alethea considered Cait too harsh and strict on her, al-ways nagging and chastising. In Caitríona's forthright opinion, Thea was flighty and inconsiderate, too easily taken with whims and capri-cious fancies, and all-too-often indulged when she should have been corrected. Indeed, Alethea should not have been aboard the ship in the first place—except that when she found out that Duncan was planning to take Caitríona to the Holy Land to see all the places he and Padraig had visited during his long pilgrimage, the younger girl had moped and whined and sulked until her father relented and agreed to take her, too.

Cait sat listening to Alethea's deep, regular breathing for a moment, and then reached out and rested her hand on the girl's shoulder where the thin coverlet had slipped aside. The skin was warm beneath her palm, and Thea's face appeared so peaceful and content, Cait was loath to disturb her rest. *No,* she thought, *let her enjoy the last serenity she will know for a very long time. The grieving will come soon enough.*

She rose, moved silently to the sea chest at the foot of her bed, opened it, withdrew a clean mantle and small-clothes, and then left Alethea to her rest. She crossed the narrow companionway to her father's quarters and went inside. She stood for a long while, just looking at the room, but apart from the sea chest and a pair of boots in one corner, there was nothing of Duncan to be seen.

Cait lifted a large, shallow brass bowl from its peg and placed it on the sea chest, then filled it with water from the jar. She undressed then, and washed herself over the basin, letting the cool water sluice away the previous day's sweat and anguish and tears. The water felt good on her skin and she wished the bowl was big enough for her to submerge her entire body—like the great enamelled basins of the caliph's *hareem* her father had told her about once long ago.

When she finished, she dried herself with the linen cloth from the peg, and then, succumbing to her exhaustion at last, lay down in her father's bed. She molded herself to the depression left by his body in the soft pine shavings of the box pallet, and closed her eyes on the grim nightmare of the day that had been.

But there was neither rest nor sleep, nor less yet any respite from the outrageous succession of misfortune that she had suffered in all that followed her father's death. To recall the stinging injustice of her predicament made her blood seethe.

For, presented with a corpse in their cathedral, the ecclesiastical authorities had fetched the *scholae*. When questioned by the leader of the troop, Cait had named the killer, and was immediately brought before a court *magister*, who listened politely to her story, and then conducted her forthwith to the Consul of Constantinople, a blunt, practical man with a short-shaved head of bristly gray hair. He sat in a throne-like chair beside a table prepared for his dinner, and listened while she repeated her charge; she told him everything, just as it happened—only to be informed that it was not remotely possible.

"You must be mistaken, woman," the consul said frankly; his Greek, like that of the others she had spoken to, although different, could be understood readily enough. "Renaud de Bracineaux is Grand Commander of the Templar Knights of Jerusalem. He is a priest of the church, a protector of pilgrims, upholder of the faith."

"That may be," Cait allowed. "But I saw him with my own eyes. And my father named him before he died."

"So you say. It is a pity your father died without repeating his accusation to anyone else—one of the priests, perhaps." He glanced at the table, and stretched his hand toward his cup. "I am sorry."

"You mean that you intend to do nothing." She felt as if the ground were crumbling beneath her and she was plunging into a dark, bottomless pit, helpless to prevent it.

The consul gave her a thin, dismissive smile. "Even if what you allege was in some way possible, I could not take action against this man based solely on what you have told me."

"Because I am a woman."

"Because you are *alone.*" The consul frowned, and then sighed with exasperated pity. "Truly, I am sorry. But the law is clear: without the corroboration of at least two witnesses, I can do nothing."

"The church was full of people," Caitríona pointed out. "Someone must have seen what happened."

"Where are these people?" the consul inquired, lifting a hand to the empty chamber. "Where are they to be found?"

"Do not mock me, sir!" snarled Cait, her voice growing cold. "I know what I saw and there was no mistake." Taking up the skirt of her mantle she spread it before her. "This!" she said, shaking the cloth angrily. "This is my father's blood I am wearing. De Bracineaux stabbed him. If you will not do anything about it, then *I* will."

"I urge you to reconsider." Angry now, the consul rose from his chair. "Renaud de Bracineaux is a man of great esteem and even greater renown—a friend and favorite of both King Baldwin of Jerusalem and Emperor Manuel. He is a guest of the Basileus, and I would not presume to trouble him on the basis of the scant evidence you provide. Furthermore, I warn you: should you persist in repeating this accusation, you will certainly be dealt with most harshly."

"Oh, I am through with accusations," Cait informed the official icily. "I may accept your judgment, but I will not suffer the injustice."

With that, she turned her back and strode from the room. She wept in the street as she walked back to the cathedral, and then again as she sat with her dear father's body and waited for a hired cart to come and collect his remains, then to be taken to the church where he and Sydoni had been married. Following a short negotiation, an agreement was reached where, for a generous gift to the monastery, the brothers were persuaded to allow Duncan to be buried on holy ground—and according to Caitríona's specific conditions.

She left the body to be prepared for burial, and hired a chair and asked to be taken to Bucoleon Harbor; after waiting a considerable time, she had struck a bargain with the overbusy harbor master allowing her two days' berthing—again for a tidy fee.

Daylight was fading by that time, and so she returned to the Church of Christ Pantocrator to pray and wait with her father's corpse, which had been washed and wrapped in a clean linen shroud, and placed on a low board before the altar. She stayed through the night, lighting candles and listening to the monks chant the prayers for the dead. When the watch service was over, she left the church, waking the bearers she had paid to wait for her outside. They carried her through the still-dark streets down to the Venetian Quay where she roused a boatman who had ferried her to the waiting ship as day broke in the east.

Now she lay and listened to the sounds of the crewmen clumping around on deck as they set about moving the ship. She remembered the day Duncan had hired the hands—two brothers from Hordaland in West Norway. The elder, called Otti, was a large, hard-working fellow, rendered simple by a fearsome blow on the skull which, although cutting short his apprenticeship as a Viking, no doubt saved his life. The younger, called Olvir, was a dark, quiet, good-natured boy a year or so older than Alethea; since the death of their parents, he had the responsibility of keeping himself and his older sibling fed, clothed, and out of trouble.

After a time, she heard a splash, followed by the clunk of the anchor onto the deck, and soon sensed a change in the slow, rhythmical rocking of the ship. They were moving. For the briefest instant, she was tempted to go back on deck and order Haemur to sail for home . . . but no, not yet.

Soon, but not yet.

Cait slept for a while, but rose unsettled and unrested. She washed her face again, dressed in a clean undershift and mantle, and wrapped a handsome woven girdle around her waist; into this she tucked her father's purse, filled with silver, and a slender dagger which had once belonged to her great-grandmother, and which her grandfather Murdo had carried with him on the Great Pilgrimage. She then put on a gown of exquisite thin material—dark for mourning—and chose a long scarf which she folded over the crown of her head and wrapped around her throat so that the ends hung down her back. Then she went up onto the deck to break fast and wait for Alethea to rise and join her. But her sister was already awake. Little more than half-dressed as usual, Cait noticed sourly, she wore neither hat nor shoes, but merely a sleeveless shift which exposed her slender upper arms and shoulders. She was standing at the prow, tapping her palms on the rail in an attitude of agitation.

She whirled on her sister as Caitríona approached. "Where is Papa? What's happened?" she demanded. "Haemur would tell me nothing. Why are they moving the ship?"

"Thea," said Caitríona, reaching toward her sister, "listen—"

"Haemur said he was not to come with us," she blurted, her face suddenly blotching with color. "Why would he say that?"

"Come and sit with me." Cait put her hand to the young woman's arm, and started toward the covered platform before the mast.

Alethea took two steps and then pulled away. "No! Tell me now! Why are you doing this?" Her shout made the crewmen turn from their work to look at the two women.

"Please, Alethea, this is not seemly. Now, come and—"

"Tell me!" she demanded, crossing her arms over her breast.

"Very well," Cait snapped, losing patience. "Papa is not coming with us because he was attacked when we were leaving the church yesterday."

"Papa hurt? Where is he? I must go to him."

"No." Cait shook her head gently. "Papa was attacked and he was killed."

"But where is he? If he is hurt, we must go to him."

"You are not listening, Thea—"

"You should not have left him. You should—"

"Alethea," she said sharply, "Father is dead. He was attacked and killed. I was with him when he died."

"You left me behind deliberately!" the young woman shouted, tears starting to her eyes.

Stepping close, Caitríona took hold of her sister's arm and gripped it above the elbow. "Stop it!" When Alethea did not respond, she shook her hard. "Listen to what you are saying! If you cannot speak sensibly, shut your mouth."

"This is *your* doing!" Alethea wailed. "And now I will never see him again!"

Cait was instantly furious. "Do you think I brought about Father's death just to spite you?" she snapped. "For once in your life, Thea, think!"

The dark-haired young woman's face seemed to crumple inwardly. "He cannot be dead." The tears spilled over her long lashes and her shoulders began to shake. "Oh, Cait, what are we going to do?" she sobbed. "What are we going to do?"

Thea put her face in her hands and leaned into her sister's embrace. Cait put her arms around the young woman, and felt Alethea's warm tears seeping through her mantle. "We will mourn him," she murmured, rubbing Alethea's smooth bare shoulder as she stared dry-eyed upon the great, looming city spread out before her on its fabled hills, "and we will see him buried.

"Then," she added to herself, "we will avenge him."

THREE

"Tell me," whined Thea, using her most irritating tone. "I am not taking another step until you do."

"The less you know, the less you have to remember."

The two young women walked together along the wide avenue as a deep, wine-colored dusk gathered around them. The street—all but deserted when they had started out—was quickly returning to life once more as the heat of the day gave way to a velvet soft evening. Everywhere, the imperial city was shaking off its languor and reviving itself in the splendid mid-summer night.

"Tell me, Cait. I want to know."

"If I tell you," she replied wearily, "will you promise to keep quiet until we get there?"

"Where? Where are we going?"

"I am not telling you a thing until you promise."

Along the verges, meat vendors hunched over filthy black charcoal braziers which filled the air with blue smoke and the aroma of burning olive oil and roasting spices. Day laborers and wives late from the markets jostled them as they passed, hurrying home with their suppers wrapped in oiled cloth, and large, flat round loaves of bread tucked under their arms. Gangs of young men dressed in short blue tunics caroused, laughing loudly to call attention to themselves. Several caught sight of the two unescorted women and made obscene gestures with their hands which Cait saw; Thea, however, remained blissfully unaware.

Cait moved with solemn purpose, immune to the charms and curiosities around her. To Alethea, who had not ventured into the city before, everything appeared fantastic and enchanting; she had to force herself to remember that just this day they had buried their father, and that she should, as a loving daughter, assume a mournful and somber step like her sister. But it was difficult when every few paces some strange new marvel presented itself to her easily dazzled eyes.

They passed through a street dominated by the tall, well-made houses of the wealthy, each of which boasted elaborate, carved wooden balconies—veritable outdoor rooms which overhung the street—on which the families of spice, timber, and gold merchants, ship owners, and moneychangers gathered to eat their evening meal and watch the pageant below.

Meanwhile, the inhabitants of more humble dwellings fled the close confines of dark, stuffy rooms and gathered in the streets and deserted marketplaces to exchange the news of the day. Men stood in huddled conclaves around jugs of raw country wine and nibbled green olives, spitting the pits into the air. Old women squatted in doorways, their wrinkled faces shrewd and silent, watching all around them with small, dark eyes. Dirty-faced children, clutching bits of food snatched from the table, stood stiff-legged and stared, while hungry dogs tried to cadge morsels from their hands.

Every now and then they passed a walled garden and caught a fragrance on the air—jasmine, lemon blossom, hyacinth, or sandalwood—or heard the music of pipes and lute, played to the accompaniment of the tambour, sticks, and hand drum. Although they recognized the instruments, the melodies seemed quaint and plaintive and strange to the ear, unlike anything they had heard before.

After a time, they arrived at a crossroads which formed a common square. Here, the commerce of the day was far from concluded. Women whose companionship could be obtained for the price of a meal strolled idly along, jangling the silver bracelets on their arms as an unobtrusive means of promoting their wares. Across the square, a potter had set up his wheel beside a low wall on which he presented examples of his work, and nearby stood a man with bits of painted wood dangling from strings in his hand; by pulling the strings, the carved pieces seemed to dance—much to the delight of the spectators gathered around him.

There were also chairs for hire lined up alongside a wall beneath the overhanging boughs of a huge sycamore tree. The bearers were huddled around a small fire in the street, resting after their day's work, talking and laughing as they passed a jar around.

Alethea took one glance at the row of chairs and instantly felt the strain of having walked so far. She stopped in mid-step. "Could we?" she said, tugging on Cait's sleeve. "I am just exhausted."

Cait moved on, inclined to ignore her sister's entreaty.

"Oh, Cait, please? We have been walking all day. My feet are sore."

Caitríona hesitated. She turned back and looked at the chairs. Her vacillation was all that one of the more enterprising chair owners needed. Leaping to his feet, he hurried to where the two young women were standing. "My friends!" he called. "You wish to hire a chair. Mine is best." Dark and thin, he smiled at them as he spoke in rough, rustic Greek. "I am Philippianous. Come with me, I will show you now."

"Very well," said Cait, when she had examined the chair and found it satisfactory. "How much?"

"Where you wish to go?" asked the eager Philippianous. "You tell me that, I tell you how much."

"Blachernae Palace."

At this, the young man's eyes grew wide. "You have business there tonight perhaps."

"Yes," said Cait. "How much?"

"Thirty denarii," he said, growing sly.

"Ten."

"My lady," complained Philippianous, "it is getting dark. We are tired and have nothing to eat. Twenty-five denarii. It is a good price."

"Fifteen denarii—for both of us—"

"Ten apiece," countered the chair owner.

"Very well," relented Cait. Slipping a small leather purse from beneath her girdle, she began counting small silver coins into her hand. "Ten apiece—to take us there *and* return."

"My *lady*," whined Philippianous. "We are poor and hungry. We have had nothing to eat all day. We cannot work all night with nothing to eat."

"Then take your rest," replied Cait, regarding the group of bearers who were listening to the negotiation with undisguised interest. "I am certain one of your friends would be more than happy to oblige."

"Cait, please!" whispered Alethea, embarrassed that her sister should haggle like a fishwife over such a trivial matter.

Sensing victory, the bearer pointed to his chair. "It is a nice chair. Very comfortable. We will take good care of you."

"If you do well," Cait promised, "I will give you extra for a meal. But you must take us to the palace first."

"Done!" The chair owner spun on his heel and clapped his hands. He called to his laborers, who rose from among the men gathered around the fire. One of them took a last gulp from the jar before passing it along, and then he and his three companions shuffled to a wide red-painted chair with a green cushion on its wooden bench seat.

Alethea nudged her sister in the ribs, and pointed at a green chair. It was newer, slightly larger, the pole rings were shiny brass, and the cushion was yellow satin. Cait nodded. "Wait," she said, and pointed to the green chair. "That one."

"My sister," complained the owner. "That one is very special—for the empress herself, eh?"

"If the empress wishes to hire it, we will gladly give it to her," replied Cait, stepping into the chair. She held out the little stack of coins.

Philippianous sighed, but gave his men the nod to go ahead. Taking up two long brass-tipped wooden poles from among those leaning against the wall, they slipped them through the rings, lifted the chair, and started off. "Enjoy your journey, my friends."

"You come, too. I will give you an extra ten to announce us at the palace," Cait said, adding a few more coins to the stack in her hand.

"Philippianous is at your service, empress," said the chair owner, accepting his payment with a polite bow. The bearers moved out, and the owner ran on ahead, leading the way and clearing idlers from the path.

Alethea was instantly ecstatic. "This is wonderful! Cait, we should travel like this *everywhere*," she said, almost hugging herself.

Cait made no reply. She turned her eyes to the slowly darkening street ahead, and thought about what had been accomplished this day, and what was still to come.

"Why did you not say we were going to the palace?" asked Alethea brightly.

"Some surprises are best kept secret," Caitríona replied.

Alethea snuggled closer, enjoying the mysteriousness of it. "Is the royal family there?"

"No," replied Cait. "I have to see someone."

"Who?"

"A man called Renaud de Bracineaux."

"It is to do with Papa's death?"

"Yes."

Cait turned once more to her meditation on the day's events. As soon as the ship had been secured in its new berth in Bucoleon Harbor they returned to the church where Duncan was lying on his bier in the sanctuary, waiting for burial. She allowed Haemur to accompany them—more for Haemur's sake than for her own. The old sea captain had liked and admired her father very much, and it would have been a needless cruelty to have denied him the consolation of attending the burial.

So, leaving Olvir and Otti to look after the vessel, they had proceeded to the church where they were received by the abbot himself and conducted into the darkened sanctuary where burned but two tall candles, one either end of the shroud-wrapped corpse. Upon entering the chapel, Alethea had begun to cry. Once they were seated, the cleric had read a simple service for the dead, at the conclusion of which the body of their father had been taken up by the brothers and carried to a small burial ground in a portion of the garden outside the monastery scriptorium where a fresh grave had been dug in the dry, rocky earth.

After a lengthy prayer in Greek, Cait said another in Gaelic, whereupon Alethea, weeping uncontrollably now, had placed on the body a handful of summer flowers and foliage wrapped in a length of white silk. The monks lowered the body into the hole and, while the abbot read a passage from the holy scripture, the brothers slowly filled in the grave. Haemur stood with bowed head and folded hands, and both Caitríona and Alethea knelt as the monks heaped the dirt high over the bundled corpse, tamped it down, and then planted a new-made wooden cross in the mound.

The service concluded, the abbot led the little funeral party to the refectory where they were given some wine and honey cakes with raisins to refresh themselves. Afterward, Cait delivered the monetary gift they had agreed upon—together with an additional sum for the grave to be continually maintained—whereupon the chapter's infirmarer was summoned. A stoop-shouldered man of middle age with sad dark eyes, the infirmarer presented the women with a small box made of lead; a *chi-rho* had been embossed in the soft metal, and the container sealed with solder.

"I thank you, brother," Cait said, accepting the small casket from his hand. She then thanked the abbot for his care and kindness, and the three were conducted by the porter through the gates of the monastery and out into the light of a hot summer day. Cait moved out into the sun-bright street in a thoughtful mood, Haemur solemn and silent beside her.

Alethea, who had dried her tears, walked along the tree-lined streets with a buoyant step. The great tide of sorrow which surged over her unexpectedly now and again had ebbed for the time being, and she felt light-headed—as if the heavier humors had been drained off, and now she might float away on the breeze. "It was a fine funeral," she observed, once they were through the gate. "Do you not think so, Cait?"

"It served a purpose."

"*You* could have done better, I suppose."

Not wishing to argue with her sister, she merely said, "Papa wished Padraig to conduct his funeral."

"Oh," said Alethea. She had not thought of that. "Of course."

A Célé Dé funeral was a very sacred and special occasion, combining not only prayers and hymns, but stories, songs, and special readings. It culminated in a feast at which family and friends gathered at the banquet table to celebrate the life of the departed and share their fondest recollections. The feast generally began at dusk and continued through the night, finishing at dawn when everyone went out to witness the breaking of the new day and sing their brother and fellow pilgrim on his journey home.

Cait felt sorry that her father had not been able to receive such a funeral; it was his due. Still, she meant to do what she could.

"What is in the box?" asked Alethea. "Strange they should give us a gift."

"It is not a gift," said Cait quietly.

"What is it then?" The younger woman snatched away the box which Cait held reverently in her hands. She turned it this way and that, looking for a way to open it.

"Thea, please." Cait put her hand on her sister's arm and turned her around. She held out her hand for the box. "Give it to me now."

"No," the young woman sulked, jerking the box away. "Not until you tell me what's inside."

Cait frowned, regarding her sister with sour disapproval. "It is Papa's heart," she said softly.

29

"What!" shrieked Alethea. Cait held out her hand, and Thea shoved the box into it with disgust. "You had them cut out his heart?" she cried, tears welling at once. "You cruel and thoughtless creature! How could you do such a thing!"

"It was his dying wish," Caitríona explained simply. "He wanted his heart to be buried in the church at home."

Alethea put her face in her hands and wept. Despite her aggravation, Cait felt sorry for her sister—always getting things twisted around and making herself look foolish. She passed the box to Haemur who was standing awkwardly to one side, shifting his weight from one foot to the other in embarrassment.

"Take this back to the ship, put it in a safe place, and wait for us there," Cait told the grizzled old pilot. "Remember what I told you. It will likely be very late when we return, so keep a light burning at the prow."

Haemur accepted the lead box with a little bow, and said, "As you will, my lady. Return when you like, you will find the ship in order and awaiting your command."

Cait smiled; the old seaman seemed to be going out of his way to demonstrate his acceptance of her as the new master of the vessel. For that, she was grateful. She thanked him and sent him on his way, and then she had begun her work of revenge.

The previous day, the consul had told her that de Bracineaux was a friend of King Baldwin and a guest of the emperor. To find the Templar commander all she had to do was discover which of the many imperial residences was being used by the friends, relations, and entourage of the newly wedded couple. With Thea in tow, she had then begun the tedious and tiring inquiry—a delicate investigation which necessitated shrewdness, tact, and a finely honed sense of diplomacy—particular skills which Cait possessed in fair measure, when she cared to use them.

It was late when they left the Magnaura Palace precinct where Cait had at last been able to tease out the information she required. They had stopped to buy a little fruit and bread and cheese at a market they happened by, and then continued on their way to the Blachernae Palace where the members of the royal wedding entourage were staying as guests of Emperor Manuel Comnenus.

Now, as evening descended around them, Cait settled back in the chair, and allowed herself to think about what lay ahead. She closed her eyes and rehearsed the decisive moment in her mind, trying to imagine it down to the smallest detail so that she should not be taken by surprise.

They were closer to the palace than they knew, and soon Philippianous halted the chair and pointed to an enormous square structure in brick and stone rising from behind a stout wall. "The palace, my lady," he said, as if he were the proud owner.

Caitríona observed the flat, undistinguished façade, with its alternating colors of brickwork, and its high-peaked roof shingled with red tile, and decided that it looked more like the Earl's great house in Orkney than the favorite residence of the Holy Roman Empire's exalted ruler.

"This is the palace?" wondered Alethea aloud. Like Cait, she had imagined something far more grand and imposing.

"Indeed, yes," Philippianous assured them. "The Palace of Blachernae is renowned. People come from all over the world to see it."

There were four soldiers standing in the street before a gate wide enough and high enough to allow the royal carriages of kings and princes to pass through with ease. "Be so kind as to announce us," Cait instructed.

"It would be a pleasure, my lady," replied their expansive guide.

"Say that Ladies Deborah and Constance de Payens have arrived for their audience with Commander de Bracineaux."

At this, Alethea, who had been daydreaming about the rich pearl-studded gowns the empress reputedly wore, sat up sharply. Her Greek was not as good as her sister's, but she understood this last without any difficulty. "What are you saying?" she demanded. "Those are not our names."

"Quiet, Thea," snapped Cait. "Do as you are told."

Philippianous' smiling features arranged themselves into a knowing smirk. He opened his mouth, but Cait cut him off before he could comment. "Announce us," she commanded.

Cait turned on her sister. "Now listen, Thea," she warned. "Keep your mouth shut, and do what I tell you, or I will leave you here by yourself. Understand?"

"I still cannot see why we have to—"

"I mean it!" Cait raised a threatening finger.

Alethea nodded sourly.

"Good. I will explain everything later."

Philippianous had made their names known to the porter, a hulking drone who waved the chair and its occupants through the gate—eyeing the nubile younger woman lustfully as the two passed. Inside the palace grounds, they proceeded at once to the courtyard and the palace entrance where they were halted by guards, and where, once again, the doors were opened without further question when the commander's name was given.

"Be so kind as to wait here," Cait told the bearers. "God willing, we may not be long. If you are ready to depart the moment we return I will double your fee."

"Most gracious lady," replied Philippianous grandly, "we will await your appearance with confident expectation." He led them to the massive copper-gilded iron doors, where they were escorted into the palace without delay.

Once inside, they were met by an aging courtier who demanded to know their business. "We are invited to an audience with Commander de Bracineaux," Caitríona replied crisply.

The courtier cocked his head to one side and gave the two young women a long, dubious glance. "Even so?"

"The invitation was issued by the Master himself." Cait leaned forward and placed her hand on the man's arm, putting her mouth close to his ear. "He said to tell anyone who asked that we are—" she paused precisely long enough to leave no doubt in the courtier's mind that it was a lie, and then added, "his *nieces*."

The elderly courtier pulled away as if burned by her touch. He drew himself up to speak, and Cait thought he might refuse them then and there. Instead, he merely turned on his heel and led them across the entrance hall to a long flight of wooden stairs. Without a word, he indicated that they were to ascend. Cait thanked the servant and, taking the dumbstruck Alethea's hand, proceeded up the stairs without looking back.

They emerged on the next floor and stepped into a large, wood-panelled vestibule connecting three long corridors lined with doors. Two yawning servants leaning against a gilded column regarded the newcomers lazily, but made no move to help them. Cait presented herself and asked in which of the apartments the Templar de Bracineaux might be found. The chamberlain raised a hand, indicated the central corridor, and said, "Sixth door."

Thea close behind, Cait proceeded down the corridor, drawing a deep breath to calm herself. It was going better than she had hoped, but an instant's carelessness would ruin everything. They passed several doors, and heard coarse singing emanating from behind one of them; from behind another came a loud crash followed by raucous laughter and stamping feet.

So, the local gossip is true, she thought. *The Franks sleep when they should work, eat when they should sleep, and roister when they should pray. They rarely wash, talk too loud, blow their noses on their clothing, and rut like pigs.*

As they approached the sixth door, Alethea squeezed Cait's hand. "Someone is coming!" she whispered.

Caitríona looked quickly down to the far end of the corridor where a figure had just appeared in the passageway. As the figure approached she saw the tray of cups in her hand. "It is just a serving girl."

She waited until the girl drew near and paused at the sixth door, whereupon Cait approached her quickly and asked whether the cups and jar were bound for the commander's chamber. "Indeed, my lady," replied the girl.

"Leave it with me," said Cait, taking the tray from her. "We were just about to join him. You may go."

The girl looked at the two women, and then surrendered to their unarguably superior rank. She delivered the tray with a tight bow, and retreated quickly the way she had come. As soon as the girl was gone, Cait laid the tray on the floor; she quickly shrugged off her costly mantle and handed it to her sister; next, she removed the dagger from its sheath at her side and tucked it into her girdle at the back so that it would be out of sight, yet ready to hand.

"What are you doing?" asked Alethea, eyeing the dagger.

"I told you. I have to talk to someone." Cait picked up the tray. "Stay here and keep watch. Knock on the door if anyone should come."

Alethea made to protest, but Cait's raised eyebrow persuaded her to hold her tongue. Glancing nervously both ways along the corridor, she said, "Hurry, then."

Balancing the tray with one hand, Cait reached for the latch and, taking a deep steadying breath to calm her pounding heart, pushed the door open and stepped quickly inside.

FOUR

The room was large and dark, and opened onto a smaller inner chamber which in turned opened onto a balcony overlooking a garden court. The double doors separating the rooms were thrown wide, and two men were sitting at a small round table on the balcony, enjoying the soft evening air. Even by fitful torchlight, she recognized the broad shoulders and untidy mane of white hair belonging to Renaud de Bracineaux. With a glance at Alethea, who made a last anxious plea to hurry, Cait closed the door behind her and stepped inside.

At the sound of the door closing, Commander de Bracineaux called, "Here, girl."

Steadying the tray, she moved through the darkened room toward the balcony. De Bracineaux's back was to her, and the other man—a younger fellow with a large, beak-like nose, fair, straight hair and a fine, silky wisp of a beard—was leaning on the table with his arms crossed. Neither man was armed, and both were deep in conversation. A quick strike from behind, and she would be gone again before the Templar knew what had happened.

"Think what it is worth," de Bracineaux was saying.

"More than I can imagine," the fair-haired one replied. "I should think the pope will give you anything you want. The reward will be yours to name."

"Ha!" de Bracineaux sneered. "If you think that conniving old lecher is going to get his poxy hands on it, then you, my friend, are an even bigger ass than his high holiness."

One step, and another, and she would be in position. Before she

34

could reach the table, however, the second man looked up. "I have not seen you before," he said, rising abruptly.

Cait halted.

"Let me help you with that heavy thing." He grinned and stepped toward her, but the Templar grabbed his arm and pulled him back to his chair. "Sit down, d'Anjou," he growled. "Plenty of time for *that* later."

The younger man lowered himself to his seat again, and Cait proceeded to the table, remaining behind de Bracineaux and out of his sight. She placed the tray on the table, and made to step away, her right hand reaching for the hilt of the slender dagger at her back.

As her fingers tightened on the braided grip, the Templar cast a hasty glance over his shoulder. She saw his lowered brow and the set of his jaw, and feared the worst.

Silently, she slipped the dagger from its sheath, ready to strike. But the light of recognition failed to illumine his eyes. "Well?" he demanded. "Get to your work, now. Light the lamps and leave us."

Cait hesitated, waiting for him to settle back in his chair. When she did not move, the Templar turned on her. "Do as I say, girl, and be quick about it!"

Startled, Cait stepped back a pace, almost losing her grip on the weapon.

"Peace, Renaud," said his companion. Reaching out, he took the Templar's sleeve and tugged him around. "Come, I have poured the wine." He raised his cup and took a long, deep draft.

De Bracineaux swung back to the table, picked up his cup and, tilting his head back, let the wine run down his gullet. *Now!* thought Cait, rising onto the balls of her feet. *Do it now!*

Her hand freed the knife and she moved forward. At that instant, without warning, the door burst open and a thick-set, bull-necked Templar strode into the room behind her. Cait whipped the dagger out of sight, and backed away.

"Ah, here is Gislebert now!" said d'Anjou loudly.

The Templar paused as he passed, regarding Cait with dull suspicion. She ducked her head humbly, and quickly retreated into the darkened room.

"Come, sergeant," called the fair-haired man, "raise a cup and give us the good news. Are we away to Jerusalem at last?"

35

"My lord, baron," said Gislebert, turning his attention to the others. "Good to see you, sir. You had a pleasant journey, I trust."

As the men began talking once more, Cait was forgotten—her chance ruined. She might cut one or even two men before they could react, but never three. And the sergeant was armed.

Still, she was close. The opportunity might never come again.

Reluctant to give up, she busied herself in the adjoining room, steeling herself for another attempt. Fetching some straw from the corner of the hearth, she stooped and lit it from the pile of embers. There was a lamp on the table, two candles in a double sconce on the wall by the bed, and a candletree in the corner. She lit the candles first, taking her time, hoping that Gislebert would leave.

She moved to the table and, as she touched the last of the straw to the lamp wick, became aware that someone was watching her from the doorway. Fearing she had been discovered at last, she took a deep breath, steadied herself and cast a furtive glance over her shoulder.

She did not see him at first. Her eyes went to the men who were still at the table on the balcony, cups in hand, their voices a murmur of intimate conversation. They were no longer heeding her. But, as she bent once more to the task at hand, she caught a movement in a darkened corner of the room and turned just as a man stepped from the shadows.

She stifled a gasp.

Dressed in the long white robe of a priest, he held up his hand, palm outward in an attitude of blessing—or to hold her in her place. Perhaps both, she thought. A man of youthful appearance, his hair and beard were black without a trace of gray and the curls clipped like the shorn pelt of a sheep. His eyes, though set deep beneath a dark and heavy brow, were bright and his glance was keen. He stepped forward into the doorway, placing himself between Cait and the men.

When he moved she felt a shudder in the air, as if a gust of wind had swept in through the open door; but the candles did not so much as quiver. At the same time, she smelled the fresh, clean scent of the heathered hills after a storm has passed.

"Do not be afraid," said the man, his voice calm and low. "I merely wish to speak to you."

Cait glanced nervously beyond him to where the Templar and his companions sat at their wine.

"Blind guides," he said, indicating the men. "They have neither eyes to see, nor ears to hear."

"Who are you?" As she asked the question, she glanced again at de Bracineaux and his companions; now laughing heartily, they appeared oblivious to both her and the stranger.

"Call me Brother Andrew," he said.

At the name, Cait felt her throat tighten. She gulped down a breath of air. "I know about you," she said, struggling to keep her voice steady. "My father told me."

"Your family has been in my service for a long time. That is why I have come—to ask if you will renew the vow of your father and grand-father."

"What vow is that?"

"I asked young Murdo to build me a kingdom where my sheep could safely graze . . ."

"Build it far, far away from the ambitions of small-souled men and their ceaseless striving," Cait said, repeating the words she had learned as a child on her grandfather's knee. "Make it a kingdom where the True Path can be followed in peace and the Holy Light can shine as a beacon flame in the night."

He smiled. "There, you see? You do know it."

"He did that. He built you a kingdom," she said bluntly, "and died an old man—waiting for you to come as you promised."

"Truly, his faith has been rewarded a thousandfold," the White Priest told her. "But now it is your turn. In each generation the vow must be renewed. I ask you, sister, will you serve me?"

At the question, Cait felt a hardness rise up in her, like a rock in her chest. She hesitated and looked away, not daring to meet the White Priest's commanding gaze.

"Caitríona," chided Brother Andrew gently, "I know what is in your heart."

When she did not answer, the monk shook his head sadly and moved a step closer. "Thus says the Lord of Hosts: 'As surely as I live forever, when I sharpen my fiery sword and my hand grasps it in judgment, I will take vengeance on my enemies and repay those who hate me.'"

She set her jaw and clung to her silence.

"I ask you, sister, do you believe that the Great King is able to per-form justice for his servants?"

Her answer was quick and biting. "If his justice is as ready as his protection, his servants had better sleep with a shield in one hand and a sword in the other."

"His ways are not our ways. Whatever misfortune befalls one of his own, the Allwise Creator is able to bend it to his will. He will not suffer evil to prevail," he replied.

She could feel his eyes on her, but she was determined not to be swayed by anything he said. "And yet it *does* prevail."

"Look at me, Caitríona," the monk commanded. She raised her eyes slowly. He was watching her with an intensity which burned across the distance between them. "I ask but once more: will you serve me?"

Both her father and her grandfather had stood before the White Priest, and both had answered his call. How could she do less?

"I will," she replied at last.

"Then put aside your wrath, and believe. For it is written: 'Vengeance is mine; I will repay, says the Lord. In due time their foot will slip; the day of disaster is near and their doom rushes upon them.' Behold," he said, pointing to the table behind her, "this is the work I am giving you. When it is finished, you shall receive the desires of your heart."

She turned to look where he was pointing and saw a parchment document—a formal-looking communication in Latin. The image on the broken seal looked regal, and the signature at the bottom of the document was in red ink—as were the words *Rosa Mystica*.

Cait picked up the letter and turned to ask what it was the White Priest wanted her to do. But he was gone, and she was alone once more. She looked at the letter in her hand, but before she could read any of it, de Bracineaux shouted from the other room. "Here! You! Get away from there!"

"For the love of God, de Bracineaux, leave the wench be," said d'Anjou.

"I will see her off," said Gislebert. He rose from the table and lumbered in from the balcony.

Taking up the tray once more, Cait whipped the folded parchment out of sight beneath it. She turned and made a slight bow toward the men, then bolted from the room. Gislebert watched her go, and then moved to the door, closing it firmly after her.

She stepped out into the corridor once more. Alethea was hovering in the passageway, wringing her hands and looking as if she had swallowed a mouse. "Are you all right?" she asked as Cait emerged from the chamber.

"No thanks to you," snapped Cait. "You were supposed to warn me."

"He surprised me."

"Yes, he surprised me too."

"Now you are angry," pouted Alethea. "He came up behind me and caught me lingering by the door and told me to get about my business. What could I do?"

They moved quickly off along the corridor. Returning to the vestibule, Cait laid the tray aside and, while Thea kept watch, drew on her mantle once more and tucked the parchment away; then the two women descended the stairs and retraced their steps outside where, as arranged, the chair and bearers were still waiting. They climbed into the chair, and Cait instructed Philippianous to take them to the Bucoleon Harbor.

"Well?" demanded Alethea, as they passed through the gate and back into the street once more. "What happened? Did you see him?"

"I saw him," muttered Cait.

"Well, what did he say?"

"Nothing."

"You were in there a long time. He must have said something," insisted Alethea.

Out of the corner of her eye, Cait caught Philippianous leaning toward them so as to overhear their discussion. "Not now," Cait told her sister. "Later."

"I want to hear it now."

"Shut up, you stupid girl," Cait blurted, changing to Gaelic. "They are listening to us."

"All very well for you," squeaked Alethea indignantly, "Lady Caitríona gets to do whatever she likes, while *I* have to be her dutiful slave."

Cait turned away from her sister and watched the activity in the streets instead. Fires bright in iron braziers and countless oil lamps illumined the night with a garish glow. In some of the broader avenues, musicians played—pipe and lute, tambor and lyre—and people danced, hands upraised, stepping lightly as they spun and turned. Occasionally, an enterprising merchant would approach the passing chair and offer his wares: bangles and necklaces of colored glass beads, pots of perfumed unguent, satin ribbons, and tiny bunches of dried flowers for the ladies' hair.

The variety and charm of the baubles distracted Alethea from her sister's stinging rebuke, and she would have stopped and bought trinkets from them all, but Cait instructed Philippianous and his bearers to move on. As they neared the seafront, the streets became quieter and darker—the houses meaner, the people more furtive, sinister. Arriving at the harbor, however, the seamen and sailors drinking wine and playing dice on the wharf gave the quayside a less threatening atmosphere.

More than one lonely seafarer licked his lips hopefully as the two women stepped from the chair. One or two of the younger men called to them, offering wine and an evening's entertainment. "As agreed," said Cait, dropping a stack of small silver coins into Philippianous' outstretched hand. "And, as promised, a little extra for your trouble." She dropped a few more coins into his hand.

"This," she said, taking out a single gold *solidus*, "is for forgetting you ever saw us. Do you think you can do that?"

"Most certainly, gracious lady." He reached for the coin eagerly.

She snatched it back. "I beg your pardon?"

A sly smile appeared on his face. "Is someone speaking? I see no one here."

She let the coin slip through her fingers. "Excuse me, I think you must have dropped something."

"How clumsy of me," replied Philippianous, bending to retrieve the coin. When he straightened, the two women were already hurrying away.

Cait and Alethea moved quickly toward the ship *Persephone* at the end of the wharf, ignoring the shouted pleas and propositions their presence provoked. Once aboard, they were met by Haemur. "Thank God you are safe," he said, hurrying from his place at the stern. "It grew dark, and when you did not return, I feared something ill had befallen you."

Cait thanked the pilot for his concern, and said, "We are perfectly well, as you see. But now, I want you to wake Otti and Olvir, and move the ship away from the wharf and into the bay."

"Now?" Haemur thrust out his hands. "But, my lady, it is too dark. We cannot—"

"Enough, Haemur." Cait stopped him with an upraised hand. "I would not insist if it was not important."

With that, she went to the brass lamp hanging from a hook on the mast, lit a candle from the basket on the deck, and proceeded to her quarters below, leaving an unhappy pilot staring after her.

"I am sorry, Haemur," Alethea offered sympathetically. "You had best do as she says, or there will be the devil to pay."

"Very well," replied the seaman. He hurried off to rouse his crew, and Alethea joined her sister in their quarters.

"You could try to be a little more—" she began, and then stopped as she saw Cait bring out the folded parchment from beneath her girdle. "Where did you get that?" she asked, then guessed. "You stole it!"

"Hush!" Cait snapped. Opening the letter, she sat down on the edge of the box bed to read it.

Alethea watched her sister for a moment; then, indignation overcome by curiosity, she joined her on the bed. "What is it? What does it say?"

Cait ignored her and continued to read silently to herself. When she finished, she looked up from the page. "Thea, do you know what this is?"

"How can I? You tell me nothing."

Cait made no reply. She was reading the document again.

"Well?" demanded Thea after a moment. "What *does* it say?"

"They have found a very great treasure—"

"Who?"

"The greatest treasure in the world—that is what he says."

"*Who* says? Who wrote it?"

"A cleric called Bertrano. He calls it the Rosa Mystica."

"The Mystic Rose?" mused Thea, none the wiser. "What does that mean?"

Cait shook her head, scanning the document again. "He says only that it is beyond price—see?" She pointed to the letters in the tight Latin uncials of the scriptorium, and read out the words: ". . . that which is beyond all price, the treasure of the ages, our very real and manifest hope for this present age and the kingdom to come, the Mystic Rose."

Thea shrugged.

"Obviously, it is a name employed to conceal the true nature of the treasure."

"And this letter tells where to find it?"

"It does—I think." She pointed to the portion of the document written in a different language. "I cannot read the rest, but I think it must tell where the treasure is to be found."

The younger woman regarded her sister suspiciously. "Why *did* we go to the palace tonight? And do not say it was to steal this letter, because you did not even know it was there."

Cait stood and began folding the letter carefully.

"You are going to have to tell me sooner or later," Thea pointed out. "You might as well tell me now."

"We must hide this where no one can find it."

"Cait," said Alethea, adopting a disagreeable whine, "tell me—why did we go to the palace?"

Cait sat down again. Placing the parchment square on her knees, she held it in both hands as if she was afraid it might unfold itself and fly away. "Listen carefully. I will say this but once. We went there to confront Father's murderer and hold him to justice." She gazed steadily at Alethea and added, "I was going to kill him."

Alethea gaped in amazement at her sister's audacity. "The knife . . . It is true—you were going to stab him . . ." Her voice trailed off as the full impact of her sister's ruthlessness broke upon her. "Oh, Cait—"

"Renaud de Bracineaux murdered our father," she continued. "Papa named him before he died. The magistrate refused to accept the word of a woman; he refused to do anything—so I had to do it myself."

"Oh, Cait," Thea whispered, her voice made small by the magnitude of her sister's cold-blooded confession. "God help us."

Caitríona gazed down at the document she held in her lap. "I think," she said, "he already has."

FIVE

"Is that the one?" demanded Renaud de Bracineaux, squinting at the rank of hire chairs across the square.

"It is, my lord commander," answered the porter of Blachernae Palace. "He comes to the palace sometimes."

"Bring him here." The commander sat on his horse in the middle of the street, sweating in the bright sunlight. His head hurt from last night's wine, and he felt bilious from too much rich food. Baron Félix d'Anjou, he thought—and not for the first time—was a profligate toad and his usefulness was swiftly coming to an end.

Also, the sooner he had his hand on the thieving bitch who had stolen his letter, the better he would feel.

He had not discovered the theft until this morning when he rose and went to wash himself. Passing the table, he had noticed the square of parchment was missing. He had summoned Gislebert at once. "The letter," he said pointing to the table. "What happened to it?"

"I thought you put it away."

"If I had put it away, would I be asking you what happened to it? Think, man!"

"That serving girl last night—" Gislebert began.

"Oh, very good, sergeant," roared the commander, pushing Gislebert toward the door. "Instead of standing like a lump of ripe cheese, go and find her."

Gislebert had scurried off and returned a short while later with word that although no one knew the servant in question, the porter had seen two women arrive in a hired chair. "He says the chair came from Tzimisces Square—not far from here," the sergeant reported. "He has seen it before."

"Have horses readied," barked de Bracineaux. "We are going to get that letter back."

"What of the porter?" asked Gislebert. "He is waiting outside."

"Bring him with us."

Now he sat sweltering in the saddle, and watched the porcine gate-man waddle across the square, leading a slender young Greek with the air of a jovial pirate. *These people, these Greeks—a supremely deceitful race*, thought de Bracineaux darkly, *natural-born thieves and cut-throats each and every one.* The easy, carefree grace of the young man— the insufferable indifference of his long, loping stride, and the subtle expression of superiority on his swarthy features filled the commander with a rank and bitter loathing. *It seems*, he decided, *an example is in order here.*

The thought made him feel better. Perhaps all was not lost. After all, the thief could not possibly know what it was she had taken, could not possibly imagine its unrivalled importance, its inestimable value. It had been the rash act of an ignorant and opportunistic slut, and she would pay for her impudence—he would see to that. First, however, he would teach the sly young Greek a lesson he would never forget.

"Do you recognize him?" grunted the sergeant as the porter trundled nearer.

"I have seen him before. He is the one."

"Greetings, my lord, a splendid day for a ride in a chair. Where would you like to go?"

"Shut up, you," said Gislebert sharply. "You will speak when spoken to—understand?"

"That is not necessary, sergeant," said de Bracineaux wearily. "He is not to blame." Regarding the slim dark youth before him, he said, "What is your name, boy?"

The youth bristled at the derisory word but, considering the angry-looking men before him, swallowed his pride and said, "I am Philippianous. How can I help, your majesty?"

The commander's eyes narrowed; he could not tell if the youth was making fun of him; more likely, he decided at last, the young fool really thought he *was* a king. "You brought two women to Blachernae Palace last night. Where did you take them when they left?"

"I do not recall."

"Liar!" snarled Gislebert, drawing back his hand.

Philippianous glared at the Templar sergeant. "Is it my fault if a man cannot remember where he put his whores?"

Gislebert gave out a growl and swung at the young man, who jerked back his head, letting the blow sail harmlessly by. Before the sergeant could regroup for another swing, his commander called him off, saying, "That will do, sergeant. He is used to being paid for his service, so we will pay."

De Bracineaux put his hand into the leather purse at his belt, withdrew it and flipped a gold *solidus* to the young man. "I trust that will help restore your memory," he said.

Philippianous caught the coin in his fist and examined it before replying. "They must be very important to you."

"Where did you take them?"

"I brought them here," he sighed, as if the conversation no longer interested him, "because that was all the money they had." He turned to go.

"A moment!" said de Bracineaux. "I think you may be of further service to me. I will pay you for your trouble, never fear." To the porter, he said, "Take him back to the palace and wait with him there."

When the two had gone, the Templars continued on. "He was lying," Gislebert said.

"No doubt," replied the commander placidly.

"I could have made him tell us."

"We will, but not here. The boy is well known hereabouts, and too many people have seen us already. If the women are close by, I do not want them warned off by a street fight."

"What do you intend, commander?"

"Give him inducement enough to consult his memory, and we will soon have the letter in our possession once more."

They rode on to the church of the Holy Apostles, which was no great distance from the square, attended a lengthy mass, and then broke fast at an inn which was frequented by many of the Templars who were now more or less permanently stationed in the city. They met several of their order and entertained them with a meal of fresh bread flavored with caraway and honey, soft cheese, and wine diluted with lemon water.

After breaking their fast, they returned to the palace to find a very irritated Philippianous, who had been made to stand in the courtyard in the hot sun while he waited.

"Here you are," said the commander, strolling into the courtyard, "I had almost forgotten about you. Do forgive me."

"I would have left long ago, but that pig of a porter would not let me go. What do you want from me? I have already told you all I know."

"This for your trouble," said de Bracineaux, holding up a gold coin. "And two more if you can remember where those two young women went after they left here."

"Keep your filthy money," Philippianous spat. "I am leaving." He pushed past the sergeant and started toward the courtyard entrance.

"No," replied the commander calmly, "I do not think we are finished yet." He made a gesture with his hands and three Templar soldiers appeared in the doorway behind him. "Take hold of him."

Philippianous made to dart away, but the Templars seized him and bore him up. "I am a citizen!" he shouted, struggling ineffectually in their grasp. "I have done nothing wrong!"

To his sergeant, the commander said, "Bring me some coals." As Gislebert hurried away, he added, "If d'Anjou is still abed, rouse him. He would not thank us to miss this."

Commander de Bracineaux went to his room and removed his spotless white tabard. Picking up his leather gauntlets, he tucked them into his belt, and then attached the hanger for his dagger.

He drew the knife from its scabbard and tried the edge, admiring the fine craftsmanship of the weapon as he ran his thumb along the honed and polished blade and thought back to the first time he had seen it, along with five others in a box delivered to the ship by a young lord he had tried to recruit in Rouen—the same self-righteous fool of a young nobleman whose meddling had caused him so much trouble all those years ago.

At long last, that old debt was settled.

A thin smile touched his lips, for until that very moment he had not considered the fact that it was none other than Duncan who had brought him the knife when it had been left behind; he had been so eager to please.

The commander replaced the dagger and, as he walked from the room, he wondered if Duncan, as he lay dying, had fully appreciated the grim irony of the situation. Had he, as his life ebbed away, savored the delicious absurdity of being slain by the very weapon he had supplied?

The Shrine of Mary the Virgin served as a private chapel for the residents of Blachernae Palace, and the crypt below it was a labyrinth of connecting vaults which housed tombs for minor royalty. It was a suitably dark and private place where the proceedings would not be disturbed.

Commander de Bracineaux made his way down the narrow steps leading to the first and largest chamber of the crypt. He paused at the small altar with its gilded crucifix and its ever-burning lamp, making a haphazard sign of the cross. Then, setting aside the crucifix and lamp, he took up the altar stole—a narrow strip of cloth with a sturdy cord binding—and proceeded to the chamber beyond, where three Templars were holding an extremely agitated Philippianous, while a fourth stood guard at the doorway.

"Release me!" shouted Philippianous as the commander stepped into the room. "I have done nothing! I am a citizen, and I demand that you release me at once."

"Save your breath," de Bracineaux replied. Handing the altar stole to the Templar at the doorway, he said, "Bind him and put him over there." He pointed to a low, flat-topped sarcophagus of gray stone. "Then leave us."

The soldiers bound their captive securely hand and foot and quit the chamber. When they had gone, de Bracineaux moved to the head of the sarcophagus. "Many noble and illustrious men are interred in this crypt," he said, leaning on his elbows. "Of course, they were dead before taking up residence here—but I do not think anyone will mind if we make an exception for you."

"What do you want me to tell you?" said Philippianous. "You want to know where the women went? I will tell you. Let me go, and I will tell you everything."

"In God's good time."

Gislebert arrived just then, carrying a small iron brazier filled with burning coals and suspended by a length of chain. "Ah, here is Sergeant Gislebert now," de Bracineaux said. "Put the coals there." He indicated a place on the stone beside the young man's head. "Where is d'Anjou?"

"D'Anjou is here," said a voice from the doorway, and a bleary-eyed baron staggered into the room. "God's wounds, but my head hurts, de Bracineaux. What is so almighty urgent that a man must be wakened and dragged from bed at the crack of noon?"

"We have an interesting problem before us," replied the commander. "I thought you might like to see how we solve it."

The baron tottered to the sarcophagus for a closer look. "What has he done—stolen the keys to the palace?"

"I have done nothing!" shouted Philippianous. "In the name of God and all the saints, I beg you, release me. I will tell you anything. I do not even know the women. I never saw them before."

The commander drew the gold-handled dagger and handed it to d'Anjou. "Exquisite, is it not?"

"I took them to the harbor," Philippianous said. "I remember now."

"It is a very fine weapon," the baron agreed.

"I took them to Bucoleon Harbor. That is where they wanted to go."

"It was made by an armorer in Arles—a very artist with steel," de Bracineaux said, taking up the knife once more. "It has served me well so many times over the years, yet still looks as good as new."

De Bracineaux thrust the dagger into the burning coals. "You know," he said, as if imparting a closely held secret, "one must be very careful not to allow the blade to grow too hot—gold melts more readily than steel; or, so I am told. In any case, it would be a shame to damage the handle."

"I think they had a ship waiting for them," shouted the young Greek, growing frantic. "For God's sake, let me go. I can find them for you."

"It never ceases to amaze me, d'Anjou," said the Templar commander, pulling on his gauntlets one after the other, "how very talkative people become when they finally grasp the utter hopelessness of their position."

"Positively garrulous," replied the baron with a yawn.

"But then it is too late." De Bracineaux pulled the knife from the burning coals; the blade shone with a dull, blue-red glow. "The problem now," he continued, "is turned completely on its head."

"Turned on its head?" inquired d'Anjou idly.

"Yes." He spat on the blade and the spittle sizzled as it struck the hot metal. "They simply will not shut up."

"Listen to me," said Philippianous, his voice tight with desperation; sweat rolled from his face and neck in great fat beads. "Wherever they went, I can find them. I have friends in many places. They hear things. Let me go. I will talk to them. I can find these women for you."

"You see?" said de Bracineaux. "A very fountain of information." He nodded to Sergeant Gislebert who, stepping quickly around the sarcophagus, seized the Greek's hands which were bound at the wrist, and jerked his arms up over his head. The young man, pleading for his life, began to thrash and wail.

"In the end, there is only one way to assure silence," said the Templar commander, lowering the knife to the young man's chest. The hot blade seared the thin fabric of his mantle. The cloth began to smolder.

"They went to Bucoleon Harbor," shouted Philippianous. "Please, spare me! Listen, my uncle owns many ships. His name is Stakis—ask anyone, they will tell you he is a very wealthy trader. He will reward you handsomely to let me go. Whatever you ask—I swear before God, he will pay it."

"But we do not need your money." He drew a line with the hot blade down the center of the young man's chest, searing the skin. The air filled with the stench of burning flesh.

Philippianous screamed, "In the name of God, I beg you. Spare me!"

"I do not think God can hear you," said the Templar, pressing the hot knife deeper. Blood oozed up from the wound, spitting and sputtering as it touched the hot metal.

"Oh, why not let him go?" said d'Anjou. "I have not had a thing to eat or drink, and the stink you are making turns my stomach."

"Very well," replied de Bracineaux. He lifted the knife away and plunged it back into the coals. "Still, it would not do to have our glorious and renowned order ridiculed by the filth of the street. Once people find out the Templars can be lied to with impunity, we will be mocked from Rome to Jerusalem—and we cannot allow that. So, I think an example is in order."

"No!" shrieked Philippianous. "No! Please, I will not tell a soul. I will not breathe a word to anyone."

"For once I believe you," said the commander. His hand snaked out and, snatching the knife from the brazier, he pressed the glowing tip hard against the young man's teeth, forcing his jaws open. The hot blade slid into his mouth, searing his tongue. A puff of smoke rolled up, and the blade hissed. Philippianous gave a strangled scream and passed out; his body slumped.

Only then did de Bracineaux remove the knife. "He has soiled himself," he observed, wiping the blade on the young man's clothing. "He stinks. Get him out of here, sergeant." He turned away from the inert body on the gray stone slab. "Come, d'Anjou, I am thirsty. I think I would enjoy some more of the emperor's excellent wine."

"My thoughts exactly, de Bracineaux." The baron turned and shuffled from the chamber, followed by the commander.

Gislebert regarded the unconscious Greek. "What do you want me to do with him?"

"Throw him back in the street," replied the commander over his shoulder. "He will serve as a mute, yet nonetheless persuasive reminder to all who think to defy the Order of the Temple."

SIX

She pressed the hem of her mantle to her nose and paused, putting a hand to the mildewed wall as her stomach heaved. So the Saracens would not think her weak, she swallowed back the bile, steadied herself and walked on into the suffocating stench of the dungeon. For the first time since leaving Constantinople, Caitríona doubted whether she was doing the right thing.

That first night aboard ship, with the vision of the White Priest still burning in her mind, her course had appeared obvious, the way clear. Ignoring Alethea's pestering and petulance, she had taken the letter to her father's quarters to examine it alone in greater detail. By the gently wavering light of three lamps and four candles, she had read the document three times—most of it was in Latin, save for a small section in an unknown script. She puzzled over the obscure portion trying to make out the curious text; it was not Latin, or Greek, much less Gaelic or Norse—the only languages she knew.

The letter had been written by a Portuguese cleric called Bertrano, Archbishop of Santiago de Compostela, and addressed to none other than Pope Adrian IV. After the usual greetings and salutations, the archbishop announced that the "secret of the ages" had been revealed—a marvelous treasure had been discovered in Aragon, a part of eastern Iberia which had been, until recently, a Saracen domain. His reason for writing, he said, was to seek the aid of the Holy Father in the protection of this treasure, which he called the *Rosa Mystica*. Owing to the increased instability of the region, he greatly feared the Mystic Rose would be captured, or destroyed, and "the greatest treasure in the world would be lost for ever"—a calamity which, he said, would never be forgiven.

The archbishop asked the pope to send faithful and trusted servants guarded by a fearsome company of knights to retrieve the treasure and carry it back to the Holy Land so "that which is beyond all price, the treasure of the ages, our very real and manifest hope for this present age and the kingdom to come, the Mystic Rose, might be re-established in Jerusalem" where it rightfully belonged.

As she pored over the text, she wondered what this treasure might be, and why the White Priest wanted her to become involved in this affair. The more she thought about it, the more strange and fantastic it all became. In de Bracineaux's chamber, Cait had accepted his appearance as normal and natural as meeting a friend in an unexpected place. But now it seemed anything but natural. *Put away your wrath, and believe,* he had told her, and promised that when she was finished she would receive the desires of her heart.

Well, what she desired most was revenge. *Lord,* she prayed, folding the parchment letter carefully, *make me the instrument of your vengeance.*

She wrapped the letter in a piece of cloth and hid it under her father's clothing and belongings at the bottom of his sea chest, then lifted out her most precious possession. It was a book—*her* book, written by her father during his sojourn in the caliph's palace in Cairo. Removing it from the heavy cloth bag, she ran her fingers over the tough leather binding with its fine, tight rawhide stitching—the work of the Célé Dé monks of Caithness. She carefully untied the braided leather cord, opened the cover, and began turning the heavy, close-written parchment pages.

The original, faithfully rendered by the Cypriot monks, remained in the abbey church at Banvarð. The ever-thoughtful Padraig had ordered the good brothers of Caithness to produce a copy of the Lord Duncan's manuscript which he had then bound on one side and presented to Duncan to give as a gift to the daughter for whom it had been written.

Her father had read it aloud to her when she was a little girl. But as she grew older and her command of Latin increased, Cait had been able to read more and more of it for herself. She could not count the winter nights she had spent before the hearth, wrapped in her mother's old shawl, tracing the fine-scripted lines with a fingertip. While her body was confined to a draughty, wind-battered house in snowy Scotland, in her mind she wandered lost in the labyrinths of the caliph's palace, or followed the Amir's caravan across burning deserts with the severed head of proud Prince Bohemond on her back.

Over the years she often found herself going to the book as to an old friend. Indeed, she could recite much of it from memory. But this night, as she opened the heavy leather cover and felt once more the solace of the familiar, there was a fresh urgency to the words she knew so well. For though it comforted her to hear again her father's changeless voice, speaking to her across the distance of oceans and years, she realized for the first time that these well-known words could instruct and guide her. In these self-same pages she had first learned of the White Priest, and tonight, this very night, she had met him for herself, and renewed her family's long-held vow.

She gazed with increasing excitement on the heavy volume in her lap and understood that it had suddenly become more than the tale of her father's youth. It was a signpost directing her along the paths of her family's destiny. She could feel that destiny thickening around her like the tide on the turn, when, just before it begins to flow, the water swells and stills with concentrated force.

Yes, and once the tide has begun to run, she thought, *no power on earth can hold it back.*

She closed her eyes and turned the pages, letting the book fall open where it would. Opening her eyes once more they lit upon the word *Damascus.*

If she was to undertake the pursuit of the Mystic Rose, she would need help. And Damascus was where she would find it.

Cait had spent the night in a fever of excitement as the plan took shape in her mind. Just before dawn she had emerged from her quarters to wake Haemur and his crew and tell them to prepare the ship to sail at first light. "Are we going home, my lady?" asked Haemur; Olvir and Otti looked on hopefully.

"No," she replied. "I have business to conclude first. We are going to Damascus."

That was twelve days ago, and with the help of favorable winds and several nights of moonlight sailing they had reached the well-protected port of Tyre with its imposing fortress built on a spit of rock extending out into the bay. There, leaving the ship in Olvir's capable hands, Cait arranged to join a group of Venetian traders on their way to Damascus to buy cloth and spices. For a fee, she and her small entourage consisting of Alethea, Haemur, and Otti were allowed to travel under the protection of the traders. The journey through the arid hills passed uneventfully and they had, after seven days in the sweltering heat, at last reached the gates of the city where her father had languished for a time, awaiting a ransom that never came. Once inside the walls, Cait held off the myriad distractions of the vendors, street hawkers, and moneychangers, and immediately set about finding a place to stay and hiring the services of an interpreter who could help her conduct negotiations.

Her search quickly produced a young Syrian physician by the name of Abu Sharma, who had spent many years studying in Cairo and Baghdad. Abu spoke several Arabic languages, as well as Latin, and helpfully agreed to take leave of his practice for a few days and place himself at her service.

"My patients are demanding, of course," he told her. "But perhaps I can steal a day or two from the sick and dying to help you. It would be a pleasure. To tell you the truth, it would be a blessing. I am run off my feet from first light to last—every day it is the same. I would welcome the change."

Cait noticed that despite the pressure of his demanding patients, he still found time to sleep in a quiet corner of the bazaar during the day. After paying him a token retainer, Cait had instructed him to meet her at the palace the following morning. He was waiting outside the palace gates when she and the two seamen arrived. "Allah be good to you, noble lady," he said. "Abu Sharma is at your service. Please tell me now, how am I to help you?"

Cait had taken him aside and explained what she wanted him to do, and how they were to proceed. "Simplicity itself," remarked Abu when she finished. "You may rest your trust in me completely. Abu Sharma will help you obtain the best possible price."

"Do that," Cait told him, "and you shall receive double your fee."

"Watch and be amazed!" He made a low bow, and they joined the long parade of dignitaries, merchants, and suppliers of various goods and commodities making their way into the palace—a grand if slightly formidable edifice of stone covered in mortar which had been tinted green so that it gleamed in the sun like a massive block of jade. They passed through a double set of arched timber gates, and into a palm-lined courtyard filled with scribes at tables.

"It is because of the earthquake last month," Abu said, and explained that owing to the damaged reception hall, all court affairs were taking place in the outer yard where scribes toiled away at their tables, busily recording the representations of each visitor wishing to do business of one sort or another with his exalted highness, Prince Mujir ed-Din.

The party presented itself to one of the prince's many functionaries who, upon hearing the reason for their visit, conducted them forthwith to his superior Wazir Muqharik. The red-turbanned official listened to their request, stroked his beard thoughtfully, then gave his consent, promptly sending them off to the prison in the company of his katib, or secretary.

Once inside the prison, they were conducted along a row of cells where local malefactors awaited judgment for their crimes, and then down a flight of stone steps to the lower prison where the captives of war were kept in perpetual stink and gloom.

Now, Cait stood retching in the dim half-light of the dungeon, feeling the cold sweat on her clammy skin as wave after wave of doubt assailed her. Eyes watering, stomach churning, she looked down the narrow corridor; at the end of the passage was a barred and locked timber door. Once across that threshold, there would be no turning back.

This is madness, she thought. *I do not have to go through with it. I can let it end here, return to the ship and sail for home, and no one would blame me.*

But Cait was not made that way. The dauntless spirit of her clan was her spirit; it was their blood that pulsed through her veins; her heart beat with the same strong rhythms; its destiny was her destiny, too. She had accepted the charge of the White Priest, and she would do whatever that service required—so long as it brought about the destruction of the Templar commander. Failing that, she would appeal to the ancient code of justice which demanded an eye for an eye, a tooth for a tooth, and a life for a life. One way or another, she would have her revenge.

Sweeping all doubts aside as if they were straws before the cold gale of her retribution, she steadied herself, removed the bunched-up hem of her mantle from her nose and mouth, and nodded to the jailer, who placed the great iron key in the lock. The prince's secretary turned to address Cait through her interpreter. "As you will see," said Abu, translating the katib's words, "there are many prisoners from which to choose. If you wish to speak to one, you have but to point him out, and the jailer will have the man brought to you."

Cait nodded to show that she understood, whereupon the jailer pushed open the door and stepped through into the cavernous chamber. Cait followed, with Abu Sharma close behind. Haemur and Otti came next—in attendance not because they were any real use in this matter, but for propriety's sake: Cait had quickly learned that the Saracens respected only those women who appeared to possess the support and protection of men.

The lower prison was little more than a dark noisome hole; the only illumination came from the grates of the open sluice drains in the floor above. Despite the stink, the cell was cool and dry—an acceptable trade, Cait thought, for if one could not have the light, at least one did not have to endure the heat. In the surrounding gloom, the captives lay: eighteen or twenty men, all knights, all of whom had been captured in one battle or another.

As Cait moved into the high-vaulted room, the captives stared up with hopeful faces, and began clamoring for attention. The jailer waded in, roaring at the prisoners and clouting them with his ring of keys until rough order was restored. He then stepped back, and beckoned Cait forward to examine the goods on offer and make her choice.

Cait had already had plenty of time to decide what she wanted. She stepped forward, and raising her voice to the hopeful men addressed them in slow, distinct Latin. "Believe me when I tell you that I am sorry for your plight," she said. "My own father sat in this same cell awaiting ransom and release. It came for him eventually, and I pray that it will come soon for each and every one of you."

She paused to allow her words to be relayed by Abu to the jailer. "Today, however, liberation has come to a fortunate few," she told the prisoners. Then changing smoothly to a simple, but serviceable Norse, she asked, "Are there any Norsemen among you?"

Several voices answered eagerly: "Here!" said two; and "Over here!" said another.

"Stand, please," commanded Cait. Three men rose eagerly to their feet. Pointing to the nearest of them, she turned to the jailer, who motioned the prisoner to step forward.

Hobbling, his hands and feet shackled and chained, the man edged into the light. Tall and gaunt, his fair hair and beard hanging in dirty tangles, his face gray with despair and lack of light, he regarded the young woman with an expectancy almost painful to behold.

"What is your name?" Cait asked in the northern tongue.

"I am Yngvar," replied the man, his voice cracking dry. He held himself gingerly, favoring one side, as if to protect an injury.

She looked him up and down. "Are you well enough to fight, Yngvar?"

"I am that," he replied without hesitation.

"These others," she said, indicating the knights waiting their turn. "Do you know them?"

He nodded his head once. "They are my swordbrothers." Pointing with both hands to the thick-shouldered, heavy-browed man behind him, he said, "That is Svein Gristle-Bone." Nodding to the young, dark-haired man a short distance away, he said, "That is Dag Stone-Breaker."

She summoned them by name. "Svein, Dag, come here." As they shuffled painfully forth, she asked, "Where is your lord, Yngvar? Was he killed in battle?"

"By no means," replied the knight. "He is here with us even now." He turned and pointed to a man squatting on the floor a few paces away.

Cait moved to him and he looked up at her impassively. His face—what she could see of it beneath the foul mat of his hair and beard—was broad, his chin and cheekbones strong. "This man here says you are his lord."

"He speaks the truth."

"Then why do you refuse to stand with the others?"

"You did not say how many would be chosen," he replied evenly. "If any are to gain freedom today, I want my men to have first chance."

Cait nodded thoughtfully. "If I pay ransom for your men, will you join them?"

"Of course," he said. "I am their lord."

"Tell me, how did you come to be here?"

"There was a battle," answered the knight. "We lost."

"Is that all? Nothing more?"

"That was enough."

"I mean," said Cait with exaggerated patience, "is there nothing more you care to tell me about how you came to be here?"

"We are warriors, not criminals. There is nothing more to tell."

"Then let us strike a bargain, you and I," replied Cait, satisfied at last.

The knight climbed slowly to his feet. Even in chains, his clothes little more than filth-crusted rags, he held himself straight and tall. "I am Rognvald of Haukeland," he declared. "Tell me your bargain."

"It is this," said Cait. Before she could continue, the jailer, who had been talking idly to the katib, suddenly thrust himself between them, shouting and swinging his keys again. Instantly, the knight raised his shackled hands, caught hold of the iron ring, and held it firm so that Cait would not be struck. The jailer roared with frustration.

"Peace! Sala'am!" cried Abu, rushing forward. He beseeched and cajoled, and by degrees calmed the outraged jailer. "He says you must not go among them," Abu informed Cait, "or you will certainly be hurt."

"Tell the jailer I thank him for his vigilance and concern," Cait replied, stepping back to show she understood. To the knight, she said, "Here is my bargain: I require the aid and protection of several men-at-arms for a pilgrimage I intend to make. In exchange for your vow of fealty, I will pay your ransom. Serve me well, and once I have reached my destination and achieved my purpose, you will be paid for your services and released to go your way."

Lord Rognvald regarded her with the same indifferent expression with which he had greeted her.

"What say you?" she asked. "Do you wish to discuss the matter with your men?"

When he still did not reply, she demanded, "Well? What is your answer?"

"I am thinking."

The other prisoners began shouting just then, imploring to be recognized, giving Cait to understand that if these Norwegians were reluctant, many another would happily take their place. Putting out her hand to the clamoring captives, Cait said, "You see? There are plenty of others ready and willing to volunteer."

"This is what I am thinking," replied the knight, stroking his beard with a grimy hand.

It was at that moment that Cait knew she had made the right choice. "Lord Rognvald, I chose you because while I know nothing about fighting men, I *do* know something about Norsemen. And I know that if a Norseman accepts my bargain I can trust him to keep it, and I will sleep secure in my bed at night."

"That is true," replied the knight. "How do you know so much about Norsemen?"

"My great-grandfather was born in Norway, and my grandfather came from Orkneyjar—he served King Magnus on the Great Pilgrimage."

Lord Rognvald's men stood looking on, their faces pinched with desperate hope.

"Come, let us agree," said Caitríona. "I think you will find service in my employ far less onerous than your present occupation."

A ghost of a smile touched his dry lips. "My lady, I accept."

Cait turned at once to the katib. "These four men," she said. "How much is the ransom?"

Abu translated her words, and the wazir's secretary cast his eyes over the standing men. He made a mental calculation, and announced the price.

"Ten thousand dirhams," Abu said, relaying the katib's words. "Each."

"Very well," said Cait. "Tell him I agree."

"With all respect, *sharifah*, that I will not do," Abu replied. "It is impious to accept the first price—it shows disrespect for the bounty Allah has given you. Also it is an insult to the intelligence and an affront to the spirit of commerce."

"I see. Then tell him it is too much," said Cait. "I will give five thousand." ·

Abu and the katib held a short, spirited discussion, whereupon Abu turned to Cait and announced, "Katib says you are not to offend his master the prince with such a ridiculous offer. These are Christian knights, not camels. Ten thousand is the price for which noble fighting men are redeemed. He will not accept less than eight thousand dirhams."

"While I intend no disrespect to Prince Mujir ed-Din," Cait replied smoothly, "I must point out that one of these men is injured, and all of them suffer from lice, starvation, dysentery, and God knows what else. I doubt whether his highness the prince would buy camels in a similar condition. Six thousand, tell him."

"Seven thousand and five hundred dirhams for each man," countered the katib when Abu had translated her words.

"I think it is still too much," Abu confided in a low voice. "These men have been here a long time. Stay at six."

"Six thousand and not one dirham more," said Cait through her dutiful translator. Looking around the prison, she added, "I do not see anyone offering a better price. Therefore," she smiled, "I advise you to accept mine."

"Twenty-five thousand for all four," countered the katib serenely.

"Very well," said Cait. "Twenty-five thousand for these four," she held up a finger, "*and* freedom for one more of my choosing." She paused, and added with a smile, "Twenty-five thousand silver dirhams, katib, or nothing. I leave the choice to you. Personally, I think twenty-five thousand dirhams would be very useful in helping repair the earthquake damage to his majesty the prince's reception hall."

When her words were relayed to him, the katib rolled his eyes. "Yu'allah!" he sighed. "Very well, which is it to be?"

Addressing Rognvald, she said, "Is there any man here with a young family waiting for him at home?"

The knight thought for a moment. "There are two that I know of," he said, and pointed out two knights, who eagerly rose and stood expectantly.

"Do either of you have a daughter?" Cait asked in Latin.

"I do," replied one of the men.

"How old is she?"

"Six years this summer," answered the man.

"When did you last see her?"

"Three years ago."

"I will buy your release on one condition," she said. "You must abandon any claim to wealth or rank in the Holy Land and return home to your family without delay."

"God smite me if I do not fly from this hellhole the moment I am released," replied the knight, unable to keep the quaver of excitement from his voice.

"Swear it," she insisted.

"Upon my soul and every hope of eternal salvation, I hereby abandon any and all claims to wealth and rank in the Holy Land, and vow to return home by the swiftest means possible."

"Very well," replied Cait. "If you like, you may accompany us to the coast where you will find passage aboard a ship to take you home."

"Your kindness shames and overwhelms me," replied the knight. "I thank you, my lady. I am your devoted servant."

"Your safe return to your family is sufficient."

Turning to the katib, Cait indicated the man and said, "That one is to be included with the others. They are to be allowed to wash and given clean clothes. Understood?"

The katib bent his head in acknowledgment and the bargain was sealed. Turning on her heel, she walked quickly from the chamber, steeling herself against the piteous clamor of the captives as they cried out to be released. She did not stop until she was outside the prison and drinking in the fragrant air of the prince's courtyard once more.

"Please tell Prince Mujir ed-Din that I thank him for indulging my request so admirably. And I will thank Wazir Muqharik to command the captives to be readied for their release by midday when I return with the money."

"It shall be done," replied the katib when Abu had delivered her words.

The party then left the palace and returned to the inn where Caitríona had taken rooms. Leaving Abu and Otti to keep watch in the courtyard outside, she and Haemur brought out the chest containing the items carefully selected for the purpose from among the treasures Duncan had assembled to pay for their pilgrimage to Jerusalem. Alethea watched as her sister withdrew a gold bowl rimmed with alternating rubies and sapphires, and a ceremonial dagger with pearl-studded handle and crystal blade.

"Now what are you doing?" Thea asked, yawning with boredom.

"I am selling a few things to pay for knights," Cait explained, passing the objects to the ship's pilot, who placed them in a cloth bag which he knotted and tied.

"Are you going into the city?" asked Alethea. "I want to go. I hate staying here alone. If you are going, I am going, too."

"No," replied Caitríona crisply. "We are staying here."

"I cannot see why we need knights anyway," grumped Alethea.

"I told you, it is not safe for us to travel alone," replied Cait. "We need the protection of a bodyguard." With that, she and Haemur returned to the courtyard, where Cait instructed Abu Sharma to accompany Haemur to the principal marketplace in the city and negotiate the best terms possible for the sale of the precious objects. "We need at least twenty-five thousand dirhams, as you know," she said. "Bargain well, and I will give you a dirham for every ten you receive over the necessary amount."

"Done!" cried the young physician. "Place your full confidence in me, sharifah. We shall return in triumph."

"Otti," she said, turning to the seaman, "I want you to go with Haemur for protection. Let no harm come to him. Understand?"

The simple seafarer nodded dutifully, and took his place beside the pilot. She watched them depart, and then went back to her room and lay down on her bed with eyes closed, hoping to escape the heat and noise of the busy streets outside the inn.

It was no use. The barking of dogs, the braying of donkeys, and the restless fidgeting and sighing of Alethea kept her awake. So, abandoning the attempt, she rose and, taking her sister with her, went to find the innkeeper to arrange for a special meal to be served that evening for her soon-to-be-released warrior band.

SEVEN

"Sharifah!" cried Abu Sharma, his voice loud in the courtyard. "Come quickly!"

Cait awakened at the sound. The chamber door was open to the courtyard outside. "Thea!" she muttered.

Rising, she pulled on her shoes and hurried out to find the courtyard filled with the horses, camels, and baggage of a caravan of Arab merchants newly arrived in the city. The travelers, dressed in dark robes and pale yellow turbans, were standing in the yard overseeing the unloading of their pack animals while the innkeeper passed among them with cups of lemon water and tiny honey cakes. The sun was hovering above the rooftops, and the heat of the day slowly fading.

"Here, sharifah," Abu called again. "Come and see what I have done for you!"

The young physician and the old pilot stood holding a small wooden casket between them. Otti loomed behind in an attitude of hovering protection. Haemur was grinning like a child with a naughty secret, and Abu was puffed up and strutting like a cockerel. Alethea stood nearby, gawking at the Arab travelers in their opulent, richly patterned robes. The younger men among the merchants were, in turn, ogling Alethea who, owing to the heat, had put off her mantle and come out wearing only her undershift; her long smooth arms were exposed and her legs bare from her shapely calves to her slender ankles.

"Thea! Get inside," Cait ordered. To Abu and Haemur she said, "Bring it in. There may still be a few people in Damascus who have yet to learn our business. Perhaps we might keep it that way."

The two men lugged the chest into Cait's room, and lay it at her feet.

The others crowded around as Abu pulled the hook from the hasp and swung the lid back on its hinges. "Behold!" he cried. "Silver and gold for her majesty!"

Indeed, the casket was filled with silver dirhams and a scattering of gold dinars. "How much is here?" asked Alethea excitedly, her eyes wide at the sight of so much money.

"Thirty-three thousand dirhams," replied Haemur with unaccustomed enthusiasm. "It was all Abu's doing. You should have seen him, my lady; he bargained like a champion—"

"That is me: Abu Sharma, Champion of the Bazaar!"

Otti laughed out loud. "He is crazy, this one."

"That may well be," agreed Cait, removing a handful of coins from the chest.

"But this is wonderful, Cait," said Alethea. "Do you not think so?"

"I am delighted." She counted out coins amounting to eight thousand dirhams, put them in a leather bag which she tied, and returned the rest to the box. To Abu and Haemur she said, "I might have been more delighted if you had accomplished the task in good time." Taking up a shawl to wrap around her shoulders, she said, "Close the box and bring it."

Abu's face fell slightly. "You do not wish to hear how the Mighty Abu wrestled the demons of avarice, greed, and desire in the marketplace?"

"*I* do," said Alethea.

"Later," Cait said, moving to the door. "I wish to secure the release of the captives before they close the palace gates."

Motioning Otti to help him, the young Syrian took up the casket. "I know," he said, brightening once more, "I will tell you on the way. It will pleasantly pass the time."

"Excellent," said Thea happily.

Cait turned and handed her the bag of coins. "You are staying here."

"Ohhh," Thea whined in frustration. "Cait, please, I want to go."

"And keep the door closed until I get back."

Thea frowned.

"I mean it, Thea. I will not have you wandering around outside alone."

"Otti could come with me," she suggested hopefully.

"I need Otti with me."

At Caitríona's command, Abu hired a small carriage from among those waiting outside the inn. She and Haemur rode in the carriage guarding the box, while Otti and Abu walked alongside. Abu, eager to aggrandize himself in the eyes of his patroness, embellished his story shamelessly. However, the tale that emerged bore at least a passing resemblance to what had actually taken place.

As directed, the three men had taken the precious objects Cait had given them from among the items in her father's store, and they had gone to the marketplace, where, in the street of goldsmiths, they sought out the expert valuation of one of the more highly respected craftsmen there. The fellow had examined the items, expressed interest and, when he asked the reason for the sale, had been told the simple truth: to raise funds for the ransom of prisoners. "Fifteen thousand," offered the goldsmith, upon receiving this information. Abu duly pointed out that the objects were far more valuable than that, but the fellow refused to barter. The offer remained firm. "The walls of Damascus would be easier to move than that pinchfist," Abu declared.

Undeterred, they took their business to another goldsmith across the street, who welcomed them with small glasses of spiced wine, sat them down, and proceeded to spend a considerable time examining the items they had for sale. They were fine pieces, exceptional pieces, he told them. The finest materials and craftsmanship, beyond the shadow of a doubt. "Why are you parting with them?" he asked, and was told, as before, that the money was needed to ransom captives of war. "Fourteen thousand," replied the gold dealer. "Each?" asked Abu Sharma. "For both," sniffed the dealer. "And I am doing you a favor at that."

Nor would he improve the offer. "A rock in the sea would have more compassion," Haemur asserted with a sorry shake of his head.

The next goldsmith they visited offered a slightly improved sixteen thousand—but only when told they had already received an offer of fifteen from a nearby competitor. This is when Abu grew angry. They went out and walked along the street for a while to give Abu time to consider the situation. Haemur was all for going back and letting Cait decide what should be done, but the young Syrian had the bit between his teeth now, and he was determined not to be bested.

They walked to the end of the street, and then down another street, and yet another, coming to the less respectable dealers of gold, gems, and precious objects—places where formerly wealthy people often found buyers for treasures acquired in more prosperous times. Abu chose one of the most disreputable-looking of these, and told Otti to stand across the street and stare very hard at the shabby little shack and not to move. Next he instructed Haemur to accompany him, but to stand by the door and say nothing. It was agreed. Abu drew a deep breath and held it until Haemur feared he would burst, and then, gathering up the box, he darted across the street and into the dealer's dwelling.

"This fellow looks up to see Abu rushing in all red-faced and out of breath," said the young Syrian, "and it is 'Allah help you, my friend, what has happened?' " So, Abu explained that he had something to sell, but was concerned that nothing should be known of his visit—not to anyone, not ever. The dealer said that he himself could not imagine any reason why anyone should learn of any transactions they might undertake. He took special pains to point out that his customers often required sympathy and understanding. Ask anyone, he said, they would tell you that Faraq Irbil is the soul of discretion and silent as the tomb.

Apparently satisfied, Abu opened the sack and agreed to allow the dealer to examine the goods—but first would he mind going to the door and looking outside, please? "This he does," said Abu, "and as the fellow peers out he sees Otti standing across the street glaring at the door of his hovel. 'Oh, no!' I cry. 'We must vanish at once!' I close the sack and jump up to leave.

"The dealer is not content to allow his opportunity to disappear so abruptly. 'Wait a moment,' pleaded Faraq, 'there is nothing to fear. Let me see what you have. Maybe I can help.' 'But no,' I said, 'It is too late! Too late! I am sorry. I had hoped to raise a little money, but now . . . Allah help us, it is too late! Forgive me for troubling you.' "

Abu chuckled at his own shrewdness. "I close up the sack and rush to the door. 'Please do not leave,' the dealer cries, clutching at my sleeve. He has glimpsed the golden bowl with the gem-edged rim, and is loath to let it vanish as quickly as it has appeared. 'I can see you are troubled,' Faraq says to me. 'Perhaps events have overtaken you, eh? Yes, I thought so. But there is nothing to fear. You are safe here. Come, sit down. You say you wish to raise money. You have come to the right place. I am a dealer in fine gold, jewelry, and precious stones. Let me see what you have brought.'

" 'Very well,' says Abu, 'I may as well show you—but remember: no one must ever know I was here. A woman's honor is involved. She is a wealthy woman, you see? The fault is not hers. Forgive me, I wish I could say more.' So, Abu brings out the sapphire-and-ruby-rimmed bowl, and says, 'It is worth sixty thousand. You know it. I know it. Alas, the time for bartering is past. I will take forty.'

" 'Forty!' Faraq pretends to be shocked. 'If only that was possible. Alas, my purse is not so capacious as those in the upper street. I am a man of more slender means. Twenty is the best I can offer. You think it over while I go and see if that belligerent fellow is still waiting for you across the street. Oh, yes, he is still there. It seems you must choose between us now.'

"But, Abu Sharma, slayer of demons, is not finished yet. He brings out the crystal dagger, withdraws it from its sheath of gilded leather, and lays the pearl-studded hilt beside the golden bowl. 'I see that sacrifices must be made,' says Abu. 'But it is forty thousand I must have. So: twenty for the bowl, and twenty for the knife.'

"The dealer's eyes grow round. This is a most auspicious day, he is thinking. 'Truly, my friend, these are exquisite pieces. Therefore, against my better judgment, I will give you fifteen apiece. More I cannot do.'

" 'O, woe, woe! Doom and woe! Why did I ever stray from the paths of righteousness? Alas, I am undone! Cursed was the day of my birth. I must have been fathered by a scorpion!'

"Abu wails and moans, he throws himself about the room, tearing his hair and gnashing his teeth. He scoops up the precious objects and throws them into the bag once more and points accusingly at the silent Haemur. 'You see? You see? You see how I am destroyed? Now we must make haste and flee the city! Our last hope must be in flight.'

"The dealer, deeply impressed and alarmed by these words, puts up his hands and says, 'Wait! Wait! I have a brother who might be willing to help us. From him I can get three thousand more. I will add that to the sum already offered, yes? Let us agree and put your troubles to flight, my friend.'

"Under the gold dealer's ministrations, Abu allows himself to be calmed. Thirty-three thousand dirhams it is. The dealer goes out and returns but a few moments later with the gold and silver in a chest. Together he and Abu count out coins amounting to thirty-three thousand dirhams and, with much praising and blessing Haemur and Abu depart, carrying the chest between them." The young Syrian smiled broadly. "And the rest, sharifah, you have seen."

"It is a remarkable tale, Abu," Cait declared. "If even half of it is true, you have earned your reward. I will pay you as soon as we have redeemed the captives and returned to the inn."

At the palace, however, they found the courtyard deserted and the wazir's secretary less than pleased at having been kept waiting half the day to complete the arrangements he had begun for the release of the war captives. "Thirty-five thousand dirhams," he informed Cait when she and the others had been brought into the hall where Wazir Muqharik received his visitors.

"I beg your pardon, katib," answered Cait, speaking through Abu, "but twenty-five thousand was the amount we agreed upon."

"*That* was before you kept the prince's chief official waiting," he replied imperiously. "Thirty-five thousand. Pay it, or go."

Caitríona motioned for Otti and Abu to bring the chest forward and place it on the table. This they did, and Cait threw open the lid and upended the box, spilling the coins in a glimmering rush over the table. "Twenty-five thousand," Cait declared. "That, along with my most sincere and profound apologies for the inconvenience you have suffered, should be more than sufficient. I pray you will accept both."

Having made his point, the katib accepted the money and the apology. "The captives have been washed, and clothed. They also have been waiting," he said, speaking through Abu. "If you would please proceed to the gate, they will be brought out to you."

Cait thanked the katib and returned to the palace gate where, a few moments later, the five knights were escorted from the guardhouse by a company of spear-bearing Saracens led by the jailer. They were delivered without ceremony in simple Arabic garb of long, belted tunics and sandals—cast-off clothing and well worn, but clean. They were still unshaven, but they had been scrubbed to a glowing luster, and had made a gallant, if only partially successful, attempt to comb the tangles from their long hair and beards. They hobbled from the courtyard and out through the palace gates without looking back.

Their long imprisonment made walking difficult—to a man they moved with an odd lolloping gait as if their legs were made of wood, ill-fashioned and poorly hinged. Their muscles were unequal to the exertion and after only a few hundred paces they had to rest to catch their breath. Cait sent Abu ahead to a nearby market square to hire two carriages; when he returned, the knights eagerly, if painfully, clambered aboard. When the carriages began to roll, leaving the palace walls behind, the former captives overcame their infirmities sufficiently to revel in their freedom by giving vent to enthusiastic whoops and battle cries. Their exuberance drew stares from the people in the streets, many of whom muttered imprecations against ill-mannered foreigners, and fools who could not hold their wine.

Blissfully ignorant of the disapproval swirling around them, the jubilant company drove like conquering heroes through a city they had never thought to see again.

EIGHT

Upon arriving at the inn, Cait discovered that the rooms she had be-spoken for her enlarged retinue were now occupied by the merchants who had arrived earlier in the day. The innkeeper was vaguely apologetic, but unwilling to turn his guests out; moreover, the special meal Cait had arranged was now being prepared for the merchants. "I begged to be excused, but they insisted," he said, spreading his hands in a gesture of abject helplessness. "They paid in gold dinars. What could I do?"

"I suppose honoring your promise to me never occurred to you?" inquired Cait tartly.

"Exalted lady, you must try to be reasonable," protested the innkeeper in his rough, marketplace Latin. "These are very important men from the East. It is said that one is the supplier of pepper and saf-fron to the Sultan of Rhum, and the others are the owners of caravans that carry silk and spices from Kush to Samarkand. They are celebrat-ing a royal commission to provide the court at Baghdad with damask cloth and cinnamon."

"Spare me your mealy mouthed excuses," snapped Cait. "These merchants who cannot be denied—where are they?"

"Cait, no," murmured Alethea; she had been watching for her sis-ter's return and hurried out to meet the knights, who, having eased themselves from the carriages, stood gazing at the evening sky with the transparent delight of children.

"The merchants, my lady? But—" He looked to Alethea for help.

"Cait, please . . ." Thea tugged anxiously on her sleeve.

Ignoring her sister, Cait demanded, "Where are they?"

"Why, they are resting in the inner court. But—" began the innkeeper.

"As it is our meal they propose to eat, they will not mind if we share the celebration." Turning to Abu, Cait said, "Come with me, we will secure our invitation to the feast."

The horrified innkeeper started after her. "My lady, this you cannot do. It is—"

Cait turned on him, and let fly. "You will *not* presume to tell me what I can and cannot do! I have five noblemen who require beds tonight. Not merchants: noblemen. Knights! They are newly released from captivity and are not of a mind to sleep in your stinking stable. So, if I were you, my oily friend," she jabbed a finger into his flabby chest, "I would not waste another moment worrying about my precious propriety, but would start trying to save my worthless skin. For unless you find rooms where my men will be comfortable, I will give them leave to peel you like a grape."

With that, Cait turned and marched directly into the inner courtyard to a flurry of protestation from a red-faced, horrified innkeeper. The courtyard had been spread with rugs and cushions for the comfort of the merchants and their guests, who were reclining around large brass trays filled with cups and jars, and bowls of olives and roasted pine nuts.

At her sudden appearance, all conversation ceased. The merchants looked up to see a woman livid with rage sweeping into their midst. For a moment they merely stared, and when it appeared that she was not about to leave, one of them rose to his feet and addressed her courteously. Abu translated.

"Most gracious lady," he said, "you honor us with your radiant presence." A swarthy man of middle years, his ample form swathed in costly robes of glistening blue and black and crimson, he touched his fingertips to his forehead and made an elaborate flourish with his hand—a flash of gold from the rings on every finger. "I am Ibn Umar al-Farabi, purveyor of rare spices from the Orient. How may I be of service to you?"

"It seems the rooms which I have engaged for my party have been given to you and your friends."

"Indeed?" remarked the merchant with mild surprise when Abu had relayed her words. "Nothing was said of this to me. I am sorry, but I fear there is little to be done about it now. We have already paid for the rooms, you see."

"Also, the meal which you will be served was bespoken by me," she told him bluntly.

"Again," replied the trader, "it is unfortunate, but we were not told of this—otherwise we would certainly have made other arrangements. As it is, we have paid for the meal and it is even now being prepared. There is no remedy, I fear." He inclined his head sympathetically. "Please accept my deepest regrets."

The other merchants were listening now; she saw one of them smile with a smugness that brought her already seething rage to a roaring boil.

"You may keep your regrets. I have no use for them," Cait snapped. "However, I may be persuaded to accept an invitation to join you at table tonight—sharing the cost, of course."

The Arab twisted a gold ring on his finger. "Truly, you are as astute as you are determined. Therefore, it pains me to confess that we cannot offer you the invitation you suggest. For, according to our faith, it is a sin for a follower of Muhammed, peace be upon him forever, to entertain an infidel beneath the roof of his house."

Abu relayed the merchant's words, and added for Cait's benefit: "This is not strictly accurate. I believe he is testing you, sharifah."

Cait considered this observation, and countered, "If this is all that prevents you, allow me to put your pious soul at ease. We are not infidels, as you conveniently suppose, but *Ahl al-Kitab*, People of the Book." Indicating the dusky red sky overhead, she said, "Also, the roof you see above you was created by God himself, and it is his good pleasure that all his many children might sit with one another beneath it so that harmony and understanding may increase."

A shrewd smile spread slowly across the Arab's smooth face. "I perceive that you are a most formidable advocate," said Ibn Farabi, bowing low. "I yield to your superior judgment. Therefore, let it be as you say." Spreading his jewelled hands wide in welcome, he said, "Please join us, and what was to have been a simple meal among friends will become a banquet."

Cait thanked the merchant for his liberality and sent Abu to bring the knights. They trooped noisily into the courtyard, still reeling with the heady intoxication of freedom. Haemur and Otti came next with a mortified Alethea trying to remain invisible behind them.

Upon seeing their dinner companions, however, the Norsemen's jubilant expressions faded abruptly. Cait heard the ugly growl of muttered oaths. "It is not what I planned," she told them sternly, "but it comes to this: dine with them, or go hungry. You decide."

As they stood staring dully at their reluctant Arab hosts, the first platters arrived—two large brass trays bearing a veritable mound of apricot-stuffed partridges, and a wicker basket heaped with bread in flat round loaves. The trays were served by the innkeeper's wife and daughters, dressed for the evening in shimmering green satin with strands of gold coins on their brows and in their hair.

"Well?" demanded Cait. The aroma of the roast fowls filled the courtyard, and the knights' gaze shifted from the Arabs to the mounded platters. "What is it to be?"

"Lady," Rognvald answered, recovering something of his former exuberance, "tonight I would sup with the Devil himself for a taste of this feast." Turning to the others, he said, "Not so?"

They all agreed, so Cait bade her band of prison-haunted knights, land-locked sailors, and mortified sister to follow her and, with Abu's help, presented each in turn to al-Farabi, who welcomed them and introduced them to his four fellow merchants and their companions. The two parties sat down uneasily together. One of the knights reached straight for a roast fowl, and would have gulped it down, but for Cait's sharp tap on his wrist. "This is not prison slops in a trough, it is a banquet. We are guests, not prisoners. Therefore, you will behave as if you have dined in civilized company before." She turned her withering gaze on the rest of them. "You may look like denizens of the dung heap, but try to remember you are noblemen, and let us refrain from giving these Arabs the satisfaction of slandering us when we leave."

Alethea, blushing crimson, lowered her eyes and shrank even further into herself. But the knights accepted the reproach with good grace. Duly chastised, they assumed a more courtly demeanor and began to imitate their Muhammedan hosts. They washed their hands in the basins provided, and proceeded to dip from the platter with their right hand, placing the food on a flat of bread balanced on their left.

More platters and bowls were brought—herbed vegetables soaked in olive oil and grilled over coals, fish and olives in mustard sauce, and slivered cucumbers in salted cream and vinegar. A careful, if not altogether convivial, silence descended over the meal as the hungry Norwegians filled empty stomachs with food they would have gladly given sight and sanity to eat only half a day ago. The merchants, not to be outdone at their own feast, kept pace with their ravenous guests, and the food rapidly disappeared. Indeed, the hungry company was just finishing the platter of partridges when the centerpiece of the meal arrived: a whole roast lamb stuffed with rice, leeks, pistachios, and spiced sausage surrounded by a sunburst of spit-roasted doves glazed with sweet mulberry jelly.

As this grand dish was laid before the delighted company, the innkeeper appeared, and meekly inquired if the meal was satisfactory. "Is all to your liking?" he asked, tugging at his moustache with apprehension.

"Bring us wine," Cait told him, "and, God willing, all shall yet be well."

"At once," said the innkeeper, hurrying away.

Within moments, wine was pouring from tall pitchers into cups and bowls. The Muhammedans did not drink the wine, but continued to sip their *sharábah*, an infusion of violets in sweetened water; the knights, however, more than made up for the Muslims' restraint by quaffing the luscious dark liquid in deep drafts until it ran down their untidy beards.

As night drew in around them, casting the company into deep shadow, the innkeeper brought torches which he placed in jars of sand around the courtyard; the resulting flames cast all in a rosy glow, allowing Cait to study her ragged band of knights.

There was Yngvar, first chosen, a big man, tall, with hands easily twice the size of her own. His fair hair was long and looked as if it had been gnawed by rats. As she had noticed in prison, he favored his left side somewhat—wincing now and then when he laughed. But that did not stop the laughter. His face was open and honest, and his deep-set eyes seemed like chips of northern slate beneath the overhanging ledge of his brow.

Next to him sat Svein: darker, more thoughtful, genial, but reserved. Cait suspected that however much he might nod and laugh with the others, the greater part of him remained aloof and watchful. The weight of his captivity lay heavy on him; his broad shoulders drooped from carrying the burden of that long oppression. And although he said little, Cait could tell from the wry, knowing expression when she

74

talked that his understanding of Latin was better than his fellows, and perhaps equal to her own.

Beside Svein was Dag, whose knowledge of Latin appeared to extend only so far as the end of his well-shaped chin. Nor, Cait suspected, was he troubled by an overly energetic intellect. But, where the others looked like they had been pulled fresh from the hostage pit, he appeared as hale as a man who had just woken from a long nap. Younger than the others, he was undeniably handsome, and enjoyed the confidence his dusky good looks bestowed. Even so, Cait was pleased to see he displayed none of the conceit that good-looking men so often cultivated. He was easy with himself and the others, his smile at once genuine and effortless. Beside Dag sat the unknown knight, guarded, silent, happily making himself an unobtrusive, humble presence.

And then, next to her, Rognvald. Tall and gaunt, his flesh seemed to hang on his bones, but the bones were strong. Cait imagined that a few weeks of good food, clean air, and rest would restore his former strength and chase the prison pallor from his face. And it was, she decided, a good face—a true Nordic face with generous features and a long straight nose. He was past the first blush of youth—his sand-colored hair had begun to thin somewhat, and the lines were beginning to deepen on his face—but, just sitting next to him, she sensed a steady and resolute spirit, and his quick blue eyes hinted at hidden depths.

While she might have hoped for a more imposing bodyguard, Cait was satisfied. They were near kinsmen, after all; with their familiar Scandic features they might have been brothers, uncles, or cousins, and she felt she understood them. In the strangeness of this foreign land, she found their presence comforting and reassuring and she was confident that once they had exchanged their prison clothes for attire more natural to their rank, they would begin to resemble something more impressive than the moth-eaten coterie she saw before her now.

After the first pangs of hunger were appeased, the meal took on a more cordial atmosphere. The warmth of food and wine and the pleasant surroundings of the courtyard worked a charm of peace and calm. Conversation became more cheerful, filling the evening with an amiable companionship which expanded to embrace them all.

In their elation over the extravagant and sumptuous fare, the Norsemen completely forgot their qualms about eating with Arabs, and the sedately dignified merchants gave every appearance of enjoying the company of the raucously enthusiastic northerners. Though they could not speak to one another, save through Abu's mediation, the Arabs offered their boisterous guests choice morsels of succulent lamb, or tiny spiced sausages. For their parts, the knights loudly acclaimed the virtues of their hosts with endless salutes of their cups. All around the circle, smiles came easier and laughter more frequent—even Alethea, from the security of her place beside old Haemur, had shaken off her embarrassment and was enjoying herself.

As she sat watching the others eat and drink and laugh, Cait felt the hard-twisted knot she had carried within her for many days begin to loosen and unwind. She found herself wishing Duncan could be there to enjoy it. *Papa would have loved this,* she thought, and suddenly the grief which she had succeeded in stifling since Constantinople rolled over her in a great fathomless wave. Tears welled suddenly and unexpectedly in her eyes. To hide them, she bent her head over her cup and let them fall.

"Lady," murmured Rognvald beside her, "are you well?"

She nodded, dabbing the tears away with the back of her hand.

"Celebrations always make me cry, too," he confided. She glanced up quickly to see if he was mocking her, but could not tell from his thoughtful expression.

"I suppose I am just a little tired," she said.

"It has been an eventful day for all of us." He raised his cup, held it up to her, then drank a silent health in her honor, before filling his bowl with more roast lamb.

As the moon rose above the finger-thin tops of the cypress trees lining the courtyard and showered the company with its gentle glow, a man in a white turban and long black cloak appeared in the arched doorway. Instantly, Ibn Farabi rose from his place, and clapped his hands for silence. Gesturing for Abu to join him, he made a formal announcement in Arabic, which Abu translated: "Friends and esteemed companions," the merchant said, "I have now the very great pleasure of presenting to you the renowned seer and conjurer, Jalal Sinjari, who has kindly consented to perform for us this evening a few of his legendary feats."

The innkeeper and his family, and several of the other guests at the inn, slipped in through the door to stand along the perimeter of the courtyard and watch the dark magician who stepped forward, bowed, and made a fluttery movement with his hands. Suddenly there was a blinding flash of light, and two small boys appeared beside him, one on either side. Dressed in white tunics and trousers, barefoot, their hair shaved to a single thick knot which hung from the back of their heads, they knelt and touched their foreheads to the ground. Sinjari stretched a hand over each of the boys and, still kneeling, they floated up into the air.

Then, producing two large squares of blue silk cloth from beneath his cloak, he covered first one boy and then the other. He lifted his hands and the boys drifted higher still, and then hung there, suspended in the air while Sinjari, his arms spread wide, walked beneath them to the chorused murmurs of his small crowd. He stepped back, holding his hands high, turned his face heavenward, drew breath, and gave out a mighty shout. In the same instant, he leaped forward and, seizing a corner of the silk in each hand, whipped the coverings away.

There was a popping sound and a flurry of white flower petals whirled and spun around the magician. Cait felt a puff of warm air on her face and was bathed in the fragrance of roses. The unexpected marvel delighted even as it astonished, and Cait laughed out loud. She laughed again when the conjurer turned around and . . . there were the two boys clinging to his back!

They somersaulted to the ground and, while the diners and onlookers applauded and rattled their cups against the brass trays, the boys ran off to fetch a large, urn-shaped wicker basket which they dragged forward between them. One removed the basket's lid, and the other retrieved a small pipe-like flute which the conjurer began to play with a raspy, low, droning sound. The noise, while not entirely pleasant to Cait's ear, nevertheless made her feel as if a subtle movement was taking place in the earth beneath her, and all around; the trees and walls and air seemed to quiver with the sound.

For a long time nothing appeared to be happening, but as the buzzing notes from the pipe began to quicken, there came a movement from the basket which drew gasps and shrieks from the onlookers as what appeared to be the head and thick sinuous form of a gigantic serpent rose slowly above the rim of the basket.

But it was not a snake—it was a heavy braided rope, the end of which had been knotted and bound. Up it went, slowly undulating as it rose ever higher, as if drawn upward by unseen hands. Eventually, the top of the rope reached up beyond the small sphere of torchlight, and there it stopped, stretching itself taut. Without taking his lips from the pipe or interrupting the strange low melody, Sinjari nodded to the boy beside him, who began to climb, wrapping his arms and legs around the rope and gripping it with his bare feet.

Higher and higher he climbed until he reached the top. Cait could see his small form dimly outlined in the moonlight as he clung there above the courtyard. Only then did the conjurer cease his playing. He called up to the boy, who answered him, his small voice drifting down to them. Handing the pipe to the other boy, Sinjari took hold of the rope with both hands and began to shake it, shouting angrily at the boy above.

The frightened child cried out, but the conjurer paid him no heed. Indeed, the more he cried, the more Sinjari shook the rope, each jerk growing more violent until those looking on were shouting, too—for the magician to desist and let the boy descend.

Their pleas were too late, for Sinjari gave the rope a final terrible jolt and the hapless child shrieked and lost his grip, plummeting to the courtyard like a stone, the rope collapsing over him. But when Cait looked, she saw only an empty tunic and pair of trousers. Of the boy there was no other sign.

The spectators gaped in amazement and declaimed to one another in voices thin with shock as the other boy picked up the crumpled clothes and threw them into the basket, and then fed in the rope, coiling it round and round. Sinjari meanwhile walked to one of the torches and pulled it from its container. Returning to the basket, he pointed to it, and the boy with the rope climbed inside, pulling the last of the rope in with him.

The magician replaced the domed lid and, taking up one of the blue silks, covered the basket with the cloth. He called out to the boy inside, who answered. He called out again, and the boy answered likewise; he called a third time, and before the boy could make his reply, Sinjari whipped away the cloth and, throwing off the lid, thrust the torch inside.

Cait, fearing the boy would be burned, threw her hands before her face. Otti leaped to his feet and prepared to charge to the boy's rescue—and was restrained with difficulty by Haemur and Abu—while the others cried out in dismay for the child's sake. But the magician, impervious to their anguished shouts, stirred the torch around and around, filling the basket with flames.

Then, withdrawing the torch, Sinjari placed his foot against the basket, and kicked it over. The wicker vessel rolled lightly aside. Both boy and rope were gone—and in their place, a real, living snake, its skin glistening dully in the torchlight as it slithered slowly into the courtyard. The crowd gasped and drew back in fright.

Stooping to the serpent, Sinjari seized the beast by the tail and picked it up. Holding it at arm's length as it writhed in the air, he began to spin it—gently at first, but with increasing speed, he spun the creature, its sinuous length blurring in the flickering torchlight. Then all at once, he stopped and . . . Behold! It was a serpent no longer, but a handsome wooden staff, which he tapped on the ground three times with a solid and satisfying thump.

Next, he raised the staff and held it across his outstretched palms. He elevated it heavenward once, twice, three times, whereupon there was a sharp, resonating crack. The staff snapped in two, spouting sparks and plumes of flame from the broken ends. The flames showered tiny glowing embers of gold which bounced on the ground with a fizzing sound, creating a curtain of white smoke. And when the smoke cleared, there, standing before Cait's astonished eyes were the two small boys, unharmed and neatly dressed as before.

The gathering cheered and applauded, and Cait laughed and clapped her hands with delight. Otti dashed forward to examine the two young lads and their mysterious basket, as al-Farabi congratulated the renowned conjurer on his extraordinary feats. Cait turned to speak to Rognvald and found him looking, not at the spectacle before him, but at her.

For an instant his eyes held hers, and then he smiled and glanced away, leaving the distinct impression that he had been subtly appraising her. Before she could think what to say to this, al-Farabi clapped his hands for silence. "My friends!" he called, with Abu's help, "Jalal Sinjari has kindly consented to apply his skills as a seer for us this evening. Please, remain seated and he will come among us."

The magician bowed and proceeded to the reclining diners. Pausing before one of the merchants, he said, "You wish to know whether your sojourn in the city will bring an increase in fortune. I tell you, friend, it already has!"

There were murmurs of approval from the others in the party, and he turned to the man beside him, and said, "Your wife will not thank you for bringing home the servant girl. Unless you marry her and make her a wife, you will not have a moment's peace."

The man sputtered with chagrin, but his friend roared with laughter. "He has seen through your cunning plan, Yusuf!" he cried. "Marry the girl!"

The magician moved on, and was soon standing before Cait. Pressing his palms together, he bowed respectfully to her. "Most noble lady," he said, speaking through Abu, "you are as lovely as the jasmine that blossoms in the night. Please, give me your hand."

Enthralled, Caitríona extended her hand to him. Taking it in both of his own, Sinjari pressed it, and then turned it over. He traced the lines of her palm lightly with a finger and Cait saw the merriment die in his eyes. He stared at her palm and then looked into her face. His touch grew instantly cold.

"Your other hand, please?" he said, glanced at it, thanked her, and stepped away abruptly, saying, "A long and happy life awaits you, good woman. Allah wills it."

Dismayed and confused by this brusque dismissal, Cait felt the color rising to her cheeks. Aware that the others were watching, she smiled weakly and tried to shrug off the waves of distress rising around her. After all, she told herself, it was only a ruse, a trick for entertainment's sake—like the snake and disappearing boys—the sly deception of a practiced performer.

And yet, despite all that reason assured her, she could not shake off the feeling that Sinjari had seen something in her future that had caused him to abandon what he had been about to say.

The magician moved on, foretold a few more futures—the innkeeper would have another son before the year was through, and one of the merchants would become an amir—and then quickly thanked his audience for their most gratifying praise and attention, and dismissed himself. Ibn Umar al-Farabi walked with him to the doorway and bade him farewell. While the two men talked together, Cait, unable to resist, summoned Abu and, when Sinjari took his leave, she followed him out into the yard.

"A word, sir, if you please," called Abu on her behalf.

The conjurer turned. "Ah, I expected as much." He smiled wanly. "Accept my humble admonition: do not persist in your inquiry. Sometimes it is better not to know."

"I understand," replied Cait, through Abu, "but I must know."

"Noble lady, a seer glimpses only shadows, nothing more. What can I tell you that you could not guess?"

"Please."

Sinjari sighed. Taking her hand once more, he turned up the palm and gazed into it. After a moment he began to speak in a low, solemn voice that caused Cait's skin to tingle with stark apprehension. "You have placed yourself in great jeopardy," he said. "Already the forces of chaos and destruction gather about you—they soar like vultures circling in the air, waiting for their feast." He regarded her sadly. "If you persist in the way you have chosen, death will mark you for his own. Death is a shrewd and pitiless hunter. None escape his snares."

She pulled her hand from him as he finished, and thanked him for telling her, then bade him good night and turned away.

"It is not too late to turn aside," the magician called after her. "The future is written in sand, not stone."

NINE

"Forget the woman, I say. She is nothing to us."

Commander de Bracineaux regarded his companion with a stony basilisk stare. "She has stolen the pope's letter."

"She might have stolen the pope's golden chamber pot for all the good it will do her." Félix d'Anjou leaned his long frame against the stone rail of the balcony and, eyeing the fruit in the glass bowl on the table before him, drew a knife from its sheath at his belt. The red-and-blue striped sunshade rippled lightly in the breeze, as if it were struggling to exhale in the stifling heat of the day.

"She has the letter and she has gone to Damascus."

"My point exactly," replied Baron d'Anjou, spearing a ripe pear on the point of his dagger. He cut a slice from the soft flesh, and lifted it to his lips on the edge of the blade.

"Are you finally insane, d'Anjou?" inquired the Templar commander. Inert in his chair, his white tunic open to the waist, sweat was rolling off him in drops that spattered the dusty tiles like fat raindrops on hard desert pan.

"Perhaps," allowed the baron judiciously. "But it occurs to me that if she has gone to Damascus it can mean but one thing."

"Which is?"

"She does not have the slightest idea what she has stolen." D'Anjou cut another slice from the soft fruit, ate it, and tossed the rest over the rail into the garden below. "That is to say, the woman has no idea of the letter's value, or what it means. She is nothing but an opportunistic thief—and *not* a very clever one at that. Probably she cannot even read."

"That is precisely why we must get it back," de Bracineaux pointed out.

"Why?" The baron picked his teeth with the point of the knife.

"Before someone else finds the letter and realizes its worth. My God, d'Anjou," he blurted in frustration, "what have we been talking about?"

The Baron of Anjou sniffed. He stabbed a fig and raised it on the end of his knife. "All the more reason to forget the girl and go for the treasure instead—*before* someone else gets there first."

The commander regarded his fair-haired companion for a long moment. There was definitely something unnatural about him. In all the time Renaud had known him, he had never seen Félix d'Anjou sweat. The sun might scorch like an oven, but the pallid baron seemed always at his ease. By the same token, nothing ever rankled him; nothing ever perturbed, bothered, aggravated, or upset him. He seemed to have no feelings at all, but met each and every trial with the same unassailable equanimity. Some might consider such supreme and disciplined poise to be courage or confidence, but de Bracineaux knew it was neither.

"Unless, of course, you merely wish to gratify your deep desire to punish the slut for trespassing on your good nature," d'Anjou continued, "then I could quite understand such a pointless preoccupation." The baron took a bite of the fig, then flipped it over his shoulder and sent it spinning into the garden to join the pear. "But with things as they are, I daresay you would be better employed pursuing this Mysterious Rose Blossom, or whatever you call it."

"God's wounds, d'Anjou," replied de Bracineaux slowly, "but I begin to see a sort of sense in what you say."

He splashed some more of the chilled lemon water into the tall silver beaker in front of him, lifted it and rubbed the cool metal over his forehead before gulping down the sweet-sour liquid.

"We could leave as soon as troops arrive from Jerusalem," said the baron. His blade hovered above the fruit bowl ready to strike. "The weather will stay good. We can reach Asturia—or wherever this cleric may be—well before autumn."

"As to that," the Templar commander rejoined, "I have twenty men garrisoned in the city. That is a force of sufficient strength. I cannot imagine we would need more. We can depart as soon as provisions are put aboard. We can leave tomorrow morning."

"Better still." D'Anjou's dagger flashed down, splitting the smooth skin of a plum. He raised the fruit; red juice trickled down the blade like blood. "What of the emperor?"

"We will simply tell our host that we have been called away on urgent Church business, and beg his leave to depart at once. I am certain his niece and her new husband will find ways to amuse themselves until we return. Anyway, the Poor Soldiers of Christ have better things to do than provide escort for over-pampered newlywed royals." He sipped from his cup, adding, "It is beneath us."

De Bracineaux set down the beaker and rose as if he would set off for the harbor that very moment. He looked at the white sunlight beating down on the rooftops of the surrounding wings of the palace. The heat shimmered in waves before his eyes. He promptly sat down again. "Gislebert!"

He had to shout twice more before rousing the sergeant from his nap in the next room. "There you are. Fetch me a runner, sergeant. I have a message for the emperor."

Emperor Manuel Comnenus reclined on a couch beneath a sunshade of blue silk stretched between gilded poles. The thin fabric rippled in the light breeze of the garden as he lay with his hands folded over his compact, well-muscled chest, listening with half-closed eyes as a robed official read to him from a large scroll entitled *Ecloga Justinian*. The aged courtier's thin, nasal voice droned in the quiet of the sun-soaked garden, keeping the emperor from his midday sleep. Two small, half-naked children splashed in a fountain under the watchful eye of a white-robed servant in a broad-brimmed red hat.

At the approach of the *papias* he roused himself, rolling up onto his elbow. The official bowed low, his chain of office almost touching the ground. "Well?" demanded Manuel irritably.

"Grand Commander de Bracineaux has arrived, Basileus."

"Good. Let him wait on the terrace."

"Basileus," said the courtier, "the sun . . ."

"Yes? What of the sun?"

"It is very hot on the terrace, your majesty."

"Let him wear a hat."

"Of course, Basileus."

84

The old man had stopped reading while this exchange took place, and as the *papias* departed, the emperor turned to the reader and said, "Pray do not stop, Murzuphlus, even for a moment, else we shall never get through this."

He returned to his reclining position and listened for a while longer, and then, when he was ready to hold audience, he rose and thanked the old man, saying, "We will return to this tomorrow." Calling an order to the white-robed servant to take the children inside out of the sun, he then proceeded to the terrace. As he entered the gallery, he was met by two courtiers—the *protovestiarius* and the *silentarius*. The first held out a long sleeveless robe of purple with pomegranates embroidered in thread of crimson and gold; Manuel drew on the robe and stood patiently while the laces were tied. Meanwhile, the second offered him a blue peaked hat with a brim like the prow of a ship in front, which the emperor allowed to be placed on his head.

The silentarius bowed and then, walking backward while holding aloft his ebony rod of office, he led the emperor to the terrace where an extremely hot and uncomfortable de Bracineaux was waiting.

"Ah, there you are, commander," said the emperor; he made it sound as if he had been searching for the Templar for most of the day.

De Bracineaux swallowed down his annoyance. "It is a pleasure, Basileus, as always." He smiled, sweat streaming from his red face.

"It is very pleasant out here," Manuel said, walking to the terrace rail. Below the city walls he could see the Golden Horn gleaming like beaten metal in the hot sunlight. He watched the boats which ceaselessly worked the wide stretch of water. "We never grow tired of the view."

"It is a fine view, Basileus."

"It is, yes." The emperor stood at the rail, hands clasped behind his back, gazing out across the water to the hazy blue hills beyond, lost, so it seemed, in a reverie.

De Bracineaux waited a few moments, but when the emperor appeared to have forgotten him, he cleared his throat and said, "You wished to see me, Basileus, I believe."

"Did we?" wondered the emperor. He turned to the commander and regarded him mildly. "You should put off that heavy surcoat, commander," he observed. "You look like an ox on the spit."

"It is warm, yes, Basileus," agreed the sweating Templar. The sun beat down on his red, uncovered head.

Manuel smiled. "We received a message that you wished to leave Constantinople."

"With your kind permission, Basileus. A matter of some importance has arisen which requires my presence elsewhere."

The emperor accepted this. "Are we to know the nature of this important matter?" His glance became keen as he watched the Templar commander try to avoid answering the question.

"It is a procedural matter, Basileus," replied de Bracineaux with slight hesitation. "I would not presume to inflict the minutiae of our Order on you, your highness."

"Procedure can be fatiguing, we find." The emperor drew breath and turned once more to the folded hills rising above the wide sweep of the Golden Horn. "Nevertheless, you may consider that we have matters of importance which require your presence here, Grand Commander de Bracineaux."

"But your highness—" de Bracineaux started to object.

The emperor cut off his protest with a wave of his hand. Without looking at his visitor he said, "My niece and her new husband will be returning to Tripoli in a few days. You agreed to escort them, and we are inclined to hold you to your agreement."

"With all respect, Basileus," countered the Templar, "I must beg to be excused."

"But you will not be excused, commander," replied Emperor Manuel placidly. "Your *procedures*," he gave the word caustic emphasis, "will no doubt wait until you have fulfilled the duty for which you have been retained."

"No doubt, Basileus," replied the Templar stiffly. "You are right to remind me of my duty. I will abide."

"We are pleased to hear it," Manuel said, turning once more to his visitor. "We are having a banquet tomorrow evening, for which we have arranged a display of arms. We understand you Franks are fond of martial entertainments. What is the word you use?"

"*Tournament*," replied de Bracineaux.

"Ah, yes, we must remember that," replied the emperor, his face lighting with pleasure. "We are having a tournament. We are certain you and Baron d'Anjou will enjoy it, commander."

"I wait upon your pleasure, Basileus," said the Templar. "If there is nothing else, I will trouble you no further." He made a small bow and started away.

"It does a soul good, we find," said the emperor, "to bend to a higher authority from time to time. You must try it more often, commander."

TEN

"We are being followed."

The voice stirred Cait from her brooding contemplation of the white, heat-bleached sky and the powder-dry road ahead. Cait lifted her hood and turned in the saddle to see that it was Rognvald who had addressed her.

"Forgive me. I would not intrude, my lady, but there is someone following us." He addressed her in Norse, and his accent sounded, to Cait's ear, like the old fishermen who used to take refuge at Banvarð when foul weather drove them into the bay. They were also from Norway, and the sound of the knight's voice reassured her; it made her feel as if she were speaking to some ancient relative.

"How many?" She cast a hasty glance over her shoulder—but saw nothing save the owner of the horses they had hired, and his two sons, bringing up the rear on their donkeys. Behind them the dust-dry track stretched back and back across the undulating hills to Damascus—now a small shimmering gleam in the heat-haze far behind them.

Rognvald said, "Just one." He regarded her curiously. "Did you think there would be more?"

"Never mind what I thought," she told him firmly.

"I believe," he replied, "you will have to tell me your secret sooner or later. Perhaps if you told me now, I could help you with it."

"I have no secrets." She looked back at the trail behind her and saw a small dark figure disappear swiftly over a faraway hilltop. "At least none I care to discuss with you."

"As you will."

They rode on for a time, and Cait turned her thoughts next to the necessary steps ahead. Acquiring her bodyguard of knights was just the beginning. They would have to be properly clothed and armed, and they would need horses—all of which would be expensive; she would have to sell more, if not most, of the remaining valuables from her father's chest. She had offered to buy new clothes for them before leaving the city, but the knights preferred their rags to Saracen garb, which was all that Damascus had to offer. Nor could they buy any weapons—the Arabs were forbidden to sell to Christians under pain of death by a decree of Prince Mujir ed-Din. Cait had her dagger, but that thin blade was the only protection the party possessed. Once they reached Tyre, however, they could buy anything. The horses, at least, could wait.

"Why did you ransom us?" asked Rognvald.

"Hmm?" wondered Cait, half aware he had spoken to her. "I already told you."

"This pilgrimage of yours, yes. But as you will not tell me where we are going, I can only assume some deeper purpose."

Cait thought for a moment. "As a young man, my father visited the Holy Land," she explained simply. "He never reached Jerusalem, and always wanted to return and finish the pilgrimage. Last year he decided to do it, and to take Alethea and me with him; he wanted to show us the places he had visited."

"Including prison?"

She frowned. "My father was once a prisoner there."

"So you said. Where is your father now?"

Cait's frown deepened. When she did not reply, Rognvald looked at her and saw her face clenched with concentration. She seemed to labor so long over the question that he drew breath to withdraw it; before he could speak, she said, "We stopped in Constantinople to see the city and refresh our provisions. While we were there, one of Emperor Manuel's many nieces was married, and we went to the ceremony. It was held in the Cathedral of Saint Sophia, and thousands attended."

She did not look at him when she spoke, but kept her eyes on the road ahead—although her sight had turned inward. And there was a softness to her voice that was not present before, a sadness.

"The service was over, and I followed the crowds out into the street to see the bride and groom away. My father remained inside, however, and when I returned, I saw him talking to a man. By the time I rejoined him, the man was gone and my father had been stabbed."

"The man stabbed your father?" wondered Rognvald, incredulity creasing his brow. "In a church?"

"He died in my arms," affirmed Cait, nodding sadly. "We buried him the next day in the graveyard of a monastery, and then sailed on to Damascus."

"I see." The knight nodded thoughtfully. "So, in honor of your father's wishes, you are continuing the pilgrimage to Jerusalem."

Cait frowned. "No," she said, then hesitated, unwilling to say more.

"Ah," Rognvald guessed, "here is where the secret arises."

"There is no secret," Cait insisted.

"Then tell me. Where are we going?" He regarded her with benign interest. "Come, my reluctant lady, you have entrusted your life and that of your sister to us; you might as well entrust your secret."

"I will tell you," Cait decided at last, "but not now. Once we are aboard ship—then I will tell you."

Lord Rognvald accepted her decision. "Agreed." He smiled. "I will look forward to hearing it."

Cait turned to look behind again. "What are we going to do about our follower?"

"There is a stream just ahead," he said, pointing to a line of small, scrubby trees gray with dust. "It is growing hot. We can rest there and see what comes."

Cait agreed and the traveling party proceeded slowly to the line of trees. The stream turned out to be dry, the bed full of dusty rock and withered grass. But the patchy shade provided some relief from the heat and the savage onslaught of the sun. They dismounted and, while the owner of the horses and donkeys gave each of his beasts a handful of grain from a bag, the knights and seamen found places to rest under the trees. Rognvald rode a little apart and took up a position where he could watch the road.

Retrieving the waterskin from behind her saddle, Cait pulled the stopper and took a long draft; the water was warm, but it wet her lips and tongue, and washed the dust from her throat.

Owing to their long captivity, the knights were unaccustomed to the heat and sun, and unused to the saddle. They limped manfully to the little grove and flopped down, to lie exhausted in the mottled shade. After only half a day outside, their prison pallor was replaced by the radiant pink of sunburn. Cait watched them doubtfully; it would be weeks, she reckoned, rather than days, before they were back to fighting fitness. Thus, despite her impatience to hurry back to the ship, she resolved to adopt a slower pace for their sake.

Handing the waterskin to Otti, she told him to take a drink and pass it on, then sat down with her back to a treetrunk and closed her eyes. In a little while, she heard someone beside her and looked around to see Dag settling his lanky frame beneath the same tree.

"Why Stone-Breaker?" she asked after a time.

He smiled, his blue eyes crinkling at the corners. "Well, now," he said, "I was born in Jutland, where there are a great many mounds and stones and such belonging to the Old Ones. It is a very fine place—sometimes a little cold, but the hunting is good. Once when I was out hunting with my brothers, we caught sight of an elk and gave chase. Even though I was the youngest, I was in the lead, ya?" He smiled at the memory, and Cait smiled, too, for he also sounded like the Norse fishermen whose voices rose and fell over the dips and crests of their words like a ship plowing the ocean swell.

"Well, now," he continued, "as I raced along I passed one of these standing stones and as luck would have it my horse stumbled in a badger hole at that very moment, and I was thrown from my saddle. Well, I hit this stone, see." He slammed his fist into his hand with a loud smack to demonstrate. "I smashed into it head first and knocked it down. The stone fell and I fell. They thought I was dead, but when they came to look, they saw that I was still alive. And when they raised me up, they saw the stone was broken under me." He grinned, his fine straight teeth a winning flash of white. "I have been Dag Stone-Breaker from that day."

Hearing their talk, Yngvar edged nearer to join them, and Svein, too. Cait noticed that Alethea, whose understanding of Norse was nowhere near as good as her own, was nevertheless listening with rapt attention to the handsome nobleman. "Tell how you got *your* name, Svein," said Dag with a nudge of his elbow.

"Nay," he replied, "it is never so exalted as Dag's tale." But at the encouragement of the others, he sighed and said, "My father kept hounds—every year he had to train up three good dogs to give King Sigurd in tribute. He had several fine bitches, but his favorite was a sweet-natured brown called Fala. A few months after I was born, Fala lost her litter. She was very disturbed over it, and would not eat or drink at all. My father gave her good meat on the bone, but still she would not eat.

"This went on until my father thought he would have to put her away. He held off as long as he could, but it had to be done. So, he went to get his sword and a strap to take her out behind the barn. But when he came back, he could not find Fala. They looked everywhere and finally found her in my bed with me; she had brought me her bone.

"We were both in there together chewing on that bone—Fala on one end and me on the other, chewing away. I have been Svein Gristle-Bone ever since."

He made the face of a boy gnawing a bone, and Alethea laughed out loud; the others, who had heard the story before, laughed too. "What about Rognvald?" asked Cait. "Does he have another name?"

The knights looked from one to the other and shrugged. "If he does," replied Yngvar, "I never heard it."

"How did you come to be taken captive?" she asked. When no one made bold to answer, she said, "If it makes an unpleasant tale, you do not have to tell me. Still, do not think to spare me on account of it. My father was captured by the Seljuqs as a young man—that is how he came to be in the Damascus prison—so I know how abhorrent it can be."

"Your father was captured, too?" wondered Yngvar. "That is a tale I would like to hear." Nodding, the others added their agreement.

At that moment, however, there came a shout from the road, and they all rushed to the edge of the wood to see Rognvald riding toward them with a stranger in tow. Cait saw the pale yellow tunic and trousers, the bristly dark hair, and started out to meet them.

"I caught him hiding behind that hill," said Rognvald, speaking Latin for the benefit of his captive. He pushed the intruder forward. "He was spying on us."

"I was resting only!"

"What are you doing here, Abu?" Cait demanded.

"My donkey ran away because of him." The young Syrian crossed his arms over his chest and pouted.

"Answer me, Abu. What are you doing here?"

"Please, sharifah, do not send me away. You will need someone to speak for you. I can do this easily. Please, let me go with you."

"What about the sick and infirm who depend on you—the patients who keep you running morning to night?"

He frowned. "Do you have any idea how difficult it is to win favor as a physician in a place like Damascus? You need an amir or two at the very least if you hope to survive."

She regarded him sternly. "Do you even *have* any patients?"

"To tell you the truth," he replied, "no."

"And are you a physician?" she said, her tone defying him to lie to her.

"I studied medicine in Baghdad. I did," he insisted. Dropping his voice, he added, "—a little. It is a very difficult occupation. You have no idea."

"Studying was too hard, so you abandoned it."

"I did not!" he maintained. "Was it my fault my teacher was executed?"

Yngvar had heard enough. "Allow us to send him on his way, my lady."

"Not just yet," she said. "I want to hear the end of this. Svein, Dag, go find his donkey and bring it. You," she said to Abu, "come with me."

They returned to the grove and sat down once more, Abu before Cait, and Rognvald and Yngvar on either side—a magistrate and her officers, dispensing justice. Alethea leaned on one elbow beneath a nearby tree, feigning disinterest in the proceedings. Under Cait's questioning, it soon emerged that while languishing in the Baghdad prison for stealing eggs—"How was I to know the chickens belonged to the *qadi* of Baghdad?"—Abu had chanced to meet the celebrated Muslah Abd Allah Ud-Din Ibn Arabi al-Tusi, court physician to the royal family.

The famed physician had been sent to prison following a failed attempt to poison the caliph. "It was a grave mistake, an injustice of unrivaled magnitude," Abu declared with surprising vehemence. "The *khalifa* was not well liked, it is true. And those who would have rejoiced at his funeral were as numerous as the desert sands. But dear old al-Tusi could no more have poisoned anyone than a faithful dog pee in his beloved master's cooking-pot. He was a sage and scholar of the highest distinction—a very saint." Abu shook his head sadly. "When the poisoners failed, they needed a scapegoat and supplied the royal physician. Indeed, he made a perfect sacrifice; he was too affronted at the suggestion to even defend himself."

"So you met the physician in prison," Rognvald confirmed. "Were you never his pupil?"

Abu shook his head. "Not in the way you mean."

Yngvar picked up a strong stick.

"But he taught me just the same," Abu added quickly. "Muslah allowed me to help him as he tended the other prisoners. He also taught me Greek. I learned a very great deal from him."

"What about Cairo?" asked Cait suspiciously. "Were you ever there?"

"Oh, indeed, yes, sharifah. It is a very great city. I could be your guide if you want to go."

"But you never studied there."

"Alas, no." Abu's face fell. "I went there to study, it is true, but I fell in with some bad fellows who worked for a man who owned a brothel—the finest brothel in all Egypt!"

"Now, my lady?" said Yngvar, slapping the stick against the side of his leg.

"Still," Abu Sharma offered, "it was a good school in many ways. I learned a very great deal."

Cait was silent for a moment; she regarded the contrite youth before her. "Why should I let you come with us?" she said at last.

"These men you have redeemed from prison," he said, indicating the knights. "Yet before you stands a man no less needy than they were when you plucked them from Mujir's dungeon."

"You were well paid for your services. How can you say you are needy?"

"In all the time I was in Damascus," he said solemnly, "I never met anyone like you. Sharifah, you say a thing, and you do it. You have a purpose, whereas I have none. I try, God knows, but I have failed at everything. If you let me come with you, then I, too, will have a purpose." His deep, dark eyes pleaded. "Let me go with you. On my father's head, I promise you will not regret it."

Caitríona frowned, regarding the young man with mild exasperation.

"If you have any more dealings with Arabs," Abu suggested pointedly, "you will most certainly need someone to speak for you."

"Very well," said Cait, deciding at once. "You can join us."

"Thank you, sharifah. Oh, thank you very much," Abu said. Darting forward, he snatched up her hand and pressed it to his lips. "You have made the right decision, you will see. God wills it, amen!"

"Go and help Svein and Dag find your donkey," she ordered, extricating her hand.

Rognvald stared at her for a moment, then rose without a word and stumped off. "What is wrong with him?" wondered Cait.

"He is a little upset, I think," suggested Yngvar.

Cait rose and went after him, and caught up with him at the horse picket. She stood and watched while he made a pretense of inspecting the animals. "Well? Whatever it is, you might as well spit it out."

"There is nothing to say." He did not look at her when he spoke.

"You think I made a mistake."

"So, now you know what everyone is thinking."

"Am I wrong?" she demanded. "Look at me and tell me I am wrong."

"Honest men do not consort with thieves."

"Neither do they consort with the refuse of the hostage pit," she replied crisply. "Yet, I did not hear you complain about that."

The nobleman's countenance darkened at the jab. Before he could reply, she said, "Hear me, I am in command here and I will not have my authority questioned. Understood?"

"Perfectly," Rognvald replied, then added, "my lady." He bowed stiffly, turned, and walked away.

Cait returned to her place beneath the tree and sat down. "You made him angry," Alethea pointed out.

"He will learn who is in command."

"You should be nicer to people. You might want them to be nice to you one day."

"Spare me your homilies, Saint Alethea."

Thea sniffed and shut up. Cait leaned against the trunk, and closed her eyes, but she kept thinking of all the other things she wished she had said to put haughty Lord Rognvald in his place.

After a time, the others returned with Abu's donkey. They rested through the heat of the day, and moved on again when the sun began its descent in the west. A few small ragged clouds had drifted in from the coast after midday, bringing with them a slight freshening of the air. Thus, the party resumed their journey in better comfort than before, and continued on until darkness made the road difficult to see.

They camped then, a little distance from the track, in a grove of ancient olive trees which were fed by a tiny spring. While the others set about watering the horses, Haemur, Otti, and Yngvar prepared a meal. The moon had risen by the time the food was ready; they ate by moonlight, and stretched themselves beside the dying fire to sleep. Caitríona lay awake for a long time, watching the stars slowly turn in the heavens. The moon rose above the far-off hills, causing the night creatures to stir. Somewhere out in the unseen wilderness a bird called, filling the silence with its sad, forlorn song. Tears came to Cait's eyes, for she heard in the sound the cry of her own wounded soul, and she felt a cold hard ache inside—as if a sliver of ice had pierced her breast and lodged itself deep in the hollow of her heart.

She would feel the ache, she told herself, until she—God's instrument of Holy Vengeance—had sent de Bracineaux's black soul to judgment.

The night passed, but gave her no rest, and she rose to begin another day on the trail ill-at-ease and irritated. They broke camp and started off; it was not long before she found herself riding beside Rognvald once more.

"We will get you some weapons when we reach Tyre," she said when the uncomfortable silence grew too great to bear. "The markets are good there. We should be able to buy whatever you want."

Rognvald thanked her, but made no further reply.

"I would have preferred to get weapons in Damascus," she continued, "but the merchants are forbidden to sell arms to Christians." She paused, glancing sideways at the tall Norseman. His proud silence was beginning to irk her.

"I suppose," she said, trying to draw him out, "Abu might have bought something for us somewhere."

Again, he waited before he answered. "No," he said at last. "It is better this way."

"Better?" she challenged, her vexation flaring into anger. "In what way better? Knights without weapons are not much use." He looked at her calmly, and that irritated her the more. "Well?" she demanded.

"If any of Prince Mujir ed-Din's soldiers had caught us with so much as a pruning knife between us while we were still in the city, we would have been thrown into prison again—or worse," he told her. "I think it is better this way."

For some reason this reply annoyed her, too.

"Well, then," she said tartly, "if we are attacked on the road, I will just leave it to you to explain to the cut-throats just how much *better* it is *this way*."

She snapped the reins and made to ride away, intending to leave him behind with the sting of her retort. But the knight reached out and took hold of her mount's bridle, jerked back on the reins and brought both horses to a halt.

Surprised, and instantly furious, Cait glared dangerously at him and was about to lash out at his impertinence, when he looked her in the eye and said in a low, deliberate voice, "So long as I have breath in my body, no harm will come to you."

He paused to make certain she understood, then added, "That is my solemn vow, and I do not make it lightly." He looked at her again, and she felt herself unsettled by the intensity of his gaze.

"My lady," he said, releasing his hold on her mount's bridle. He snapped the reins and rode on alone.

ELEVEN

Dusty, saddle-sore, hungry, and with a throbbing thirst clawing at their throats, Cait and her small company arrived at the port of Tyre. It was late in the day and, after the stifling, airless heat of the dry plain, the wind off the sea was cool silk on her skin. As they rode through the wide main street of the city which led down to the harbor Cait saw the white glimmer of sun on water just ahead, and heard the cry of gulls, and was instantly transported to the coldwater bay below Banvarð in Caithness.

The elation she felt at this sudden memory faded with the realization that her father would never see his home again, never again sail into that generous bay, never again sweep his darling Sydoni off her feet and fold her in his strong arms. *Poor Sydoni*, Cait thought, *she does not even know Duncan is dead. She is waiting for him to come home and he never will.*

She felt the sadness rising up in her like a spring, but like the girl in Abbot Emlyn's tale of the overflowing well, she dropped the heavy stone lid back into place and the upsurge of grief subsided. There would be time one day to lament her father's death and mourn him properly. But that day would have to wait. Grief was an extravagance she could not afford—there was too much to do, too many responsibilities, too much ground to cover. Later she would grieve, she told herself, when her work was finished. *You will be avenged, Papa*, she vowed once more.

As they drew near the harbor, she sent Haemur and Otti to buy food and drink for their supper, while she and the others proceeded to the wharf. Upon dismounting, she dismissed the hostler, paying him a little over the agreed amount for the use of his horses, thanked him and sent him on his way. She also gave the last-chosen knight a handful of silver coins and sent him on his way, saying, "Should you be tempted to desert your family again, remember your vow and know that God will hold you to account." The knight bowed and, thanking her lavishly, hurried away along the wharf in search of a fast ship to take him home.

She then climbed aboard the waiting *Persephone* to be welcomed by Olvir, who had been left behind to watch over the vessel in her absence.

"Are you certain they are knights?" wondered the seaman, observing the Norsemen as they clambered onto the deck. "They look more like pig thieves."

"They have been in prison," Cait informed him. "How do you think *you* would look if you had been left to rot in chains for three years?"

"Who is that dark one? Is he also one of ours?"

"That is Abu," Cait replied. To prevent further discussion, she added: "He is a physician and interpreter, and will prove very useful in dealing with the Arabs."

Olvir counted the extra mouths that would need feeding every day. "Maybe I can teach him to cook, too."

Cait glanced at the sun, and then at the ships crowding the harbor; one of them caught her eye. Hanging from the top of its mast was a white flag bearing a crimson cross: a Templar ship. The sudden recognition brought her up short. She told herself that it was unlikely de Bracineaux was aboard that ship; even so, it served as an unwelcome reminder that the murderous commander had allies everywhere, and he would not be idle. Because of the knights' inability to travel at speed, it had taken far longer to reach the ship than she had anticipated and, seeing the Templar ship, she was loath to waste another moment.

"Show the men where they can stay, get them some water to drink, and fetch some soap so they can wash," she told Olvir, making up her mind at once. "Then make ready to sail."

"This late? My lady, the day is soon over," protested Olvir. "We have few provisions and little fresh water on board. Let us leave tomorrow when all is in order."

"Will no one obey a simple command without crossing swords?" Cait scowled at the obstinate sailor. "I want to depart as soon as

Haemur and Otti return from the marketplace. Now go and do as I say."

A grumbling Olvir hurried off, and Cait went to her quarters to wash and change her clothes. It was cool and dark below deck, which she found soothing after days in the relentless sun. She undressed and laved the water over herself. There was a little soap left, and a clean cloth, and she luxuriated in scrubbing her face and washing her hair. Most of the water in the basin ended up on the floor before she was finished, and when Alethea came in she complained of the puddles. But if she had made ten times the mess and used up a week's supply of water, Cait would not have cared: it was well worth the delicious thrill of being clean again.

She dressed in fresh linen and, feeling civilized once more, left Alethea to bathe, and returned to the upper deck. The Norsemen had assembled and were stamping their feet on the planking, pounding the rail and mast with their fists, and remarking on the admirable qualities of the ship.

Presently, Haemur and Otti appeared with armfuls of provisions for the evening meal. They had bought bread and wine and olives in the market, and a sack full of sardines from a fisherman just returning with the day's catch. Cait commanded the knights to clean the fish, and the seamen to help Olvir cast off.

Rognvald heard the order and came to her. "I thought we were to buy clothes and weapons in Tyre."

"I have changed my mind."

"I think you should reconsider. This is a good place; the city is secure and the markets are renowned. We can get everything we need here."

"We can get what we need in Cyprus, too. We will stop there."

"And what if we should be overtaken by Arab pirates before we reach Cyprus?" he inquired.

She had not thought of that, but was determined not to let Rognvald have the last word. "As we are sailing by night, the pirates will never see us."

"It is a foolish risk," he told her. "If it was my ship, I would not put her, or her passengers, in such needless danger."

He turned and walked away, leaving Cait furious with him for the second time in as many days. While Svein and Dag gutted the sardines, the others helped Olvir, Otti and Haemur make the ship ready to sail. In a little while, sleek *Persephone* slipped her moorings and moved out of the harbor. Despite what Rognvald said, Cait was glad to be aboard ship and under sail again.

Once they had entered deep water, Olvir began preparing the charcoal brazier to cook their meal. Soon the deck was awash in the sweet scent of oily smoke and charcoal, and the sardines were sizzling on spits. One by one, the Norsemen were drawn away from the rail and their last lingering looks at the pale Syrian hills, now glowing red in the light of a crimson sunset. They gathered around the brazier, watching the fish hungrily. Olvir opened the wine jugs, and soon the wooden cups were making the rounds. While his men sampled the raw Syrian wine, Rognvald strolled around the ship, examining the fittings and ropes.

After their unpleasant exchange, Cait hesitated to join him, but then considered it would make shipboard life too awkward to be avoiding one another every time they disagreed. So, she followed him to the prow where he had stopped and was gazing out to sea. "My father loved this ship," Cait remarked, joining him at the rail. "So much, in fact, that he had two more built just like it. Still, he preferred the original."

"I can see why," the Norwegian lord replied amiably. "She is a handsome craft—suitable for most any water, I should think."

Otti appeared with his jug of wine and wooden cups. "It is not so bad, this," he said, pouring wine into the cups.

"To your good health," said Cait, raising her cup.

"And freedom," added Rognvald.

"Health and freedom." Cait took a mouthful of the wine and almost spat it back into her cup. She swallowed hard and gasped.

Rognvald smiled placidly. "It is somewhat rough, I think."

"It is ghastly!"

"Perhaps it would be better mixed with a little honey and water," he said. "Permit me." Taking her cup, the Norseman walked to where the others were dosing their drinks to taste. She observed him among his men: genial and unassuming, his authority genuine, and therefore unpretentious and unaffected.

Perhaps I have not made such a poor bargain after all, she thought to herself as she watched him returning.

"Try this," he said, offering her the cup. "I think you will find it more palatable."

She took a tentative sip; he watched her reaction. "Oh, that is much better. Very much better." She thanked him, and they both sipped from their cups. "If Galician wine is half so good, we should not go thirsty."

"Is that where we are going?" he asked. "Galicia?"

Realizing she had said more than she intended, Cait looked at him over the rim of her cup. Well, it was no use denying it now. "Yes," she told him. "After Cyprus we sail for Galicia. Do you know it?"

"No," he replied, shaking his head. "We saw the coast from a distance, but the king was eager to reach Jerusalem, and so we did not stop."

"I have never been there, either," said Cait. "My father was there once, on his way home from the Holy Land. He said it was a fine place—all steep hills, deep valleys, and rocks, a great many rocks. But the people, he said, were friendly to a fault."

At that moment, Olvir called out, saying the supper was ready. Glad for a chance to break off a conversation which she did not care to pursue, Cait turned and walked to the platform before the mast where Olvir was handing around the wooden skewers. Accepting a fresh-roasted sardine, she retired with her cup and a piece of bread to the pilot's bench where she sat down to eat. The others remained clustered around the brazier, watching hungrily as Olvir set more skewers of fish on the coals. The knights, growing garrulous as the wine loosened their tongues, joked and laughed as they plied Olvir and Otti with questions about their homeland.

On the platform, Alethea sat with Abu and both appeared so deeply absorbed in their discussion that neither one was eating; the skewers were untouched in their hands. Cait was just thinking that she would have to have a word with Thea about encouraging an unseemly familiarity with the servants, when Rognvald approached and asked to join her.

"If you like," she said indifferently. The Norseman regarded her with pursed lips, but said nothing. "What?"

"It is a large enough ship. I can easily find another place to sit."

"Please," Cait relented. "I insist."

His smile was ready and affable. "Since you insist, I accept." He sat down happily beside her, put his cup on the deck and began pulling steaming bits of fish from the skewer. He chewed quietly for a while, and when Cait thought he might let their former discussion pass without comment, he said, "If Galicia is so full of friendly people, why do you need a bodyguard of fierce and terrible Norwegians?"

Cait could feel his eyes on her, but she stared straight ahead and deliberately stripped off a piece of fish and put it in her mouth and chewed slowly to give herself time to think how to answer. Rognvald sipped from his cup and waited.

"We are going . . ." she began at last, then paused. It was no good trying to concoct a plausible explanation on the spot. "The truth?"

"Well, why not?" said Rognvald. "It saves so much time and trouble in the end. Yes, let us begin with the truth."

She looked at him sideways. "The truth is, I do not know."

He nodded thoughtfully, considering this odd revelation. "Then," he said after a moment's reflection, "if you do not mind my asking, why are you going?"

The way he said it—neither opposing, nor disapproving—made Cait smile. She could hear Duncan adopting the same tone, and she liked it. "As to that," she said, "I am not altogether certain."

"That would follow." He slapped his knee with his palm. "Well now, it is good to have that settled." He thanked her for telling him and rose abruptly, saying that if she should ever receive any further leading in the matter he would much appreciate a word.

"Are you always so headstrong and haughty?" she called as he stumped away. When he did not stop or look around, she relented. "Oh, very well. I will tell you."

He turned around and retraced his steps. "Everything," he said, standing over her.

"Yes," she conceded, "everything. Just sit down so I do not have to shout up at you."

Rognvald sat, leaned back against the tiller rail, clasping his cup in both hands. "Proceed."

"First," Cait said, "I must know if you hold any regard for the Poor Soldiers of Christ and the Temple of Solomon."

"The Templars?" He glanced at her curiously, and saw that she was in earnest. "No, my lady," the nobleman answered, shaking his head slowly. "I have known but two or three of them—they were in prison with us, but were quickly ransomed by their order. They were Franks, it is true, but seemed like honorable men nonetheless." He shrugged. "They are said to be formidable warriors, but I cannot say one way or the other. Are there Templars in your explanation?"

"There are," confessed Cait. "One, at least, but probably many more by now. They are the reason for this . . . this . . ." she searched for a word and did not find one.

"*Pilgrimage?*" suggested Rognvald, supplying the term she had used before.

"It is no pilgrimage," Cait admitted.

"No?"

She looked across the deck to where the knights were now lolling around the brazier, their voices loud with raucous talk. Rognvald was right; she had entrusted her life to these knights, she might as well trust him with the rest. She stood. "Come with me. It will be easier if I show you."

She led him below deck to her father's quarters where she opened the wooden sea chest containing his clothes and belongings. Reaching down into the chest, she felt along the side of the box and brought out a flat parcel wrapped in one of her mantles. While a bemused Rognvald watched, she untied the knotted fabric and withdrew a flat parchment tied with a red silk band.

"This," she said, placing the document in his hands, "is why we are going to Galicia." She indicated that he should open it.

He untied the silk band and opened the stiff parchment. "A letter," he said, scanning the salutation, "to the Patriarch of Rome."

"Yes," she confirmed, "and it leads to a prodigious treasure."

TWELVE

"That which is beyond all price," intoned Rognvald, following his finger along the heavy parchment, "the treasure of the ages, our very real and manifest hope for this present age and the kingdom to come, the . . . what? *Rosa Mystica* . ." His voice trailed off and he looked to Cait for an explanation.

"I do not know what it is, either," she confessed. "He calls it the greatest treasure in the world. I mean to have it."

"And the Templars? What of them?"

"The letter was in the possession of a Templar commander," Cait explained. "I got it from him."

"You stole it," guessed Rognvald.

"Yes."

The Norseman nodded slowly. "This priest, Bertrano—do you know him?"

"All I know about him is there." She pointed to the elaborate signature in red ink: Bertrano de Almira, Archbishop of Santiago de Compostela. "First we find the man who wrote this letter and induce him to tell us where the treasure can be found. Then we go and get it."

Rognvald frowned and looked at the letter again. "Simple plans are often the best," he mused.

Cait caught a note of censure in his tone. "You disapprove?"

"Of the treasure? No." Tapping the signature with his finger, he said, "But have you considered that Archbishop Bertrano may not feel like telling you what you want to know?"

"You asked me what I planned to do, and I have told you." Cait stood and, hands on hips, glared down at the disagreeable knight. "I do not require your approval, my lord, but I will insist on your obedience. And I will thank you to keep your opinions to yourself."

They came in sight of Cyprus the second day after leaving Tyre, and that evening *Persephone* sailed into the harbor at Famagusta. The rumored pirates had not appeared, and the crossing proved wholly uneventful—which Cait counted a victory for her decision. The next morning, as soon as the markets opened, she sent Rognvald and the knights into the city to search out the best armorer. "Take Abu with you, and when you have found the one," she instructed, "send Abu to fetch me. He will find me in the street of tailors."

The knights departed in high spirits, and Cait and Alethea disembarked a short while later, with Otti as an escort, and proceeded to a narrow dog-leg of a street where the city's tailors plied their trade. They passed along, examining the goods on display carefully, and asking the prices.

"Oh, look, Cait," said Alethea, holding up a white linen mantle with tiny blue flowers embroidered around the neck. "It is beautiful, is it not?"

A young Greek fellow squatting in the doorway leaped up just then, crying, "No! No! No! This is not for you. God forbid, my fine lady, you should ever wear anything so coarse and unflattering." He seized the mantle and tossed it back onto the pile of folded garments. "This!" he said, producing a mantle in butter-colored satin. "This is for my lady."

Alethea was delighted. "Oh, Cait, look!" She clasped the delicate mantle to her and gazed down at its shimmering length. "It is wonderful."

Sensing a potential sale in the offing, two tailors from across the street hurried over. "You like this, lady? We have more," said one. "And better than this," added the other. "Much better. Here, come, we will show you."

The young Greek stepped between his customers and the other merchants. "Get back, Theodoros. Away with you." He pushed them back. "I saw them first. Go. Leave us in peace."

"If he cannot help you," called Theodoros, "come to us. We have better goods."

"If I cannot help them, I will personally bring them to you. Now, go."

Having sent away his rivals, he turned to his customers, and made a polite bow. "I am Didimus. What can I show you? A new cloak perhaps? I have several I think would appeal."

"Where did you learn your craft?" asked Cait, examining the stitching on the mantle Alethea still clutched tightly in her hands.

"My family lived in Jerusalem—six generations, all tailors," the young man said. "When the city fell to the Franks, we were among those fortunate enough to survive. We fled to Jaffa, and then here. Now, I am the only one left." His long, sad face brightened. "But I have a son. God willing, he will learn all I have to teach and he will become the best tailor in Famagusta, like his father."

"It is good work. But we are not looking for ourselves," she said, and went on to explain that she required clothes for four men. "Everything," she said, "from cloaks to belts."

"Small-clothes as well?" he asked politely.

"Small-clothes as well. Everything."

"It will be a pleasure, my lady," he said, bowing low. He ran to the door and called to someone inside, then returned with a stool for Cait. "Please, be seated. I will bring you some things to examine, and we will begin."

He hurried away again, and returned with an armload of cloth which had been half-sewn into cloaks. While he was showing Cait his wares, a young dark-haired woman emerged with a tray containing a jar of sweetened lemon water, and small honey cakes which had been baked until they were dry and crisp. She placed the tray on the ground beside Cait and knelt down to pour the drinks and offer the cakes, before retreating hastily inside.

While Cait sipped her drink and made her selections, Alethea munched honey cakes, and chose beribboned shifts and flowered mantles for herself. In the end, Cait decided on five cloaks: one red, two green, two blue with thin rust-colored stripes; five short mantles, all white; five pairs of long breeches cut from a stout, tightly woven wool which had been dyed a deep brown. "Now the belts," she told Didimus. "They must be leather, and they must be stout."

"Alas, I do not have belts such as you require, but my wife's brother works in leather. If it please you, my lady, I could take you to his shop and you can tell him what you want. Also, if you need shoes for these men of yours, he would be happy to oblige."

So, that is what they did. Cait paid for her selections, arranged for the knights to come along later to be fitted for their clothes. At the shoemaker's workshop she chose the leather for the belts, and was discussing the cost of new boots when Abu appeared to say that Rognvald had found an armorer with whom he was pleased to deal. "They are waiting for you now."

It was not an armorer who greeted Cait, but a merchant named Geldemar who traded with smiths and weapons-makers from many places, including Cairo, Constantinople, Tripoli, and Damascus; the continual warring in the Holy Land brought a steady commerce to his door that made him wealthy, discriminating, and fat. He conducted his lucrative business from a large house at the end of a street of metal-workers. The house, protected by a high wall and three imposing servants with dogs, boasted two floors; the lower rooms were crammed with weapons and armor of all kinds. "Your men have been kind enough to express an interest in my wares," Geldemar told her, lifting a jewelled hand to a hall bristling with lances, pikes, halberds, and swords. "As you see, I have assembled a fine collection." He smiled, regarding Alethea with a keenly appreciative eye. "My ladies, you are welcome to examine my goods. I trade with only the finest craftsmen. Please, satisfy yourself that this is so."

Alethea, uninterested in weaponry, yawned as Cait moved to a nearby rack which contained a dozen or more Frankish broadswords; other racks contained both smaller and larger swords of Arab and Byzantine design. She picked up one and hefted it in her hand; the weight was good, and the wooden pommel tightly bound with rawhide. Thoroughly bored now that there was nothing for her, Alethea wandered into the next room where Yngvar and Dag were selecting shields from among the many different varieties on offer— from small, round Byzantine *dorkas*, and long oval *targs* which covered half the body, to the enormous curved square wooden *scutum* of ancient Roman design.

"My compliments to you, Geldemar," said Cait, replacing the sword. "You have amassed a distinguished armory."

Rognvald appeared just then, holding a slender, thin-bladed lance. Caitríona joined him. "We will find everything we need here," he said. "With your permission, my lady, I would like to deal with this fellow."

"Very well," replied Cait. "I will leave it to you, my lord. If you like, Abu can stay and help with the bargaining."

"No need," answered Rognvald. "Geldemar and I understand one another."

She turned and addressed the merchant. "I will leave the choice of arms to the discernment of my knights," Cait told him.

Geldemar smiled, pressing his hands together. "Very wise, my lady."

Producing a small purse, Cait handed it to the merchant. "As a gesture of good faith here are ten gold *solidi*. Let this be a partial payment for the items they select. The rest will be paid when the goods are delivered to the harbor." Indicating the tall knight looking on, she said, "Lord Rognvald will make the arrangements."

"I am your servant, my lady," replied the merchant, accepting the money. To Rognvald he said, "Now, perhaps if you would tell me what you require, I will consider how best to help you."

Cait left the men to their business and, summoning Alethea and Abu, resumed her procurement of provisions. They visited a butcher, miller, baker, sellers of spices, honey, oil, and green goods, and suppliers of smoked and salted meat and fish. They arrived back at the ship only a few moments before the knights returned. Each carried a new sword and dagger—which the merchant Geldemar had trusted them to take away—and their spirits were higher than she had yet seen them. They vied with one another in proclaiming the virtues of their weapons.

"This blade shines like a flame," announced Svein, brandishing the weapon in the slanting sunlight. "I shall call it *Loga*."

Yngvar said that his sword would be called *Fylkir* because, as he boasted, "It will always be first into the fray."

Dag said his was to be called *Hollrvarda*, because of the three, his blade was the only true defender. This provoked an argument over what sort of names were best for weapons, and what the other items in the armory were to be called. The discussion was still going on when Rognvald and Geldemar arrived in a horse-drawn wagon carrying the remaining arms and armor: helms and shields for all, swordbelts with heavy bronze buckles and hangers for their daggers, battle axes for Svein and Yngvar, a mace for Dag, and ten good stout lances. There were hauberks in heavy ringed mail, with hoods, and mail greaves to cover their legs.

Cait went down to the wharf to meet the wagon and pay the balance due for the weapons. "We have done well, my lady," Rognvald informed her. "He put up a good fight, but we vanquished him in the end."

"It was four against one," Geldemar said happily, "what could I do?" She noticed the rosy blush on his nose and cheeks, and guessed he had been standing very near a wine jar recently.

"How much is owing?" asked Cait.

"One hundred and fifty-five gold solidi, my bounteous lady," said the merchant grandly. "And a rare bargain it is, if I say so myself."

"Indeed?" Cait looked to Rognvald for confirmation.

"Our friend here was rendered helpless by a fit of generosity of a magnitude unseen in Cyprus for more than a hundred years," declared the knight, patting Geldemar on the shoulder amiably. "I do believe he is trying to become a saint among merchants."

Geldemar laughed loudly at this, and as the knights unloaded the wagon Cait opened her purse and began counting out the gold coins into his hand. Then he thanked Cait for her custom, bowed low and kissed her hand, and with Rognvald's help climbed into the wagon. Off he drove, with much waving and wishing of good fortune, disappearing along the quay. Cait and Rognvald watched him go; as soon as he was out of sight, Cait said, "I know little about the cost of weapons, but a hundred and fifty-five seems a good price to me—a *very* good price indeed. I thought it might be two or three times as much."

"To be sure," replied Rognvald easily. "But sometimes, after a few friendly jars, a fellow begins to understand that there is more to life than gainful trade."

"I see."

"Anyway, Geldemar has more than enough gold, but very few friends."

"At least not many who will drink with him in the middle of the day, I suppose."

They returned to the ship to find the knights rolling up the mats and clearing the foredeck; that accomplished, they immediately set themselves to honing skills dulled by long captivity.

Cait decided to withdraw to her quarters below deck where it was cooler. "Come, Thea," she said, "let us leave the men to practice their swordplay."

When Thea made no reply, she looked to see her sister gazing raptly at the knights, who had stripped to the waist in the heat. "He is handsome, is he not?" she said.

Cait saw where her sister was looking. Dag, his spare, muscular torso glistening with sweat, was lunging back and forth across the deck in a vigorous display of stab and thrust—as much for Alethea's benefit, Cait surmised, as for the drubbing of his invisible opponent.

"Thea, come away," snapped Cait. Abashed at her sister's barefaced stare, she took the younger woman by the arm and pulled her down the steps. "Have you no shame?" she demanded as soon as they were below deck. "He is hired to do my bidding, and I will not have you making cow eyes at him."

"I was never making cow eyes!" replied Thea, rigid with indignation. "Not that *you* would know anything about it. You will die a dried-up old hag and have no one to blame but yourself."

The remark was calculated to cut deep and it did. "Take that back."

"No."

"Take it back!"

By way of reply, Thea screwed up her face in a sour expression of defiant disobedience. Before she knew it, Cait's hand snaked out and struck her on the cheek with a resounding slap. Without another word, Thea turned and disappeared into her chamber, slamming the door behind her.

Cait, upset and angry, stood fuming in the companionway, fighting down the urge to go in and throttle her sister. Instead, she returned to the upper deck, and was speaking with Haemur about the voyage ahead when Rognvald approached carrying a long cloth bundle in his hands.

"This is for you, my lady," the tall Norseman said. Drawing aside the cloth wrapping, he presented her with a short, slender sword. "It was made as a gift for Queen Melisende of Jerusalem, but was taken as loot when the baggage train that carried it was overrun by Saracens. Geldemar only recently acquired it."

He placed the elegant, keen-edged blade in her grasp. It was half the size of a man's weapon, lighter, shorter, and balanced for a woman's hand. She swept it back and forth smartly. The quick, responsive weight sent an unexpected thrill through her. She had tried swords before—men's blades—and thought them cumbersome and ungainly.

111

"It is fine, is it not?" said Rognvald approvingly.

"A very marvel," she murmured. *With this blade,* she thought, *I will hold de Bracineaux to account.*

"When Geldemar saw that I liked it for you, he insisted that you should have it."

"In recognition of a wonderful new friendship, I should think."

"No doubt," agreed the knight.

Cait raised the sword before her face. The way the sunlight slid over its polished surface and danced along the razor-sharp edge brought a smile to her lips. "You must teach me to wield it properly," she said.

"It will be my very great pleasure," said Rognvald, inclining his head.

Two days later, after fittings from both tailor and shoemaker, a visit to the barber for shaves and haircuts for the knights—who were finally beginning to look almost civilized again—and numerous deliveries by provisioners bringing wine and water by the cask, ground meal by the barrel, hard-baked bread, salted pork, fish and sausage, dried peas and beans and other staples, and delicacies such as honey, almonds, pepper, and ground spices—Haemur raised anchor and *Persephone* drifted slowly out into the bay. Once clear of the long spiny ridge of the headland, he unfurled the sails and they set out for the Pillars of Hercules and the rocky storm-fraught coasts beyond.

PART II

September 2, 1916: Edinburgh, Scotland

"Gentlemen, the time has come to appoint a new leader."

It was Evans, our Second Principal, speaking in low, solemn tones which filled the Star Chamber with a sepulchral sound. "The war which has already cost so many lives has claimed one more, and we now taste the grief of those who mourn throughout our nation. I tell you, brothers," he said, looking to Pemberton's empty chair, "it fills my mouth with bitter ashes."

He turned his sorrowful gaze from Pemberton's place and said, "The rule of our order dictates the terms by which the new leader is to be appointed. But before proceeding any further, we will observe a time of silence in honor of our fallen leader."

We all bowed our heads and offered up the memory of that fine, noble man to the Allwise Creator in whose presence he now delighted. The silence in the room swelled to become a hymn of deepest admiration and the most profound esteem, a veneration beyond utterance.

I do not know how long it lasted, for time was overwhelmed by eternity and no longer held any meaning to me. I simply became aware that Evans was speaking, and once more returned, reluctantly, to the concerns of this world and the matter before us.

"Unless anyone has cause to object," Evans was saying, "we shall proceed in accordance with the directives established in the Rules of Order. I shall now read the pertinent portion from the Articles of Investment: 'If it should happen that the First Principal shall die in office, the Second Principal shall hold in his stead the seal and charter of the Brotherhood of the Temple and the Order of the *Sanctus Clarus* until such time as the surviving members of the elect be met to nominate and appoint one from their number who shall assume the mantle of authority and resume the leadership of the Order, guiding its protection, preservation, advancement, and the furtherance of all its aims.' "

Here the compact Welshman looked up. "Hear me, all of you? Signify by saying, 'Aye.' " This we did, and he continued, "I shall now read from the Articles of Initiation. 'If it should be found that, prior to the election and investment of the First Principal, any of the Seven have not attained to the Master, or Final Degree Initiation, and unless any impediment shall be admitted, that initiation shall be offered without delay.' Hear me, all of you? Signify by saying, 'Aye.' "

While we all affirmed our understanding, I did so in a slightly bemused state, for until that moment I had neither heard nor suspected there were any higher degrees than the one I now occupied, the Seventh. Despite the slightly archaic and abstruse language, it did not take a legal mind long to realize that Evans was talking about *me*. In other words, if the First Principal is to be elected from among the remaining members of the Inner Circle, then they must all be of equal rank and status. Obviously, I did not enjoy that particular rank.

Indeed, the very next instant he turned and addressed me personally. "Brother Murray," he said, "I am mindful of your standing. Having attained the Seventh Degree, and having performed loyal and exemplary service since your investment, I declare before this assembly that you are deemed worthy of consideration for initiation into the Final Degree."

Still slightly awed by the implications of Evans's announcement, I could only nod as Zaccaria hastened to ratify this astonishing declaration, saying, "I stand as second to the initiation of our esteemed brother."

"We recognize the sanction and affirmation of Brother Zaccaria," Evans said. "Therefore I must ask you, brothers, is it your will and pleasure that Brother Murray attain to the Final Degree? If so, please signify."

All around the table the members of the Inner Circle declared their endorsement of the proposal, whereupon I was asked to stand. "Brother Murray," said the Second Principal, "seeing no impediment to your elevation arising, I now ask you: to the best of your knowledge is there any reason why you may not advance to your initiation?"

"No, brother. I stand ready to accept the mandate of my superiors." It is the customary answer to questions of this kind within the Brotherhood; the only difference is that now I knew the men around me to have been my superiors and not, as I had mistakenly imagined for so long, merely my peers. While I accept that my initiation was a formality which was being carried out to fulfill the dictates of our Rules of Order, I nevertheless experienced the familiar excitement of the novitiate facing the unknown.

Obviously, I did not know the form this initiation would take. Remembering my induction to the Seventh Degree, however, and the harrowing ordeal it engendered, my enthusiasm was tempered by experience. That is not to say I was afraid: I was not. I trusted the men around me implicitly. Even so, the frailty of the human frame having been much on my mind of late, I was only too aware of the limitations age had introduced. Though I was the youngest member of the Inner Circle, I was neither as energetic nor as agile as in my youth, and any qualms I felt were those which attended men of my age when contemplating even the most ordinary exertions.

Evans took me at my word, however. "So be it," he said. "Let the initiation commence."

He closed the book from which he had been reading out the Articles. "The nature of initiation to the Final Degree requires that the candidate should remain in seclusion neither more nor less than three complete diurnal periods, the purpose of which is to allow the candidate to reflect on the commitment he is about to make, and to seek the safeguarding of his soul through making peace with his Allwise Creator." He looked to me for an answer. "Do you understand?"

"I understand, brother, and I am ready to proceed."

"So be it." Turning to the others, he said, "We will adjourn until this hour in three nights' time when we will reconvene to undertake the initiation of our esteemed brother."

The meeting ended then, and I received the congratulations of the others. They wished me well and departed, disappearing into the night by their various routes. In a little while Evans and I were left alone. "I was sorry to hear of the death of your wife," he said; our business concluded, we could speak more informally. "It must have been a very great shock to you."

"Yes," I replied. Although I had no idea how the other members of the Inner Circle learned of these things, I had long ago accepted that they did. "I am only beginning to realize the extent of my loss."

"Time will heal," he told me. "I do not offer that lightly. Though many people profess the same sentiment blithely and without consideration, it is true nonetheless. Given time, the wound will heal. The scar will remain, but you will no longer feel the pain."

I thanked him for his expression of sympathy, and said, "As it happens, I was prepared to relate a most curious incident concerning Pemberton's death. I wanted to hear what the other members made of it."

"Oh, indeed? Well, would you mind telling me?"

"Not at all," I answered, and went on to explain about Pemberton's ghostly appearance at the country house, and my subsequent interview with Miss Gillespie. I reported the queer message the young woman had passed on to me. "He spoke to the young lady; he said: 'The pain is swallowed in peace, and grief in glory.' That's what she thought him to say, but it makes little sense to me."

Evans rubbed his smooth chin and his eyes became keen. He loved a good puzzle, and I was happy to share it with him and let him mull it over for as long as he liked. "Now that *is* a poser," he allowed. "Providing, of course, that is what Pemberton said."

"Granted," I replied. "What one says and what one is heard to say are not necessarily the same thing."

"Quite." He smiled, his round, friendly face lighting with simple good pleasure. "I shall have a good think. Now then, let me show you to your cell."

I had learned over the years that the little church where we met contained several underground passages leading to a number of chambers, sub-chambers, and catacombs. Thus I was not surprised to learn that the cell he mentioned was of the old-fashioned variety: a simple bare room with a straw pallet piled with fleeces for sleeping; a small table with a large old Bible bound in brittle leather, and a single, fat candle in an iron holder; a low, three-legged stool; in the corner a tiny round hearth with narrow stone chimney above; and, next to it, a supply of wood and kindling. Beside the hearth was a covered wooden stoup filled with water; a wooden ladle hung by its handle from a leather strap. Atop the stoup lay a cloth bundle. The rock walls were white-washed, and a simple wooden cross adorned the wall above the bedplace.

In all it was a clean little room, reached after a short candlelit walk along a passage which joined a flight of steps leading from the Star Chamber, which was itself below the chancel of the church. "All the comforts of home," Evans said, tipping his candle to the one on the table, "but none of the distractions."

"I've always wondered what it would be like to be a monk. Now I will find out."

"You will enjoy your stay, Gordon." He stepped to the doorway. "There is food in the bundle, and you will find a latrine in the next cell along." He bade me farewell then and left me to begin my time of preparation. I listened to his footfall recede down the passageway, and heard the door shut a moment later, and I was alone.

I occupied myself with setting a tidy little fire on the hearth. This I did as much for the light and the cheery company of the flames as the warmth provided. I unwrapped the bundle and saw that it contained three large round loaves of bread, a lump of hard cheese, a half-dozen apples, and three dried fish. Not only would I sleep like a monk, I would eat like one, too.

I tried the bed, stretching myself out on the fleeces; it was simple, but comfortable—the straw was fresh, and there was a rough woven coverlet, should I need it. I was not particularly tired, so I got up, took the candle, and had a look at the latrine—again, a simple but service-able affair which would meet my basic requirements. Returning to the cell, I placed the candle on the table once more and took up the Bible. I perched on the edge of the bed, adjusted the candle so that I could see the pages and opened the cover—only to discover that what I had taken for a Bible was in fact a large, heavy, antique volume entitled, *The Mark of the Rose*.

Curiosity pricked, I turned the pages and examined the text. I am no expert in these things, but I had plowed through enough musty, dusty old books in various legal libraries to recognize a hand-printed tome when I saw one. There was neither colophon, trademark nor printer's stamp that I could see. Judging from the antique typeface and the way the heavy pages were bound, I guessed it had been printed anywhere from the mid to late 1700s. Considering its age, the pages were in remarkably good condition—indicating, I assumed, a pro-longed and conscientious effort at preservation.

I returned to the title page and found printed beneath the title the words: *prepared from the manuscript of William St. Clair, Earl of Orkney.*

The choice of words was interesting. It did not say that William had written the manuscript, but merely implied ownership. From this, I deduced that the manuscript in question was an older document from which the book I now held had been produced.

Thoroughly intrigued, I began thumbing the pages indiscriminately, and before long began reading. My pulse raced as, one after another, I began encountering the old familiar names: Ranulf . . . Murdo . . . Ragna . . . Duncan . . . Caitríona . . . Sydoni . . . Padraig . . . Emlyn . . . and others whose lives had now become so intimately known to me that I thought of them as friends.

I understood then how I was to use the time I was being granted. Settling back on my bed, I pulled the table close and, propping the book on my knees, turned to the first page and began to read.

THIRTEEN

Twenty-six days out from Cyprus, *Persephone* passed the Pillars of Hercules, leaving the calm blue waters of the Mediterranean behind and entering the green-gray foam-traced depths of the cold Atlantic. Almost at once, the fair warm weather changed. Brilliant blue, cloudless skies gave way to low, heavy gray ceilings of endless overcast; cold winds gusted out of the northwest, kicking up a rough chop which hammered the prow and kept the ship pitching and lurching from crest to trough for days on end.

No stranger to heavy seas, Haemur reduced the sail—once, and then again—and kept a firm hand on the tiller and an experienced eye on the heavens. When the rain and mist finally cleared, the Iberian coast came into view. Two days later they sighted the entrance to the great shallow saltwater bay which the locals called the Sea of Straw.

Weary of the wind and rain and bouncing deck, Cait gladly gave the command to make landfall, and in a little while they came in sight of Lixbona, with its wide and busy harbor tucked into the curved arm of coastline on the Tagus river. The white Moorish city, rising on terraced hills, glistened in the sun with a fresh, rain-washed gleam. The air seemed sharper, more invigorating, too—heralding an early autumn, Cait thought.

Persephone's eager passengers stood on the deck as the ship passed through the narrows and into the bay, and watched the city grow larger as more of the gently undulating hills were revealed to them. "There is the *al-qasr*," said Abu Sharma, pointing to the citadel sitting square atop the steep promontory overlooking the harbor.

"Do you know this place?" wondered Rognvald.

"No," he said, and explained that the word simply meant "fortress" in Arabic. "And, look, there is the central *mosq*." He pointed to a large, domed building with a tall, pointed tower rising beside it like a finger pointing toward Heaven. But the tower, or *minaret*, as he called it, was topped by a large wooden cross, and another had been erected in the center of the mosq's bulging dome. For when the city fell to the Christians there had been no gross destruction; instead, the practical people of Lixbona merely converted the Muslim buildings to new uses: the fortress became the king's palace, and the mosqs were made into churches.

Thus, Lixbona resembled a true Damascus of the north: wide marketplaces, covered bazaars, mosqs, synagogues, and chapels scattered among the tall, white-washed houses with their elaborate screened balconies and flat roofs, on which families gathered after the day's work was finished. And like Damascus, it was a city of brisk commerce, too. The rolling brown Tagus was a well-traveled road along which the people of the fertile southern valley shipped grain, meat, wine, and green produce all the way from the craggy Sintra mountains to the coast.

Upon reaching the great river harbor, Haemur could find no berths along the huge timber wharf, so took a place among the ships anchored in the bay; while the seamen made *Persephone* secure, the others prepared to go ashore. After a few attempts, the knights succeeded in attracting the attention of a ferryman, who took them to the wharf. It was the first landfall since leaving Cyprus and it took some time to get used to solid, unmoving ground beneath their feet. For the knights, the day began and ended at the first alehouse they encountered on the street leading up from the harbor. Meanwhile, Cait and Alethea, accompanied by Olvir and Otti, purchased fresh provisions to be delivered to the ship. That finished, and with no wish to hurry back, they walked along the market stalls and marveled at the variety of goods. Feeling generous, Cait allowed Alethea to buy a sky-blue beaded shift and mantle, and gave Olvir and Otti a similar amount to spend on two used, but serviceable, daggers. Ever since the knights began their arms training, she had noticed how the seamen lusted after their Norse companions' handsome weapons, and considered it would be no bad thing to arm her sailors as well.

By evening, they were back aboard the ship, and remained in the harbor for the night. Having discovered the Norsemen's fondness for ale, Cait thought it best to move on as quickly as possible, putting out to sea again at first light the next morning to continue their journey north along the coast. The evening of the second day, they arrived at Porto Cales, where again they stopped for the night. Haemur's chart was good, but not so exact that he felt confident to navigate the treacherous, often lethal waters of the rock-strewn coast ahead; he wanted to talk to the local fishermen and find out all he could about their destination. So they put in for the night and, while Abu and Haemur, with chart in hand, spent most of the next day conversing with the boat owners and sailors of the town, the others prowled the marketplaces— except for Svein, Dag, and Yngvar, who prowled only as far as the waterfront inn and remained blissfully occupied drinking ale until Rognvald came and fetched them back to the ship.

"The best counsel, my lady," reported Haemur on his return, "is to go up coast to Pons Vetus and hire a guide for the way ahead."

"There are many ways to Santiago de Compostela," Abu put in. "The entire city is a shrine to Saint James the Great and many pilgrims come there to reverence his bones. It is second only to Jerusalem, they say."

"Can we go and see it?" asked Thea. "Oh, Cait, can we?"

Ignoring her, Cait said, "And did anyone happen to mention which of the many ways to the city we should take?"

"The best way for us is by river," answered Abu. "They say the river is wide and deep enough to take the ship, but the channels can be difficult for the unwary."

"It will cost a little," Haemur said, "and no doubt I could do it myself if pressed to it. But if it please you, my lady, I would feel better for the use of someone who knows the water hereabouts." He paused, then added, "Your father would not thank me to wreck his beloved *Persephone* and forsake you and your lady sister in a foreign land."

"Nor would I, Haemur," replied Cait. "But thanks to you, I am certain that will not happen. I am happy to trust in your good judgment."

"Very good, my lady. God willing," he said, as if resigning himself to an irksome task, "I will take on a guide at Pons Vetus."

Two days later, that is what they did. The fisherfolk of the busy little port knew the region well, and when it was discovered there was silver to be had for showing the strangers the way, Haemur had no end of offers from which to choose. Eventually, he decided on a man of mature age, like himself, who had for many years fished the coastal waters and supplied the Galician markets with his catches.

"Wise you are," the fisherman told them when he came aboard at sunrise the next morning. "To many folk the river is just a river. They learn otherwise to their disadvantage. The Ulla is chancy—especially above the bend. But never fear, Ginés will see you safe to port without a worry."

With that, the old seaman took his place beside Haemur; and although neither man could comprehend the other, with Abu and Olvir's help, and much use of the signs, nudges, and nods recognized by sailors the world over, the two men soon formed a rough understanding of one another. Ginés directed the old Norse pilot around the peninsula, and up through the scattered rocks and islets on the other side. It was slow work, and the tide was out by the time they reached the river mouth. "It will be dark before the water is high enough again," Ginés told them. "The weather is going to change. We will find no better place to stay tonight. If you are asking me, I would say to drop anchor right here and proceed when it is light—weather permitting."

Although the sky seemed clear and the day mild enough, they accepted the old fisherman's advice, and prepared to spend the night idly drifting in the sluggish river current. After supper, Cait soon lost interest in listening to the sailors trade sea tales and watching the knights drink wine; she summoned a complaining Alethea and went below deck to bed. In her sleep, she dreamed that she and her father had completed the pilgrimage and returned home. She awakened when she felt the ship begin to move again and went up on deck to find what at first sight appeared to be a dream come true: they were back in Caithness.

The sky was thick and dark and low; clouds lay on the hilltops and it was raining gently. The hills themselves were green and steep, and covered with splotches of yellow gorse and the criss-crossing patterns of sheep trails etched in the thick turf. The rounded bulges of granite boulders broke the smooth surface of the hills, like the tops of ancient gray skull-bones wearing through their moss-green burial shroud. White morning mist searched down the slopes, twisting around the stones with long, ghostly fingers.

In all, the landscape of Galicia evoked her homeland so suddenly and solidly that before Cait knew it, tears were running down her cheeks. More mystified than melancholy, she nevertheless felt the inexplicable pull of her far-off homeland and marveled that this place should appear so remarkably like Scotland.

"Here, my lady," called the old pilot from the helm, "I never saw a place looked more like home. If I knew no better, I'd say we were come to Caithness."

"He is right," remarked Olvir. "I was thinking the same thing."

Cait nodded and moved quickly to the rail so that Haemur and the others would not see her crying; she stood wrapped in her mantle gazing at the mist-covered hills as they slid slowly past. When the knights came on deck to breakfast, she was dry-eyed once more and ready to embark on the next stage of the journey.

It was after midday when the ship came to the small river town of Iria. "There is a hostler at the crossroads in the town. You can hire horses from him," Ginés told them. "Compostela is not far, and you will soon be there."

As it happened, the hostler had only two horses left for hire. Not wishing to wait until others became available, Cait took the two: for herself and Rognvald. The others, she decided, could remain behind with the ship, and she and Rognvald would travel more quickly without a crowd to slow them. Thus, they set off early the next day and undertook the ride through thickly wooded countryside. The road was old and straight, a Roman road, but well-maintained and busy, passing through several little hamlets and holdings in the valley bottoms.

They rode through forests of beech and oak, damp from the rain and heavy with the smell of ferns. As the day progressed, the clouds parted and the sun grew warm. They began to pass bedraggled travelers on foot, some cloaked in brown and stumping along with long wooden staffs, wearing wide-brimmed cockle hats. Most of those they passed had scallop shells sewn on their hats and on their cloaks. No doubt, she reckoned, these were some of the pilgrims Abu had mentioned; but what the crude symbol might signify, she could not imagine. They also overtook farmers carrying braces of chickens, trudging along beside their wives lugging baskets of eggs, or bunches of onions, or carrots, or bushels of beans, and once an oxcart piled high with turnips, and another with yellow squash as big and round as heads.

They made good time and reached the walls of Compostela before sunset. The city gates were still open and upon passing through, they immediately entered a wide stone-paved street leading to a great square, in the center of which stood an enormous basilica. On this pleasant summer's eve, pilgrims without number thronged the square; those who were not waiting their turn to go into the church were either encamped on the bare earth of the square, or crowding around one of the scores of booths and stalls which had been set up to sell food, clothing, or trinkets—such as painted scallop shells, brass badges, drinking gourds, or sandals—to the restless pilgrim population that ebbed and flowed through the city like a brown, beggarly tide.

"He must be a miracle man, this saint of theirs," observed Rognvald in amazement at the hordes. "I have not seen anything of this kind since Jerusalem, and even there it was not like this."

Besides the holy wanderers, there were traders, moneychangers, merchants, vendors of food and drink and the produce of the surrounding fields, and laborers of every kind. For the precinct of Sancti Iacobi was rapidly becoming a town in its own right; with a dozen or more grand buildings in various stages of construction, the square seemed more like a building site than an ecclesiastical precinct.

In the streets surrounding the square numerous inns had been built to serve travelers of better means. Cait decided on a small establishment with a red rose painted on a placard above the door. "This is the one for us," she said, and Rognvald went in to inquire about rooms for the night.

"They will have us," he reported, "for two silver denari a night—each. There are others who will take less."

"I am content," she replied. Lord Rognvald signaled a young man who came at a run to take their horses; as he led them away, Cait and Rognvald went in to make the acquaintance of the innkeeper, a small bald man with a large mustache and a swollen jaw from an abscessed tooth. He was wearing a poultice of herbs soaked in vinegar and wrapped in a cloth tied to the top of his head. "Peace and comfort, my friends," he said thickly, trying to smile through his pain. "I am Miguel. Welcome to my house. Please, come in and sit while I make your rooms ready. There is bread on the table and wine in the jar. I also have ale, if you prefer. Supper will be served at sundown."

He beetled off, pressing a hand to the side of his cheek, and Cait and Rognvald found places at one of the two large tables in the center of the hall-like room, one side of which was taken up by a great hearth on which half a pig was sizzling away over a bed of glowing coals. Owing to the cost of the rooms the inn was not crowded, and the guests were of a higher rank than the mendicants who swarmed to the monastery porches and hospices. Their fellow-lodgers were merchants and wealthier pilgrims for whom a visit to the shrine of the blessed saint was not a particular hardship.

Still, after the fresh air of the open sea, Cait found the smoky confines of the inn almost suffocating and was heartily glad when, after a supper of roast pork, bean soup, mashed turnips, and boiled greens, she could at last leave Rognvald and the traveling tradesmen to their stoups of ale and news of the world and retire to her room. Not much larger than her quarters aboard ship, it was swept clean, and the box which made the bed was filled with fresh straw and the coverings were washed linen.

She undressed, hanging her mantle and shift on a peg on the door, and happily sank into the bed—only to spend an all-but-sleepless night scheming how best to get Archbishop Bertrano to reveal the secret of the Mystic Rose. She had had plenty of time to ponder this since leaving Constantinople. But as many plans as she had made, that many had been discarded along the way. Now it was time to decide, and she was still far from certain what to do.

The following morning, as they walked across the busy square, an anxious Cait schooled a thoughtful Rognvald in the necessity of gaining the cleric's confidence before broaching the true subject of their visit. "He must not suspect we are anything but genuine pilgrims," she said. "We will get the measure of him first, and then decide how to proceed. Understand?"

"Aye," replied Rognvald, absently, "I understand."

They strolled through the gathering crowds to the huge oak doors of the archbishop's palace hard by the great basilica which, according to the pilgrims at the inn, contained the holy remains of the blessed *Iacobus Magnus,* Saint James the Great, disciple and companion of Christ. It was the apostle's venerable bones that drew the penitent pilgrims in ever-increasing numbers. At the palace, they presented themselves to the much-put-upon porter, who eyed them with weary indifference. "God be good to you. I am Brother Thaddeus," he said in clipped, precise Latin. "How may I help you?"

"Greetings in the name of Our Lord and Savior," said Rognvald, stepping toward him. "We are looking for Archbishop Bertrano. It is a matter of some importance."

Thaddeus regarded his visitors blankly, and said, "He is not difficult to find, but you must take your chances like everyone else."

"We would be happy to make an appointment to see him when it is more convenient," suggested Cait.

The priest smiled pityingly. "You misunderstand. The archbishop is overseeing the construction of the new monastery. He is seldom to be found in residence." The monk lifted a hand toward the tower of timber scaffolding in a corner of the square and then closed the door.

They walked to the place and were soon standing on the edge of a cleared mound where, amidst vast heaps of gray stone and a veritable forest of timber, the stately curtain walls of a sizable chapel and bell tower were slowly rising, block by heavy granite block. The place was seething with workers: an army of masons, stone-cutters, and sculptors, scores of rough laborers, and dozens of haulers with their mules and teams of yoked oxen—all of them moving in concert to the loud exhortations of a large, fat-bellied man dressed in the simple black robes of a rural cleric. His jowls were freshly shaved, and his round face glowed with the heat of his exertion.

"Leave it to me," Rognvald told her as they approached. "I have a bold idea."

"What are you—wait!" Cait began, but it was too late. Rognvald was already hailing the priest, who turned to regard his visitors with a scowl that would have curdled milk in a bucket.

FOURTEEN

"*Pax vobiscum!*" called Rognvald, cupping a hand to his mouth. With the creaking of windlass and wagon, the groaning of the ropes, the lowing of oxen, braying of mules, and the dull continuous clatter of hammer and chisel on stone, the Norseman had to shout to make himself heard above the din. "We are looking for Bertrano, Lord of this Holy See."

"God be good to you, my friend. You have found him." Turning from his visitors, he cried, "Not there! Not there!" Bertrano waved his hands at a group of workmen shoveling white powdered lime into a pile beside the half-raised bell tower. Despite his rank, the archbishop appeared perfectly at ease amidst the clamor and dust of the building site. Indeed, the only thing that set him apart from one of his many laborers was the wooden cross swinging by a beaded loop from his wide leather belt. "On the other side! It goes there—" Bertrano pointed to a heap of sand, "there—on the other side, you see?"

"I commend you, archbishop," offered Cait politely when they had succeeded in gaining his attention once more and finished introducing themselves. "Your monastery will be a marvel of the builder's art."

"A very marvel, indeed, good lady," agreed the archbishop sourly, "*if*, by some miracle, it is ever finished." Red-faced, puffing, and sweating—for all the sun had only just risen—the fat man wiped his forehead with a damp sleeve and shouted a terse order to a mule driver who was just trundling past, dragging a length of timber with a chain.

"Why should it not be finished?" she asked.

"Ask the king!" cried Archbishop Bertrano. "It is his interminable campaigns that keep us limping along like lame lepers when we should be racing like champions to achieve God's glory."

"If not for the king," suggested Rognvald, "the Muhammedans would still rule this part of the world, no?"

The harried archbishop threw him a withering glance. "What do you know about it?" He cast a disdainful eye on the tall knight's sword. "There is more to life than brawling, battling, and wenching."

Before the knight could beg his pardon, the archbishop softened. "Forgive me, son, I have allowed my temper to get the better of me. God's truth, I am a tyrant until I've broken fast; afterward, I am mild as a lamb."

"We would not think of keeping you," Cait began. "Perhaps we might return later when—"

"Nonsense," replied the archbishop, striding away. "Come, we will break bread together and you can tell me the news of—where did you say you have been?"

"The Holy Land," said Rognvald confidently.

"Ah, yes, the Holy Land." Bertrano led them to a small wattle and thatch hut across the way, in the center of what would one day become the monastery's cloisters; there three monks had prepared a table for the archbishop. At his approach, the monks hastened to fetch the archbishop's throne-like ecclesiastical chair from inside the hut; this they placed at the head of the table. The chair was high-backed and bore the image of an eagle on each armrest; a fine cross was carved into the massive top rail; gilded and surrounded by hemispheres of cut and polished jet, the golden cross looked as if it were encircled by a string of shiny black pearls.

"I had the workmen put up this hut so I might oversee the work," Archbishop Bertrano said, indicating the sturdy little house. He gathered his robes and settled his bulk in the chair; the monks drew the table up to his stomach, and then darted back inside to begin serving the food. "You simply would not believe the morass of problems that require my attention." He waved his guests to places on stools either side of the table, rinsed his hands in a bowl of water offered by one of the monks, and then wiped them on his robe. "Eternal vigilance, my friends, is all that separates us from everlasting chaos."

"I imagine it can be very taxing," replied Cait sympathetically.

"Just *you* try building a bell tower," growled Bertrano, "and then come and teach me about taxing."

Cait, stung by the remark, felt her face growing red. The archbishop gulped and smacked his forehead with his hand.

"God help me, I have done it again! I beg your kind indulgence, my lady. Please, let us sit in contemplative silence, I pray you, until we've got something in us to dull hunger's sharp edge."

The three sat quietly, and presently the monks brought bread and boiled eggs, sweetened wine, and a porridge made from dried peas, onions, carrots, and bits of salt cod. Oblivious to his visitors, the archbishop fell to, sopping up the peas porridge with chunks of bread, which he sucked dry and then gobbled down, pausing every now and then to peel an egg, break off a bit of bread, or take a gulp of wine, before plunging in again.

Cait and Rognvald ate sparingly, watching the archbishop for any sign that he deigned to notice them once more. When, after a third bowl of porridge and second cup of wine, he appeared to be slowing his onslaught, Cait ventured a compliment on the food; Archbishop Bertrano held up his hand for silence, raised the bowl to his lips and drained it in a long, greedy draft. He wiped his mouth on the tablecloth, sighed, sat back in the great chair, and beamed beatifically at his guests while flicking crumbs from his robe. "Ah, now, you were saying?"

"The meal was delicious," said Cait. "The eggs were boiled to perfection."

"We get a lot of eggs," observed the archbishop. "The people bring them to the monastery. God knows what they think *we* want with them. But there you are." Turning to Rognvald, he said, "Now then, you say you have come from the Holy Land, I think."

"I have," replied the knight, pushing aside his bowl, "and I would the tidings were better. There is much fighting, as always, and the Crusaders win as often as they lose, it is true, but they lose all the wrong battles."

"Any battle lost," opined the archbishop, "was a wrong battle, I should have thought."

"True enough," agreed Rognvald affably. "Still, the winnings do not cover the losses, if you see what I mean. Everywhere, territory falls to the Muhammedans, and the Christians are once more subjugated and enslaved."

Bertrano appeared disheartened by the news. "Is Jerusalem still safe?"

"It is—for the time being. But soon it will be merely a solitary rock in an ocean of Islam. It cannot last."

The Norseman spoke with a sincerity that surprised Cait. She watched with growing admiration for his intelligence and subtlety as he drew the archbishop into their trap.

"*Perditio, perditio,*" sighed the archbishop, wagging his head sadly. "But, tell me, can nothing good be said?"

"The cities of the coast—Tripoli, Tyre, Acre, Jaffa, Ascalon—all remain safe. The Arabs are masters of horse and desert, but they are indifferent sailors. Thanks to the Genoan and Venetian fleets, the Saracens can make no advancement there. So, for as long as the ships can pass unhindered, the coastal cities will remain in Christian hands."

"Ah, well, that is something at least," answered the archbishop contentedly. He, like Cait, regarded Rognvald with a new admiration. "You speak like a commander. Perhaps *you* should be leading the Armies of Christ against the infernal hosts of the infidel."

The knight smiled, but shook his head. "No, I have seen enough of battle; I want nothing more to do with it—with any of it. For my troubles, I spent nearly three years in a Saracen prison, and indeed, I would still be there now if not for the love of my good lady wife." He reached across the table to take Cait's hand. "She traveled all the way from our home in Caithness to Damascus and ransomed me from Prince Mujir's dungeon, and for that I shall be eternally grateful to her."

He squeezed her hand, and Cait pretended a smile of wifely love, which surprised her with its naturalness and ease.

"No, I shall not go back there again," Rognvald said. "But others were not so fortunate. I saw many good men die in that stinking prison—too many. One of them—and it grieves me full well to say it—was none other than the Grand Commander of the Kingdom of Jerusalem."

"Impossible!" cried Archbishop Bertrano. "It cannot be."

Rognvald regarded the cleric with unflinching conviction. "Alas, it is all the more lamentable. In fact, it is because of his death that we have come."

The archbishop raised his eyebrows in mystified amazement. "Pray tell me how this has come to be."

"The tale is sorry, but soon told," replied the knight. "The commander arrived sorely wounded—there was a storm and his ship had foundered on the rocks, somewhere between Tripoli and Tyre, I think. A great many men were drowned outright and, as ill luck would have it, the Saracens who found them killed a number as well. The few survivors were taken captive and brought to Damascus." He frowned, as if remembering a tragedy. "They had fought valiantly to prevent themselves being captured . . ."

"As only a man of his courage and stature would," offered the archbishop.

"The battle was fierce, as I say. Several were gravely injured—Commander de Bracincaux foremost among them. His wounds were too great; he could not recover. He lingered only a few days, and then died."

"I am grieved to the very soul to hear it," sighed the archbishop. "Jerusalem will not see a finer soldier, and more's the pity."

So persuasive was the Norseman's forthright tale, that Cait found herself feeling sorry for the plight of the poor Templars and their mortally wounded Master. "It is a very great loss," she agreed, her voice soft with sorrow.

"I will say a special mass for them," declared the archbishop, "and order a day of perpetual intercession on their behalf before the Throne of Grace." He nodded absently to himself. "It is the least I can do."

The three were silent for a time, and then the archbishop stirred himself and asked, "Did he say anything before he died?"

"Oh, yes," Rognvald assured him. "As noblemen, we were held in the same cell. You can well imagine that the ransom price for such an important man is exceedingly large—as much as for a king. The Saracens were hopeful his release would earn them a fortune."

"Greedy dogs!" snarled the archbishop. "I would to heaven that God might rain unending calamity upon their unbelieving heads. I truly do."

"You will also appreciate, knowing de Bracineaux as you undoubtedly do, that his last days were eaten up with anxiety lest the Templars should hear of his capture and pay the money. He thought the ransom excessive, and worried that it would impoverish the order unnecessarily. He said to me, 'I pray I may die quickly and cheat the devils of their due.' He said he would not rest in peace if he knew the money paid for his release would be used to carry on the persecution of brave Christian knights."

Dumbstruck, the archbishop leaned back in his chair and thumped his head gently against the carved rail of his chair. "Even as he lay dying," he said after a moment, "even then, he took no thought for himself."

"You know better than I the kind of man he was," said Rognvald with touching conviction.

"*That*, sir, is the kind of man he was!" cried the archbishop, his broad face suffused with a ruddy rapture. "Noble through and through."

"He told me something else," Rognvald confided, leaning nearer. "His last days were difficult, as you might expect; talking, however, gave him some peace. It comforted him to unburden his soul." He leaned closer still, as if he feared he might be overheard. The archbishop bent his head nearer. "This is why we have come."

"Indeed?" wondered Bertrano. "Then tell me, my son. If it is a confession, I will hear it."

"The matter that most upset him concerned a letter."

"A letter?"

"A special letter," confirmed Rognvald. "From you, Archbishop Bertrano."

"From me!" The cleric sat back and gazed at the knight in amazement. "In Heaven's name, what can it mean? Are you certain this letter was from me?"

Rognvald nodded in solemn earnest. "He was very agitated about it," said the knight. "Toward the end he spoke of nothing else. I think it pained him to leave his task undone. And that is why he confided in me. There was no one else, you see. He wanted me to carry on the work that he had begun."

Bertrano grew thoughtful; he gazed out toward the unfinished tower. "Did he tell you what he had undertaken?"

"Alas, no," answered the knight. "He made me swear upon my life and the life hereafter that if ever I was to receive my freedom, I was to come to you, Archbishop Bertrano, and tell you what had happened. He said that you would explain all I needed to know." The knight spread his hands, as if humbly offering himself for the churchman's inspection. "Here I am."

"Great God in heaven!" cried the archbishop, leaping to his feet and almost overturning the table in his effort to extricate himself from his chair. "No! No!"

Both Rognvald and Cait drew back in alarm. Rognvald stood, hands outstretched to calm the suddenly ferocious cleric. Cait, astonished at the abrupt change in the archbishop's demeanor, jumped up and started after him, furiously trying to think what the Norwegian lord had said to so completely antagonize the archbishop as to send him fleeing from the table.

"Please," she called, "wait!"

Archbishop Bertrano threw her a hasty glance over his shoulder. "No! It is all going wrong!"

"We meant no offence. Can we not return to our discussion?"

"Not you," the archbishop said, "the tower!" He thrust an angry finger before him. Cait looked where he was pointing, and saw an ox-drawn sledge loaded with stone. The driver was tossing the rough blocks onto a heap of fresh-cut stone. "Come to me after vespers. We will dine together and I will tell you everything. I must go!" He raced on, shouting, "You there! Stop! Desist, I say, or I shall excommunicate you at once!"

FIFTEEN

"I confess I find it difficult to believe," Archbishop Bertrano was saying. He looked from Cait to Rognvald, and shook his head. "That a man like de Bracineaux should be cut down so cruelly . . . I am sorry; it is most untimely, and it saddens me greatly."

"Nor are you alone in your grief," offered Cait sympathetically. "I have only recently lost my father."

"Accept my deepest condolences, my child," said the archbishop. "More wine?"

He reached for the silver jar and filled all three cups, beginning with his own. He took a long draft and, wiping his mouth on his sleeve, said, "Now then, I have been thinking about this letter you have mentioned. It can only be the letter I wrote and dispatched to the pope some time ago. Did the commander tell you what this letter contained?"

"Only that it was a matter of highest and utmost importance," offered Rognvald. "I think he feared revealing too much lest our captors somehow discover the secret."

"In that, he showed the wisdom that made him such a formidable leader of men." The archbishop took another drink, and laid the cup aside. He fixed his visitors with a stern and cautious stare. "Are you certain he said nothing more about the contents of the letter?"

"By my faith, no, my lord archbishop," answered Rognvald truthfully. "He breathed not a word to me."

The table around which the three were gathered was large, round and splendidly made of polished oak; it nearly filled the chamber. Before them was sweetened wine in a large silver flagon, and a platter of ripe figs. Although modest, the room bordered a walled garden, and for this reason the archbishop often used it to welcome his more intimate guests. Sparrows returning to the roost twitched and twittered in the branches of the orange trees outside, adding to the heightened anticipation for Cait.

"Well, you have said it. For it is indeed a matter of utmost and highest importance," the churchman continued. "And now that I know my message has gone astray, as it were, I shall send to the pope to inform him of the tragedy."

Cait swallowed hard. Did he mean to tell them nothing after all? Before she could think how best to proceed, Rognvald, nodding sympathetically, said, "No doubt that would be best."

It was all Cait could do to stifle a scream of frustration. She took a drink from her cup to hide her aggravation.

"Then it is settled," Bertrano concluded happily. "I shall write to the pope at once and send it by swift courier."

Rognvald smiled diffidently, and Cait narrowed her eyes at him over the rim of her cup, silently urging him to speak up before it was too late.

"The Templars will be choosing a new Master of Jerusalem soon enough, I expect," the knight replied. "We can but pray it will be someone who shares de Bracineaux's integrity and zeal." He paused, then added, "I tremble to think what would happen if the reward of your hard work was to be usurped by an emperor-loving Judas."

"But what do you mean?" wondered the archbishop, a crease of worry appearing on his brow.

"Just that," said Rognvald. "Nothing more."

"Do you think there might be a chance that could happen?"

Rognvald shrugged. "I should not like to say."

"Come now, sir," stormed the archbishop, striking the tabletop with a fist. "If you know something, you must tell me."

"I fear I have said too much already." Rognvald raised his hands in surrender. "I beg you do not force me, for I would not like it to be thought that I slandered another man's name. In truth, it is none of my concern, and I will say no more."

"No, sir!" blurted Bertrano, growing agitated. "That will not do at all. I must know if my purpose is likely to go astray."

"I assure you, my lord archbishop," answered Rognvald a little stiffly, "I have told you all that can be said." He appeared about to say something further, but thought better of it, and closed his mouth instead.

The archbishop saw his hesitation and pounced on it. "Ah, you *do* know something!" he crowed. "Tell me, my son; keep nothing back. I am a priest, remember; with me, all confessions are sacred."

"It was only a thought," began Rognvald. He turned to Cait, as if seeking her approval.

"Go on, my darling," she urged him sweetly. "Let us hold nothing secret from this honest and upright churchman."

The archbishop gazed at him benevolently; his features, warmed by the wine to a fine mellow glow, arranged themselves in an expression of compassionate understanding. "It is for the good of all," the archbishop intoned in his best confessional voice. "Allow me to hear your thoughts and we will decide what to do."

"Let it be as you say," said Rognvald, as if relieved to have the thorny decision behind him. "Here is the nub: it occurred to me that there might be a way to ensure the harmony and, shall we say, the original integrity of the enterprise so cruelly curtailed by the Saracens."

"Yes? Go on," urged Bertrano, "I am listening."

"If you agree, I might fulfill that certain task which troubled his last days, and which death forced him to abandon." The archbishop shook his head in sorrow over the sad plight of the suffering Templar's trouble-filled last days. "In short," Rognvald continued, "I could serve in de Bracineaux's place."

Before the churchman could respond to this, Rognvald turned to Cait, stretched out his hand and took hers, saying, "I am sorry, my love. I know I should have discussed it with you, but the notion just occurred to me."

The cleric gazed at the knight thoughtfully, and then, with a clap of his hands, declared, "I am liking this. Continue."

"It seemed to me that a letter, even by swiftest courier, would take several months to reach the Templars—*if* it should reach Jerusalem at all. It could so easily go astray and fall into the wrong hands."

"Too true," agreed Archbishop Bertrano. "I feared as much with the first epistle. But if you were to act for me in this, it would hasten our undertaking to a favorable outcome."

"Am I to have nothing to say in this matter?" Cait said, adopting the manner of a neglected and much-put-upon wife. Turning to the churchman, she said, "You must forgive me, archbishop, if I find the prospect of losing my husband less than agreeable. He was three years in prison," she lowered her eyes modestly, "and I have only just got him back."

"I can but apologize, my love," answered Rognvald, "and beg your pardon." To the archbishop he said, "My wife is right. I pray you will excuse me, and release me from the duty I have so rashly proposed."

The trusting cleric, distressed to see the perfect solution to his dilemma receding as swiftly as it had presented itself, raised his hands in a fatherly gesture of mediation. "Peace, dear friends. Let us not make any hasty decisions we will soon regret. I am certain there is nothing to prevent us proceeding along a harmonious and, dare I say, mutually beneficial path."

To Cait he said, "My dear, I can well understand your reluctance in this regard. But once you learn the nature of the prize before us, you will understand. Moreover, you will embrace our purpose with a zeal you cannot now imagine."

Cait regarded the cleric doubtfully. "Since you put it that way," she allowed, none too certainly, "perhaps you had better tell me about this *prize*, whatever it might be."

"Oh, my lady, it is not to be spoken of lightly," said Bertrano, growing earnest. "For it is a wonder long concealed from the world, but pleasing God to reveal in our time to further the glorious conquest of his Blessed Son over the heathen infidel."

He raised his cup and gulped down more wine, as if fortifying himself for what he was about to divulge. Delicately wiping his mouth on his sleeve once more, he leaned forward in an attitude of clandestine solemnity. Cait and Rognvald drew nearer, too.

"The Rose of Mystic Virtue," he announced, savoring the words. Eyes shining with excitement, he looked from one to the other of his guests, and seeing the uncomprehending expressions, exclaimed, "Here! Does the name mean nothing to you?"

"Upon my word, it does not," Cait confessed, beguiling in her innocence. "What does it betoken?"

"The holiest, most worshipful object that ever was known," declared the archbishop. "It is nothing less than the very cup used by our Lord and Savior in the holy communion of the Last Supper."

Yes! Cait's heart quickened. *At last! Oh, and what a rare treasure indeed. Beyond price, to be sure. The treasure of the ages,* she thought, remembering the description on the parchment, *our very real and manifest hope for this present age and the kingdom to come.*

It was all she could do to keep from laughing out loud for the sheer joy of having discovered the secret. *Oh, yes!* she thought, *this is what I have been called to do. Like my father and grandfather before me, I am to seek a prize worth kingdoms!*

Adopting a more solemn tone, she said, "But how do you know? I mean no disrespect, my lord archbishop, but it has been lost a very long time, as you have said. Forgive my asking, but how does anyone know it is the selfsame cup?"

"It is a fair question," allowed Bertrano, "and one I did not hesitate to ask myself. But the good brother who brought this discovery to my attention is stalwart and trustworthy. I have known him for many years as a priest of unquestionable faith and character. Furthermore, he is most adamant about the provenance of the holy relic. In fact, it was his revelation that prompted my letter to the pope.

"You see, ever since the reconquest began, the Moors have been pushed slowly but steadily further and further south and east. Many of the Moors who used to live on the plains and in the valleys have fled to the hills and mountains to escape the king's relentless pursuit. Thus, unless its loss can be prevented, it is only a matter of time before the most sacred and holy relic ever known falls into the hands of the infidel."

"I understand," replied Rognvald thoughtfully. "Then the pope must have passed the letter on to Master de Bracineaux."

"Who else?" asked the archbishop. "No doubt the pope entrusted the task of recovering the holy relic to the Templars. It follows, since the commander would be charged with guarding this inestimable treasure once it has been returned to its proper position as the centerpiece of our faith. Indeed, that, to my mind, will be the most difficult part—protecting it from the Saracens, heathens, pagans, and Greeks who would undoubtedly try to steal it so as to mock our glorious salvation."

"Do you know where it is?" Cait asked, unable to keep the tremble of excitement out of her voice.

"No." Archbishop Bertrano shook his head. "And I do not wish to know. Owing to Brother Matthias' careful directions, however, it should be easy enough to find."

"The directions—were they in the letter?" said Cait, thinking of the obscure text she had not been able to read.

Again, the archbishop shook his head; he reached for the flagon and refilled his cup. "No," he said, between gulps of wine, "I did not think it wise to trust information of such importance to a mere letter." He lowered his cup, and smiled with sly satisfaction. "Instead, I told the pope where to find Brother Matthias; the good brother knows where the cup is to be found. And I wrote the directions in a secret language."

Cait was about to ask the nature of this secret language, but Rognvald spoke first. "Very wise," he agreed. "You seem to have thought of every-thing." He poured himself more wine, and filled Caitríona's cup as well. "But now, everything has changed. If we are to help protect the Mystic Rose, then we will need to know where to find Brother Matthias."

"In time, my impatient friend," replied the churchman. "All in good time. First, you must find fearless and trustworthy men to help you. From the little Matthias has related, I believe the Sacred Cup resides in Aragon far away—in the mountains somewhere, if I am not mis-taken—and there are a great many Saracens between here and there. You will need troops."

Rognvald slapped the table with the flat of his hand. "Ask and it shall be given," he declared jubilantly. "As it happens, I have men with me—countrymen who were imprisoned with me in Damascus. They are sworn liegemen, tried and true; I trust them with my life."

The archbishop raised his hands in benedictory praise. "Truly, you have been sent by God himself for this very purpose." Turning to Cait, he said, "My lady, you can no longer have any objection to your noble husband pursuing this enterprise. It is blessed and ordained by the Lord God himself, and Heaven stands ready to pour out grace and honor and glory upon any who undertake this service."

Rognvald regarded Cait with the look of a loving husband. "What say you, dear heart? Will you allow it?"

At the knight's use of the intimate term—the one her father had so often used in their talk together—her throat tightened and it was a moment before she could answer. "Yes," she replied at last, gazing at Rognvald with genuine admiration, "I will allow it. How could I, a mere woman, stand against Heaven's decree?"

SIXTEEN

Having taken their leave of Archbishop Bertrano, Cait and Rognvald stood up from the table and walked through the dark and quiet streets of Compostela alone. Save for occasional roisterers, whose loud singing echoed from the walls and galleries round about, they had the city to themselves; respectable townsfolk were asleep in their beds.

"Lying to an archbishop, now," Rognvald said, shaking his head in mock remorse, "that is a very low thing."

"De Bracineaux dead in prison," remarked Cait. "If I had my way he *would* be." She regarded the tall knight with a new appreciation. "Wherever did you think of that? I confess, when I heard you say it, I thought you had taken leave of your senses."

"I know we agreed that we should pretend the pope had commissioned us to look into the matter on his behalf, but that did not sit well with me. It raised more questions than it answered."

"You might have warned me," she said, her tone more irritable than she felt.

"In truth, I did not think of it until I said it."

"Well, it all came right in the end," she allowed. "What is more, it was a better tale by far. Indeed, you told it with such conviction, I began to believe it myself."

"Thank you, my lady," said Rognvald, pleased to have earned her guarded praise.

"God willing," she added, "we will be far away from here before anyone learns otherwise."

They walked the rest of the way in silence, listening to the roisterers and the crickets chirruping in the long grass beside the walls. Upon reaching the inn they found the doors barred and locked, but Rognvald's insistent rapping on the door eventually roused the disgruntled landlord who took his time letting them in. Caitríona, enraptured with their triumph and exhilarated by Bertrano's revelations, lay down on her bed and tried to compose her mind. It was no use. Her thoughts whirled with gleaming images of the wonderful treasure waiting for her, the Mystic Rose, Chalice of Christ—even the sound of the words on her lips made her feel quivery inside with an almost unbearable excitement. The most holy object in the world and she, herself alone, had been given the task of finding it, and protecting it.

Oh, but that was not all, far from it. For, once she had the sacred relic in her possession, she could use it to lure Renaud de Bracineaux to his richly deserved doom. Her thoughts teemed with ways to bring about his demise. Time and again she brought his fleshy, gray-bearded face before her mind's eye and imagined his astonished expression as the realization broke upon him that he had been bested by the daughter of the man he had so rashly, thoughtlessly, viciously murdered. Just how and where this fateful meeting would take place, she could not determine. But time and again she imagined the moment when cold, implacable justice would find its fulfillment.

Swiftly and without warning, the dagger clasped tight in her hand, she would strike. The narrow blade would enter his gut—just as his own knife had pierced her beloved father's side—and de Bracineaux's imposing bulk would crumple to the floor. As he lay dying, she would stand over him and watch the light of recognition come up in his eyes only to fade as his lifeblood spilled out in a slowly deepening crimson pool.

But perhaps this was not punishment enough. Perhaps she would force him to confess his crime and beg for his life. She could see him: stripped of his robes of office, humbled, on his knees, holding up his hands to her, beseeching, wailing, pleading for mercy—before she slit his throat like a hog at the slaughter.

She lay for a while, savoring the sweet, hot tang of revenge. *Lord*, she prayed, *the blood of a good man cries out to be avenged. You, whose judgment against the wicked is everlasting, make me the instrument of your vengeance.*

And then, as the gray dawn's light began seeping in under her door, she decided to wake Rognvald. They could be on the road by sunrise, and back in Iria and under sail by evening. With favorable weather, they could be in Bilbao in a few days, and from there it was an easy ride to Vitoria, where the archbishop had told them they would find Brother Matthias.

"What if the Templars reach this Brother Matthias first?" asked Rognvald once they were on the road again.

"I cannot see how that is possible," replied Caitríona smugly. "We have the letter, and we know where Matthias is to be found—de Bracineaux does not."

"No? I wonder," mused Rognvald. "He must have read the letter. If he read it, then he knows enough to find the monk to lead him to the treasure."

"Bertrano said the directions were in a secret language," protested Cait, her confidence beginning to erode.

"Secret to us, perhaps. But not to the pope and perhaps not to the Templars." Rognvald was silent for a time, then said, "I think we must assume the Templars are searching for the treasure as diligently as we ourselves. They may even find it before we do."

"They will *not* find it first," declared Cait.

"Can you be so certain?"

Thanks to Rognvald, a dark cloud of doubt dogged the return to Iria, and Cait begrudged every moment spent on the trail. By the time they arrived back at the ship, she was anxious to set sail immediately. But those who had remained behind had first to be collected from the town; the knights were easy to locate—a search of the waterfront inns brought them from their cups—but Abu and Alethea were more difficult to find. By the time she spotted them, Cait's anxiety had long since boiled over into desperation.

She heard a laugh that brought her up short. It was Alethea, no mistake, and Cait glanced quickly around to see her sister strolling across the town square with Abu Sharma at her side. They were talking, and Thea was laughing and swinging a cloth parcel. The mere sight of the two of them together, and Cait's anger flared to white heat. "What in Heaven's name are you doing?" she demanded, flying at the two young people.

Alethea, smiling, oblivious to her sister's rage, glanced at Abu and laughed again. "Oh, Cait, you have to hear this. Tell her, Abu. Tell her about the spitting monkey you saw in Damascus."

The young man, more mindful of the elder sister's mood, wisely declined. "Another time, perhaps," he said, the smile evaporating from his face.

"Oh, please, Abu," insisted Alethea blithely. "Tell her. You will like it, Cait. It will make you laugh."

She glared at her sister. "I do not want to hear it," she replied, her voice flat with menace.

"What's wrong with you—sit on a bee?" quipped Alethea.

Cait turned on Abu. "Leave us! Get back to the ship."

"At once, sharifah." He ducked his head in a hurried bow and swiftly removed himself from the vicinity.

Taking her sister's arm, Cait marched the complaining Alethea to a deserted corner of the near-empty square. "Must you always humiliate us?"

"Me!" gasped Alethea. "What did I do? Anyway, *you* are the one always causing trouble all the time."

"He is an *infidel!*" Cait hissed. "Can you understand that?"

"Who?" demanded the younger woman. "I have no idea what you're talking about."

"Abu!" spat Cait. "You cannot be seen going around with him like that. It is disgraceful. I forbid you to be seen with him."

"*You* forbid *me!*" Thea charged, her voice going shrill with indignation. "You are not my mother and father."

"No," snapped Cait. "Father is dead and your mother is a world away. Like it or not, you answer to me. I will not have you behaving like a lowborn slut."

"Abu is friendly," countered Thea weakly; she was beginning to wither under the lash of her sister's fury. "I like him. He is kind to me, and he makes me laugh."

"He is a Muhammedan!" Cait's voice was a stinging slap in her sister's face. "He is also a servant, and I will not have you consorting with him in public."

"Who else have I to talk to?" Thea moaned, tears starting to her eyes. "You are always rushing about, and the knights only care about drinking and fighting."

"They do not," said Cait, "and anyway what they do is none of your concern." She took Alethea's arm and squeezed hard. "Now you listen to me. You are a lady of a noble family, and you are to keep yourself

145

chaste and above reproach. Abu is impertinent and brazen enough as it is without you encouraging him."

"He is *not* a Muhammedan," Alethea insisted, her lip beginning to tremble as the tears started. "He is a Druze—which is a kind of Christian. He told me."

"He could be the Patriarch of Constantinople for all I care," Cait snarled. "He is still a servant, and you are not to have anything more to do with him." She glared hard at the sniffing, unhappy Alethea. "Do you understand?"

Her sister nodded and pushed the tears away with the heels of her hands.

"Very well," said Cait, softening at last. "You have made a poor beginning, but that is no reason you cannot amend your manner and conduct. See that you do."

They walked back to the waterfront and boarded the ship. Owing to the delay, it was well after midday when *Persephone* slid from her mooring and out into the river. With Ginés' help, however, they reached the headlands as the sun began its downward plunge to the sea. Rather than look for a place to berth for the night, Cait ordered Haemur to sail on, and they reached deep water as the sun dipped below the horizon.

"We dare not go further, my lady," Haemur said. "It will be dark soon."

"Ginés says there will be a full moon tonight," Cait countered.

"That is as may be," allowed the pilot. "But the waters hereabouts are dangerous. We should drop anchor in the next cove and start as soon as it is light."

Cait hesitated. The wind was fair and the weather mild, with a good moon they could be well up the coast by morning.

"Haemur is right," said Rognvald, who had been listening to the exchange. "Full moon or no, it would be foolhardy to try the rocks at night. Pay the fisherman to stay on, and he can show us the fastest way to Bilbao."

Much to Haemur's relief, Cait relented and gave orders to drop anchor for the night. With a promise of double payment, she induced Ginés to stay aboard and lead them to Bilbao, and at first light next morning he and Haemur began the long and tedious process of picking their way among the great rocks and tiny islands strung out along the Galician coast like so many shards of broken crockery.

Two days later, they rounded the protruding northwestern hump of the Iberian Peninsula and entered the great, sweeping expanse of the Bay of Vizcaya. Each day they watched the tiny fishing villages of the coast passing one by one in slow and stately procession, glistening white against the earthy greens and browns of the Cantabrian mountains rising behind them like a dull swath of wrinkled cloth.

The sea remained calm, allowing Haemur to sail by night. Once Cait awoke at midnight and, wanting some air, went up on deck to find Lord Rognvald at the helm taking a turn to rest the old pilot, who was asleep on a nearby bench. She watched the tall knight for a moment, before going back to her bed without a word.

Seven days after leaving Iria, they came in sight of the port. "There it is," Ginés informed them. "That is Bilbao."

Cait and Alethea looked where the old seaman was pointing; beyond the clusters of crude fishing huts scattered along the coast, they saw a dark smudge of smoke hanging above the low hills divided by the deep-channeled river.

"Not much of a city," concluded Alethea, dismissing it with a disdainful sniff.

"Perhaps not," allowed the Galician, "but it is the gate through which you must pass."

A short time later, they sailed into the cup-shaped bay of the Nervión river estuary and proceeded to work their way along the wide, slow-flowing channel to Bilbao. As at Iria, they hired horses for the ride to Vitoria. This time, Cait paid for enough mounts for all to go, save the four sailors who stayed behind to watch the ship. It cost a great deal for so many horses, but Alethea obviously needed watching, and she did not like the idea of leaving the knights behind to waste their days in the alehouses of Bilbao. And Abu's usefulness as a translator, along with whatever rudimentary skills as a physician he possessed, argued for his inclusion.

"I do not know how long we shall be away," Cait told Haemur. "God willing, it will only be a few days or so. But it may be longer."

"Take all the time you need," the old pilot told her. "It matters not a whit to me. As I told your father, my lady, never fear: though the Lord return and sound the heavenly trumpet to call the faithful home to paradise, you will find old Haemur here and waiting still."

"Thank you, Haemur," Cait replied. "Even so, should we be gone longer than I expect, I am leaving enough money to keep the ship in harborage and for any provisions you will need. And," she added, "you know where Duncan's sea chest is kept if ill befalls and you need more."

"Worry not," the old seaman replied. "In a lively harbor such as this, there are always nets to be mended and hulls to caulk. If our hands keep busy, we should not want for anything. There is just one small matter, however . . ."

"Yes?"

"Ginés was hoping to stay on with us awhile, if you have no objection."

"I have no objection whatsoever. He has given us good service, and I am grateful." She nodded to the Galician fisherman, who was standing quietly aside, looking on. "If he wishes to stay, so be it."

"Thank you, my lady," said the pilot with some relief. "In a place like this it helps to have a friend who can speak the tongue of his countrymen, if you know what I mean."

"I understand. He can also help you keep the young men out of trouble."

"That he can, my lady."

Caitríona bade him farewell, and then took her leave of Olvir and Otti—the latter of whom was not at all happy to be left cooling his heels in port while the others rode away. "Otti," Cait said, "who will guard the ship, if not you?"

He tried to think of some way to dispute this fact, but could not rise to the challenge. "But *you* will need me, too," he insisted.

"I do need you, it is true," she said gently. "I need you here, Otti." She rested her hand lightly on his arm in confidence. "The others are not as strong as you, and if any trouble should arise, you must protect them and guard the ship."

Feeling that he was failing to persuade her, he lowered his head in sullen defeat.

"Listen to me, Otti," she said, "I am counting on you to look after the others." When she saw that he understood, she added, "Now then, I have left Haemur a little money for ale for you and Olvir. If you do well, he will give it to you."

At the realization that she had made provision for him and Olvir, that they were not to be forgotten in her absence, Otti's face lit with simple pleasure. He accepted this compromise happily and Cait joined the others at the end of the wharf to begin the ride to Vitoria—accompanied by the hostler who, for a small additional fee, had agreed to be their guide.

So, as she climbed into the saddle, Cait took a quick mental inventory of her company. First came the hostler, a short, stocky man named Miguel, a pleasant fellow with a ready, if somewhat toothless, smile—he had been kicked by a horse and was missing both upper and lower front teeth; he rode a hinny and led a pack mule bearing equipment and supplies for the camp. Following the hostler were Yngvar and Svein who had tied long strips of blue cloth to the heads of the lances they carried; the improvised pennons fluttered in the light breeze. Alethea, hair gathered beneath a low-crowned green hat with a veil to keep the sun from her face, had managed to make her place beside Dag, who, Cait noticed, had lately begun to reciprocate her sister's undisguised interest. Next came Rognvald, tall and upright in the saddle, a wide-brimmed leather hat high on his head, the sleeves of his shirt rolled to his elbows. The knights all had shields slung upon their backs, and swords at their sides; Cait, dressed in a simple red shift and mantle, her dark hair swept back and held in place by small silver combs beneath her hat, carried the sword Rognvald had given her, its gleaming slender length sheathed for protection of blade and rider. Both Svein and Dag led pack animals carrying the rest of the armor and weapons; and Abu, his face all but hidden beneath a large straw hat, brought up the rear, leading two more mules laden with provisions, provender, and drinking water for the journey.

Freshly shaved and dressed in the clothes she had bought for them in Cyprus, their weapons gleaming in the strong sunlight, Cait thought her knights a fine and handsome sight. As she took her place beside Rognvald, she was filled with a sudden and unanticipated joy, and a sense of righteous certainty, almost inevitability—that her feet were established on a path which had been prepared for her long ago. She was where she was meant to be, and doing what she had been born to do. Tightening the scarf holding her pale yellow, wide-brimmed hat, she raised a hand to show that she was ready. The hostler cracked his whip, and the company set off.

SEVENTEEN

The road was good and the sun hot; the company traveled quickly, passing through numerous settlements of the deep river valley. At several of these, the sky darkened and they smelled the sharp stench of sulphurous smoke; black ash rained out of the air, and they saw heaps of spent slag darkening the hillsides. The river turned an ugly rusty color and barges loaded with pigs of rough iron floated slowly toward the harbor.

They soon left the last of the iron-working settlements behind, and the sky became clear and the air clean once more. Despite their long absence from the saddle, the knights rode easily and lightly, talking and joking as they went along, and making the hills echo with the sound of their banter. Cait liked hearing them; it confirmed in her the feeling that she had done well to save them and give them back their lives.

That first day, they rode as long into the evening as they could and then made a simple camp: grass sleeping-mats arranged around a stone-ringed fire with the star-flecked sky for a roof over their heads. They were on the move again as soon as light permitted the next morning, and the second day passed like the first; the only difference they noticed was that the settlements were smaller and further apart. On the third day, the hostler pointed out a tiny projection rising like a dark sliver from a distant hill. "That is the bell tower of the church of Vitoria," he told them.

The rest of the day they watched the tower slowly grow as they came nearer. They also began to smell a foul odor as they approached, for the town was supplied with no fewer than three tanneries which used water from the streams to wash the hides, and dumped the scraped offal and waste in the water to be carried away downstream. The heat of the sun raised a stink that could be smelled for a great distance around, which the party did its best to ignore.

It was only when they reached the town square that they gained some respite from the smell. The tower stood on one side of the square; attached to it was a church, which was connected to a monastery where, according to Archbishop Bertrano, they would find Brother Matthias. Cait slid down from the saddle, and dropped the reins on the dusty ground. "Rognvald, come with me. The rest of you wait here," she said, and went straight to the monastery gate and presented herself to the porter. He listened politely, and then conducted her and Rognvald to the friar.

"Brother Matthias is not here," said the clean-shaven friar who met them outside the chapel. "He *was* here—earlier this spring, for a time—but he is gone now."

"Gone?" wondered Cait, as if trying to think what the word could mean. Frustration sharp as despair arrowed through her.

"Gone," the friar confirmed. "I am sorry. Good day to you."

Caitríona stared at the insipid smiling cleric and thought of all the time and effort—not to mention expense!—she had employed just to get this far . . . only to be told by some fool of a priest that her pains had been for nothing.

It took a moment before she could trust her voice to speak. "I would thank you to tell me where we might find him," she said, masking her acute disappointment with a smile. "We have journeyed a very long way to see him."

"It makes no matter how far you have traveled," replied the friar carelessly, "he is not here and that is that. Now, if there is nothing else, I have duties elsewhere—" He made to leave, but Rognvald reached out a hand and took hold of his brown robe, bunching it in his fist and holding the monk firmly in his place.

"Perhaps," the knight suggested, "your duties are not so pressing that you could reconsider the lady's question with the courtesy it deserves."

The friar spluttered indignantly; he gaped at the knight, saw that he was in earnest, and blurted, "Oh, very well. He is at Palencia if you must know."

"This Palencia," said Rognvald, releasing the priest, "is it far?"

The friar smoothed his robes and glared at his assailant. "It is nei- ther near nor far."

"Neither near nor far," repeated Cait, her brow lowering. "Is that what passes for an answer in this festering stinkpot of a town? Or are you more of an idiot than you appear?"

"It is a middle distance, I would say," sniffed the friar. "Satisfied?" Rognvald raised his hand, and the friar quickly added, "I have never been there. Ask in the town—one of the merchants will tell you."

"One would think information more valuable than gold the way you hoard it," Cait replied, her anger beginning to simmer. "Tell me, miserly friar, when was the last time you gave a generous answer to a friendly question?" As the friar huffed and puffed, she added, "It is as I thought—you cannot even remember!"

Cait turned abruptly and started away. Rognvald fell into step be- side her. They had walked but four paces when the priest called after them, "You are not thinking of going to Palencia."

"We are," Cait replied. She halted and turned around, regarding the cleric suspiciously. "Why?"

"It is not allowed," the friar informed them, allowing himself a gri- mace of satisfaction. "The king has forbidden anyone to travel there."

"And why, I pray you, is that?" demanded Cait, moving closer. Be- fore the friar could reply, she held up her hand. "No! Do not tell me, for I am keen to guess. Let me see . . . I know: the road has been scrubbed and put away for safekeeping." She took another step closer. "No? Then how about this: the king is annoyed with Palencia and wishes to punish it by denying it any visitors." She took another step closer. "No? What then? Is the sky the wrong color? Or perhaps the moon makes all the citizens mad?" She was now face to face with the priest once more. "Well, which is it?"

Realizing he was once more on precarious ground, the friar quickly explained that, alas, King Alfonso VII had died last year, and his son, Alfonso VIII, was king now. "Until the king can re-establish order," the monk told them, "all roads to the south and east remain under control of the Muhammedans and bandits who prey on pilgrims and mer- chants."

"I travel with my own army," Cait replied, a fearsome frown bend- ing the corners of her mouth. "The bandits will not trouble us."

"Then I wish you Godspeed," the monk replied blandly, some of his former insolence returning. "Only, you must first obtain a writ of passage from the king."

"I cannot tell if you are more fool than knave," replied Cait darkly, "or whether it is the other way around. But if you value your ears, explain."

"The writ can be had for the payment of a small tax—that is all I know."

"Very well," said Rognvald, "we will go and see the king, and obtain this writ."

"I do not think it will do any good," the friar offered. "The king sees no one but his mother and her attendants."

"Why?" Cait asked, her frown deepening dangerously. "Is he ill?"

"Ill? By no means, my lady." The priest shrank from her threatening glare. "God keep him, he is in the best of health. But he is only three years old."

"Agh!" shrieked Cait. "This is absurd! We are going to Palencia—with or without your mewling infant monarch's blessing." She turned on her heel and stormed away. "Stupid man."

Rognvald caught up with her a few paces down the street. "I will go and speak to the magistrate and see what he advises," he offered. "If you like, you could wait with the others in the square."

"Go then," Cait agreed, and Rognvald hurried off in the direction of the town's civic hall—a blocky fortress surrounded by a high wall of red stone, and a shallow dry moat. Cait walked slowly back to the square, which was now all but deserted; most of the townspeople had gone to their homes to escape the heat of the day, leaving only a few stragglers and gossips behind. The latter were standing in the center of the square, holding forth with several idle tradesmen.

She found the rest of her party readily enough. A tall market cross stood in the center of the square above the great round stone basin of a fountain. The knights, Abu, and Alethea were sitting around the base of the cross beside the fountain watching the hostler water his horses and pack mules in the basin. Cait joined them and sat down in the shade at the base of the cross to wait. It was passing midday; most of the market stalls had closed already, and in the rest, the merchants were dozing on their stools. An air of drowsy contentment hung like a gauzy curtain over the square; Cait leaned back against the cool stone, and took a deep, calming breath. She closed her eyes and listened to the droning of the knights' voices as they talked.

"You are sadly wrong, Svein," Yngvar was saying. "The Romans were never in this place. It was the Goths."

"Victoriacum," replied Svein knowingly. "Does that sound like a Goth name to you?"

"Maybe the Goths spoke Latin," countered Yngvar. "Did you ever think of that?"

"Maybe you are not as clever as you think," replied Svein. "Did *you* ever think of that? Here now, Dag, what say you? Is it Roman, this place, or Goth?"

"Who cares?" answered Dag. "They are not here now—I am."

"Oh, yes," said Yngvar, "that is something. One day people will find this place and say, 'Dag the Conqueror was here.' I tell you it was Goths."

Eyes closed in the cooling shade, Cait felt her steaming frustration slowly give way to the soothing air of the place. The ransomed knights were, she reflected, much stronger now, and becoming more themselves with every passing day. If nothing else, the long sea journey had been restorative, allowing them to recover their strength as the good food and air and water healed their hurting spirits. Whatever awaited them on the road ahead, they would, she felt, be ready to meet it.

Abu, however, was rapidly becoming an unwanted problem. Since the confrontation in Iria, he had grown increasingly truculent. Allowing him to join them had been a mistake; there was no denying it. With every mile further from the Holy Land, his usefulness dwindled that much more; and unless she could think of something for him to do, he would soon be far more trouble than he was worth. She was just thinking it might be best to send him back to Bilbao with the hostler, when she heard Rognvald hail them from across the square.

Cait opened her eyes and saw the tall knight striding toward them. He paused to lave water over his head and face before turning to her. "I have no good news, my lady," he said, his face and hair dripping. "I was able to speak to the magistrate, who confirmed that a writ must be obtained. However, he refused to help us. He said that he could not allow us to travel until the bandits had been eradicated and the roads secured once more.

"It seems the Archbishop of Castile has requested the formation of a holy order of knights to guard the roads—the Knights of Calatrava,

154

he called them. They have sent an embassy to Rome to secure the church's authorization—"

"But that could take months," Yngvar pointed out.

"If not years," said Svein.

"Too true," agreed Rognvald. "But until the new order receives the blessing of the pope, the magistrate insists no one is to be allowed to use the roads."

"If we cannot secure the king's permission, we will simply go without it."

"Even that may not be so easy," Rognvald went on to explain, "for, without the writ, none of the tradesmen in this place will sell to us. They risk confiscation of their goods and, perhaps, imprisonment into the bargain."

Cait, unable to fathom the idiocy of the Spanish authorities, was not of a mood to comply. "Good!" She stood, making up her mind at once. "I want nothing more to do with this flyblown dirt clod of a town anyway." The others sat looking on. "To your horses," she told them, "we go on to Palencia."

EIGHTEEN

Despite the extravagant protestations of the hostler, who received the rumor of bandits with, Cait thought, exaggerated emotion, he nevertheless seemed happy enough to permit the company to purchase his animals. "Seven horses and five pack mules," he said, tapping the side of his nose thoughtfully. "I could let you have them for . . ." His eyes narrowed as he calculated the figure. "Five gold marks each for the horses, and one for each mule—forty gold marks in all!" he proclaimed triumphantly.

"A moment," said Cait, and summoned Abu, who seemed to know the trade value of everything. "He says forty gold marks—what do you think?"

"Not a bad price," granted Abu, "but not a good one."

"The horses are in good condition," Rognvald said, stepping near, "but one is blind in one eye, and two of them will need shoeing soon. I cannot say about the mules."

"They are fair," said Abu, "for mules. Offer him thirty."

"Do you have that much left?" asked Rognvald.

She nodded and turned back to the hostler. "Master Miguel," said Cait reasonably, "you have us at your mercy. We need the animals in order to continue, and there is no one else who can sell to us." She removed the coin bag from beneath her girdle and untied it. "Therefore, I will give you thirty gold coins."

"My lady," replied Miguel with his toothless grin and shaking his head, "if it was my decision alone, I would do it. But I have a wife and children to feed, and without my animals I cannot earn my crust. Forty gold marks, please."

"Since you put it that way, I will give you what you ask," she said, but before he could reply, she raised an admonitory finger. "But I make one condition."

"Yes?" The eagerness faded from the hostler's face.

"As you know, we will be returning to Bilbao where the ship is waiting. Therefore, once our business is completed and we have no further use for the horses, we will sell them back to you for, say . . ." she glanced at Abu who showed three fingers, "thirty gold marks. Agreed?"

"Twenty-five gold marks," countered Miguel.

"Done." Cait counted the gold coins into the hostler's hands, and bade him farewell. By way of thanks, Master Miguel accompanied them a fair distance from the town to see them well on their way to Palencia before turning back to make his way home.

The ride through the long, lush Nervión valley proved peaceful and wholly agreeable. Never did they see any sign of the fearful bandits; the countryside appeared quiet and serene as the last of the fierce summer's heat dissipated, leaving behind a beautiful, mellow autumn which settled over the countryside like a warm, comfortable cloak. Apart from a few sudden showers which sent the party galloping for the shelter of overhanging chestnut boughs, the days remained bright and clear. Occasionally, they awoke to a crisp nip to the morning air which Cait found both refreshing and exhilarating, but for the most part the days remained warm from early morning to well after dark.

Every now and then, Cait would look up from her solitary meditations to discover a silent partner beside her: sometimes Abu, or one of the knights, but more often Lord Rognvald. He seemed content merely to ride with her, never speaking until she invited his conversation, which she usually did, and in this way Cait began to discover the depths of the man she had redeemed from a slow death in a Muhammedan prison.

"What is it like where you were born?" she asked him one day. The morning air was cool, and the sun warm on her face; the leaves on the birch and ash trees were just beginning to turn and she felt like talking.

Rognvald cocked his head to one side and looked at her with a quizzical expression. "My home?" he said after a moment. "Or the place where I was born?"

"Most people are born at home," she said. "Were you not?"

"My home is in Haukeland, near Bjørgvin in the south, but I was born at Kaupangr, where Olav the Holy is buried. It is a most sacred place and a great many people make pilgrimages there. My mother was a very devout lady."

"Your mother was on pilgrimage at the time of your birth," Cait assumed, curiously delighted by the notion.

"In truth . . ." replied Rognvald, shaking his head, "no." He smiled, and Cait caught the cheerful gleam of his eyes, blue as the cloud-scoured Spanish skies above, as he said, "You see, the king also had hunting lodges there, and he would invite noblemen to come hunting with him. It came about that my father was summoned to attend one of the king's great winter hunts.

"Well, one of the old vassals—a wise woman with uncanny powers—had foretold bad luck for a winter birth, and that doubled for a child without a father. My mother took this to heart, so naturally my father was loath to leave her alone."

"Naturally," echoed Cait, staunch in her conviction that childbirth ought to take precedence over trivialities like hunting.

"Yet even so, the hunt was to take place during the Yuletide celebrations, and fortunate indeed were those allowed to observe the Christ Mass with the king—a rare and singular honor, and one not to be spurned, for otherwise it would certainly never come again. So, my father did what anyone in his position would do."

"Heaven forbid it!" said Cait.

"He took their bed from the house and lashed it to the deck of his ship and covered it with a tent. Then he wrapped my mother warm in his huge bearskin cloak, tucked her safely in bed, and sailed off to Kaupangr to visit the king."

Cait laughed out loud, her voice falling rich and warm on the leaf-covered trail. Rognvald thrilled to hear it, and several of the others riding along behind raised their heads and smiled. "So, you were born at the king's hunting lodge," she guessed.

Again, the knight shook his head. "My mother would not endure the noise—all the shouting and singing, you know. When men hunt they get thirsty, and King Magnus was never one to stint on anything. His öl was sweet and dark and good, and served in foaming vats that never were allowed to run dry. The noblemen and warriors feasted and reveled every night with the same zeal as they pursued the harts and hinds by day. This made the lodge a very clamorous place."

"King Magnus, you say."

"King Magnus was a cousin of my father," he said. "In the same way, King Eystein is now my cousin."

"Is now?" wondered Cait. "Was he not always your cousin?"

"No," explained Rognvald, "he was not always the king."

Cait laughed again, and they rode on, happy in one another's company. The knight related how his mother, having refused the king's boisterous hospitality, was lodged instead at the nearby convent. "And that was where I was born," he told her, "two days after the Christ Mass. I am told the queen herself attended my birth and presented me to my mother. So, perhaps my birth was not so unlucky after all."

"Indeed, not," murmured Cait. She grew silent, thinking about the strangeness of life and its many unexpected turns.

After a time, Rognvald turned in the saddle and asked, "Something I have said has made you thoughtful, I see."

"I was just thinking that if not for King Magnus, you and I would not be riding together at this very moment."

"Then he is a far greater king than I imagined. I must remember to lay a gift at his shrine and thank him for his fortuitous assistance." He looked sideways at her and asked, "But how do you reckon we owe our meeting to Magnus?"

"It was Magnus who befriended my grandfather," she told him, and went on to recount how it was that Murdo had come to follow his father and brothers on the Great Pilgrimage, traveling on a ship in the hire of the king. "We lost our lands in Orkney," she told him, "but the king was just. He gave us Caithness instead."

"That was very good of him," replied Rognvald approvingly. "He must have liked your grandfather very much."

"Well," Cait allowed, "it was mostly the king's fault we lost the land in the first place. It was the least he could do."

"No," laughed Rognvald suddenly, "it was never that. You must not know many kings." He regarded her, trim and comely in the saddle; her cloak falling low on her shoulders—for all it was a warm day—and her dark hair neat beneath her silver combs. "Do you like Caithness? Or would you rather have Orkney?"

"My grandfather might feel differently, I cannot say. But Caithness is home to me; I have never known any other."

"My family owns an estate on one of the Orkneyjar islands," the knight confided. "They tell me I visited there once with my family, but I cannot even remember which island it was."

They talked amiably, passing the time as they rode along, each enjoying the easy companionship of the other—until Alethea grew bored riding by herself and decided to join them, whereupon the pleasant mutual feeling gradually shriveled under Alethea's irritating whining about the heat, the dullness of the countryside, the sun in her eyes, how thirsty she was, how rough the saddle, and how disagreeable her mount.

"I cannot see why we have to ride anyway," she complained. "You should have bought a carriage instead, and then we could travel like queens."

"If only everything was that easy."

Three days after entering the Valle de Mena, they came to the walled trading town of Burgos, paused briefly to replenish their provisions, and then set off again before anyone made bold to stop them. Four days after that, they arrived at Palencia.

The town had faded somewhat from its glory under the Roman legion of Lucus Augusti. The crumbling garrison still stood; having served several generations of Muhammedan rulers as a stable and armory, it was now a monastery in sore need of a new roof. The old Roman walls remained in good repair, however, and protected the town and its inhabitants from the Moorish raiders infesting the hills, preying on the foolish and unwary.

Owing to the king's ban on travel, the local farmers and merchants were effectively cut off from their trading partners to the west. Consequently, they seized on the newcomers' arrival with an interest that far exceeded the significance of their visit. As Cait and her entourage dismounted in the town square, one of the onlookers ran to inform the magistrate that important visitors had arrived. The magistrate and his young assistant came on the run to offer an official welcome.

The town's governor was a smooth-shaven man with a frizzled fringe of dark hair which he tried to keep under a red cap shaped like a deeply notched bowl. Pushing the eager townsfolk aside, he cleared a place for himself in the crowd and then addressed the visitors. "Most noble lady," he began, bestowing on Cait the sort of bow usually reserved for royalty, "friends, travelers, allow me to introduce myself. I am Carlo de la Coruña, magistrate and governor of this fine and prosperous town." His deputy smiled and bowed, too, in anticipation of being introduced to the handsome noblewomen and their broad-shouldered, fearsome entourage, but his superior plowed ahead without so much as a wink in his direction.

"On behalf of the worthy citizens of Palencia," the magistrate announced, "I welcome you and your excellent company. Furthermore, I invite you all to be our special guests at a feast to be held in your honor tonight. Please, rest and take your ease while you are here. Be assured we will do all we can to assist you in every possible way for as long as you care to remain with us."

Cait thanked him kindly, and said that she and her traveling companions would be delighted to attend the feast, and asked whether there might be a convenient moment for herself and the magistrate to discuss matters privately. "As it happens, a few small concerns have arisen. I would be grateful for your counsel, Magistrate Coruña. I am certain they will pose no difficulty for a man of your obvious wisdom and authority."

The magistrate's cheeks took on a rosy glow under Cait's well-aimed flattery. He ducked his head in hasty assent, and said, "With pleasure, my lady. If you would deign to join me in the courtyard of my house during *sixta*, we might discuss your concerns over a cooling drink."

Cait smiled, but hesitated. Spending the rest of the day with the obliging bumpkin of a magistrate might have its uses, but foremost among her concerns was locating the priest called Brother Matthias. Lord Rognvald saw her hesitation, however, and, leaning close, confided, "Go and see if you can charm him into getting us a wagon and some tents."

"The priest—"

"I will find him."

Cait smiled at the eager official. "My sister and I would be honored, magistrate."

"Your men, however, may wish to observe the—ah . . . usual formalities at our most excellent inn," suggested the magistrate delicately.

"I am certain they would like nothing better." Turning to Rognvald, she instructed him to take his men to the inn and see that the formalities were, in fact, observed. "Take Abu with you, and make certain everyone is washed and prepared for this evening's festivities." As the knight inclined his head in assent, Cait added in a whisper: "Find Matthias. Tell him we wish to speak to him tomorrow. I will see what I can do about the wagon and tents."

Turning to the magistrate, Cait smoothly linked his arm in hers and allowed him to escort her across the square—much to the satisfaction of the townspeople, pleased to see their governor esteemed by such distinguished and obviously important visitors. Upon reaching the archway which marked the entrance to the square, Carlo turned to his assistant. "Grieco! What are you doing?"

The young man looked blankly at his superior. "We are having drinks, Uncle Carlo, are we not?"

"No, no, no! Not you! You must run to Master Pedrino at the bakery and tell him we will need twenty chickens roasted for tonight's feast."

"Yes, uncle," replied the youth, visibly disheartened. "Twenty chickens—is that all?"

"For heaven's sake! Must I do everything myself? It is to be a feast, Grieco. Tell him we want three sheep as well." He paused, considering the quantity of meat to be provided. "Yes, and a pig—a big one, not a skinny runt like last time. Oh yes, and five dozen loaves. No, six dozen, tell him."

"Yes, uncle."

"Why are you waiting? Go! Hurry! There is everything to get ready." The young man made to dash away. "Wait!" cried his uncle. "Go to Tomas at the inn and tell him we want wine for sixty guests. He is to bring it to the banqueting hall. And olives, too. Everything!" He fluttered his hands at the havering youth. "Be off with you now! Hurry!"

The gangly Grieco flapped away down a side street, leaving Cait and Alethea and Carlo to proceed at a more leisurely pace to the magistrate's house where they were received with all cordiality by Carlo's sister, Manuela, who acted as housekeeper, cook, and companion to the busy official. The ladies were conducted directly to places on a low bench under the leafy boughs of a lime tree in the corner of a terracotta tiled courtyard. While Manuela saw to the refreshments, Carlo, drawing up a greenwood chair, settled himself in the pleasant company of his captivating guests.

"Now then," he said expansively, "about these tiresome concerns—please, tell me everything that troubles you." Cait smiled and opened her mouth to reply, but her host held up his hand, and said, "Remember, it is the Magistrate of Palencia you are speaking to—by authority of the Castilian Crown. Therefore, tell me everything, and we will see what can be done."

He waved his hand imperiously, settled back in his chair, and closed his eyes. "Please to begin."

NINETEEN

"My dear archbishop," said Commander de Bracineaux smoothly, "I am very pleased to meet you at last."

"And I am astonished to meet you at all," answered Bertrano, eyeing the Templar narrowly. "You are supposed to be dead."

De Bracineaux laughed. "Then I think you will find me a most corporeal ghost." As if to demonstrate his material presence, he reached out and took the churchman by the arm and squeezed it. "I assure you, my lord cleric, I have a good deal of life left in me yet."

Archbishop Bertrano, seated in his throne-like chair outside his hut, regarded the hand on his arm; his flesh seemed to squirm under de Bracineaux's hand—as if he had been touched by something from beyond the grave. "Indeed, sir," replied the archbishop, pulling his arm away. "But how am I to know you are who you claim to be?"

"Ah, yes, of course," sighed de Bracineaux as if the question had plagued him down the years. "What proof will you accept?"

"It is not up to me," grumbled the archbishop.

"Perhaps you would not mind telling me how you came by word of my demise," suggested the Templar commander.

"But I *do* mind, sir," snapped Bertrano. "I do not see that I owe you any explanations. It is for you to prove yourself, or get you hence."

"A moment longer, if you please," said de Bracineaux. "I do not know how this confusion has come about, but I can guess: there was a woman—not pretty, but young still, with dark hair. She had a letter—*your* letter—the one you wrote to the pope asking for help to save a treasure called the Mystic Rose. This woman told you I was dead." Regarding the churchman closely, he said, "I believe I am close to the mark."

164

Archbishop Bertrano fingered the wooden cross at his belt, but said nothing.

Turning to d'Anjou, the commander said, "You see, baron? It is as we feared—the thief has already been here before us. We are too late. The damage is done."

"Be of good cheer, my lord," answered d'Anjou with practiced, if slightly oily, sympathy. "All is not lost." He turned sad, imploring eyes to the archbishop. "With God's help we may yet be able to recover the holy relic."

"You are right to remind me," replied de Bracineaux glumly. "We wait upon God's good pleasure—and upon this prince of the church." Turning once again to the archbishop, he said, "It rests with you, noble cleric. We are in your hands."

Bertrano frowned and pulled on his beard. He gazed long at the two men before him and made up his mind. "Then I will not keep you waiting, my lords. I tell you now I want nothing more to do with you."

"I protest—" began Baron d'Anjou.

The archbishop cut him off. "Hear me out. You come galloping into my city with your horses and men, covered with dust and stinking of the trail. You come making demands and shouting orders at everyone, raising an unholy turmoil in the streets. You command audience and bully my monks until I abandon my work to see you." He glared at his two unwelcome visitors.

"Well, I have seen you," concluded the archbishop brusquely. "And I do not mind telling you that I do not like what I have seen." He rose from his chair and stepped from the table. "Now, sirs, I will thank you to excuse me. I have a church to build."

D'Anjou made to object once more, but de Bracineaux waved him off. "I see we have provoked you, my lord archbishop," he said. "Pray forgive us. If we have acted in haste and without sufficient forethought, it was because we have been long on the trail with but a single thought burning in our hearts—to recover the holy relic for the good of the church."

The archbishop's scowl turned to anger. "So say you," he answered. "But I do not know you. The Renaud de Bracineaux I knew perished in a Saracen prison!" He stepped toward the door of his hut. "I bid you good day, gentlemen, and Godspeed." With that he stepped through the door, slammed it behind him, and was gone.

"How extraordinary," remarked d'Anjou quietly. "I do believe the man is insane."

"Perhaps," agreed de Bracineaux. "But there is more to this matter than we know. We must consider carefully what has happened before we decide how to act." He rose stiffly from his chair and rubbed his hand over his face. "I am tired, d'Anjou, and in dire need of a drink."

"Come, de Bracineaux," replied the baron rising at once. "I sent Gislebert to secure rooms for us at the inn across the square. Follow me, and we shall have wine and meat before you know it."

The inn was as much stable as hostel, with rancid straw on the floor and a grubby, ill-kept fire on the hearth. It was crowded with rough-handed laborers from the nearby cathedral who sat in dull exhaustion with pots of warm ale between their thick paws, drinking quietly to ease the throbbing in their joints. Several knights from the town had heard about the Templars' arrival and had come to see for themselves what manner of men they were. They were talking loudly and drinking wine as they took the measure of the much-vaunted Grand Commander of Jerusalem.

"This is a noisy place," grumbled de Bracineaux into his cup, swallowing down the wine in gulps. "And it stinks. Trust Gislebert to find the worst."

"I have seen better, certainly." D'Anjou gazed around the room with mild disgust. "We could try somewhere else," he suggested. "Or would you rather stay at the monastery with the men?"

"Good Lord, no. I have had a bellyful of simpering, damp-eyed monkery." He drank again and set the cup down heavily. "We will stay here the night and if all goes well tomorrow we will not be forced to endure another night in this pesthole of a town."

Baron d'Anjou refilled the cups. "Have some more, de Bracineaux, and tell me how you plan to persuade this disagreeable priest of your sincerity."

The commander pushed aside the cup. "No more of this vile stuff. See if the innkeeper has anything better."

D'Anjou rose and made his way to the board behind which the innkeeper and his haggard wife dispensed food and drink to their guests. He returned to the table with a small brown jar and two small wooden cups. He pulled the stopper and poured out a pale golden liquid, then passed one of the cups to the commander, who sampled it, then tipped his head back and swallowed the sweet, fiery liquor down in a gulp.

"That is more to my liking," de Bracineaux said. "What is it?"

"He called it dragon's milk—if I understood him correctly. The rude fellow's Latin is atrocious." D'Anjou took a delicate sip. "Not bad, whatever it is." He refilled his companion's cup. "It seems our friend the archbishop believes you to be someone else."

"What else should he believe? The man thinks me dead."

"You think it was the woman?"

"Of course, who else? She spun a tale for him and he believed her, the old fool. And you are a fool, too, baron; I should never have listened to you." The commander tossed down another bolt of the liquor. "Now we must find a way to convince him of his folly."

"I wonder what else she told him—and, perhaps more to the point, what he has told her?"

De Bracineaux shrugged. "Once we gain the archbishop's confidence, all our questions will be answered." Placing his hands flat on the table, the commander shoved back his stool and rose. "I am going to bed."

He turned to make his way toward the door at the back of the room leading to the three sleeping rooms—one a common room with six grubby pallets of wood shavings and straw, and two small private chambers with slightly better furnishings. As he moved through the room, one of the Spanish knights called to him.

"They say the Templars are God's own soldiers," the young knight said loudly. "Have you come to enrol the brave Spanish in your holy army?"

De Bracineaux glanced around and saw four large young men sitting at a table, watching him with scowling faces. He saw the ruddy blush of wine on their smooth cheeks and knew they were half in their cups, so decided to ignore them and moved on.

"My lord Templar!" shouted the knight. There came a crash as his stool toppled over behind him. "I asked you a polite question. Perhaps you would have the decency to answer."

The inn grew hushed as de Bracineaux turned. "Are you speaking to me, pigherd?"

The knight stepped around the table and into the Templar's path. "I am Alejandro Lorca, sir. You will address me with the respect that is due a nobleman."

"Out of my way." De Bracineaux put a hand to the young man's chest and pushed him aside. He fell sprawling on his backside, but sprang to his feet with surprising agility. He came up fast, knife in hand.

The Templar commander backed away a step.

The youth grinned stupidly. "Ah, now we shall see the famed courage of the Knights of the Temple."

He lunged forward, the blade sweeping the air before him. De Bracineaux dodged to the side, took the young man's arm, spun him around and shoved him hard into d'Anjou, who stepped forward at that moment. The two collided, and the youth went down clutching his side and gasping.

D'Anjou peered blandly down at him.

The young knight pulled his hand away and gaped at it in disbelief; his fingers were covered with the blood which was rapidly spreading from the gash in his side.

"Impudent pup," intoned the baron coolly. "I ought to slit your throat." He bent down and the young man flinched. D'Anjou smiled wickedly and with a flick of his hand wiped the blade of the short dagger on the wounded knight's tunic. "Perhaps next time," he said, then stepped over his victim and continued toward the door, the incident already forgotten.

De Bracineaux regarded the young knight with loathing. "You want to be more careful, pigherd. You could get hurt."

The two men disappeared into the room at the back of the inn. The knight's friends and the rest of the patrons rushed to the young man's aid as soon as the door was closed. Lifting him upon their shoulders, they hurried from the inn to the physician's house in the next street to have his wound stanched and bound before he bled to death.

The next morning the innkeeper greeted his two prickly guests with extreme deference, bowing and bowing until d'Anjou asked if the man's bowels were loose.

"No, my lord," replied the innkeeper, mystified by the question.

"Then kindly stop bobbing around like a goose with distemper and bring us some bread and a bowl of sweet wine." The man bowed again and darted away. "Mind the bread is fresh." D'Anjou called after him. "Not that worm-gnawed crust you gave us last night."

De Bracineaux walked to the entrance, pushed the door open and gazed out across the bare earth street. Beyond the low roofs of the surrounding dwellings, the timber scaffolding of the cathedral soared heavenward. "I think," he mused, "we shall pay another visit to our quarrelsome archbishop this morning, and see if we can persuade him to see things in a different light."

"How, pray, do you propose to do that?"

"While you slept, I have been thinking. On the evidence of the disturbance here last night, it occurs to me that the people of Santiago do not fully respect the Poor Knights of Christ and the Temple. A lesson in courtesy would not go amiss, I think."

"I am intrigued," said d'Anjou with a yawn. "Tell me more."

"You must learn to rein in your enthusiasm," replied de Bracineaux, glancing back over his shoulder. "It will do you harm one day."

The innkeeper reappeared a moment later bearing an armful of fresh loaves and two jars of sweet wine, which he poured into his best cups. "There is honey for the bread, my lords, if you please," he said with a bow.

"Bring it," said the baron.

They broke fast on bread and honey and sweet wine while the innkeeper watched them twitchily until they rose to go. "Was everything to your liking, my lords?" he asked anxiously.

"You keep a foul rats' nest of an inn," d'Anjou told him. "It would be a boon to travelers everywhere if I burned it to the ground."

The innkeeper drew back in horror at the suggestion.

"Pay him," said the commander, moving to the door.

Baron d'Anjou reached into the purse at his belt, withdrew two coins and offered them to the innkeeper. As the anxious man reached for the coins, the baron tilted his palm and spilled them into the dirty straw at his feet, then turned and followed de Bracineaux into the gray autumnal mist.

They proceeded to the monastery where, following prayers, the gates were just being opened for the day. The Grand Commander strode into the cloistered square and called in a loud voice for his men to come forth. They appeared from various doorways—some from the chapel, some from the refectory, some from the dormitory. Marshalling his troops, de Bracineaux ordered them to saddle their horses and arm themselves for battle. This they did without question, although there was no indication of alarm; the town seemed peaceful and quiet.

Within moments this placid repose vanished in the clattering tumult of troops rushing to saddle horses and don armor. They assembled in the street outside the monastery gates and many of the townspeople, hearing the commotion, came out to watch the strange soldiers array themselves for war.

As soon as they were armed and mounted, Master de Bracineaux, with Sergeant Gislebert on one side and Baron d'Anjou on the other, took his place at the head of his company—four ranks of five Knights Templar, each wearing the long coat of fine chain mail and, over it, the distinctive white surcoat with the cross of red upon the chest; armed with lance and sword, and carrying the long-tailed oval shield—painted white and bearing the red cross—they rode out, passing slowly along the streets of Santiago de Compostela and proceeding toward the town's great square and the building site of the new cathedral. As the mounted troops moved slowly on, they gathered a crowd of curious townspeople along the way so that by the time they reached the unfinished square the onlookers outnumbered knights by more than ten to one.

The laborers were already at work; their fires and iron braziers were scattered around the site at places where they could warm themselves from time to time and cook their meals. The dull morning rang with the sound of heavy hammers on wood and stone, the creak of wooden wheels, and the braying of donkeys as the timber scaffolding and stacks of cut stone rose slowly higher, and ever higher.

Archbishop Bertrano stood at the broad base of the tower, shouting at one of the masons who gazed down at him from the unfinished wall high above. The mason pointed beyond him into the town square, whereupon the churchman turned and beheld the mounted Templars and their entourage of townsfolk. Hands on hips, he waited for the knights to draw near.

"You again," he growled. "I told you I wanted nothing more to do with you."

"Good morning to you, too, archbishop," answered de Bracineaux cordially. "I hope you passed a pleasant night."

"It is none of your concern," snapped the archbishop, eyeing the mounted ranks of armed soldiers.

"I myself did not sleep so well," the commander confessed.

"Guilty conscience, no doubt," remarked the cleric.

"On the contrary," said de Bracineaux. "I could not sleep for thinking how I might prove myself to you."

"Then you have forfeited a good night's sleep for nothing," the archbishop told him. "Be gone, and let me return to my work."

"And then, as I was at my prayers, the answer came to me," continued the commander, speaking evenly and slowly so any of the many onlookers who understood Latin might understand. "The example of Our Lord Christ himself provided the way to verify the truth of my claims."

"That I very much doubt, sir," sniffed the archbishop. "More likely it was the Devil you were listening to."

"Diligent churchman that you are," the Templar continued, as if he had not heard a word the archbishop said, "you will certainly recall the incident recorded in the holy text where the Lord Jesu is approached by a centurion of the Roman army."

Bertrano frowned. Drawn by the crowd and commotion, more people were streaming into the square. "I know the text," he said. "Do not think to instruct me."

"This Roman soldier, as you will recall," continued de Bracineaux blithely, "had a trusted servant for whom he had developed a certain affection."

"Yes, yes," snapped the archbishop impatiently. "I know the story."

"Do you?" remarked the Templar. "I wonder."

"The servant had fallen ill," said the archbishop, his irritation growing, "so the Roman sought out the Lord Christ and asked him to heal the man."

"Indeed, yes," replied de Bracineaux, smiling, "the Lord said he would come to his house and perform the necessary healing at once." He paused, his smile becoming fierce. "And do you remember what the soldier replied?"

"Of course!" snapped the archbishop. "Stop this mummery. I see what you are doing."

"The Roman soldier stood before Jesu and said, 'My lord, I would not presume to have you set foot in my house. But just say the word, and my servant will be healed.' The Lord marveled at the man's faith, and the centurion explained; he said, 'I myself am—' "

Not to be outdone before his own flock, the archbishop took up the recitation, "He said, 'For I myself am a man under authority, with many soldiers under me. I tell this one "Go!" and he goes. To another, I say, "Come here," and he comes to me. To my servant, I say, "Do this!" and he does it.' " He regarded the Templar shrewdly. "Am I supposed to be impressed by a small recital of holy writ? Well, then, I am not impressed in the least. Even the Devil can quote scripture—as we all know."

"My dear archbishop," coaxed de Bracineaux, "you miss the point of the lesson. You see, like that centurion, I am a man under authority, with many soldiers under me. Arrayed behind me are but a few of them. I say to this one: come—" he turned and summoned the first soldier from his place behind him, "and, behold!—He comes."

The soldier dismounted and ran to the commander's side. "I say to him: stretch forth your hand!"

The Templar lifted his arm shoulder-high and stretched out his hand. De Bracineaux drew his sword and touched the keen-edged blade to the man's wrist. He then raised the sword high overhead and prepared to strike off the soldier's hand. Without a quiver of fear, the Templar gazed impassively at the archbishop.

"Do you think maiming this unfortunate soldier will sway my opinion in any way?" said Bertrano coldly. "I tell you it will not."

The commander slowly lowered the blade. "Perhaps you are right," he conceded. "What is a man's hand when the fate of the most valuable relic in all Christendom even now hangs in the balance?"

Handing the naked blade to Gislebert, he dismounted and stepped before the waiting Templar. "Have you been shriven?" he asked simply. The man nodded once. "Then, as your superior in Christ, I command you to kneel before me and stretch out your neck."

Without hesitation the Templar dropped to his knees and, placing his hands behind him, he lowered his head and stretched out his neck before the commander. Meanwhile, Gislebert, having dismounted, brought his commander's sword; taking his place beside the commander, he held the sword across his palms.

A body of monks from the nearby monastery arrived in the square just then and, seeing what was happening, raced to prevent the impending slaughter. "Keep them back," the commander ordered, and six mounted Templars broke ranks and rode to head off the onrushing monks.

Indicating the man kneeling before him, de Bracineaux said, "As you, a prince of the church, wield power over the priests beneath you, likewise does the commander wield power over those who serve under him. For, I ask you, my lord archbishop: who but the rightful lord holds the power of life and death for those beneath his authority?"

The archbishop glared furiously at the Templar, but held his tongue.

"Very well," concluded de Bracineaux. "What I do before you now, I do to prove my authority."

Taking the sword from Gislebert, he grasped it in both hands and made an elaborate sign of the cross above the kneeling soldier. Then, slowly raising the blade above his head, he cried, "For the glory of God and his Kingdom!"

The blade hovered in the air, and the archbishop rushed forward like an attacking bull. "Your authority!" charged the archbishop, his voice ringing in the restless silence of the square. "Your authority! You wicked and perverse whoreson!"

The blade faltered and halted in its downward stroke. The Templar turned to face the oncoming archbishop.

"For the glory of God?" roared the angry cleric. "Get thee behind me, thou Satan! It is for *your* glory, not God's, and I will not stand aside and watch you spill the blood of the innocent for your vain amusement."

Genuinely taken aback by the indictment, de Bracineaux lowered the sword. "You accuse me of vanity, priest," he growled. "How many men have you killed in the raising of this monument to *your* vanity?" He waved a hand airily at the curtain wall and tower of the unfinished cathedral.

"It is a temple to the Everlasting God, sir," replied the archbishop. "Four men have died, and five hundred have labored long to establish an altar which will last forever—their lives and labor an honorable sacrifice to the Author and Redeemer of Life."

The archbishop bent down, raised the kneeling soldier to his feet, and pushed him out of the way before turning on the Templar once more. "Do not presume to elevate your wicked exercise by comparing it to the exalted and holy obedience of my faithful laborers. I know you for what you are, sir, and I condemn your arrogance and pride."

De Bracineaux bristled at the cleric's heated accusations. "Why you bloated old goat," he said, his voice strangled with rage, "no man talks to me this way. I am the Master of Jerusalem! Do you hear?"

"Were you the very emperor himself, I would speak," declared the irate archbishop. "For when vile pride usurps a man's humility and true affection it is the duty of a priest to speak, to name the sin and call the sinner to account."

The Templar's eyes narrowed dangerously; his hand tightened on the hilt of his sword. "I came before you in friendship and humility," he said, forcing the words between clenched teeth, "and I was shunned. Now, as I stand before this crowd of witnesses, I am reviled."

His jaw muscles worked, grinding his teeth with suppressed rage. "I command armies and ships, fortresses and cities; I have but to lift my hand and kingdoms are overthrown; I speak and heathen nations tremble. And I swear before Almighty God, were it not for the sake of the Holy Cup, you would be kneeling before the Throne of Heaven even now, proud priest."

Archbishop Bertrano raised a triumphant finger. "Now do I truly believe you are the Master and Commander of the Knights of the Temple. For who else but a man long accustomed to the wicked conceits of high position could stand in the presence of God and boast as you do? Your pride, sir, is a stink in the nostrils of God Almighty, and unless you repent on bended knee, it will drag you down to hell."

De Bracineaux, livid and shaking, reached out and snatched hold of the archbishop's robe and pulled him close. "Tell me where the Mystic Rose is to be found, or I swear by my right hand that before you draw another breath I will carve that devious tongue from your lying mouth."

The archbishop, his lips pressed into a firm, defiant frown, glowered at the Templar with smoldering indignation.

"Well, priest?" de Bracineaux said, his breath hot in the cleric's face. "It was your letter that brought me here, and I have not come this far to fail. I ask but once more." He tightened his grip on the archbishop's robe. "Where is the Holy Cup?"

"As God is my witness, I tell you I do not know where the relic is to be found," answered the archbishop. "That knowledge resides with the monk Matthias; he alone knows the whereabouts of the Sacred Vessel, and he is not here. He is in Aragon."

"Then you will tell me where this brother is to be found," the commander said. Even as he spoke, his eyes took on a sly gleam. "Better still, so that no further misunderstandings threaten the harmony between us, you will *show* me the way. Considering that this singular opportunity has come about through your interfering offices, I think it is the least you can do."

Releasing the cleric, he called to Gislebert. "Ready a horse for our friend. His highness the archbishop is joining our pilgrimage."

"You cannot command me," the archbishop spluttered. "I have work to do."

"Then I suggest you make haste to discharge your obligations without delay." He turned on his heel, and gestured to the Templars looking on. "Bring him."

One of the pack mules was hastily saddled and made ready for the archbishop, who, protesting the outrage being practiced upon him, was forcibly manhandled onto the back of the beast. Then, at the sergeant's signal, the ranks of Templars moved slowly off.

The monks gave out a loud cry of dismay, pushed past the mounted soldiers and ran after their beloved archbishop, clamoring for his release. The soldiers paid them no heed—until some of them ran up to the churchman's mule and tried to haul him from the saddle. At a word from the Master, Gislebert called a command and the last rank of Templars wheeled their horses, raised their shields and lowered their lances, instantly blocking the street and preventing the townsfolk and monks from impeding their retreat.

Meanwhile, the rest of the cavalcade rode on. Archbishop Bertrano, realizing there was no rescue forthcoming, called to his monks for building work to continue in his absence. He was still shouting instructions when his listeners disappeared from sight.

TWENTY

"Impossible!" cried Carlo de la Coruña. "Holy Mother of God, bear witness! I cannot allow it."

Surprised by the magistrate's sudden vehemence, Cait glanced at Thea, who rolled her shoulders in a shrug of perplexed resignation. "Why ever not?" wondered Cait, somewhat more innocently than she felt.

"You will certainly be killed, all of you. The bandits are very fierce. They are brigands. Cut-throats!" Carlo's wicker chair creaked as he squirmed with agitation. "No, it is impossible. My conscience would give me not a moment's peace if I let you go. I would never forgive myself. Indeed, God himself," he said, thrusting a finger heavenward and crossing himself solemnly, "would never forgive me."

"The road is safe enough," Cait pointed out. "We saw no sign of anyone all the way from Bilbao—neither bandits, traders, nor anyone else."

"You see? The king's ban is working. We are starving the bandits into submission."

"No doubt," said Alethea, stirring herself from her listlessness, "the thieves have already moved on to more profitable pickings elsewhere." She yawned. "Otherwise we would have seen them."

The little man shook his head from side to side. "No, no, no, no, no. It is too dangerous. I cannot allow it. You must stay here at Palencia until the Knights of Calatrava can escort you and your lovely sister properly and in all comfort and safety."

"May I remind you, magistrate, we already possess such an escort," Cait insisted gently. "And if you agree to allow us to buy the supplies we need, then we will be as well provided on the road as we would be here behind the walls of your excellent city." She displayed her most winsome and beguiling smile. "You are very kind, Carlo, and your concern shows a generous and compassionate heart." She reached out and pressed his hand warmly. "But, you see, there is really no cause to be fearful on our account."

"*Madre mía*," sighed the magistrate. "The king would boil me alive in hot oil if he found out."

"The king," Alethea replied blithely, "is only three years old."

They feasted that night in the banqueting hall of the old palace; Palencia had been a favorite royal residence many years ago—from the time when Alfonso III expelled the Moors and took over the amir's house for his own. Rognvald and the knights had spent the day roistering with some of the higher-ranking townspeople and had made a fair few acquaintances among Palencia's knighted nobility—a small but ferociously loyal brotherhood. Most of these had been invited to the feast, and so the warriors carried on their revel late into the night.

In all it was a grand repast, and when the celebrants arose from the crumb- and bone-strewn tables and staggered out into the darkened streets of Palencia, new friendships had been forged and vows of eternal brotherhood pledged. The next morning, Caitríona, Alethea, Rognvald and Dag rode out to an estate a short distance south of the city where, as Rognvald had learned from one of the local noblemen, Brother Matthias was reported to be building a church for the vassals.

The estate was not far, and Magistrate Carlo offered to ride with them and show them the way; Cait was desperately trying to find a way to politely, but gently, discourage him from this course, when he was called away on urgent business to settle a dispute between a pair of brothers over the use of a cow which they had bought. "Let us go quickly now," Thea said as the officious governor hurried off, "before he comes back."

The way was well marked, and they had no difficulty finding the church, for, but a short distance from the trail, they observed a heap of rubble and several piles of rough lumber. In the midst of these heaps, a ragged curtain of laid stone was being raised.

Leaving Dag on a nearby hilltop to keep watch on the trail and warn them should any trouble approach, they rode onto the building site where, on a plank balanced between two sections of wall, stood a young man wrapped in the brown robe of a priest. The hem of the robe was drawn up and tucked into his wide leather belt, revealing a pair of muscular, but dirty, legs and equally filthy bare feet. The day being warm, he had withdrawn his arms so the upper half of the wool garment hung down around his trim waist.

"*Pax vobiscum*," called Rognvald as they reined up.

The monk straightened from his work and turned to greet his visitors, holding in his hands the stone he was about to lay. "*Pax vobiscum*," he replied, glancing from the knight to the two women. His dark hair and wispy beard had been lightened by long hours in the sun.

"We are searching for a priest called Brother Matthias," said Rognvald. "I am wondering if you could help us find him."

"Your search is at an end, brother," replied the monk in easy, Spanish-tinted Latin. "I am Matthias."

"God be good to you," said Cait. "We have something of importance to discuss. Is there a place we might talk?"

"I have no secrets before God, sister," the monk replied, turning back to his work. "And, as you can see, there is no one here but the Good Lord and me, so whatever is in your heart, speak." He placed the stone onto a bed of oozing gray mortar which he had prepared, then scooped the excess mortar from the side of the wall and packed it around the stone.

"Are you building this church all alone?" asked Alethea. "Is there no one to help you?"

"God is helping me, sister," answered the monk. He lowered himself onto the plank, and then dropped to the ground; moving to the nearest heap of rubble, he chose another stone, hefted it on to the plank, and then clambered up once more. "The people come when they can, but it is soon harvest time and they are needed in the fields."

"We have come from Archbishop Bertrano in Santiago," said Rognvald.

"Have you indeed?" said the monk, turning toward them again. "Then you have traveled a fair distance." He straightened and regarded them with renewed interest. "I would share a cup of wine with you," he said, "but all I have is water." He pointed to a gourd hanging from the wall by a strap. "Still, you are welcome to it."

Cait thanked him, but declined. "I fear we come bearing bad news," she said.

"Bertrano is dead?" guessed the monk. He picked up the stone from the plank and gazed at it sadly. "How did it happen? Was it one of the builders?"

"The good archbishop was hale as ever when we last saw him," Cait assured the priest quickly. "Unfortunately, it is Commander de Bracineaux who is dead." She noticed Alethea's quick and questioning glance, and prayed her sister would, just this once, keep her mouth shut. "I am sorry," she said, ignoring Alethea. She hated deceiving the priest in this way, but the ruse must be maintained if they were to secure his help.

A puzzled frown clouded the monk's open, guileless features. "I do not understand."

"There was a shipwreck," Rognvald said, and explained how the Templar commander and the other survivors were attacked by Muhammedans. "Sadly, the commander died of his wounds."

"I am aggrieved to hear it," offered the monk, resuming his work.

Alethea watched him set another stone in the wall. "You seem to take your grief in your stride," she observed.

"Thea, hush!" whispered Cait furiously.

Matthias glanced at her, his sun-browned features breaking into a grin. "No doubt I would be more sorrowful if I had the slightest idea who this man de Bracineaux might be."

"You do not know him?" asked Cait.

"Good lady, I know him less well than I do the knight beside you," said the monk, "and him I know not at all."

"Forgive me, brother," said Rognvald quickly. "I am Rognvald, Lord of Haukeland and Orkneyjar. And this is Lady Caitríona, and her sister Lady Alethea of Caithness in Scotland."

"May the Lord of All Holiness bless you and keep you, my friends," said the priest, inclining his head in an ecclesiastical bow.

"As it is nearing midday," said Cait, "I wonder if we could entice you down from your lofty perch with an offer of a meal. We have brought some food—would you care to share it with us?"

"The work of God cannot be diverted." Matthias dropped down to the ground once more, selected another stone, and hoisted it onto the plank.

"You *do* eat, do you not?" asked Alethea.

"Sometimes," allowed the monk, "when time is not so pressing. Still, I want for nothing. God supplies all my needs."

"If he feeds you like he helps with the building," Thea observed, "then I am not surprised you have but little time for food. Indeed, it is a wonder you do not waste away altogether."

Matthias laughed. "O, ye of little faith," he said, clambering back on to his rough plank. "We must work while we have the light. For I tell you the truth, night is soon coming when no man can work."

To Cait's surprise, it was Rognvald who parried this lighthearted thrust. "Blessed Yesu said, 'My food is to do the work my father has given me.' Perhaps, what we have to tell you is also the work of God. Therefore, let us also eat—and perhaps we will discover what Our Heavenly Father would have us do with the light we yet possess."

The priest stood upon his plank and beamed. "A man after my own heart. I yield to your wise counsel."

As the priest climbed down from his suspended walkway again, Cait indicated a solitary scrub-oak tree a little apart from the building site. "Come, Thea, we will prepare the meal. We can sit in the shade."

They dismounted and, taking the bundles from behind her saddle, Cait led her sister past the mounds of stone and timber to the tree. "Thea, there is no time to explain. But whatever Rognvald or I may say—just you consider it the truth. Better yet, Thea, keep your mouth closed."

"I know the Templar isn't dead," she said. "Is that what you mean?"

"Yes, and there is more. I will explain everything later. Believe me, I do not like it any more than you do—"

"I like it just fine," remarked Alethea glibly. "And so do you—I saw your face when you told him. You enjoy it! So, do not try to pretend being holy and contrite all of a sudden. I know better."

"Oh, very well, have it your way," Cait told her. "We will talk later. Just see you do not interfere."

"Why would I interfere? Anyway, he is a fine and handsome man—do you not think so, Cait?"

"He is a priest!" hissed her sister. "You cannot treat with him like other men. In fact, you must not treat with him at all."

Alethea shrugged, and they unwrapped the bundle and began spreading the meal beneath the tree. Shortly, the knight and priest finished their inspection of the far-from-finished church, and joined them. "Bertrano sent you to tell me this?" the priest was saying.

"He did," answered the knight. "You see, the archbishop took your concern to heart and sent to the pope for guidance in the matter of the Holy Cup."

"You know about the Mystic Rose?" wondered Matthias. "Bertrano told you?"

"Commander Renaud de Bracineaux was Master of Jerusalem," the knight said. "He told me of the pope's letter before he died. He asked me to take word to Archbishop Bertrano, and Bertrano has sent me to you."

The priest nodded. "I begin to see now. I did not know the archbishop would involve anyone else. I told him in confidence."

"And so it remains," Cait quickly assured him. "I am certain the good archbishop would not have confirmed us in this task if there was a better way."

"Although you might not know it," the knight added, "the Muhammedans have been troubling the region of late. Travel has become very difficult. No doubt the archbishop took this into account."

"I suppose you are right," agreed Matthias. "There has been trouble, true enough. Thanks be to God, we have been spared until now."

"Why did you think Archbishop Bertrano was dead?" wondered Alethea.

"Thea, not now," hushed her sister.

Matthias grinned again, his teeth white against the sun-darkened patina of his skin and curly wisp of a beard. "So long as that cathedral of his remains unfinished, the man is a very plague to all the poor workmen who must labor under his tireless zeal." He chuckled to himself. "In truth, it is only a matter of time before one of his harried builders smites him with a hammer, or throws him from a scaffold."

"Even so," said Rognvald, "the cathedral rises day by day. It will be a magnificent church."

"That it will," agreed Matthias with a sigh of resignation.

The marked lack of enthusiasm did not go unnoticed. "You do not approve of such enterprise?" asked Cait.

"Lady, I confess I do not. The expense is beyond belief. For the cost of one cathedral, a thousand churches like mine could be built and a hundred monasteries, convents, and hospitals besides." He sighed again. "But cathedrals woo the wealthy, and everywhere kings are vying with one another to see who can build the most ostentatious monuments to their own vanities."

"The food is ready," said Alethea pleasantly. She smiled at the tanned and hardy priest. "Please sit, brother, be our guest."

Taking up one of the small loaves of bread, the monk raised it on high as if it were the host of the holy sacrament, and blessed it, whereupon they all sat down to a simple, but perfectly satisfying meal. They had brought bread and smoked fish, olives, cheese, and plums. There was watered wine to drink, and while they ate, they listened in enthralled silence as Matthias told an enchanting and wondrous tale.

TWENTY-ONE

"I first learned of the Holy Cup four years ago," Matthias said, rolling an olive between thumb and forefinger before popping it into his mouth. "This was in Old Alfonso's day, mind, when the king's peace still held—and I was traveling in the high hills to the east, beyond the Ebro valley, where there are many villages without churches. But in one of the places—a small settlement in the mountains reached by a single sheep trail which is all but impassable most of the year—I found that the people already knew Christ and his teachings.

"I asked how this had come about, and the head man of the village told me that they had preserved this knowledge from long before the Muslims came—"

"But that must be," said Rognvald breaking in, "what? Three hundred? Four hundred years?"

The priest nodded; he broke off a bit of bread and chewed thoughtfully. "You know something of history, my friend. Yes, four hundred years—as you shall see. And for all those hundreds of years the people have remained faithful though surrounded by Muhammedans on every side—like a tiny rock of Christianity in a turbulent Muslim sea."

"Extraordinary," breathed Alethea, hanging on the handsome young priest's every word.

"Miraculous," agreed the monk placidly. "I confess that, at first, I scarce thought it possible. So, during my sojourn with them, I took every opportunity to question the villagers about this—subtly, of course, for I did not care to make them wary. Gradually, they began to trust me, and to tell me more. And the more I learned, the more extraordinary it became.

183

"In time, they came to realize my interest in them was genuine, so one night the village chief came to me and asked if I wanted to learn a secret which would answer all my questions. I told him I would welcome it—*if* he wished to show me. But if it would disturb any of his people in any way, I did not care to know it; for I valued their friendship far more than any secret they might possess."

Alethea clucked her tongue with impatience at such irrelevant civility. "*I* would have made him show me at once."

"And *that*," replied Matthias with a wink, "is why you would still be waiting to discover the secret. You see, the hill people are not like others. I believe they are the remnant of a more ancient race. They are secretive by nature, but they can be very loyal and they have extremely long memories. They remember the slights and injuries of centuries as if they happened yesterday, and they never forget a kindness.

"So, my answer was just the right one, for the chief looked at me and said, 'I would not show you if I had not already asked everyone. I asked them, and everyone has agreed—even Gydon, and he never agrees to anything!' Well, it was the middle of the night, and I thought he meant to show me in the morning, but he instructed me to tie up my shoes and put on my cloak and, taking neither lantern nor torch, we walked out into the darkness and up into the hills behind the village with nothing but the light of a pale quarter-moon to guide us.

"I saw neither trail nor path; like a blind man, I had to maintain a tight grip on the chief's shoulder to keep from stumbling with every step. We walked a fair distance, or so it seemed, and came at last to a hidden valley—nothing more than a crease between two steep bluffs— and high up on the side of one of the bluffs was the entrance to a cave.

"I could not see it—for all it was dark as the bottom of a well—but he assured me it was there, and by virtue of small steps cut in the bluff, he led me up to the cave. Though it was a tight squeeze through the rough doorway, once inside the chamber we could stand upright. My guide knew the cave well, and by means of some materials left there, he soon lit an oil lamp so we might view what he had come to show me."

"What was it?" asked Alethea, rapt, her eyes gleaming.

"A small altar had been cut in the rock at the back of the cave, and the entire wall whitewashed and painted with the sign of the cross so as to make a sort of shrine. This painting was of a delicate and intricate craft the like of which I had seen but once before—in an old, old text in the scriptorium of the monastery where I received my priesting. This text was one of the monastery's principal treasures: a gospel of John copied out by the hand of Saint Samson of Dol.

"It was a very beautiful ornament, and I imagined that this was what he had brought me to see—and it was wondrous enough! But no. The chief indicated that I should move nearer the altar, which I did; and on the altar was a curious object. At first I took it for a knife—it was long," the monk held up his hand to indicate a dagger-length span, "and like a knife, it tapered along its narrow length. A closer look revealed that it was not a knife, however, for although it had a sharp point, it had no edge like an ordinary blade, and no handle."

"What was it?" demanded Alethea, hugging her updrawn knees and rocking back and forth in anticipation.

Matthias, enjoying the suspense, gave her a smile. "That is what I asked him. The chief stretched forth his hand, and said, in a prayerful and reverent voice, 'This is the spike which pierced Our Blessed Redeemer's feet as he hung on the cross for our salvation.' Just like that."

At these words, Cait felt a tingle of excitement trickle up along her spine. *This is ordained*, she thought. *We are meant to be here. This is a sign.*

"How did it come into their possession?" asked Rognvald.

"That is what I asked," chuckled Matthias. "I said to him, 'My friend, tell me, how did it come to be here?' Crossing his arms over his chest, the village chieftain bowed low before the altar and spoke out a prayer in a language I have never heard before. And then, pointing to the spike he said, 'Iago gave it to us.' "

"Iago?" echoed Cait. "You mean, Saint James—the same whose tomb is at Compostela?"

"The same," replied Matthias, enjoying the wide-eyed wonder of his listeners. "The old Galicians called him Iago, and hold that after the infant church was driven from Jerusalem, Saint Iago fled by ship with a number of other followers of the Way. They landed in the north and wandered here and there, performing signs and wonders, and preaching the gospel of salvation through belief in the Risen Lord Christ.

"He lived among the Galician tribes for many years, and toward the end of his life decided to return to Jerusalem. His proselytizing landed him in trouble with the Jewish authorities, who had him arrested and taken before Herod Agrippa, who tried him and put him to death. So that his grave should not become a place of worship, Herod refused to allow him a proper burial."

The priest paused to take a drink of wine before continuing. "When word of the sainted man's unfortunate end eventually reached the new-founded churches of Iberia, the people grew very distraught. They came together and chose a delegation of twelve strong and righteous men, led by a priest of undoubted holiness. The delegation was sent to Jerusalem to claim the body of their beloved Iago.

"Through many travails they persevered, and were at last granted permission to recover the corpse of the great saint, which they placed in a specially prepared casket and carried back to Galicia to be buried in the place where he and his followers first made landfall, and where his bones have been venerated ever since."

"Was it really the true spike?" Alethea wanted to know. "It might have been any old scrap of iron."

"There is no deceiving you," declared the priest. "You put the Blessed Thomas to shame." Leaning close, he said, "To tell you the truth, I had my doubts, too. I asked how it was that after such a long time they could be certain that it was the selfsame spike of the crucifixion—and do you know what the chief did?"

Alethea shook her head. The nearness of the priest made her stomach flutter, and she noticed how the sun had burnt the hair on his bare arms to a fluff of golden curls. "What did he do?" she asked, almost swallowing her voice.

"He told me to pick it up. He said, 'Iago was a powerful prophet, and he foresaw the time when the Galicians would suffer under the Moors. He gave us this inestimable treasure so that we should never forget the teaching he left behind, for he knew the gospel he preached would help us endure and survive. And he told the truth.' Then the village chieftain stretched out his hand toward the relic and bade me to pick it up."

"Did you?" asked Cait.

"Lady, I did. I stood before the altar and I reached down and plucked up the spike and held it in my hand. It was heavier than I imagined, and cold to the touch. 'Now I know you are a holy man,' said my host, 'or else you could not lift it.' I did not know what he meant; but before I could ask, he bade me make as if to steal it away.

"Still holding the spike in my hand, I turned away from the altar and started toward the doorway and, wonder of wonders, the spike began to grow warm. In the space of a single step, the cold iron grew so hot as to scorch my palm. I looked and the metal now glowed red as if fresh from the smith's fiery forge."

"What did you do?" said Alethea.

"What *could* I do? I swiftly returned the sacred object to its place on the altar lest my hands be burned to unfeeling stumps. Lo and behold! No sooner had I replaced the relic than it resumed its former appearance. 'Touch it,' said my host, and I did." The monk stretched forth a tentative finger, recalling the gesture for his astonished audience. "What did I find? The ancient iron was cold once more."

"A very miracle," said Rognvald with satisfaction.

"You are a trusting soul," replied the priest. "I would I were more like you in this regard. Unfortunately, ever since childhood I have suffered the affliction of a suspicious nature. I could not let the matter rest. I saw a stack of kindling wood lying on the floor next to the cave entrance; so I took up a stout chunk of wood in each hand and returned to the altar—thinking to get the object between the two pieces and remove the iron spike that way without burning my hands."

"Did it work?" asked Alethea, slightly breathless with awe.

"Sister, it was even more wonderful than before. For no matter how hard I tried, I could not move that spike. Though I applied all my strength, the holy relic would not be diverted by so much as a whisker's breadth. The wood splintered, and my fingers grew raw, but I could not move it.

"The village chief watched me with great amusement. He laughed at my efforts, and then calmly walked to the altar where I was struggling and, bowing before it, took up the spike and placed it once more in my hand as if it were no more than a feather. 'Were you less holy than you are,' he told me, 'you would not be able to lift it, for to the man of evil intent, it contains the weight of the world.' I replaced the holy relic then, and knelt down before the altar and thanked the Heavenly Father for allowing me to witness this great and powerful sign.

"When I finished my prayers, we departed the cave, and returned to the village, reaching the settlement just as dawn rose over the eastern hills. I thanked the chieftain for showing me the marvelous relic, and vowed I would treasure it always, and tell anyone who cared to listen so that faith might increase. As I said this, a great smile spread over the chieftain's face, and he said, 'Do you see that sunrise? Our poor relic is as the darkness of the valley through which you walked compared to the shining glory of the gra'al.' "

The three rapt listeners repeated the strange word.

"Like you, I had never heard of this gra'al, and did not know what it might be," the priest told them. "I asked what was betokened by this word. My guide made the sign of the cross and said, 'It is the Lord's Cup—the Cup of the Communion of Saints, which was blessed by the Christ at the table of the Last Supper.' "

"The Mystic Rose," whispered Cait.

Brother Matthias nodded. "I thought he meant that the village possessed another secret in the form of this relic, and so I asked if he could show me. But he merely smiled, and said that it was not his to show, for long ago the cup was removed by the will of God, and taken to a refuge where it could be guarded lest the Moors learn of it and seek to steal or destroy it. My excitement made me rash, and in my unthinking haste, I asked him to show me where the Blessed Cup had been taken. I asked him to lead me there at once. My guide recoiled from my unseemly alacrity. It seemed then that he feared he had revealed too much. He quickly bade me farewell, and would say no more."

"Agh!" cried Alethea in protest. "You should have made him tell you!"

"In the end, I did learn the rest of the tale. A few days later, he came to me after dark. I was at my prayers, and he came into the room where I was staying and said that he could not rest knowing that he had betrayed the Sacred Cup. 'How betrayed?' I asked. 'I am a priest of the church. All things touching the holy are safe in my hands.'

"Even so, I failed to convince him, and so I suggested that the best way out of his dilemma was for me to learn the rest of the tale from someone else. 'That way,' I told him, 'the burden is lifted from your shoulders because you were not the one to tell me.'

"Well, he saw it as his redemption in the matter, and told me that if he was a man wanting to learn secrets of this nature, he knew a place deep in the high Pyrénées where all such questions could be answered. The way he said it gave me to know that this secret place in the mountains was where the cup now sheltered, so I agreed, and he instructed me on how to find this place. I listened with utmost care to all he said, and when he left, I quickly prepared a pen and wrote down all he had told me. I wrote the directions in the margin of the gospel text I always carry with me so that I would not forget them, and a few days later I concluded my work and set off to find the Sanctuary of the Cup."

"Did you find it?" asked Cait.

"I did, my lady," answered Matthias. "I found it just as he said I would."

"And did you see the cup?" asked Rognvald.

"I did," replied the priest, his voice falling to a whisper. "I saw it in all its manifold splendor, and I worshiped it. I fell on my face before the sacred object, and when I arose three days had passed."

"Three whole days!" challenged Alethea, disbelief edging into her tone.

"In the mere blink of an eye," affirmed the monk. "And then I rose and went out, healed and satisfied in heart and mind and soul. I rose as a man renewed and reborn, and with a holy fire burning in my belly. Since then, I have traveled the land, preaching wherever I am welcomed, and building churches for those who have none."

He spread his hands humbly. "I am as you find me, a much-changed and chastened man." He drank again, allowing the others to ponder what he had told them.

"Why did you write to the archbishop?" asked Cait after a moment's reflection.

"Ah, that—that has vexed me greatly," Matthias confessed. "Following my rebirth, the zeal burned so great within me that I could not rest but that I should begin straight away to preach to the poor and build churches for them, and thus bring them to knowledge of the Loving Creator.

"Naturally, I could not set about this new work without the permission of my superior. So, I composed a thoughtful letter and sent it to Archbishop Bertrano, asking for his permission and seeking his blessing. In my rapture, I told him about the Mystic Rose of Virtue—that I had seen it, and been changed by it. In short, I told him everything—and more, for I was enraptured and unable to keep this glorious news to myself, and he is my superior, after all.

"Well, after I sent the letter—not at first, but some time later—I began to fear that I had said too much. What if the letter went astray? What if the news of the Sacred Cup should become known to men of evil intent, low thieves who would steal or destroy? But the deed was done, and I could but trust God to make it right."

Cait lowered her eyes modestly, hoping the priest would not see the waves of guilt washing over her. They had come, like low thieves, to steal the cup for themselves. The simple, trusting faith of Brother Matthias put her to shame, and she was on the brink of admitting it to the priest, confessing her sin and asking for absolution when her sister spoke up.

"*God* has sent us to you," declared Alethea with quiet but undeniable conviction.

Cait glanced at her in furtive amazement, only to see that the young woman was in utter and solemn earnest—and this astonished her even more. Mouthing untruth with such brazen audacity must be the worst kind of blasphemy, certainly. She was still trying to take in the enormity of Alethea's sacrilege when Lord Rognvald said, "Archbishop Bertrano also feared for the safety of the cup. He told us that, owing to the reconquest of the land, he considered it only a matter of time before the Holy Cup fell into the hands of the Moors." The knight smiled, his broad countenance shining with the light of a golden day, and the joy of blessed assurance. "That is why he sent us. With God's help, we will rescue the cup and bear it away to safety before any ill can befall it."

Grinning, Brother Matthias leaned forward and embraced his visitors—first Alethea, then Rognvald, and then Cait. "I, too, believe God has sent you," he said. "I have often worried that I had done wrong by sending word to the archbishop; and as often as I worried I prayed God would grant me his peace in the matter. In you, my friends, this peace has finally come. I thank God for it, and for you."

Unable to bear seeing the unsuspecting priest deceived and deluded still further, Cait made bold to lay bare the fraud that she and the others had perpetrated. "Please, it is not what you think," she began.

"Nothing ever is, sister," replied the monk cheerfully. "Where God is concerned, surprise abounds. Our Heavenly Father delights in the unexpected, the unforeseen, serendipitous circumstance and happy accident."

"Ours is a God of surprises," Alethea affirmed.

Cait stared at the others, unable to speak.

"My friends, I am convinced the Lord has sent you. What is more, I feel he is sending me, too." The monk's grin widened still further. "I will lead you to the Mystic Rose."

190

TWENTY-TWO

When the party departed Palencia four days later, they were mere travelers no longer; they had become pilgrims, destined for a holy place. And, for at least two of their number, the journey had taken on profound spiritual significance.

Rognvald and Alethea maintained that the sudden stirring of reverence and devotion was a genuine awakening. "I see it so clearly now," Alethea insisted. It was the night before they were to leave, and the three were talking alone in the magistrate's walled courtyard. "We have been chosen to save the Holy Cup and deliver it to safety."

"How can you say that?" demanded Cait, "when you know I was the one who took the letter from the Templars?"

"As the Holy Word says: What you intended for evil," Rognvald intoned, "God has destined for good. So be it."

"And you!" Cait charged. "*I* bought your release, not the angels, and that for one purpose only—to help me steal the relic."

"God works in mysterious ways his wonders to perform," replied the knight placidly. "As for myself, I never doubted that Our Great Redeemer had a hand in your scheme. Surely, it is the divine will that we should rescue the Sacred Vessel from the iniquity of desecration."

Cait shook her head in disbelief at what she was hearing. "You sound more like a priest every day, my lord," she grumbled. "Perhaps you should join a monastery where your preaching would be more appreciated."

"Only a fool mocks what he does not understand," the knight replied, unperturbed by Cait's outburst. "Is it so difficult to believe that, in spite of your intentions, Our Great Lord has ordained us to this task, and even now guides us to our destination?"

It was no use talking sense to them, Cait decided, they were so full of holy foolishness that they could not see the blunt, obvious, mud-ugly fact that the whole enterprise was founded on a mass of lies, half-truths and deceptions, large and small, and all of them growing out of a theft, which itself originated in an act of revenge.

While it might be true that the theft of the letter was instigated by the White Priest—a fact Cait preferred not to mention to anyone—the naked, shabby truth was that she hoped from the first, and hoped still, to employ the Sacred Cup to aid in avenging her father's murder at the hands of de Bracineaux. As she had come to see it, the White Priest's commission provided her with the means to an end she had desired from the first.

Yet, she puzzled over the others' peculiar insistence that their venal and self-serving journey had in some way transmuted itself into a true pilgrimage. In Alethea's case, she suspected the girl was simply enam-ored with the handsome young monk and his simple, almost childlike ways. Rognvald was a different matter; she could see no reason for his conversion from cunning accomplice to pious pilgrim. She had as-sumed it was part of his guise—much the same as that which he had adopted to win Archbishop Bertrano's confidence. The knight, how-ever, remained adamant that his manner was in no way calculated to deceive; and in this he appeared sincere. Indeed, he bristled at the sug-gestion that his virtue had ever been a sham. "Lady, you do wrong to doubt me in this," he had told her—again, in all sincerity.

With her fellow-conspirators stricken by this inexplicable saintli-ness, Cait could find no reasonable way to discourage the zealous Brother Matthias from joining the company; and, as the prudent monk seemed wholly disinclined to reveal any details pertaining to the Holy Cup's whereabouts, she had no choice but to welcome him with as good a grace as she could muster.

Nor was the priest the only newcomer to the group. By the time they were ready to depart, thanks to the Norwegian knights' innate friend-liness and Magistrate Carlo's well-intentioned efforts, the party had acquired an escort of six additional knights who happily agreed to ac-company the travelers as far as their next stop.

"Four warriors—what is that?" he told her. "It is enough to get you into trouble, but not enough to get you out." Before she could protest, he surged on. "No, do not thank me. Since you will not listen to sense and reason, sending these additional men is the least I can do. I could not in good conscience allow you to continue your journey otherwise."

Thus, owing to her growing entourage, Cait had become the reluctant owner of three additional pack mules and a converted hay wain to carry all the extra provender and provisions needed to feed the increased numbers of men and animals. She had also taken to heart Magistrate Carlo Coruña's counsel that she should purchase tents. After Logroño, the next town on the way, he told her, settlements of even modest wealth and substance were few and very far between.

"The weather will not stay fair forever," he warned. "Sooner or later, the autumn rains must come. Sleeping under a leaking sky is not for a noble lady, Heaven forbid! But you are indeed fortunate, for I know a man who makes the most wonderful tents—a cousin of mine, as it happens, but a tentmaker without peer. I will take you to meet him, and you will see for yourself."

In the end, the tentmaking cousin had only two completed tents to sell. The number of pilgrims traveling through Palencia on their way to or from Santiago had so declined since the king's ban, that he had not made any new tents for some time and was seriously considering giving up the business altogether. He was overjoyed to sell his last tents to Cait and her company, and explained that if she could wait but a month longer, he could have more ready for her. She declined politely, but purchased the remaining two for a generous price and added them to the growing mountain of equipment and supplies.

The tents were fashioned in a sturdy, rustic way: tall, peaked leather roofs stretched between two stout poles and anchored on all sides with tight-braided ropes; side pieces of heavy wool cloth were then attached to the upper portion by way of eyes and ties, so that the interior might be opened or closed to the outside depending on the desires of the inhabitants. Whatever the structures may have lacked in elegance, they more than made up in durability; the roof portions were good Spanish leather, and the cloth was tough and impervious to wind or rain. Cait and Alethea took one tent for themselves and were pleasantly surprised by the additional comfort provided. The other tent was given to the men, who took it in turn to use it, five sleepers sharing each night.

Equipped, provisioned, and rested, they set off the next day. At first, the wilful defiance of the king's decree made the ride seem daring and eventful. But as the days passed, the continual vigilance and stealth began to pale—much like the sun-struck wilderness through which they journeyed: a dust-dulled aridity of empty hills and parched valleys filled with tinder-dry plants in subdued shades of ochre and tan and brown.

Because of their greater numbers, the company traveled more slowly than before. The Spanish knights knew many songs and games, and enjoyed teaching them to their Norse swordbrothers. They told stories about the people and places of old Galicia, often vying with one another to see who could tell the most outrageous lies about their homeland. The weather remained warm and dry, the fiery heat of summer slowly giving way to the fresh, cool days of autumn.

As before, they met neither bandits nor pilgrims, and had the road to themselves from dawn's first gleam to twilight's last glimmer. Thus, the days passed pleasantly, if not as swiftly as Cait would have liked. If not for the fact that the cost of provisions threatened to overwhelm her ready resources, Cait would have enjoyed the journey far more.

Keeping everyone fed and watered became the occupying concern of each and every day. The supplies disappeared at a shocking rate, and Cait began to feel she had made a grave mistake taking on the extra men and horses.

Fortunately, finding good water for so many thirsty throats posed no difficulty; the road was rarely out of sight of a stream or river. Although most had dwindled to little more than a trickle awaiting the autumn rains, at least the animals could be easily watered and the knights were not forced to spend the greater part of every day searching for wells, springs, or drinking holes.

Likewise, once they entered the Ebro valley they could follow the substantial Río Ebro to Logroño—another once-magnificent Roman town which had decayed under the long years of Muhammedan dominion. Upon reaching Logroño they stopped to bathe, wash their clothes, rest, and replenish provisions. As at Palencia, the travelers were welcomed with genuine warmth by the local citizenry who had not seen any travelers for many months and were eager for news of the wider world. During their brief stay, Cait followed Brother Matthias' advice to consult the abbot at the local monastery about the road ahead. The trails beyond Logroño into the lower valley, and eastward into the mountains, were not so well traveled as those they had used so far, and Cait was grateful for any knowledge of the most likely stopping-places along the way.

Because the abbot was not receptive to the idea of women visiting his scriptorium and holding converse with the monks under his charge, he declined to allow Cait to join the visiting party, so Rognvald and Matthias went in her stead.

"They say we can get meat and meal at Milagro on the Río Aragon," Rognvald told her on the eve of their departure. He and Matthias had spent most of the day studying the monastery's maps and charts of the region. "And then again at Carcastillo."

"It is four days to Milagro," Matthias said, "and Carcastillo is two or three days beyond that."

"We will stop there," said Cait. "Our provisions will last that long at least."

"The abbot suggests stopping at both places," the knight offered. "Once we are into the mountains it will become very difficult. We will get nothing more until Berdún and then but little."

"But with fewer in our party," Cait pointed out, "that should not become a problem."

"Ah, yes," said Rognvald, glancing secretively at the monk, "I have been meaning to speak to you about that very thing."

"Yes?" Cait regarded him dubiously.

"I have been thinking that it would be good to keep the Spanish knights with us."

"Oh, no," declared Cait. "I agreed they could come with us this far, but no further. They must go back." Although she enjoyed their genial and entertaining presence, the Spanish knights cost a great deal more than she had anticipated.

"They are good warriors," said Rognvald.

"They are good trenchermen, it seems to me," countered Cait. "We have not seen so much as a Moorish shadow since leaving Santiago. Do not think me a pinchfist in this matter. I enjoy their companionship as much as anyone, but it comes at a price—nearly two hundred marks since joining us."

The knight frowned, but held his tongue.

"Lady Caitríona," said Matthias, "forgive me if I speak above my place. But the abbot has strenuously advised us to turn back. He says the mountain passes have become very dangerous in these last days with many lawless and evil men waiting to prey on unwary travelers."

"With such an army as I possess, we are far from unwary," Cait pointed out.

"All the more reason to retain the Spanish warriors—if they are willing." Regarding Cait with sly solemnity, he added, "It is but a small price to pay for the saving of the Blessed Cup."

His mention of the sacred relic brought a twinge to Cait's raw conscience. Matthias did not yet know her true intentions for the vessel. She hesitated; to insist on sending half her force away might arouse the priest's suspicions regarding the nature of the enterprise which had caught him up. Until she had the cup in her possession, she could not risk losing his aid and affection. Turning to Rognvald, she asked, "Do you commend it, my lord?"

"Most heartily, I do," he replied.

"Very well, then," she decided. "Speak to the men. If they are willing, and agree to abide your command, then they may continue for as long as necessary."

Thus, when she and Alethea rode out of the gate the next morning to resume the journey, they did so with a company of twenty horses and pack mules, ten knights, and one priest and an interpreter driving a wagon laden with supplies of food and drink. By Cait's rough reckoning, enough ready gold and silver remained from that which she had brought from her father's chest to allow them to reach their destination—so long as it was no further than Matthias' vague intimations. What they would do after that, she did not know.

This cast her into a melancholy, fretful mood—a condition that did not improve when, day after day, they failed to be confronted by any of the region's much-feared bandits. Indeed, they met with no greater mishap than a sudden drenching when the sky opened and dumped a month's supply of rain on them in two days. Riding was so miserable that they camped for a day and a half, staying in their tents for the most part, until the weather cleared and they could continue. The rains filled the all-but-empty river basins, and made fording the streams more of a problem than before. At one crossing the wagon struck a submerged rock and pitched Abu headlong into the rapids; an alert Dag flew after him and plucked him sputtering from the water a few hundred paces downstream.

Each day, they moved on, following the track as it rose slowly higher and yet higher into the hills. The women gradually became accustomed to life on the trail. Cait learned to sleep with her sword, and Alethea eventually ceased complaining about each small discomfort; both became adept at darting quickly into trailside bushes to attend to their more intimate needs, rejoining the company before anyone knew they had gone. The knights grew used to one another's ways, and an easy camaraderie developed between them which made the daily tasks of establishing and breaking camp tolerable, if not enjoyable. From time to time, as the mood took him, Brother Matthias preached and recited Psalms, and he taught the Norsemen simple hymns in Spanish. Despite the ever-worsening weather, everyone remained in good spirits for the most part.

Upon arriving at the place where the rivers joined, they turned north to follow the Río Aragon up into the foothills of the Sierra de Guara, pausing briefly at the hilltown of Milagro, where, in order to conserve her dwindling supply of gold and silver coins, Cait made the knights work for the townspeople. In exchange for the necessary provisions, the men mended walls, fixed leaking roofs, and chopped firewood for the coming winter. After a week they had accumulated enough supplies, and the company moved on.

The weather in the high hill country was growing damp and windy. Matthias' staunch refusal to tell them precisely where they were going began to rankle Cait more and more. The priest was adamant that the location must remain a secret to the very end, but intimated that their final destination was still a good many days beyond Carcastillo. So, at their next stop they took the opportunity to trade labor for goods— this time in order to obtain heavy cloaks made from the dense wool of the region's sheep. Both Cait and Alethea thought the cloaks smelly beyond belief—an unappealing mixture of rancid fat and burnt dung— but the cloaks were warm even when wet, and kept the sharpening wind at bay. As the party ascended ever upward into the cooler heights, the women slowly became accustomed to wearing the noisome garments through the day and, more often than not, sleeping under them at night as well.

The weather became steadily cooler as autumn advanced; the skies grew dark and moody, and often there was rain—sometimes in fierce pelting bursts, and sometimes in dismal misty drizzle which set in early and lingered, making everyone and everything miserable, wet, and cold. Alone among the members of the company, Brother Matthias seemed not to mind the discomfort. In fact, he reveled in it, regarding the mild distress as a chastening discipline. The worse the storm, the louder he sang his psalms and chants, sometimes delivering whole sermons to the sodden, empty trail and drifting clouds. The Spanish knights apparently derived great satisfaction from this curious demonstration, a thing which Cait could not understand.

"How far?" Cait demanded of the priest one evening. They had stopped at a clearing beside the muddy rivulet which was their trail, and the knights were making camp after a dreary day's ride. Abu was trying to light a fire, and most of the Spanish knights were searching the nearby forest for dry wood. The low gray sky threatened yet more rain and the ground was soggy underfoot. The looming peaks rising in the near distance were wreathed in fog, and the wind among the rocks and canyons soughed with a desolate whine.

"Not far now," he replied with an exuberance that set her teeth on edge. "A few more days."

"How many days?" she said stubbornly. "I want to know. You are leading us there anyway, so you may as well end this absurd secrecy and tell me how much longer we must endure this incessant rain and chill."

Matthias regarded her with soulful, compassionate eyes. "Peace, you are disturbed over nothing. We will arrive in God's good time, never fear."

"Oh, I am not disturbed," Cait insisted, her voice threatening and low. "My feet are wet, my clothes are muddy, I am cold and tired, and I do not think it too much to ask how far we have yet to travel. Is it two days? Ten? Twenty?"

"Sister," the monk said, "calm yourself. There is no—"

"I am *not* your sister. I am your patron, and I want an answer."

Alethea came rushing up just then. "Cait, what is wrong? Why are you shouting at Brother Matthias?"

"All is well," the priest told her. "It is a misunderstanding, nothing more." He laid a soothing hand on Cait's arm. "Forgive me, my lady. By my estimation, we are perhaps six days from our destination. No more than ten."

"Six or ten days," Cait repeated dully, removing his hand from her arm.

"Fifteen at the most."

"Which is it, priest?" demanded Cait. "Ten? Fifteen? Five hundred?"

"It is difficult to say, my lady. So much depends on the weather. The mountain trails can be treacherous this time of year."

"Aghh!" Cait cried in frustration, and fled the conversation.

Rognvald caught up with her as she stormed from the camp. "Is something wrong, my lady?"

"No," she snapped, charging through the underbrush into the woods. "Nothing what so ever." She spat each word as if it were a pellet of venom. "All is happening in God's good time," she said, adopting the mincing tone of a dissembling cleric. "Apparently!" She shoved aside a low-hanging pine bough and let it fly.

The knight walked along beside her a few paces. "We could remain in camp tomorrow if you like," he suggested, "and move on when the weather improves."

"Why must you always take his side?"

"His side? God's side?"

"No—*him*!" She jerked her head in the direction of the monk who was now talking blithely to a warmly receptive Alethea. "The idiot priest!"

"I take no one's side without due cause and consideration," the Norseman told her firmly.

She glared at him, and surged on ahead. Rognvald started after her again. "Leave me alone!" she said, turning on him. "A woman needs a little privacy now and then—have you ever considered that?"

Rognvald begged her pardon and retreated. She went on until she came to a thick bank of elder bushes. Loosening her girdle and swordbelt, she removed her small-clothes, then hitched up her cloak, mantle, and shift, and was preparing to squat when she heard the shriek. At first she thought it the cry of a hunting eagle, for the sound seemed to have fallen from the low sky overhead. She listened, holding her breath. In a moment, it came again.

"Thea!"

Hurrying, she rearranged her clothes once more, and ran back along the track. She had wandered further than she knew. It took longer than she expected to reach the camp and as she drew nearer she heard men shouting and the clash of arms—the unmistakable sounds of battle. The camp was under attack.

TWENTY-THREE

Cait flew back through the woods. As she neared the fighting, she crouched low, and hid behind a tree. The half-finished camp was swarming with dark men in dark brown cloaks. *Moors*, she thought, counting them quickly. There were eight—and all were mounted. Two or three of the bandits held spears; the rest wielded swords and they were swooping among the knights who were struggling to fend off the marauders.

Occupied with setting up camp for the night, none of the defenders had been wearing armor when the attack began. As a result, they were only lightly armed. Most had, she saw, been able to lay hand to a sword, but none had shields, and only Rognvald had a horse.

The clash of weapons was fierce, and the shouts of the men to one another, and to their assailants, deafening; the commotion filled the clearing with a dreadful, disorienting clamor.

Above the tumult, there came another ear-shattering shriek and Cait looked to the partially erected tent. Alethea was kneeling at the tent opening, hands to her face, terrified. Dag stood before her, tent pole in hand, defending her from two swarthy assailants. Yngvar and Svein were running to join him. Just as they reached the tent, however, two mounted bandits caught them and they were forced to break off their assault to defend themselves.

The horses were picketed nearby. None had saddles, but Cait had ridden bareback from childhood. Darting to the line, she untied the nearest mount, swung herself up on to its back, drew her sword, and raced for the tent. Her attack was cut short, however, when a black-bearded Moor suddenly appeared before her and, with one swipe of his sword, knocked her weapon from her hand.

The slender blade went spinning to the ground, and the bandit, seeing that she was unarmed, reached for the bridle of her horse. Cait slashed the reins across his face, catching him on the side of the head as he leaned forward. He drew back with a curse between his teeth, and jabbed at her with the sword. She dodged aside easily, and the bandit lunged forward, snagging the bridle strap of her mount. She pulled back hard on the reins, attempting to make her horse rear, but the bandit clung on, keeping the animal's head down.

The wild-eyed brute swung around beside her, thrusting the sword at her and shouting in Arabic as he made to lead her horse away, taking her with him. Throwing aside the reins, she slid lightly off the back of the horse, landed on her feet, and started for the tent once more.

She had run but a half-dozen steps when she felt the ground tremble beneath her feet, the same instant a jarring thud between her shoulderblades lifted her off the ground. She squirmed in the air as the bandit tried to haul her onto his horse. Swinging wildly, she struck out at her attacker with her fists, striking him in the ribs. She swung again and her knuckles grazed something sharp. Twisting in her assailant's grasp, she reached for the place once more and her fingers closed on the hilt of a dagger.

The knife was out of the sheath before the Moor knew what had happened. Squeezing the hilt, she raised her arm and plunged the blade down into the meaty part of the bandit's thigh. With an astonished cry of pain and rage, her would-be captor hurled her to the ground and the knife went spinning from her grasp. She landed hard on her side, forcing the breath from her lungs.

Gasping, her chest aching, unable to breathe, she drew up her knees and cradled her head in her arms to prevent the horse's hooves from dashing out her brains. A loud whirring filled her ears, and she felt herself slipping away—as if sucked down into a dark, spinning maelstrom beneath violent waves. The whirring sound ended in a sudden crash and she felt something heavy fall upon her.

Cait could not move; the upper half of her body was trapped beneath a dense weight and when she turned her head to look, she saw the bearded Moor's sweaty face leering back at her. She felt a rush of warmth flood across her chest and stomach and looked down to see the bandit's body lying across her own, blood and bile spilling from a gash that split his torso from side to side below the ribs.

She struggled to push free of the dead weight, but it held her to the ground. A veil of darkness descended across her vision and the clash of battle grew fainter—as if the fight was swiftly receding with the onrush of night. And then the crushing burden suddenly lifted from her and she was free. Air rushed into her lungs and her vision cleared, revealing Rognvald's worried face hovering above her.

Gathering her in his arms, he raised her up. "I can walk," she gasped, gulping in air. "I am not hurt."

"This way," he said, placing her back on her feet. Holding tight to her hand, he pulled her quickly to the edge of the clearing. "Get down," he said, indicating a hollow place formed by a tree growing between two big rocks. Crouching low, she leaned back into the hollow, and with a quick chop of his sword Rognvald lopped a branch from the tree and put it over her, shielding her from view. "Stay here," he said, dashing away again.

As soon as he had gone, Cait bent back the branches so she could see. Across the clearing, the attack appeared to be intensifying. Where before she had counted eight, there were now at least twelve, possibly more—with all of them constantly circling and swirling they were difficult to reckon. Never attacking straight on, they struck glancing blows, darting in and disappearing—only to reappear again a moment later, attacking from a different quarter.

The knights were making a valiant attempt to form a defensive circle, but their numbers were too few and the need to counter the raiders' incessant darting sorties kept them off balance and unable to close the gaps in their ranks.

Rognvald swiftly crossed the clearing, dodging two bandits as he ran to join his men. Under their lord's command, they soon succeeded in closing the circle and, but a few moments later, two of the Spanish knights had gained their horses. Svein and Yngvar soon joined their comrades in the saddle, and the next whirling attack was met by four knights on chargers. They cut down two raiders, and unhorsed a third before the Moors broke off to reform the assault.

When the next onslaught came, there were five mounted knights to repel it, which they did with quick and decisive prowess, driving into the center of the bandit attack, unhorsing the foremost Moor and scattering the rest. The unseated raider fell backward over the rump of his horse and landed awkwardly, his arm bent back under his body. He lay squirming on the ground, clutching his shoulder and howling. Svein dispatched him with a short, sharp chop to the base of the skull and he lay still.

The bandits were no match for mounted knights, and knew it. From her stony nook, Cait watched as four or five spear-wielding Moors made one last half-hearted feint, allowing their fellows to gather up the plunder they had succeeded in liberating from the wagon, and then suddenly all of them were fleeing back into the surrounding forest.

As soon as the last of them disappeared, Cait sprang from her protecting hollow and ran to rejoin the others. The two Spanish knights were for giving chase, but Rognvald called them back and ordered them to stand guard lest the bandits return. Upon reaching the center of the clearing, Cait stopped and made a quick assessment of the damage. Three of the Moorish raiders had been killed, but none of the knights involved in the affray seemed to have been wounded or injured.

She breathed a sigh of relief as she looked around. The bandits had made off with some of the provisions—a bag or two of meal, a side of smoked pork, and a few smaller items—but nothing of any real consequence that she could see. Rognvald wheeled his horse and rode to where she was standing. "Lady Caitríona," he said, sliding from the saddle. "Are you hurt?"

"My ribs ache, but I am well otherwise." She turned from the plundered wagon, and looked toward the tent, suddenly remembering what she had been about when the bandit diverted her attention. "God help us, no!" she shouted, running for the tent. "Where is Alethea?"

TWENTY-FOUR

Dag lay face down on the ground before the collapsed tent, a small dark patch of blood pooling beneath his cheek. The tent pole with which he had tried to defend himself and Alethea lay broken beside him. Cait reached him first, and even as she took in the sight, her eyes quickly scoured the surrounding area for her sister. Seeing that the young woman's body was not lying battered and bloody nearby, Cait knelt beside the fallen knight. Fearing he was dead, she put a hand to his cheek. The flesh was cold and damp.

She heard Rognvald shout an order to the others to remain mounted and on guard for another attack, and then he hastened to her side. "I am sorry," began Cait as the knight handed her his sword and bent over the body of his liegeman. "I think he is—"

With expert quickness, Rognvald searched the body for wounds. Finding none, he took Dag by the shoulders and rolled him onto his back. It was then Cait saw the ugly gash over his left eye. The blood had come from this cut, and from the man's broken nose. Bending close, Rognvald placed his ear next to the man's mouth, listened for a moment, and then sat back on his heels. "He lives."

"Alethea is not here," she said. "Perhaps she has run into the forest." She made to rise, but Rognvald put his hand on her shoulder and held her down.

"Stay with Dag," he said, taking back his sword. "I will search for her." Calling Svein and the two mounted Spanish knights to accompany him, he made a swift search of the perimeter. In a few moments, Cait could hear them shouting for Alethea as they made a circuit of the surrounding woodland. While they searched, Cait occupied her-

204

self with washing the unconscious knight's wound and preparing a bandage for him. She bade Yngvar bring water and then sent him to fetch some dry moss, which she formed into a thick pad, binding it to the wound with a strip of linen torn from the hem of one of her mantles.

As she worked, she kept looking to the forest half-expecting to see her sister straggling back to camp from her hiding-place. *Where have you been?* she would demand. *We have been calling for you! Could you not hear?* Alethea, shaken but unharmed, would complain about her sister's lack of pity for her particular hardship, and all would be well once more.

In the end, however, it was not Alethea she saw, but Rognvald and Svein, hurrying from the wood, their faces tight with dismay. "Tell me you did not find her," said Cait, bracing herself for the worst.

"Lady, we did not," Rognvald replied. "The Spanish knights—the four who were gathering firewood. They were set upon by the bandits and killed before they could raise the alarm and warn us."

"All four—dead?" Despite what the knight was telling her, she only felt relieved that her sister was not among them.

"Their kinsmen are with them," Rognvald said.

"We saw no sign of the young lady," Svein added quickly. "There is hope still."

"Better than for the priest," said Yngvar, joining them.

"Matthias—why? Where is he?" She stood up and looked around.

"He has been killed, my lady." Yngvar pointed toward the plundered wagon. "His body is there."

To all appearances, the good brother had simply fallen asleep at his prayers. Hands still clasped, he lay on his side, his robe damp at the knees from kneeling on the wet ground. The killing blow had caught him on the back of the neck, almost severing his head. Yet his expression was not one of terror or anguish, but intense calm—as if, in the fervency of his prayer, he had been unaware of the tumult around him.

"I do not think he felt any pain, poor fellow," observed Svein.

"Poor fellow," Yngvar retorted. "I hope I might go in such a way. He was close to God, this one."

Svein nodded thoughtfully. "He is closer now."

Rognvald glanced at the lowering sky. "It will be dark soon. We must hurry if we are to raise the trail."

At first Cait did not understand the implication of his words. "Raise the trail," she objected. "But Alethea would not just run away."

"The bandits' trail," Rognvald corrected.

Until the knight uttered those words, the possibility that her sister had been taken had simply not occurred to her; it did so now—and with all the terrible consequence of certainty.

Instantly, her mind filled with the vile and awful defilements customarily suffered by abducted women. She stood. "We must find her. Where is my horse?"

"I will take Yngvar and the others. Svein will stay here with you."

"I am going," she insisted. "Get me a horse."

Rognvald placed his hand firmly on her shoulder. "We are armed and you are not. It would be better for you to stay and look after Dag."

"Let Svein look after him," she said, shaking off his hand. "I am going." Retrieving her sword, she strode to Svein's horse, gathered the hem of her mantle, put her foot to the stirrup and swung into the saddle. "Well? Are you coming or not?"

Rognvald muttered an oath beneath his breath and moved quickly to his mount. He wheeled his horse and started off in the direction the marauding Moors had fled. "Stay in sight of me," he said to Cait as he passed her.

At first they had no difficulty seeing exactly where the raiders had gone. They followed clear hoofprints in the rain-softened earth, making good speed through the wood. Indeed, their progress was so swift and purposeful, Cait allowed herself to imagine they would quickly catch sight of the fleeing raiders.

Too soon, however, the little light which shone through the thick overcast sky dissolved into a dismal damp gloom. And then, as darkness settled about them, the ground began to rise to meet the rocky hills; they climbed to the top of a steep, thicket-covered slope, and there the trail of hoofmarks divided. The last dregs of daylight revealed a sudden turning away from the path and into the rough, trackless hills. Here, Rognvald called a halt.

"Mark the place," he called to Yngvar. "We will resume the search in the morning."

"You would turn back now?" demanded Cait. "They must be but a short way ahead of us. We can catch them yet."

"We cannot catch them if we cannot see them," Rognvald replied.

"As it stands, we will be fortunate to find our way back to camp in the dark."

"Go back, then," Cait growled angrily. "You can all go back. *I* will go on alone. My sister is taken captive, and I will not abandon her."

"We will find Alethea," declared Rognvald, his words terse and his voice low. "But we cannot search in the darkness, and *I* will not risk all our lives in foolish pursuit."

With that, he turned and started back the way they had come. Cait shouted at him to come back, but he ignored her; Yngvar fell in behind his lord; the two Spanish knights hesitated, then followed, leaving Cait to herself.

In defiance, she urged her horse forward along the trail, but stopped again after only a few dozen paces. It was hopeless. She could no longer see the ground, much less the hoofprints; trees, shadows, hills and sky were merging into an impenetrable inky gloom—made all the darker for the lack of moon or stars to light the way.

She reined to a halt, and sat staring into the deepening murk and listening for any sound that would tell her Alethea was near. She heard only the wind fingering the tops of the tall pines as it rushed down from the cold mountain heights. When she realized she could no longer hear the knights behind her, she at last gave in. "God be with you, Thea," she murmured, and then turned around to make her way back.

Finding the trail was far more difficult than she had imagined. If not for the fact that she had just passed that way—and that Yngvar was waiting for her further on—she knew she would have spent a cold night alone in the wood. It galled her to admit that Rognvald was right, but she accepted Yngvar's silent lead and followed on.

By the time they reached the camp, a small fire was burning brightly in the center of the clearing. The bodies of the dead bandits had been removed, and Dag was sitting beside the fire, holding his bandaged head in his hands. He stood shakily as the others came into the camp.

"Where is Svein?" asked Rognvald. Dag replied that he was in the wood, digging graves.

"Paulo . . . Rodrigo," Rognvald said, turning to the Spanish knights as they dismounted, "go help Svein. We will come shortly and bring the priest for burial."

Cait heard the names and realized she did not know the Spanish knights who served her. Her cheeks burned with shame at the thought. Four of them had given their lives in her service and she did not even know their names.

In that moment, the enormity of her blind, grasping, arrogant, vengeful ambition came dreadfully, painfully clear to her. She moved to the fire, collapsed beside it, and sat staring in hollow despair. Tonight, her all-consuming hunger for revenge had cost the lives of five good men, and the abduction of her sister. *And this was just the beginning*, she thought. *Before it was over, how many more would pay?*

She heard Rognvald say, "Come, we will join them." He instructed Yngvar to wrap the body of Matthias in his robes, and then he was standing over her. "I said we would join them at the grave site."

Miserable with guilt and the heart-breaking weight of the disaster, she found she could neither lift her head nor answer. She merely nodded her acquiescence.

He stood for a moment looking down on her; she could feel his eyes, and she imagined his expression of scornful reproach. And then he was beside her, his mouth close to her ear. "Hear me, my lady," he said, speaking softly, but earnestly. "Nobility's worth is not proved by the brilliance of its glory, but by the light it lends to others in the dark night of need." Then he took her hand and stood, raising her to her feet. "Come, it is time to say farewell to our friends."

Taking Dag by the arm, she followed Rognvald and Yngvar as they carried the body of the priest a short distance into the wood where, by the light of a fire of pine branches, Svein and the two Spanish knights, Paulo and Rodrigo, were completing a wide trench between two large trees. Using their swords they had cut into the soft turf, hacking through the roots, and scooping out the earth with their hands. The four dead knights lay in a neat row to one side, bundled in their cloaks, arms crossed upon their chests. Brother Matthias was carefully laid beside them, and as Cait and Dag took their places beside the single large grave, Rognvald and the others began moving the corpses to their final resting-place.

The monk was interred first, and then the knights, two at either hand. The symmetry seemed to satisfy some desire on the part of the Spanish knights to see their swordbrothers accompanied on their eternal journey side by side with a priest. Once they had been arranged, their faces were covered by the hoods of their cloaks and loose dirt was pushed over the bodies.

Cait stood and watched in the gently flickering light as the knights packed and smoothed the mounded earth with their hands. Then one of the Spaniards took up a wooden cross he had made from a forked branch and crosspiece lashed together with a leather strap. The crude cross was set in the top of the mound and anchored with a few small stones.

They stood for a long moment in silence, contemplating the grave, and then, taking a burning branch from the fire, Rognvald held it over the mound. "In elder times," he said, "a fallen warrior would be sent on his journey to the otherworld with fire. Tonight we will honor this ancient custom, and leave our brothers and companions with a farewell flame to light their way through the dark valley of death to the City of Light."

With that, he planted the burning branch in the grave mound to one side of the cross. He straightened and stepped back. "May they enter the Great King's presence with thanksgiving. May they join the glad company of Heaven and find everlasting joy in the service of the Lord of Hosts."

Svein took up a burning branch and likewise planted it in the mounded soil. "Farewell, my friends. Though we must leave you in this strange place, we leave a flame to light your path. Go home to God."

Next, Paulo took up a brand. He stuck it in the mound, saying, "Thadeus, Ricardo, Hernando, Emari, Brother Matthias—you were my friends in life. Death has taken you away, but you will live in my memory, and in the deeds I shall do in your names. Farewell."

At last, thought Cait sadly, *I have learned all their names, and now it is too late.*

The other Spaniard removed a branch from the fire and, holding it above the mound, said: "Today I lost the friends of my youth. Tonight, I mourn the loss. Tomorrow, I will avenge them. From this moment, the blade at my side is dedicated to you, my friends, and I pray to Almighty God that it will deal justice to the cowards who cut short your lives." He plunged the burning brand into the mound. "I, Rodrigo Bilar, make this vow."

Cait knew the sentiment only too well, and shrank from the recognition. *Oh, Rodrigo,* she thought, *you do not know what you are saying.*

Yngvar and Dag each bade their dead friends a heartfelt, if simple, farewell and planted their torches. Then it was Cait's turn. Plucking a branch from the fire, she stepped to the graveside and stared at the great oblong bulge of earth. What was there to say? She did not know these men; anything she said would be a triviality, an empty gesture that would mock their sacrifice.

So, without a word, she added her torch to the circle of flame around the wooden cross. The party stood for a moment in silence, listening to the wind sighing through the unseen treetops. Then Rognvald led them back to the ruined camp where, after they had finished putting up the tent for Cait, he addressed them, saying, "Get what sleep you can. We resume the search tomorrow at dawn."

Yngvar prepared a warm gruel of pease porridge with bacon, but Cait was too tired and numb with sorrow to eat. Instead, she went into the tent and sank down onto the thin pallet of pine boughs that served for a bed. She pulled Alethea's cloak around her and lay as still as she could—as if by remaining motionless, she might calm the ceaseless whirling of her thoughts. And though she closed her eyes, she kept seeing the Moorish bandits circling and circling like ravening wolves. She heard again the dull thunder of the horses' hooves, and the desperate shouting of the knights as they strove to fend off the attack.

And, somewhere, above the clamor of battle, she heard Alethea's screams. Although she had not been aware of it at the time, she must have heard her sister's cries for help as she was carried off. She heard something else, too: a man's voice, frantically shouting for help. The hopelessness of the cry brought her bolt upright in her bed with a gasp.

"Abu!"

TWENTY-FIVE

The sound of the knights saddling the horses and preparing to strike camp brought Cait from an unquiet sleep. Her eyes felt like raw wounds, and her mouth tasted of smoke and ashes. She dragged herself onto her knees and pulled back the tent flap. The sky was dark still, but a thin line of pale red light was showing through the trees to the east. She rose and shuffled out of the tent, and felt the cold sting of the air on her face. Last night's wind had brought cold weather to the mountains; there was frost on the ground.

On stiff, unfeeling legs, she moved to where Rognvald was throwing a saddle pad over the back of a horse. He greeted her somberly, and said, "We will leave as soon as the horses are saddled. I think it best to take everything with us. I do not expect we will come back here again."

"The wagon will slow us down, will it not?"

"Dag is not yet well enough to sit on a horse. He can drive the wagon and look after the pack animals. We will mark the trail for him and tell him where to stop and wait. It will slow us, yes, but it cannot be helped."

"Abu is missing, too," she told him, her voice taking on a confessional quality.

He finished smoothing the pad and then glanced at her. "Yes," he said. "I know." He bent down, lifted the saddle which was laying on the ground beside him, and hefted it into place. "I did not think you would remember."

Another time and the reprimand would have rankled and irritated; now, however, she merely swallowed glumly. "You did not find his body when you were searching the wood," she said after a moment, "so perhaps we may yet find him. He cannot have gone far."

"He has a horse," Rognvald told her.

"How do you know?"

"There were three dead Moors, and only two horses."

"You think he took it?" Cait was baffled by this unexpected turn. "Then we shall have to divide our forces and search for them both—is that what you're thinking?"

"I am thinking," replied Rognvald, stooping to gather the cinch strap dangling beneath the horse's belly, "that where we find Alethea, there we will also find Abu."

"He followed her," Cait murmured. "Of course." She was slow to pick up the thread of Rognvald's thought, but now she had it and felt her blood warm once more to the chase.

Stepping close, she put her hand on Rognvald's arm. "I am sorry for my shameful behavior; it was not becoming a lady of rank. I allowed my anxiety over my sister's disappearance to cloud my judgment—a fact which I deeply regret."

Rognvald bent down to fasten the strap.

"I have offered my apology," Cait said, her voice growing tight. "Did you hear what I said?"

"I heard."

"Do you not accept it?"

"Lady, it is not for me to accept or reject. Am I a priest now, waiting at your beck and call to shrive you?"

Stung by his reproach, she removed her hand from his arm. "Our priest is dead."

"Yes," agreed the tall knight. "So, I think you will have to suffer your pangs of conscience as best you can."

"I do suffer them, sir. And I was taught the virtue of repentance. Obviously, *you* were not."

"See here, we all do things in the heat of battle we later regret. War *is* regret." He gave a sharp tug, pulling the cinch strap tight. "Do not look to me to soothe away your remorse with kind words and kisses."

"Oh, never you fear, my lord," she spat. "Though you die in your bed an ill-tempered old man, you will not hear me apologize again."

She turned on her heel and stormed away. Thus, the unhappy day began.

As soon as the tent was packed away and the wagon loaded and secured, the much-diminished party moved on. They accompanied Dag and the wagon a short way along the track, and arranged a place to meet later in the day before turning aside to take up the trail they had abandoned the previous evening.

The ground was more rough and rocky than Cait remembered—or perhaps it was the coating of frost which made every stone, leaf, branch and twig stand out in sharp relief. The path was much steeper, too, and as they climbed higher and ever higher, the wind began to grow stronger and more raw, whipping the horses' manes and tails.

The tracks of the fleeing Moors led up over the curving spine of a bare rock ridge; with sour disappointment growing in her breast, Cait began to suspect that the bandits had disappeared into the mountains beyond—a suspicion quickly confirmed when the party scrambled up an incline of scree and abruptly found themselves gazing down into a rocky defile through which snaked a gray stream. And across the divide—the mountains. Cait looked at the daunting slopes covered in a thick tangle of scrub-oak, hazel, and small, stunted pines, and her heart sank.

She turned in the saddle and looked down the way they had come. Far below, she could see the narrow trail as it wound along the lower shoulders of the foothills. She did not see the wagon, but reckoned it was down there somewhere.

"We will rest here a moment," called Rognvald. "Svein and I will ride to the bend—" he pointed along the top of the ridge, "and see if we can find a way ahead."

They rode off and the others dismounted to stand close to their mounts for warmth. Cait pulled her cloak more tightly around her to keep the wind out and stood staring bleakly at the soaring slopes beyond the canyon. The three knights stood talking together, and Cait decided that it was time she made herself better acquainted with those remaining in her service.

The men stopped talking as she joined them, and turned expectantly. "Please," she said, "do not stop on my account. I did not mean to interrupt."

"My lady," said Yngvar, "we were just remarking how winter comes early to the mountains."

"It seems winter has begun," Cait agreed, adding, "Alethea does not even have a cloak."

The men exchanged uneasy glances. "Is it like this in your country?" the one called Rodrigo asked, indicating the mountains.

"There are mountains in Scotland," Cait told him. "But only low hills where my family lives. Our lands are near the sea, and winters are often harsh."

"My family owns land near Bilbao—also near the sea," the knight told her. "That means we share the same sea, you and I." He smiled, and Cait realized he was trying to cheer her.

"I am sorry for the death of your friends," she said. "Thadeus, Ricardo, Hernando, and Emari." The names she knew, but had no idea which name belonged to which knight. "If not for me, they would still be alive."

The knight lowered his head; Cait saw him swallow down his grief. "I will miss them, it is true," he replied evenly. "But they were men of valor, and freely sworn. They would not hold you to blame, nor do I."

"Even so, they did not deserve to die like that," said the one called Paulo. "It is a disgrace for a knight to die without a sword in his hand."

"Only the worst coward would cut down a man who cannot defend himself," Yngvar said. "A man of honor would never do such a low thing."

A great sadness swept over Cait as she listened to the men talk. She pulled the heavy wool cloak more tightly around her throat and looked toward the mountains. The higher peaks were lost in mist which appeared to be thickening; tendrils of fog oozed down the slopes, like sinuous fingers, slowly reaching and stretching, searching out the low places, filling them, and flowing silently on. The wind blew in fitful gusts, whistling over the bare rocks of the ridge, and she could smell snow in the air.

"Oh, Alethea," she murmured to herself, "I am so sorry." She closed her eyes and prayed God to send his angels to protect the young woman from the killing cold, no less than from the hateful abuse of her heathen captors.

A short while later, they heard the sound of horses and looked to see Rognvald and Svein returning. As they dismounted, the others gathered around to hear their report. "There is a marker at the edge of the stream down there," Rognvald told them. "That is where they crossed."

"A marker?" said Cait.

"A heap of stones, my lady," replied Svein.

"But who would—" she began, and then the answer came to her. "Abu?"

Svein nodded. "We think he is marking out the way for us."

"Show me," said Cait, swinging back into the saddle.

"It is not far," said Rognvald. "But we have a decision to make."

Something in his tone gave her to know that he was talking about her. "Yes?"

"The day is growing foul. I think a storm is coming."

"We will find what shelter we can along the way. I am not giving up the search because of a little wind and rain."

"I am not suggesting we give up the search," Rognvald replied, his voice growing tight with exasperation. "But there is no need for all of us to grow wet and miserable with it. You could go back down and wait with Dag at the wagon. By the time you join him, he will have reached the waiting place and will have a fire going."

"*You* can sit and warm yourself by the fire," Cait told him. "I am going to find my sister."

"Then we move on." Rognvald motioned to the others to mount their horses, and the party continued.

Halfway down the slope, the rain started. It was not long before Cait felt the cold wet begin to seep into her cloak. Before they reached the valley floor she was chilled to the bone and wishing she had not dismissed Rognvald's offer so hastily. But now, having rejected the suggestion, she was determined not to allow him the satisfaction of proving her wrong. So she put all thoughts of warmth and comfort behind her and pulled the hood of her damp cloak lower over her head to keep the rain out of her face.

The valley was shallow and did little to slow the wind gusting down from the mountains. They came to the marker—a pile of stones at the edge of the stream; on the opposite side was another—this one in the rough shape of an arrowhead pointing upstream. They rode in the direction indicated by the marker, following along the gray stream as it wound its way around the large rocks and boulders which had fallen from the slopes above. After a while the rain turned to sleet, and they stopped in the shelter of some young pines to eat a little dried meat, but the trees offered so little protection from the stinging, wind-driven pellets of ice that they quickly decided to take to their saddles again before the horses grew too cold, and their sweaty coats began to freeze.

As the day wore on, Cait's hopes of quickly rescuing Alethea began to dwindle; they were briefly revived when another marker was found and, a short distance beyond it, the remains of a small campfire in a bend in the valley where the stream pooled. The Moors had stopped there—to water the horses and prepare a meal, no doubt—but aside from a small heap of soggy ashes and unburnt ends of branches, there was nothing to see.

Rognvald examined the tracks leading from the campsite, and concluded that the bandits no longer feared pursuit.

"How do you know?" wondered Cait. One set of water-filled hoof-prints looked very like another, and these were no different from any she had seen so far.

"The gait of the horses tells the tale," replied Rodrigo. "The riders are in no great hurry. See here," he pointed to a series of moon-shaped tracks pressed deep in the mud, "see how the leading edge of each hoof-print is scuffed—"

"I see." Cait looked more closely. "They look smudged."

"The horses are tired," the Spanish knight told her. "They are ambling—dragging their feet, yes?" He made a slow, flicking motion with his hand. "That means the riders are no longer pushing them."

"It is good for us," said Svein. "They do not know we are chasing them."

"With luck," said Rodrigo, "we may soon catch sight of them up ahead." He indicated the ridge wall which formed the end of the valley. "We will be able to see into the next valley from up there."

The trail led around the edge of the pool; the tracks in the rain-sodden bank were now easy to follow, and Cait began to feel they were making real progress at last. However, the ridge was further away than it first appeared, and the rise far more steep. By the time they reached the bottom of the ridgewall, daylight had begun to fade. Although the sleet had stopped, the wind was growing more fierce. Rognvald halted the party and, with a glance at the sky, said, "We are losing the light. It is time to turn back."

The words struck Cait like a blow. Her first reaction was to defy him, to challenge his judgment, to contradict his command. In her heart she knew he was right, however, and besides, she was cold and hungry, and no longer had it in her to fight futile battles with either men or the elements. Still, for Alethea's sake, she asked, "Might we go just a little further?"

"It is no use. Even if we gain the top, we will not be able to see anything in the dark. We must go back now if we are to meet Dag before nightfall."

That was the end of it. As before, they marked the place so they could find it the next day and turning to the high hills to the west of the pool, rode away. The sky had grown dark by the time they gained the wagon trail; the deep-rutted track was treacherous in the dark, so they were forced to dismount and cross the undulating hills on foot—which meant a cold slog along rocky, water-filled furrows.

They saw the glint of Dag's fire from a hilltop long before they reached the place. Cait watched the glimmering of flame as it grew slowly larger, step by step. Her fingers, stiff on the reins of her horse, were numb and her toes stung with the cold; she imagined stretching her feet before a blazing fire, clutching a steaming bowl of porridge between her hands, and feeling the blessed heat warm her frozen bones.

This reverie proved so pleasant, she imagined sleeping in a dry bed heaped with furs in a room warmed with burning braziers, and the delicious feeling of fur against her skin—then realized with a start that she was imagining her chamber at home in Caithness. How many times, she wondered, had she slept in that room in just that way?

Dag had the wagon unhitched and a small store of firewood collected by the time they reached the camp. Despite his throbbing head, he had spent the short span between midday and dusk doing what he could to set up the camp, and they were grateful for it. Indeed, the prospect of warming themselves by the fire so cheered the knights that, with wild whoops and ecstatic cries, they raced down the last slope to the picket line Dag had strung between the trees beside the trail; they hurried through unsaddling and grooming the horses—rubbing them down with handfuls of dry straw before watering them and tying on the feedbags. That chore finished, they hastened to thaw their freezing hands and feet before the flames.

After they had warmed themselves awhile, Rognvald said, "We will need more firewood tonight. See what you can find."

While the others moved off in search of more wood, Cait, Dag, and Rognvald set about making a supper of boiled salt pork with beans and hard bread. It was ready by the time the knights returned, and the childlike abandon with which they gave themselves to their food made Cait smile. "They are just overgrown boys," she observed as she and Rognvald followed them to the bright circle of warmth and light.

"It is good they should enjoy a dry night out of the wind and rain," the knight replied. "It will be the last we see for a while."

Cait glanced at him for an explanation.

"Tomorrow we must abandon the wagon," he told her. "I had hoped we would be able to give Dag another day or two longer to recover, but the Moors are fleeing into the mountains. If we are to have any hope of catching them, we cannot return to the wagon each night."

"Do you think it will be very many nights?"

"In truth, I hoped we would get sight of them today, and the matter would have been decided." He paused, and then as if thinking aloud, said, "We shall take with us as much food and fodder as we can carry, but the tents, poles, and irons and all the rest will have to stay behind." His expression became apologetic, and Cait realized he meant the chests of extra clothes and personal belongings.

"If that is how it must be," she replied, steeling herself for the privation ahead, "so be it. We *will* catch them. We *will* get Thea back."

"Never doubt it."

TWENTY-SIX

"I am Carlo de la Coruña, magistrate and governor of this fine and prosperous town," said the man. He made a flourish in the air with his hand, removed his fine red cap and bowed deeply. "On behalf of the worthy citizens of Palencia, I welcome you and your excellent company, and may I wish you a most enjoyable stay."

The knight took one look at the chubby, round-shouldered fellow in his peculiar hat, and decided that he was an absurdity likely to cause problems if not strenuously avoided. "Good day to you, magistrate," he replied stiffly. "As you can see, we are in need of food and lodging. I will thank you to arrange it."

The magistrate puffed out his cheeks. "Well . . ." he began to protest, but thought better of it, and said, "Of course, my lord, if that is what you wish. It will be my pleasure." Turning, he summoned his deputy to his side. "Grieco! Where are you? Come here, Grieco. I want you to take word to Master Hernando at the inn. Tell him I am sending very important guests to stay with him. Tell him—" Breaking off, he turned once more to the newcomers and said, "If you please, my lord, may I know who I have the pleasure of welcoming?"

"I am Renaud de Bracincaux, Master and Grand Commander of the Knights Templar of Jerusalem," he replied. "And this," he indicated the fair-haired, thin-faced man on horseback beside him, "is my companion Baron Félix d'Anjou. Also with us is Bertrano, Archbishop of Santiago de Compostela; unfortunately, friend Bertrano is indisposed and cannot speak to you now. I want rooms for three. The rest of my men will lodge at the monastery." Turning his arid gaze to the soggy, wind-blown street, he shivered in the autumn chill. "You *do* have a monastery in this . . ." he hesitated, "this place, do you not? And an inn?"

"But of course, my lord," answered Governor Carlo proudly. "We have a very fine monastery. It has long been renowned for—"

"Good," said de Bracineaux decisively. "You can show us where to find it." He called Gislebert to attend them. "The magistrate will lead you to the monastery. Lodge the men and then come to us at the inn."

Turning back to Carlo, the Templar said, "Come now, governor, my men have ridden far today and are in want of a hot meal and beds. Be quick about it, and you will find it worth your while."

Governor Carlo stared in astonished indignation. Who did these men think they were to order him about so? Even the king was more gracious to his subjects than these arrogant saddle-polishers. Well, if they wanted him to lead them to the monastery he would do it. But it would be the last service he would perform for them. After that, they would pay for what they received. Moreover, as they imagined themselves emperors of vast domain, they would pay royally. The thought suffused his face with a glow of magisterial satisfaction. Carlo smiled, bowed, and led the heavy footed Gislebert away.

"Simpletons," muttered the Templar, "all of them—complete and utter simpletons."

"Come now, de Bracineaux. That is overharsh," said d'Anjou. "It is a substantial enough town and we have seen far worse in recent days. I think we may well find some amusement here."

"We will not have time to amuse ourselves," de Bracineaux growled. "The moment we find this priest Matthias, we will be on our way."

"Have a heart, de Bracineaux," sniffed the baron diffidently. "We have spent the last three days slopping through mud up to our fetlocks, and I demand a few decent nights' sleep in a bed that does not float."

"We shall see," grunted the Templar commander. "First we find the priest."

"The miserable pisspot of a priest can wait," corrected d'Anjou placidly. "First we find the *inn*."

De Bracineaux allowed himself to be persuaded. He, too, was sick of the damp and filth, and the prospect of a hot meal, dry clothes, and a jug of mulled wine melted his resolve. "Very well. Two nights," he agreed. "Have one of the men bring up the wagon."

They proceeded down the crooked main street of the town to the inn where young Grieco was waiting with the innkeeper, a balding man in a big shirt with baggy sleeves and a greasy linen cloth tied around the bulge in his middle. "Welcome! Welcome, my friends!" he said, running forward to take the reins of the commander's horse. "Please, come in. Eat, drink, and take your ease." Looking past the two riders to the wagon, he said, "I see you have a lady with you. Let me assure you she will be most comfortable. I will have my wife prepare a special bath for her."

"Take no trouble," the Templar told him curtly. "It is not a woman."

As he spoke, the wagon rolled creaking to a halt behind them; the driver climbed down and went to the back where he removed the board and allowed the bellicose passenger to emerge.

"*Dios mío!*" gasped the innkeeper, taking in the imposing bulk swathed in heavy black robes. "It is the lord archbishop!" Turning on the young man beside him, he cried, "Grieco, you fool! Why did you not tell me the archbishop was with them?"

With that, he darted forward and ran to bow before the august cleric. "My lord archbishop! You honor us with your presence. Please, come in. You shall have the best room I can offer."

Archbishop Bertrano gave the man a sour smile. "I would gladly accept your hospitality," he replied, "but I believe the commander will have other plans for me."

At the innkeeper's bewildered expression, d'Anjou put his arm on the archbishop's shoulder and said, "Our cleric is on a special pilgrimage, you see. Nothing but cabbage and cold water for him, and a horsehair robe in the stable."

"The stable!" cried the innkeeper. "But, my lord, I could never allow it. Why, it would ruin me. Please, you must see that—"

"Just give him the room next to mine," said de Bracineaux wearily. "And bring us wine at once. You can stable the horses later."

"Of course, my lord," said the landlord. He hesitated.

"Well?" demanded the Templar.

"I have two rooms, my lord, but they are not next to one another. Unless, you wish to . . ."

"Just put him where I do not have to look at him, or listen to him snore."

"At once, my lord." The innkeeper spun on his heel and hurried inside, followed by Grieco, who caught the door and held it open for the important guests. De Bracineaux pushed the reluctant churchman ahead of him and, once inside, made for the low table before the hearth. D'Anjou came last and paused long enough to take Grieco's arm and pull him close.

"I will be wanting a companion this evening," he told the youth.

"A companion?" wondered Grieco. "I am certain my uncle would be most happy to oblige. I will ask him, if you—"

"The devil take your uncle, boy! I want a woman. The younger the better." He gripped the young man's arm hard. "Understand?"

He left the gaping Grieco at the door and, while the landlord bustled the silently disapproving archbishop to a room at the back of the inn, he joined de Bracineaux at a large table before the fire. He removed his gloves and put them on the table. "God's eyes, but it is good to be dry again," he said; sweeping off his hat, he tossed it onto the floor. "I thought it would never stop raining."

"You are soft, d'Anjou. You would not last three days in the East. You would have perished long before ever setting foot in Jerusalem."

"Then you can have your Holy Land, and all that goes with it," the baron replied airily. "I will stay here and delight the ladies of Iberia."

The anxious innkeeper arrived just then with a large jar and cups which he placed gingerly on the table. "Wine, my lords. It is not mulled, but . . ."

"Pour," said the Templar.

The innkeeper did as he was told, and then backed away as the commander raised his cup to his lips. He took a single sip, swilled it in his mouth and then spat it out. "Agh!" De Bracineaux pitched the contents of his cup into the fire, then threw the cup at the startled landlord. "I said I wanted wine, you dolt. Not this horse piss you serve everyone else. Now get you gone and bring me something drinkable—the best you have."

The innkeeper's mouth worked as he tried to think of a suitable reply. D'Anjou stood, shoved the jar into his hands, spun him around, and sent him staggering back the way he had come. "Look lively, man. My throat feels like old leather."

The baron sat down again and began removing his boots, which he placed by the side of the hearth. He stretched out his feet to the fire. The Templar watched him without interest.

In a moment, the innkeeper came creeping back with another jar which he offered with extreme hesitation. At a glance from the Master, he proceeded to pour, but his hand shook so badly that he missed the edge of the cup and spilled wine on the table, almost splashing d'Anjou. "Clumsy oaf!" snarled the baron, leaping to his feet. He snatched the jar from the cringing innkeeper. "Get out and leave us in peace."

The man scurried away and d'Anjou, returning to his chair, poured a cup of wine which he pushed across the table to de Bracineaux. He watched as the commander sniffed the offering, and then took a swallow. "Passable," said the Templar, whereupon the baron took up a hot poker from the hearth and plunged it into the jar.

"Mulled," d'Anjou said, as the wine sizzled. Tossing aside the poker, he poured himself a cup and settled back into his chair once more, feet spread before the fire.

They drank and let the wine do its work; when de Bracineaux held out his cup for more, the baron filled it and said, "I suppose this priest has a church somewhere close by. Has the archbishop said where it is?"

"The bloated pig's bladder of a priest professes not to know. He is more trouble than he is worth. I am sick of the sight of him."

"Regrets?" inquired the baron.

"Since Santiago he has been worthless," grumbled the Templar. "And he was very little use before that."

"I smell something cooking." The baron lifted his nose and craned his neck around.

"Probably pork," muttered de Bracineaux. "I am heartily sick of pork, too."

"What about some of that beef we saw coming into town?" said d'Anjou, sipping from his cup. "Perhaps we should have Gislebert get us some."

"He has better things to do than cater to your idle whims, d'Anjou."

At that moment, the door opened and Gislebert appeared. "Ah!" said d'Anjou, lifting his cup. "The very man himself. Here now, sergeant, de Bracineaux thinks you have better things to do than serve my trifling fancies. Is that so?"

Gislebert glared, but made no reply. "The men are lodged and the horses stabled." He looked at the wine longingly.

"What news of Matthias? Did the abbot say where the priest might be found?"

The sergeant swallowed. "He is not here. The abbot said he is expected to return to the monastery for the winter, but he has not yet arrived."

"Then we shall go and get him," said the commander. "Where is he?"

"He is building a church on lands near here. It is no great distance—half a day's ride, perhaps, not more."

"Then tomorrow we will ride out and convince this priest to join our happy pilgrimage."

"That should be no great difficulty. His grace the archbishop can simply compel him under threat of excommunication," said d'Anjou, pouring a cup of wine for Gislebert. "Sit down, sergeant. You look faint from thirst."

"Once we have the priest to lead us, we will abandon that puffing windbag at last." De Bracineaux drained his cup and, as the baron refilled it, he shouted for the landlord to bring the food. When the innkeeper appeared, the Templar said, "I have a taste for roast beef."

"I have no beef, my lord," the landlord said, wringing his hands in the cloth at his waist. "My good wife has made a rabbit stew with shallots, wine, and mushrooms. Everyone says it is excellent."

"I want beef, damn you! Beef!"

"But there is none to be had in all the town just now. Perhaps a young bull will be butchered in a day or two, and then I shall certainly get some for you." He spread his hands helplessly. "I have some sausages; and there is fresh pork. If you like, I will have my good wife make for you a fine—"

"Devil take you *and* your good wife!" the Templar raged. "I want beef, and that is what I shall have."

The innkeeper appealed to d'Anjou. "I am sorry, my lord, there is no beef in all of Palencia." His dark eyes implored. "The rabbit stew is very good."

"Bring it," the baron told him.

"At once, my lord." He turned and scurried back to the kitchen. "I will bring bread, too."

"And more wine!"

"At once, sir."

The Master glared at d'Anjou. "Never cross me like that again," he growled.

"What—and do you mean to crucify the man?" replied the baron casually. "For God's sake, de Bracineaux, there is no beef. Carving up our host will avail you nothing." He leaned back in his chair, clutching his cup to his chest and closed his eyes, savoring the warmth of the fire.

The innkeeper brought another jar and a round loaf of brown bread which he placed diffidently on the table and scurried away before drawing the ire of his difficult guests. Gislebert tore the loaf in half once, and then again; he sat chewing his portion and staring absently into the fire. The commander drained his cup and poured another.

The three drank in brooding silence until the innkeeper reappeared, holding the sides of a bubbling iron pot which he placed in the center of the table. A boy with him brought an assortment of wooden bowls, which he left beside d'Anjou's elbow before darting away again. The innkeeper produced four wooden spoons which he cleaned on the greasy scrap of cloth around his waist. Placing a spoon in each of the bowls, he proceeded to ladle out the contents of the cauldron.

"What is that?" growled de Bracineaux, eyeing the fourth bowl balefully.

The landlord hesitated. The ladle wavered uncertainly above the table. "Stew, my lord," he replied, timidly. "For the archbishop."

"You were told he was to have nothing but boiled cabbage and water," the Templar said darkly.

"Of course, my lord, but . . ." he swallowed, glancing anxiously from one to the other, "that is, I thought you were in jest."

"I do not expect you to think," the commander replied menacingly, "I expect you to obey. Pour it back, and get him the cabbage as you were told."

The innkeeper appealed silently to d'Anjou, who softened. "As this is his grace's last night with us," suggested the baron, "why not let him have the stew? Let him join us. He can tell us what he knows about this priest Matthias."

"We have asked him already," de Bracineaux said. "He has told us all he knows—which is little enough."

"Get some wine into him, and he may surprise you and sing like a lark," said d'Anjou. "It is the last chance to find out."

"Very well," said the commander. To Gislebert, he said, "Fetch the disagreeable priest and tell him he can join us if he minds his manners."

The sergeant stuffed a last piece of bread into his mouth, then rose and lumbered off; de Bracineaux regarded his companion with dull petulance. "You *are* an old woman, d'Anjou. Do you know that? You should have been a priest."

The baron sipped his wine. "I lack the mental rigor," he replied placidly. "I am too easily led astray by frivolity and caprice."

The commander stared at him, then laughed, the sound like a short, sharp bark. "God's wounds, d'Anjou." He lifted his cup and drank again, then pulled his bowl before him and started to spoon hot stew into his mouth.

In a moment, Gislebert appeared with the churchman in tow. "Sit down, Bertrano," said de Bracineaux, kicking a chair toward him. "The baron here thinks you should join us for a farewell feast. What do you say to that?"

"I say," he replied, "a shred of common decency still clings to the baron. Perhaps he may be redeemed after all."

"I would not be too certain about that." The commander pushed a bowl of stew across the table. "I want you to tell me about the priest— this Brother Matthias."

"I have already told you all I know," said Bertrano. He bent his head, murmured a prayer, crossed himself, and began to eat.

De Bracineaux reached out and pulled the bowl away again. "First the priest, and then the food."

The archbishop looked up wearily. "I can tell you nothing I have not already said before. The man was unknown to me before I received his letter. He roams about, building churches and preaching to the poor. That is all I know."

"It will be a pleasure to see the back of your disagreeable carcass," said the commander, shoving the bowl of stew toward him once more.

"You are too harsh, de Bracineaux," said the baron affably. "Our friend the archbishop is a very font of wisdom and good will. The road will be a far more lonely and cheerless place when he is gone. We shall miss his merry japes."

"Thanks to you, the building work will have fallen behind. Winter is upon us, and if the roof is not in place much of the work will be ruined."

"Has no one ever told you that it is folly to store up treasures on earth where moth and rust do corrupt?" wondered de Bracineaux, bringing a snort of derisive laughter from Gislebert.

"And is it not written: 'Because it was in your heart to build a temple for My Name, says the Lord, you did well to have this in your heart . . .' and, 'The temple I am going to build will be great, because Our God is greater than all other gods'?"

"And: 'Who,' " retorted the Templar commander, " 'is able to build the temple of God? For heaven is his throne, and the earth his footstool.' " He raised his cup in mock triumph.

"Even Satan can quote scripture," replied the archbishop sourly.

De Bracineaux bristled at the jibe. "Away with you," he growled. "Your self-righteous prattling wearies me."

The archbishop finished his stew, raising the bowl to his lips and draining it in a gulp. Then he stood. "How is it that a man can see the mote in his brother's eye, yet miss the beam in his own?" With that, he wished them a good night and went back to his room.

"Remind me to give him that lame horse when he leaves tomorrow."

"Better still," said Baron d'Anjou, "why not give him an ass so he has someone of like mind for company?"

"Well said," laughed Sergeant Gislebert. "A man after my own heart."

"You are only half the wit you think you are, d'Anjou," de Bracineaux grumbled, shaking his head.

"Be of good cheer, commander," the baron replied. "Eat, drink, and rejoice—for tomorrow the search for the Mysterious Rose begins in earnest. With any luck, you will have it tucked safely away before the season is through. We can be in Anjou before the snow flies, and winter at my estate—what do you say to that?"

"I say," replied the commander, "we do not yet have the relic. I will not revel and make merry until I hold it in my hands."

"Then let us drink to the quest," said the Baron, raising his cup. "May our joy be swiftly consummated."

TWENTY-SEVEN

Their supper was peas porridge and black bread again—and for the next three nights—as each day's search took the party further into the wild, desolate mountains. The weather grew steadily worse, each day colder than the last, the clouds lower, darker, filled with mist and rain. Wind blew down from the barren heights, buffeting them by day, and invading their sleep by night.

One cheerless day they found one of Abu's markers in a broad, grassy glen. Nearby lay the remains of a campfire; there were tufts of wool on the bushes and brambles, and sheep droppings on the ground. "Probably a shepherd taking his flocks down to the lower valleys for the winter," observed Paulo, raising his eyes to the mountain peaks which now loomed over them. "God willing, we will soon be going home, too."

The next day they rode out in the direction indicated by the marker and promptly lost the trail. By nightfall they had not found it again. "It is gone," Paulo concluded dismally.

"We must have missed a marker," suggested Yngvar.

"Perhaps," allowed Paulo. "But I do not think so."

"We will find it tomorrow," Cait said, "when the light is better."

"I am sorry, Donna Caitríona," he said, shaking his head, "the ground is mostly rock and chippings. If not for Abu, we would not have been able to trail them this long. Something must have happened to him."

"If he was injured or killed," said Svein, "we would have found him on the trail."

"The bandits must have caught him," Yngvar concluded. "This is what I think."

"Then God help him," said Dag.

"What are we to do now?" Cait asked, turning to Rognvald, who stood nearby with his arms folded over his chest to keep warm.

"I suspect they have a stronghold hidden in one of the high valleys," the tall knight replied. "We will establish a camp at the last marker, and then we will ride out from there and examine each valley in turn until we find them."

The place Rognvald suggested was a grassy dell formed by the junction of two larger glens running either side of a great, jutting spur of a peak. A fresh-running stream flowed around the foot of the mountain, so they never lacked good water; there was a sizable stand of trees on one side of the meadow where they could get firewood, and green boughs with which they constructed crude shelters to keep off the worst of the rain and wind. Not for the first time did Cait wish they had been able to bring the tents—and the extra clothing she had left behind.

The next morning they began searching out the many-fingered valleys, following the rough mountain pathways through one wind-blown canyon after another. It quickly became apparent that there were far too many canyons, gorges, dales, and hollows to be explored; so, to make the most of their efforts, they decided to pair off, each pair of searchers pursuing a different direction.

They changed horses every day, to rest the animals and allow them to graze on the lush grass of the glen. Each morning they rode out with hope renewed. This day, they were certain, their dutiful perseverance would be rewarded; but each evening they returned to collapse beside the coldwater stream, exhausted and frustrated, to spend another dank night on the ground. Each day Cait's hopes, like the late autumn sun, rose a littler lower than the day before, the light that much weaker, and more distant.

The horses ate their fill of grass and began to grow thick winter coats; but Cait and her company of knights were not so fortunate. They soon ran out of the most perishable provisions: eggs, cheese and bread; then the wine slowly disappeared, leaving only the dried meat, meal, and beans. Each night there was less to eat, and it grew increasingly apparent that if their efforts were not soon rewarded, they must abandon the search to return to the lowlands where they might find a settlement or town where they could replenish supplies.

"We have enough for ten more days, maybe," said Dag, who had become cook and provisioner for the company. They had awakened to find a fine white haze of hoarfrost on the ground; a delicate coating of frost edged the stream and spiked the bare branches of the trees. "After that . . . well, it is in God's hands, I think."

"The supplies will not outlast the weather," Paulo pointed out. "Winter is on us. The snow is coming—it could come any day—tomorrow maybe, or the day after, but soon—and when it does, it will close off the passes and we will be lucky to get out of here."

This bleak prediction cast Cait into a doleful, desperate mood, which she hated, and so she railed against Paulo for speaking it. "What do you know about anything?" she snapped. "If you were but half so observant as you think yourself, we would have found Alethea long since!"

The knight's face fell, and he looked at her with sad, tired eyes. "I beg your pardon, my lady, if I have spoken out of place."

The slender Spaniard appeared so appalled and crestfallen that Cait did not have the heart to remain angry at him. "It is I who must beg *your* pardon, Paulo," she relented, forcing down her emotion. "You merely speak a truth my heart does not wish to hear."

"The truth, yes," he agreed sadly. "But I would give the world to change it."

They searched two more days—with no greater success than before—and then Rognvald called for a day of rest. Cait did not like this any better than the icy fact of winter, but she kept her disappointment to herself this time. As luck would have it, their day in camp proved sunny and calm—easily the best weather they had seen since the raid and Alethea's abduction.

The first snow of the season fell that night, and they awoke the next morning to find the ground covered with a fine, even layer of gleaming white, and a fresh blue sun-dazzled sky. As they were getting ready to ride out, Svein and Yngvar discovered new tracks in the snow: a small herd of roe deer had ventured from the wood before dawn. The prospect of fresh meat overwhelmed all other concerns, and the day's search was swiftly abandoned so the men could go hunting. Cait declined to accompany them, forsaking the thrill of the chase for a rest beside the fire. "Keep the flames burning brightly, my lady," called Dag. "We will bring back a fine buck or two for our supper tonight."

She sat by the fire, gazing at the pale blue Spanish sky. After a while, the supply of firewood began to dwindle, and she decided that if there was going to be any roasting of venison that night she had better gather more. So, taking up the sack and rope the men used, she saddled her horse, and rode some way into the forest where she found a ready supply of dead wood. She filled one sack and dragged it back to camp; seeing the men had not returned, she decided to fetch another.

She enjoyed this humble task—the day was bright and crisp; the snow on the trees and on the high mountain peaks gave everything a glistening sheen—and allowed her mind to drift where it would, losing herself in the aimless flow of her thoughts as she moved among the trees looking for fallen branches that would be easily broken up. She thought about Sydoni waiting at home, worried by their absence—and then remembered that they had originally planned to winter in Cyprus, so those left behind in Caithness were not yet missing them.

Unexpectedly, this thought moved her to prayer. She prayed that Alethea was well, and would be found before the supplies ran out and they were forced to give up the search for the winter. *Please, Almighty Father,* she prayed, *send a sign that you are with us, and that you care.*

No sooner had Cait sent up her simple prayer, than the answer came speeding back with the swiftness of an arrow. For she heard a strange jingling sound—like tiny bells high in the air.

Amazed, she looked up quickly. The sound seemed to travel—as if an angel was gliding slowly from east to west over the treetops—but she could see nothing for the close-grown branches. She started forward, following the sound as it drifted overhead and soon found herself standing on the edge of the wood and gazing up into the crisp, blue sun-bright sky at a soaring falcon. As the majestic bird wheeled through the cloudless heavens, she noticed something dangling from its legs—the leather jesses of a trained hunting bird.

The recognition caused Cait's heart to quicken; such a hawk in flight meant a hunter nearby.

Darting back into the forest, she ran to retrieve her mount—only to discover the animal had wandered away; probably it had returned to camp, leaving her to carry her burden by herself. Taking up her half-filled sack of firewood, she began dragging it over the rough ground, scolding herself for failing to adequately secure the horse. The sack was heavy and she labored with it as she struggled back through the trees.

Upon emerging from the wood, she paused and searched the sky once more, but the hawk was gone. Unaccountably disappointed, she turned and resumed her walk, dragging the sack behind her. The track down to the camp passed by a hillock around which the stream coursed as it wound through the valley. Upon drawing even with this small promontory, she heard the light clinking jingle of the hawk's bells once more and turned toward the sound.

It was not a hawk this time, however, but a great black stallion, his glossy coat shimmering in the sunlight. At the sudden appearance of the beast, Cait stopped in her tracks and jumped back, giving out a small cry of alarm.

Then she saw the man: astride the horse, his head swathed in a shimmering black turban, a richly embroidered black cloak flung back from his shoulders and over the stallion's hindquarters. He saw her in the same instant, and although he gave no outward sign, she saw in the quickness of his keen dark glance that he had not been expecting to encounter anyone in the glen.

That he was a Moor was as obvious as the curly black beard on his face; in aspect and appearance he looked very like the bandits. But where they were sloven and cowardly, the man before her was regal, bold, a man of wealth—his cloak was sewn with silver, and his high-cantled saddle was fine black leather, ornamented with shell-like silver bosses and trimming; the horse's long, thick mane was braided, and each braid interwoven with threads of silver.

Cait stood motionless, holding her breath as the man regarded her with disarming curiosity. Turning away, he lifted his head and raised his arm into the air; he wore a heavy leather gauntlet. He uttered a piercing whistle, which was echoed by a shriek from on high, and an instant later there was a rush and rustle of wings as the falcon swooped down to take its place on its master's fist.

"I give you good greeting, woman," he said, turning his attention to her once more. His face was fine and handsome, his skin dark and smooth, his limbs slender and graceful.

"God keep you, sir," Cait replied, releasing the sack of firewood. She straightened under his scrutiny, resting her hand on the pommel of her sword.

"Forgive me for startling you," he said, "but would you mind very much if I asked you why you are encamped upon my land?" His Latin,

232

although heavily accented with a thick Eastern intonation, was spoken with a low, strong voice. The combination produced a sound which reminded Cait of the magician Sinjari, and the thought produced a feeling of recognition which made her bold.

"I beg your pardon, my lord," she replied courteously. "If I had imagined this wilderness canyon belonged to anyone, I would never have spent a moment camping here when I might have come to your house and demanded hospitality."

His smile was a white glint of teeth in the blackness of his beard. "Indeed! What makes you so certain that this Muslim would honor the request of a Christian?"

"A wise man once told me that among Muhammedans it is considered a sign of true nobility to demonstrate mercy and generosity."

"Even to enemies?"

"*Especially* to enemies, sir."

He laughed, his voice rich and deep. The sound roused the falcon on his hand. The bird shrieked angrily and flapped its wings. "Hush, Kiri, naughty girl." He reached into a pouch at his side and produced a ragged strip of red meat which he fed to the hawk. "Leave us, I wish to talk to this charming lady." With that, he flung the hawk into the air; the bird disappeared in a rushing flurry of wings and tinkling of silver bells. "Kiri is a cunning and fearless hunter," he said admiringly, "but she is also exceedingly jealous."

The Moor slid from the saddle then to stand before Cait, regarding her with a lightly taunting amusement that Cait found slightly disconcerting. "If we are to begin as enemies," he said at last, "let us at least strive for the virtuous nobility celebrated by your wise acquaintance."

"The man was my father," Cait said. "Lord Duncan of Caithness."

"Then he has my condolences," he replied with a smile.

"Sir?"

"Any man who would let such a daughter out of his sight, even for a moment, must certainly be suffering a most powerful bereavement." He smiled again, and Cait felt a strange warmth flood through her—a result, she strongly suspected, of his shameless flattery.

"I am Prince Hasan Salah Ibn Al-Nizar." He made a low, sweeping bow. "Peace be with you. May Allah the Munificent crown all your endeavors with triumph and glory. Forgive my curiosity, my lady, but what miracle brought you to this lonely and forbidding place?"

Cait gave her name and told him she was on pilgrimage from her home in Scotland.

"Caitríona," he repeated, then frowned. "That will never do. My poor Moorish tongue has not the facility to express the natural mellifluence of your wondrous name. I believe I shall call you Ketmia, instead—if I may be so bold."

Cait repeated the name uncertainly. "It is not disagreeable, I suppose. Ketmia . . . what does it mean?"

"It is the name of one of the most fragrant and beautiful flowers ever to blossom," Hasan told her. "In the East it is given to brides on their wedding day. For, like the loveliness of the flower, the memory of that day will last through all time, infusing each remembrance with its glorious perfume." His smile broke forth in a sudden blaze of delight which Cait found endearing. "When I saw you, I thought to myself, *Ketmia.*"

"Very well," agreed Cait, suitably charmed.

"Splendid!" said Prince Hasan. He made a flourish of his hand, as if in elaborate acceptance of her will, and said, "It would vastly improve the austerity of my cow-byre of a dwelling if you would accept my hospitality while you are sojourning in my realm."

"Since you ask so nicely," Cait replied, "I do accept—although, perhaps I should warn you that I am not alone. As it happens, I have a company of knights with me. Five of them—all under the authority of Lord Rognvald of Haukeland."

"Even so?" The prince looked to the right and left and back toward the camp. "Are they Djinn, these warriors of yours? By the hair of my beard, I cannot see them."

"They are riding to the hunt just now," she explained, "trying to get a little meat for our supper."

She thought she saw a shadow of displeasure pass over his face as she spoke, but it vanished in the sudden sunburst of his smile. "Then let us pray they are successful, for fresh meat will be a welcome addition to the banquet which I shall spread before you and your estimable retinue this night."

He turned and smoothly swung up into the high-cantled saddle. "Gather your things, if you please," he instructed. "I will send my katib to bring you to my house when you are ready."

Cait thanked him and watched him ride away. He stopped at the edge of the wood and whistled for his falcon, then lifted his arm and with a wave of his black-gloved hand wheeled the stallion and galloped across the meadow and was gone. She stood for a time, wondering whether she had done well in accepting the Moor's offer of hospitality. She worried over this for a while, and decided that Prince Hasan was precisely placed to help her find Alethea. Indeed, his appearance had all the fortuitous indications of an answer to her prayer.

The knights returned at midday in a jubilant mood, having killed two young stags—a humor cautiously increased when Cait informed them they would not have to sleep on the cold wet ground that night. "Tonight we are to banquet with a prince," she said, and went on to explain her encounter with Hasan.

"He is heaven-sent," she told Rognvald as the others trooped off to begin preparing the deer.

"More likely a trick of the devil," muttered the tall knight; his face clenched in a scowl of sour disapproval.

"Listen to you," she scoffed lightly. "You have not even met the man, and already you condemn him. In truth, he is the very likeness of a nobleman."

"So is the Devil," Rognvald replied.

"He has offered us hospitality and I will not hear a word against him," Cait snapped indignantly.

"He is a *Moor*," Rognvald said tersely. "Need I remind you, it is the Moors who have taken your sister?"

"That was unkind, my lord," Cait snarled. "Have I not spent every waking moment these past many days searching for my sister? Tell me what more I could have done, and rest assured I will do that, too."

Rognvald's scowl deepened. He opened his mouth to reply, but Cait cut him off.

"As it is," she continued, levelling the full brunt of her anger on him, "we are running out of food and the weather is against us. Therefore, I think it no bad thing to accept help when it is offered." She glared at him defiantly. "And yes, even from the Devil himself."

The tall knight stared implacably at her; his jaw muscles tightened with unspoken words, but he held his tongue.

"We are going to accept Prince Hasan's hospitality, and at the first opportunity I am going to enlist his aid to help find Alethea. I do not care whether you approve, or not. One way or another, I *will* find my sister."

She did not allow him the satisfaction of making a reply, but turned on her heel and stormed away. They stayed away from one another as they went about striking camp and preparing to leave. The prince's katib arrived a short time later, and found them ready, if not eager, to quit the cold and damp for the warmth of hearth and hall.

Like his master, the man was gracious and well mannered. He was somewhat older than the prince, his beard was streaked with gray and his skin was weathered and creased like an old leather glove. Though not tall, he carried himself with a posture which would have become a king. Dressed in a rich brown cloak and high riding boots, he rode a tawny brown mare, and carried a long, curved knife with a jewelled handle in his wide cloth belt.

He entered the camp with two attendants, one of whom carried a wheat-colored bundle tied with golden cord; the other led a saddled black horse. As the knights gathered to receive them, he dismounted, and in fine aristocratic Latin presented himself to Cait, saying, "May the light of Allah the Magnificent shine for you, and may his blessing of peace rest upon you." He bowed low, making an elegant motion of his hand. "I am Al-Fadil Halhuli, katib and overseer to Prince Hasan, from whom I have come with an invitation to join him at his home."

Cait received his greeting with good grace, while the knights stood looking on from a short distance. Arms folded across their chests and similar expressions of distrust fixed firmly on their faces, they followed Rognvald's lead, adopting a suspicious stance, and made no move to join in the proceedings.

Ignoring their bad manners, the katib snapped his fingers and the attendant with the bundle dismounted and came to kneel beside his superior.

"My master the prince has sent me with a gift which he hopes you will do him the very great honor of accepting." He motioned to the kneeling servant, who extended the bundle in his hands. "Please, my lady," Halhuli said, indicating that she should receive the bundle.

Cait took it in both hands, whereupon he untied the golden cord and unfolded a handsome hooded cloak of the finest wool she had ever seen; it was the color of wheat and brushed to a soft, almost fur-like finish. The hood, cuffs, and hem were embroidered with blue silk in a series of tiny swirling, filigree loops. Instantly enchanted with the gift, Cait took the cloak, shook out its folds and held it up before her.

"Oh, it is wonderful!" she said, forgetting her composure in her enthusiasm. "It is easily the finest I have ever seen—by far." The cloak was indeed exquisite—yet, it was more the completely unexpected nature of the gift that so amazed and delighted her. However, if she had seen that Rognvald's scowl had reappeared in force, she might have reined in her excitement somewhat; and if she had seen the disapproving, furtive glances the knights exchanged with one another, she might have recovered the greater portion of her natural dignity and bearing.

While the katib held it up for her, she put her arms through the sleeves and turned, drawing the splendid garment around her, luxuriating in its richness and warmth. "It is true what my master has said," he told her, "you have eyes like the very houri of paradise."

To Cait's embarrassment, she colored under this blandishment, and it brought her to herself once more. "I thank you, my lord—" she began.

"If you please, my lady," he interrupted smoothly, "I am simply Halhuli. I deem it the utmost pleasure to serve you." He turned and spread his hands in a gesture of deference, and said, "Now, if you are ready, my lords, we can proceed. My master is waiting to welcome you, and I assure you he is most eager to make your acquaintance."

With a flick of his hand, Halhuli sent his bearer hurrying to bring his horse, though it was but a few paces behind him. At the same time, the other servant dismounted and came on the run, leading the black horse. Taking Cait's hand, the katib helped her into the saddle, and then resumed his own mount. Without another word or backward glance, the prince's overseer turned and rode from the camp with Cait at his side. The knights gathered the pack animals and hurried after.

TWENTY-EIGHT

The short day faded. With high clouds coming in from the north on a bitter wind, the mountain tops were soon lost to view, and the sky grew dark and heavy long before they came in sight of their destination. Although she tried, Cait found it difficult to maintain her sense of direction. One desolate, tree-filled valley was very like another; and one twisting, trackless bare rock ridge the same as all the rest. After they had traveled a fair distance into the mountains, they paused. "It is not far now," Halhuli told her.

Turning in his saddle, he lifted his hand and said, "Behold! Al-Jelál, the palace of Prince Hasan Salah Al-Nizar."

Cait looked up to see, high on the towering ridgewall before her, a low, box-like structure squatting on the edge of an almost vertical curtain of rock rising from the valley floor. The lofty dwelling, built of the same drab stone as the surrounding mountains, was so uniformly colorless and dull that if the katib had not stopped to show her, she might never have noticed it.

The party continued on and soon reached the end of the valley and began the ascent of the ridge by way of a paved trail. Once atop the ridge, they saw that the palace—or, as Halhuli said, the *al-qazr*—occupied a natural hollow in the upper part of the slope, and had been built in the manner of a series of graceful steps rising to the top, each one slightly higher than the last. The whole was surrounded by a stone wall, the gates of which closed upon the ridge trail, sealing off the only path leading to, or from, Al-Jelál.

As a stronghold, it possessed little in the way of fortification—the wall was the only defensive structure, and it had no towers. As an example of the builder's art, it lacked any redeeming aspect. Indeed, the dismal mud-colored stone with which it was constructed appeared unspeakably dreary and cheerless beneath the low gray skies.

"The prison in Damascus had more to charm the eye than this foul nest," grumbled Yngvar under his breath. Svein and Dag grunted in agreement. Cait heard, and though she turned to glare at them for their discourtesy, she knew they were right. She looked up at the high, lonely house, and her heart sank at the thought that she had exchanged the freedom of the wind and stars for a forlorn and comfortless rock of a fortress.

The gates opened as they drew near, and they passed through and into a wide, sloping yard. A row of iron stanchions had been set up, with a torch fluttering from the top of each one; beneath each flame fluttered a golden banner with the prince's crest: a falcon soaring above a curved Moorish sword.

Beyond the row of banners stood the first of the palace buildings, the prince's reception hall. The massive cedar doors were open and white-robed servants stood with torches at either side of the entrance. As the visitors were dismounting, the prince appeared in the doorway, and came hurrying swiftly down the steps to join them. He walked directly to Rognvald and stretched out his empty hand in greeting. "My lord Rognvald," he said, "I am pleased to welcome you and your men to my home."

As the knights gathered around their lord and leader, the prince said, "I am Hasan Salah Ibn Al-Nizar, prince of the House of Tashfin. Your presence will make a most entertaining diversion during this bleak season." Indicating the dressed deer carcasses slung across the backs of two pack mules, he said, "I compliment you on your success. As it happens, my lands boast the best hunting in all of Aragon; I look forward to riding with you one day soon, my lords."

"For a certainty," replied Rognvald with but slight hesitation, "we would like nothing better."

"Splendid!" exclaimed the prince. "With your permission I will instruct the kitchen to prepare the stags to be served with our banquet tonight. Now then," he said, motioning to the waiting katib, "if you please, Halhuli will lead you into the hall."

The knights moved off, and the prince turned to Cait. "Lady Ketmia, you must forgive me for leaving you unattended, but I wished to escort you personally." Stepping before her, he caught up her hand and brushed it with his lips. "The cloak is to your liking?"

"It is beautiful," she said. "And I thank you, my lord. It is a very thoughtful gift, and much appreciated on a day like this."

"My pleasure entirely." Taking her hand, he turned and led her up the steps and in through the open doors. "The winter wind can be devilish in these mountains. The wool comes from a kind of goat that roams the peaks around here. It is very soft, but also extremely warm. I am glad you like it."

They passed through the open doors into a large vestibule. The walls were made of rough stone which had been white-washed; and the floor was polished pine. It was simple, clean and spare, if a trifle plain; but at least it was not as dire as Cait had feared, and it was warm.

There were two doors at either end of the vestibule, and through one of them Cait could see the last of the knights disappearing down a long corridor. Prince Hasan conducted her to the opposite door where two young women were waiting. Both had long black hair which was worn in a single braid, and both were dressed in the same white, loose-fitting robe the male servants wore.

At the prince's approach, the maids bowed low and remained in that posture until their lord had acknowledged them. "This is Mahdi and Pila'i," he told Cait. "They will be your maidservants during your sojourn here. I have instructed them to take very good care of you, so please allow them to fulfill the charge they have been given."

The sight of the two young women cheered Cait, and improved her spirits immediately. She had allowed herself to imagine the prince the sole tenant of his bleak, windswept haven, surrounded by the kind of rank squalor men descend to when there are no women around to maintain decency and order. The fact that she was provided with not just one, but two, maidservants, all to herself, suggested otherwise. "Are there many women here?" she asked.

"A fair number," replied the prince affably. "Yet I feel there is always room for at least one more—especially when that one brings such great cheer to the bleakness of the dark season."

It was blatant flattery, but lightly spoken, and Cait decided it would be churlish to object to it. She decided to ignore it, and instead asked, "What of your family, Prince Hasan? Is it large, or small?"

"Very large, Ketmia. Like all good Moors, our family is both numerous and industrious. Some of them live here with me, some on the lower estates in the valley, and some in Al-Maghrib."

The corridor turned and they came to another pair of polished wood doors and, as the maidservants opened one for Cait to pass through, the prince halted. "Here I must leave you," he said. "This passage leads to the women's house. It is not permitted for men to enter beyond this door."

"Why ever not?" wondered Cait.

"In a Muslim palace," the prince explained, "men and women do not share the same apartments—a practice which creates some small inconveniences, as you might imagine. Yet we find the virtues far exceed any difficulties, and the separation promotes an ease of life which is commendable in many ways. I trust you will find the women's house to your liking."

Addressing the two maids, he spoke in rapid Arabic; they bowed in response, and he said, "They will bring you to the banqueting hall when all is ready. I leave you in their capable hands."

He turned and walked away, and Cait stepped through the doorway and into a dream.

Beyond the threshold, the corridor opened onto a great oval-shaped inner courtyard with a double-tiered gallery running around the perimeter; in the center of the courtyard, an alabaster fountain splashed into a round pool. Lanterns glowed from the gallery posts, and lamps burning with fragrant oils lined pathways on which patterned carpets in red, blue, and green were laid over smooth stone. There were small palm trees and broad leafy plants in huge painted jars and, here and there, low tables and cushions where the inhabitants of the women's house might meet to recline and talk.

Cait's maidservants picked up lamps and started along the right-hand pathway beneath the overhanging gallery. Cait followed, passing a series of small doors before coming to a flight of stairs leading to the level above. The maids indicated that they were to climb the stairs; one went before Cait, and one after, to light her way. There were but four doors opening off the upper gallery; they passed two of these and, stopping at the third, the foremost maidservant motioned for Cait to open the door.

Instead of a latch handle, Cait saw only a silken cord with a tassel on the end. Encouraged by the maid, she took the tassel and pulled—the door swung open and she stepped into a room unlike any she had ever seen. There were lamps and candles by the dozen—hundreds of them, large and small—filling the room with gleaming, shimmering light. The walls were covered with glazed tiles in gem-like colors, the floors were polished wood, and the ceiling! The ceiling was wood, too, but carved into a fantastic, dizzying pattern of intersecting lines; each place a line crossed another was inlaid with a mother-of-pearl boss in the shape of a star. In the flickering candlelight the ceiling seemed to glitter with a thousand slivers of light.

The room was spacious and open, divided only by a few pierced wooden screens. As in the courtyard below, there were low tables surrounded by cushions, and these were placed on thick wool carpets displaying impossibly intricate designs. There was a woven rug hanging on the wall, too, and a row of small round windows covered with glass. Behind one rank of screens was a low cushioned platform covered in glistening blue silk. This, Cait guessed, was her bed.

She stood for a long moment, taking in the bewilderingly beautiful sight, and then gasped, "It is magnificent!" Her maidservants appeared to enjoy her amazement, and smiled behind their hands. "It is the most wonderful room I have ever seen!" They laughed at this, and Cait asked if all the rooms were as sumptuous as the one she had been given. It was then she realized her servants neither spoke nor understood Latin.

At the end of the room opposite the bed stood another screen, and behind it a carved panel set in a niche. While one maid busied herself with a wooden chest beside the bed, the other led Cait to this panel. Taking the silken cord in her hand, she pulled, and the panel slid effortlessly aside. A rush of warm, moist air flooded over Cait as she stepped into the doorway to see a smaller room—the interior of which was almost entirely taken up by a pool of water. Curling tendrils of steam rose from the surface of the pool and one look sent a melting feeling through Cait.

The next thing she knew the maidservant was removing her cloak and boots; her swordbelt, girdle, and mantle followed, and Cait found she could not shed her clothes fast enough. She moved to the edge of the pool, and shrugging off the last of her clothing, stepped down into the delicious hot water. The blessed warmth made her weak in the knees and she gave herself to it, sliding in, submerging herself slowly.

The pool had a stepped ledge at the bottom on which she sat, feeling the heat seep into her cold and weary bones. With a splash, her maid Mahdi entered the pool; in one hand she held a small brass jar, and in the other, a lumpen, loaf-shaped object. These she placed at the side of the pool and, with a stirring gesture, indicated that Cait was to sit with her back to her.

She did so, and Mahdi began laving water over her head using the pale lumpy object—Cait's first encounter with a sponge. Mahdi then poured some liquid from the jar into her mistress's wet hair and began to wash it for her. More intimate ministrations followed wherein Cait's body was lathered and washed and dried and her flesh perfumed with fragrant oils rubbed into her skin. Although sorry to leave the warmth of the bathing room, she allowed herself to be wrapped in a great fluffy cloth and led back into the bedchamber where Pila'i had chosen clothes for her from the chest beside the cushion bed.

The garments were, so far as Cait could tell, most exquisitely made and of the finest fabrics in shades of scarlet and deepest crimson—some woven with gold thread to form glittering stripes—and all of them, somehow, to be worn. Lifting one gossamer length of cloth after another, she admired each in turn, but, try as she might, she could not discern how they should be assembled.

Her maidservants soon took her in hand, however, and dressed her in the manner of an Eastern princess. Layer upon layer, the loose-fitting garments were wrapped and draped and secured here and there by way of ties and laces. Cait relished the smooth, liquid sheen of the cloth and its delicate texture against her skin as each new piece was added to the others. The maids worked together with quiet efficiency, clearly enjoying their labors, and Cait began to feel as if she were a young bride, dressing for her wedding.

Just as they were finishing, there came a knock at the door, followed by the entrance of a tiny old woman bearing a lamp. At her appearance, both serving maids bowed, giving Cait to know that she was their superior—the overseer of the women's quarters, most likely. The old woman moved forward with small, quick steps, and came to stand before Cait and, by the soft glow of her lamp, proceeded to make a lengthy inspection of the newcomer, examining Cait's hands, feet, and face. She untied the cloth belt around Cait's waist, smoothed it between her fingers, then carefully rewound and retied it.

Satisfied, she spoke a word of command to the two maids, pointing to Cait's bare feet. Pila'i scurried to the chest and brought out a pair of thin black sandals, the soles of which were soft leather, and the tops black silk with tiny pierced pearls sewn in spirals over each instep. Cait waited as the sandals were slipped onto her feet, whereupon the old woman stepped back and cast a sharp, critical eye over their efforts. Then, with a sharp nod of her head, she turned and led them from the room.

Through a series of interconnecting corridors, vestibules, reception rooms, and antechambers—so many that Cait lost all sense of direction—they came at last to a hall-like room fronted by a pair of tall, narrow doors bound in gilded leather ornamented by a pair of falcons, one on each panel, their images traced in black nails hammered through the gleaming hide.

Before each panel stood a servant who, at the approach of the old woman, stood up smartly and tugged open the heavy doors. The old woman indicated that she should enter, so Cait, followed by her two serving maids, stepped through the entrance and into what she could only describe as the interior of an impossibly large tent.

The ceiling was hung with great, swooping drapes of cloth attached to the tops of the room's numerous slender columns which took on the aspect of tent poles and from which large, many-flamed oil lamps hung on brass chains. The wide expanse of floor was covered by rugs of every size and color piled one atop another in a profligate display of wealth; and here and there around the room were clumps and clusters of enormous satin cushions.

Inexplicably, Cait remembered the first time she had entered a cathedral with her step-mother—the great church at Kirkjuvágr in Orkney. While her father was talking some business or other with the tradesmen, Sydoni had taken her to see the cathedral, and she remembered trembling with wonder at the astonishingly majestic building, so strange and mysterious she felt it must have been enchanted.

She felt the same way now, as with slow, deliberate steps, she moved into the room, eyes wide with amazement at the elaborate strangeness of her surroundings. As the doors closed silently behind her, a new serving maid appeared, greeted her in Arabic, and offered a tray containing a silver cup, a heap of bread torn into small bits, and a bowl of salt. It was, she recognized, a ritual of welcome—the Scots observed a similar custom. Taking a piece of bread, she dipped it in the salt, and then ate it. The serving girl then presented her with the cup, filled with sweetened wine. She took a drink and replaced the cup.

She heard the sound of voices in the antechamber beyond, and turned as the doors opened once more to admit Rognvald and the knights. They trooped in, following a serving boy with a blue turban. Even from where she stood, Cait could see that they had bathed and shaved and, like her, they had been provided with clothes for the festivities: of the eastern variety, well made and of good cloth, only slightly less opulent than her own. Unlike her, however, they moved uneasily in their finery as men unaccustomed to such luxury.

One by one they paused to partake of the bread and salt, and accept a drink of sweet wine. Upon seeing Cait, they immediately gathered around her and exclaimed over her exotic dress. "Oh, my lady," said Yngvar, his tone one slow gasp of pleasure, "how beautiful you look."

"No queen ever appeared more elegant," agreed Svein.

Dag nodded enthusiastically, and added, "Nor more lovely."

The Spanish knights murmured their approval, and she turned to Rognvald as he raised the cup from the tray. "What say you, my lord of somber mien?" she asked, teasingly. "I make a fine princess, do I not?"

"Passing fine, my lady," he said softly. She saw something in his eyes then that took her aback. She had meant the question to be a playful, if somewhat impish jest; but staunch Rognvald was in grave earnest. Suddenly embarrassed, she looked away just as the doors opened once more to admit their host, Prince Hasan, and with him, a slender young woman with long dark hair and large dark eyes.

The prince greeted his guests effusively, making much of the remarkable alteration in their appearances. Then he introduced the woman beside him, saying, "My friends, may I present to you my sister, Danji." The woman pressed her hands together and bowed gracefully. "Unfortunately, she does not speak Latin, but I thought her presence, and that of her handmaidens, would make this evening's festivities more enjoyable."

Turning to the knights, he said, "My lord Rognvald, perhaps you would be so kind as to present your men to me. I would know the names of those who share my table tonight."

"Of course, Prince Hasan," he replied, drawing his eyes away from the lovely raven-haired woman standing demurely beside the prince. Then, beginning with Yngvar, he presented each of the knights in turn to the prince and his sister, introducing himself last. When these formalities had been observed, the prince called everyone to join him at table, and proceeded to the center of the room where a cluster of cushions had been arranged to form an open circle.

He dropped onto a cushion in the center of the horseshoe-shaped arrangement and waved others to their places. "Here, Lord Rognvald," he called, "sit at my right hand. And, you, my lovely Ketmia, sit with Danji, at my left." When everyone had been seated, he clapped his hands and there appeared a succession of serving men bearing low tables which they placed before the diners. Hard on the heels of the men came a dozen serving maids to spread each table with a spotless white cloth; no sooner were the cloths in place than brass trays appeared, bearing sweet dark wine in silver cups.

When each guest had been given a cup, Prince Hasan opened his arms in a gesture of benevolence and declared, "Tonight it pleases Allah the Almighty and Munificent to bless this company with feasting that the bonds of friendships may be strengthened between men of faith and goodwill. Eat and take your ease, that we may rise from this table better friends than when we first sat down together."

Thus, the banquet began.

TWENTY-NINE

"Now then," Hasan said, leaning his chin on his palm, "how did you come to be wandering around in my mountains?"

They had feasted on spiced lamb and kid, and on strips of fresh venison which the prince's serving maids cooked for them over charcoal braziers set up beside the tables; when the meat was done, they transferred the roasted strip to the bowl of each individual guest using extremely long forks. The knights had not seen this before, and took an instant liking to this method of cooking and serving meat. There were also rich, highly seasoned stews of vegetables, and fragrant rice with dates and almonds, and plenty of honey-sweetened wine.

The prince's sister, Danji, summoned six of her handmaids to come and join the festivities so that the knights might have a pretty companion to share the meal. As a result, the somewhat icy wariness of the men melted in the warmth of the prince's lavish and convivial hospitality—except for Rognvald who, while allowing himself to enjoy the meal, nevertheless maintained a discreetly guarded attitude toward the prince.

"As you have discovered, my *al-qazr* is far from any roads, and travelers seldom pass this way," he continued, looking from one to the other of them as he reclined on his elbow amidst the cushions. "What brought you here?"

Despite Rognvald's cautious glance, Cait decided the moment had come to tell Hasan about her sister's abduction and secure his aid. "In all it is easily told," she began. "We were on pilgrimage following the valley road some distance from here when we were attacked by bandits. They killed five of our men, but we fought them off—only to find when the battle was over that my sister, Alethea, had been taken."

"A shameful business, to be sure," said Hasan. "But, alas, far too common in these remote regions. This is a wild land in many ways."

"The assault came at dusk," Rognvald put in, "or we might have made good the pursuit. As it was, we followed the trail until we lost the light, and were forced to give up the chase."

"A pity," sympathized Hasan. "And the next day, you resumed the search, but . . ." he sighed, "it was too late. They were always too far ahead, and eventually you lost the trail."

"That is exactly what happened," said Cait, much impressed. "How did you know?"

"Because that is the way of these brigands. They attack at dusk and make off with whatever they can carry, trusting darkness to cover their path. They ride through the night so that when dawn comes they are far ahead of any pursuit."

"Just so," said Rognvald. "We would not have come this far, only one of the servants—a Syrian fellow named Abu—had followed Lady Alethea. He marked out the way for us."

"But then the markers stopped," Cait said. "We made our camp in the place where we saw the last marker. That was five days ago. We have been searching for the trail ever since."

"You will not find it," Hasan told her. "How many bandits did you say made the attack?"

Cait glanced at Rognvald, who said, "I make it at least twelve—but there may have been more."

"Then, unless I am mistaken, it was Ali Waqqar," said the prince; his tone suggested both familiarity and contempt. "*Yu'allah!* He is the worst. He and his rabble of outcasts have been a scourge of thievery and murder for far too long."

"You know them?" wondered Cait, hope quickening inside her once more.

"Alas, I do know them—and wish to Heaven that I did not," replied Hasan, his voice thick with animosity. "Once Ali Waqqar was a fine warrior and leader of men. He led the army of Sultan al-Farama in his wars to recover Saragossa. When the sultan was finally defeated, the army dispersed and Ali Waqqar has lived as a bandit and cut-throat ever since."

"If you know them," suggested Rognvald, "perhaps you also know where to find them."

"They know the mountains well and they have many places to hide. Such is the fear they inspire, the people look the other way when they pass. Thus, they are not easy to find." The prince paused and shook his head sadly. "I am sorry, my friends. That this has happened is unfortunate; that this has happened within the boundary of my realm is unforgivable. From this moment," he said, his tone growing more adamant, "I will make it my sole concern to find Ali Waqqar and his brigands, and bring them to justice." Drawing himself up he placed his right hand over his heart and said, "Prince Hasan Al-Nizar makes this solemn vow, and I will not cease until you are joyfully reunited with your beloved sister, and your valorous servant."

"I pray you swift success," Cait told him. "Achieve your aim and you shall win a loyal and loving friend."

"Praise Allah the Magnificent! I could ask for nothing finer."

So caught up were they in pledging their fealty to one another, neither saw Rognvald's tight, slightly scornful grimace as he lifted his cup to his mouth. "Do you have a wife, Lord Hasan?" he asked abruptly.

The prince regarded him with mild surprise. "I have been married, yes—once, when I was a very young man," he said.

"Only once? I thought Muhammedans kept wives the same way herders keep cattle."

Cait, incensed at the knight's bad manners, glared furiously at him in an effort to make him desist. He took no notice.

"Some may take more than one wife. It is permitted," Hasan forced a thin smile, "although not advised. As the great Qadi Tukhmin has said, 'A house with many wives is like a ship with many oars, but no rudder.' And you, my friend, have you ever been married?"

"No," replied Rognvald, returning to his cup. "One day, perhaps—God willing. But not yet."

Hasan nodded sympathetically. "God wills all good things for his children. I am sure you will find the very woman one day, and then *qismah*—your fate will be well and truly sealed."

From somewhere outside of the hall, there came the sound of a gong. Instantly, Danji and her handmaidens rose and, bowing to the prince and his guests, they departed. The knights, sorry to see the women go, looked to their host for an explanation. "It is the Hour of Covering the Fire," Hasan told them. "From ancient times, my people have observed this practice. You see, we were once a desert people and each night the signal was given to cover the fire so that all would know when it was time to sleep." He smiled. "But, please, you are guests in this house; you must not interrupt your revelry on account of this quaint custom."

Seeing a chance to establish some small authority of his own in this strange place, Rognvald said, "We will observe your custom, Lord Hasan. For we, too, must sleep if we are to renew our search in the morning." He stood. "I thank you for your kind consideration. Certainly, it was the best meal we have had in a very long time. Now, if you please, we will leave you in peace." To Cait, he said, "I bid you good night, my lady."

The other knights, recognizing the signal, rose—albeit somewhat more reluctantly—and, following the example of their lord, took their leave. They walked from the banqueting room, leaving Cait and the prince alone.

"I cannot remember a more lavish and delightful feast, Prince Hasan," Cait said. "Your kindness and generosity have made this a night I will never forget."

The prince smiled and inclined his head. "Your praise is more than my small effort deserves." He paused, regarding Cait with a pensive expression. "Alas, I do not think your Lord Rognvald approved. He is a cold one, to be sure, but I had hoped the festivity would have warmed him a little."

"Please, I pray you, do not take a moment's thought for him. He is a frozen Norwegian who cannot accept kindness when it is offered." Cait spoke with more vehemence than she felt, but did so for Hasan's sake. "Proud men often disdain the benevolence of others."

"Ah, you are as wise as you are lovely," sighed the prince. "It is rare in my experience to find those two qualities united in one woman. For, as the poet says, 'What can be bought with wisdom's coin, that beauty does not own?' But you, Ketmia, possess both in abundance."

No one had ever called her beautiful before, and Caitríona did not know how to reply. She tried to think of something to say, growing more and more uncomfortable as the prince, blissfully silent, regarded her with delight akin to rapture, until at last, she said, "It has been a most enjoyable night, and I thank you—not least for undertaking to help us find my sister." She rose slowly. "I must sleep now if I am to be ready to ride in the morning. So, I will bid you God's rest, my lord."

"To be sure," said the prince, rising slowly. "I will have Jubayar escort you to the women's quarter."

Taking her arm, he led her to the anteroom where a very tall, very fat man was standing beside the large brass gong. He wore a pale blue turban and long, unbelted mantle. His face was beardless, revealing a livid scar running from the point of his chin to his collarbone. He regarded Cait with a sleepy haughtiness, his large, fleshy features impassive as she came before him.

"This," said the prince, "is Jubayar. He is one of my most trusted servants. He is a eunuch, and therefore has charge of the women's house. You will be entirely safe in his protection."

The big man bowed, but said nothing when Cait attempted to greet him.

"Jubayar!" the prince shouted, and then, as an afterthought explained to Cait: "He is also very deaf. But he can be made to understand if you speak loudly—although he knows no Latin." Turning once more to the large eunuch, he spoke a rapid burst of Arabic, whereupon the servant bowed and, with a last glance at Cait, began leading the way down the corridor. Cait thanked the prince once more, bade him a good night, and then hurried after her surly escort.

Mahdi and Pila'i were asleep when Cait entered the room; both young women slept on thin pallets at the foot of her bed. They roused themselves as she entered, and helped her undress, folding the numerous items of clothing and carefully stowing them away in the wooden chest. They brought out a loose-fitting silk gown which she put on and, as Pila'i prepared her cushions, Mahdi brushed her hair and then skillfully braided it so that it would not grow tangled in the night.

Leaving her maids to put out the lamps, Cait drifted off to the first truly restful sleep since leaving home. That night she saw Alethea in a dream.

She dreamed that she and her sister were in Caithness. It was a fair summer day, and the two of them were walking along the brow of the high promontory to the south-east of Banvarð. The wind was fresh and the sun bright on the water in the bay far below; she could hear the rush and tumble of the waves, and the mewing of the seabirds as they wheeled and circled in the wide, cloudless sky.

Alethea was talking about something which Caitríona could not make out; she listened in a halfhearted way as Thea droned on and on, her voice growing slowly fainter—until Cait could no longer hear her any more. Cait stopped and looked around, but could not see her sister. She called out once and again, but there was no reply.

Fighting down the panic rising in her breast, Cait tried two more times, with no better result; on the third try, she heard Thea answer. The voice came from the direction of the sea, but sounded far away. Realizing what must have happened, Cait rushed to the edge of the promontory and, fearing the worst, looked over. Instead of seeing Thea's mangled body lying on the rocks below, she saw instead a steep and narrow trail leading down to the shingle beach, and Thea herself halfway down along the precipitous track.

"Thea, wait!" she cried. "Go no further. Wait for me, I am coming to help you."

At her cry, Alethea looked back over her shoulder to where Cait was starting down the treacherous path. "Cait, no!" she called. "Do not follow me. It is for me to go on alone."

"You will be killed," Cait shouted. "Come back."

Thea shook her head gently. "No harm will come to me." She put out her hand and pointed to the bay far below. "You see," she said, "they have come for me. I must go with them."

Cait looked and saw that a boat had entered the cove, and was making landfall. There were a number of women in the boat, and they were all dressed alike in long hooded robes of gray with a small, curiously short mantle of white covering their shoulders. Two of the women climbed out of the boat and waded to the shore; they came to stand at the water's edge and, looking up, beckoned Thea to them.

"Farewell, darling sister. Do not feel sorry for me. I have never been happier."

With that, she turned and proceeded down the steep and winding trail. Cait continued to call after her, but she neither looked back, nor gave any other sign that she heard—until, after joining the two figures on the shore, she turned and lifted a hand in farewell. Cait watched as her sister waded out to the waiting boat and climbed aboard; the boat turned and made its way from the cove and out into the empty sea.

Cait stood on the clifftop long after the boat was out of sight. When she at last turned from the wide expanse of water, she saw the sky was dark with angry clouds and rain was beginning to spatter the ground at her feet. She could hear the howl of the wind rising out of the east, and knew there was a storm coming. Still, she refused to leave the place she had last seen dear Alethea.

It was not until the lightning raked the clouds with jagged talons, and thunder trembled the ground beneath her feet, that she finally turned away—only to find that the sky had grown dark and she could no longer see the path. The wind whirled around her, dashing rain in her eyes and tearing at her clothes and hair. She threw a hand before her face and staggered forward, the force of the wind almost knocking her to the ground.

Struggling to her feet once more, she took a hesitant step and then halted, for she did not know which way to go. Frightened now, lest she be swept over the clifftop and hurled to her death on the rocks below, she stood shaking with indecision, and searching the howling blackness for some sign of the path ahead.

Lightning flashed and she saw, illumined by the naked glare, the figure of a man robed in white. The figure's back was to her and he was striding purposefully away. This she glimpsed in the brief light before darkness reclaimed the hilltop.

"Wait!" she cried, lurching forward. The resounding clash of thunder drowned her words, but she made for the place where she had seen the white figure. "Wait! God help me," she cried, "please wait for me!"

The next lightning flash revealed that the man had paused a few dozen paces further on. What was more, he bore a distinct likeness to her father. *Could it be?* she wondered.

She moved toward him in the darkness, her heart quickening in anticipation. As she drew close, however, the white-robed figure moved on. "Papa!" she cried, hurrying after.

Desperate now to catch him, she gathered her wet skirts and stumbled ahead. "Papa, it is Cait! Please, Papa, wait for me."

Another jagged flash lit up the sky and she saw in the briefly shimmering light that the figure had stopped again. She ran to him. As he made to turn and move on, she lunged and, reaching out, caught hold of the trailing edge of his sleeve.

The man halted and as the sky was torn by another flash, she saw his face at last. He was a young man—much younger than her father, she could see that now—but his youthful aspect was belied somewhat by his old-fashioned dress and the way he carried himself: carefully, as if he did not fully trust his weight to the ground. Still, his dark eyes were keen, and his gaze almost distressingly direct; his hair was dark and thick, and trimmed in the tonsure of a monk.

"Oh," she gasped, "it is you."

"Greetings, Caitríona. Peace and grace be with you always," the man said. At these words, the intensity of the storm seemed to lessen. The wind calmed and she could hear him plainly. "Come now, there is nothing to fear."

"Brother Andrew—oh, please, hurry. It is Thea." She pointed back toward the precipitous edge of the cliff. "She went down there and they took her away. We must find her."

"Have no fear for Alethea," the monk told her. "They could not take her anywhere she did not wish to go."

"But we must save her," insisted Cait. "She needs me."

"Where Alethea has gone you cannot follow," he said gently. "She is at peace now."

Cait stared at him, tears starting to her eyes. "But I do not understand."

"Listen to me, Caitríona. You have departed from the True Path. Evil crouches at your heels and only awaits a chance to drag you down. Beware, dear sister."

She opened her mouth to protest, but the White Priest raised his hand. "Time grows short. The end of the race is near; the prize awaits. Like your father and grandfather before you, my daughter, you must hold tight to the Holy Light. Cling to it, Caitríona. Put your faith and trust in it alone, and let it be your guide."

At this, Brother Andrew made to step away. Cait reached out to take hold of him, but her hands closed on empty air and she was alone once more with rain and wind raging around her.

"Please," she cried, "do not leave me. Brother Andrew, help me. Help me!"

There came no answer—only the voiceless shriek of the gale and the pelting sting of the rain . . .

This was how she awoke: with the wild wind screaming over the broken crags, pounding the thick stone walls with tremendous, fist-like blows that boomed with the sound of thunder, rattling the heavy iron-barred shutters, and driving the rain through tiny cracks around the windows.

She could not tell when the storm arose, but knew that she had been hearing it in her sleep for some time. The candles had blown out, leaving her room in darkness deep as the tomb. She heard a sound beside her, and her dream came back to her in a rush. "Brother Andrew," she said aloud, reaching out, and praying the White Priest had not abandoned her.

Her fingers touched another outstretched hand; she gave a little cry and jerked her hand away. "Ketmia?" came the timorous, quivering voice.

"Mahdi—is it you?"

The frightened maidservant slipped into bed beside her. Cait put her arm around the young woman's shivering shoulders and gathered her in. As she would have comforted Alethea, she consoled Mahdi, stroking her hair and telling her there was nothing to fear. Pila'i slept on, serenely unaware of the wind and lashing rain. So, Cait and Mahdi held vigil together, huddled in bed until it was light enough to get up.

The storm gave no sign of abating with the dawn. But as soon as it was light enough to find her way around, Cait rose and allowed her maids to dress her. Then, escorted from the women's quarters by Jubayar, she hurried to find Prince Hasan so the search for Alethea could begin anew.

THIRTY

Searching for the prince, she found Lord Rognvald instead. He was standing in the vestibule entrance with two fidgety porters, the door wide open, staring out into a bleak, wind-torn void of fog and sleet and swirling snow. He turned as she came to stand beside him, and greeted her with stiff, almost frozen formality, then observed, "You are early risen, my lady—for one so late to bed."

Cait returned his chilly greeting, and said, "I could not sleep for the storm." She looked out through the open door at the roiling gray mass and felt the cold bite of the wind on her skin. A memory stirred—of a dream, or the lingering impression of a dream: something about being lost in a raging gale. It passed through her with a shiver and then was gone. "It must break soon, I should think," she said hopefully.

"Pray that it does," Rognvald told her, "for until it spends itself somewhat, we cannot resume the search."

Growing impatient at last, the porters intervened to close the doors and shut out the icy gale. Cait and Rognvald made their way to the reception hall where a fire had been lit and was now blazing with bright fury on the hearth. Two servants were adding firewood to the already towering stack under Prince Hasan's commanding gaze. At his visitors' approach, the prince beckoned them to come and warm themselves.

"It is the one regrettable verity of life atop a mountain," he said. "If the weather is bad in the valleys it is always worse here—especially in winter."

"It is often like this?" wondered Cait, extending her hands toward the fire.

"Worse, Ketmia. Winter arrives with a fury, and leaves only with the greatest reluctance. We call it *al-Zoba'a*: the Ferocious One. But the palace walls are stout, my forests keep us well supplied with firewood, and the harvest of the valleys is always bountiful, so we do not often have cause to trouble Heaven with our complaints."

"Lord Rognvald thinks the storm will prevent us from resuming the search," Cait said, hoping for a better word.

"Then he is most prudent," agreed Hasan cheerfully. "It is unwise to tempt fate on a day like this." At Cait's distraught expression, he said, "Yet all is not lost, Ketmia." He took her hand in both of his and pressed it comfortingly. "For if the storm prevents us from searching, it also prevents Ali Waqqar from escaping to the south."

"Do you think that is where they are going?"

"To be sure," replied Hasan. "Winter is mild in the south, and he will be able to sell to the slave traders." Cait had never considered this possibility before, and it brought her up short; the prince immediately offered consolation. "Have no fear, Ketmia, that will not happen. I will not allow it."

Spreading his arms wide, he took both Cait and Rognvald in his stride and said, "But come, my friends, this is a disagreeable business to discuss on an empty stomach. Let us breakfast together, and I will tell you how I plan to catch this rogue who has abducted the fair Alethea. For I pondered this matter long last night and this morning Allah, Author of Eternal Justice, has blessed me with a scheme of such simplicity and cunning it could only come by way of divine inspiration."

He led them through a door to a chamber behind the hearth. Dim light shone through tiny diamond-shaped windows of colored glass, casting the room in shades of deep blue. One wall opened onto the hearth, so that both the reception hall and the smaller chamber could share the warmth of the fire. A number of cushions had been placed around a low table near the hearth, and the table laid for a simple meal.

"Please, sit, take your ease, my friends," said the prince, dropping languidly onto a cushion. Serving maids appeared and began pouring cups of almond milk; they unwrapped stacks of flatbread spiced with anise still warm from the oven. There was dried fruit and nuts in little baskets, and a warm drink made with dried apples infused in hot water and sweetened with honey—which they served in small cups made of glass.

Cait took a bite of her bread, and set it aside. "If you please, Prince Hasan, tell me your plan," she said, unable to suppress her excitement any longer. "I must hear it at once."

"Then you shall, my dove, for it is swiftly told." Tearing a bit of bread from the flat loaf, he dipped it into the sweetened almond milk and chewed thoughtfully for a moment, before saying, "You see, it came to me that no one chases mice—it is an impossible business. What do we do instead?" He paused to allow his listeners to appreciate his subtlety. "We set a trap."

"Yes," agreed Cait, waiting for the prince to expound his philosophy.

"You are saying," mused an unimpressed Rognvald, "that we set a trap for this bandit, Ali Waqqar. We would still have to find him first—would we not?"

Prince Hasan smiled as if at an unenlightened child. "But we do not go out searching for mice. In fact, they find us, do they not? All we have to do is dangle the bait in the right place and, praise Allah, the rogue of a bandit will come to *us*. It will, I believe, save a great deal of time and effort."

"If Ali Waqqar is as cunning as you suggest, he may not care to risk the trap."

"Ah," said the prince, raising a finger in triumph, "if the bait is irresistible enough, even the most wily mouse will risk the trap." He smiled expansively. "I will simply make the bait so enticing that Ali Waqqar will have no choice. Then, when we have him where we want him, he will have no choice but to surrender Alethea."

"That will work," Cait said hopefully. "Do you not think so, Rognvald?"

"Oh, indeed, my lady," he answered stiffly. "Ask any ratcatcher." He sipped the warming apple drink, and regarded the splendidly pleased prince for a moment before saying, "Tell us more about this trap of yours."

"As you know, it is my belief that the bandits will try to sell Alethea in the slave markets of Al-Andalus—most likely in Balansiyya, or Mayurika. Forgive me, Ketmia, but a young woman of your race would bring a very great price in Tunis, Monastir, or Rabat. Naturally, the price would be even greater for a virgin. Prices in excess of thirty thousand dirhams are not unusual; and if the woman is truly beautiful, the price could easily climb to as much as fifty or sixty thousand dirhams."

"I had no idea," said Cait, a little awed by the exorbitant amount.

"Oh, yes," Hasan assured her. "And that is your sister's greatest protection. For the bandits are well aware of the value of a fair-faced virgin. Thus, we can be certain that your sister has not been harmed in any way. As the poet says, 'If evil is an oyster, hope is the pearl.' You see? Even a brute like Ali Waqqar will want to make the best price, so he will take good care of her, believe me."

"I pray you are right, Prince Hasan," said Rognvald. "Even so, I cannot see how this helps us to find Alethea."

"Ah! Impatience often begets impetuosity, my lord. I am coming to it in good time. As you yourselves have seen, for brigands like Ali Waqqar these mountains provide countless hiding places; a man might search for a hundred years and never find his quarry. But settlements are few, and all of them are within easy reach of this fortress.

"Now then," he leaned forward, grinning with wily exuberance, "Ali and his band of thieves must obtain supplies from one settlement or another. I propose to send word throughout the realm that Prince Hasan wants to buy a white slave. We will say that I have grown bored and lonely on my mountaintop and wish to divert myself with a female slave—a luxury for which I am happy to pay sixty thousand silver dirhams."

Hasan gave a little laugh and lay back. "Then we simply sit back and wait for Ali Waqqar to come to collect his fee. And when he appears . . ." he clapped his hands together smartly, "snap! We have him."

"It is indeed an ingenious plan," Cait granted. "However, there is one thing which I question."

"Only one?" muttered Rognvald sourly.

Ignoring him, Cait asked, "How can we be certain Ali Waqqar is still in the region? He might be fleeing south even now. Would it not be wise to send men to search the southern trails? If what you say about the slave markets is true—and I do not doubt it—we might catch him along the way."

"My thoughts exactly," agreed Rognvald. He tore off a bit of bread and popped it into his mouth. "Assuming that it is Ali Waqqar, and assuming that he would be making for the coast, how do we know he is not hastening there even now?"

"My friends," said Hasan, "you do not know Ali Waqqar as I know him. He has long been a bane to me and to my people. We have suffered his thieving and plundering far too long. Nothing would give me greater pleasure than to crush him like a worm beneath my heel.

"Perhaps, if I had been more vigilant in the past we might never have come to this difficult pass. But I have vowed before Almighty Allah, the Savior of the Righteous, to bring a swift end to this brigand's predation, and restore your sister to her rightful place."

Stretching his hand toward Cait, who grasped it with unseemly alacrity—so it seemed to Rognvald—the prince said, "My beautiful Ketmia, I could not endure the thought of seeing you bereft. To reunite you and your loving sister—*that* has now become the pure flame of my ambition."

Raising her hand to his lips, he kissed it. "By the will of Allah, I shall not rest until I have brought about this reunion."

Rognvald watched this immodest display through narrowed eyes; but Cait, much taken with the prince already, found her heart beating a little more quickly for his promises. Unable to stomach any more, Rognvald rose and, begging the prince's pardon, took his leave saying that he wished to see to his men. "I want to be ready to ride out as soon as a break in the storm permits," he said.

Rising, he acknowledged the prince with a bow, then turned and strode quickly from the room—almost colliding with Jubayar, who was lurking at the door. Cait watched the tall knight depart, before turning to Prince Hasan to apologize. "I pray you forgive Lord Rognvald, my lord. He seems to have forgotten himself since coming here."

"Ah, well, as the poet says, 'Warriors, like swords, grow dull with neglect.' All men of action feel inactivity an onerous burden. No doubt he will feel more at ease when he can return to the saddle."

"You are too kind, my lord prince."

"If I am, it is your good influence upon me." He kissed her hand again. "You inspire me to greater virtue, and I am happy to be so inspired."

They spent the rest of the morning together; the prince showed Cait through various chambers, halls, courts, and quarters, each more sumptuous than the last with rare woods carved and inlaid in fantastically intricate patterns, and fine colored marble. In some, the walls were smooth-plastered, and painted with rich, glowing colors; in others, the walls were decorated with ornate and costly tiles; some had windows fitted with triangles of colored glass, and others with grills of carved wood or stone.

Some of the rooms were spacious and grand, while others were intimate as bedchambers; whether large or small, however, the rooms were immaculate in cleanliness and conception, revealing the full splendor of the intellect that had created them. Each room was named, and the names were wondrous, too: Zaffira, Caravanserai, Ivory Court, the Ladies' Tower, Red Sirocco, and one called Evening Narjis—where the deep-colored tiles reminded Cait of a peacock's feathers, and so instantly it became the Peacock Room.

As they went on, Cait could not help but notice that the rooms, although exquisite to the tiniest detail, were uniformly devoid of furniture. After viewing one barren expanse after another, her curiosity grew unbearable. "Truly, I have never seen such a wealth of magnificence. Yet, I cannot help wondering where all the furnishings have gone?"

Prince Hasan put his head back and laughed, the sound of his voice full and deep. "Oh, Ketmia, you are a very marvel of practicality. Yes, the rooms are bare until the moment when I decide which shall be occupied and for what purpose. Then, the things I require are brought by my servants and arranged as need dictates."

Cait thought this practice highly resourceful, and expressed such delight at the ingenuity of it that Prince Hasan said, "Allow me to demonstrate. Now then, of all the rooms you have seen so far, which do you favor?"

Cait was ready with her reply. "Oh, it must be the Peacock Room. The colors are exquisite."

The prince appeared pleased with the choice. "Splendid! I knew you would choose that one; it is one of my special favorites, too. So! Tonight we will dine in the Peacock Room, you and I, and I will show you how this feat is accomplished."

Cait spent the rest of the day examining the books in the prince's considerable collection. Obtained in various places throughout the Arab world, each one was bound in fine leather and, although written in the graceful, flowing Arabic script which Cait could not read, she enjoyed looking at the painted pictures which adorned page after page. One book contained scenes of life along the River Nile, the Great Mosq of Cairo, and the Sphinx—and this one she especially enjoyed.

"You like this book," said Hasan, enjoying her delight. "I can see it in your eyes."

"Oh, yes, very much," she said. "You see, my father was once a guest of the Caliph of Cairo. He told me about it many times, and in these paintings I can see what he saw."

"You love your father," observed the prince. "I can hear it in your voice when you speak of him."

"I did, yes. He was a fine man. He is dead now, and I cherish his memory. It is the most precious thing I own."

"Then you must have this book so you can look at it whenever you like and remember him in a happier time."

"Oh, but I could not—" Cait protested. "A book like this—I have never seen the like. It must have cost a fortune. I could never accept such a costly gift. I have nothing to give you in return."

Prince Hasan closed the leather-bound book and placed it in her hands.

"Darling Ketmia, if you only knew how much you have already given me. Please, accept it as but a small token of my great esteem and," he gazed intently into her eyes, "my even greater affection."

Her heart, filled with tender thoughts of her father, the warmth of the prince's breathtaking generosity, and so many fragile emotions, overflowed in a sudden rush. "Pray excuse me, lord," she said, pushing the tears away, "but it has been so long since anyone has treated me with such kindness and compassion."

His gaze softened. Reaching a hand to her cheek, he said, "Oh, my lovely Ketmia, you deserve nothing less. I would that I could give you such gifts always. For although we are but briefly met, I feel as if I have known you all my life."

Flustered by this admission, Cait stood speechless. Grasping the book, she looked down and rubbed the fallen tears from the leather. In the end, she was saved having to answer the prince's declaration by the sound of a gong ringing in one of the antechambers.

The prince straightened. "I am called away. Come, I will have Juba-yar take you back to the women's quarters so that you can rest and ready yourself for this evening."

The gong sounded again, and the prince led Caitríona back through a long corridor to one of the reception halls, and there commanded the eunuch to conduct her to the women's quarters. She looked for

Rognvald, or one of the knights, as they walked back through the interconnecting maze of corridors and passages, but saw none of the other guests.

Mahdi and Pila'i were waiting when she returned. While she rested, they prepared a bath for her, and laid out clothes for the evening. Cait surrendered herself to their ministrations, and passed the rest of the day in a pleasant haze of pampered indulgence.

As evening came on, the serving maids dressed her, arranged her hair, and brought out a necklace of jewels for her to wear. And then, when she was ready, the gong sounded, and a few moments later Jubayar arrived to take her to her dinner with the prince. She followed her escort through the covered courtyard, and as they passed the alabaster fountain, she heard a rustling sound and turned in time to see Prince Hasan's sister, Danji, disappearing behind one of the leafy palms. Cait had just a glimpse and then she was gone, but received the distinct impression that the young woman had been trying to attract her attention.

She turned back to find Jubayar watching her, his wide, fleshy lips twisted in a sneer of suspicion and disgust.

THIRTY-ONE

Caitríona dined alone with Prince Hasan that night. He fed her duckling glazed with a compote of honeyed apricots, boiled rice with cardamom and pine kernels, and baked quail's eggs. He plied her with spiced wine and sweetmeats, and pledged his love for her—not once, but twice. And she had accepted his blandishments.

She returned to her bedchamber slightly dazed and giddy from the heady potion of wine and murmured endearments. With the help of Mahdi and Pila'i, she undressed and went to sleep contemplating the evening in all its glittering grandeur.

Arrayed like an Eastern princess in layer upon layer of costly silks and jewels, she had been escorted by Jubayar to her dinner with the prince. She arrived to find the Peacock Room completely bare of any furnishings whatsoever, and stood for a moment peering into the dim, empty interior, feeling vaguely disappointed; for she had allowed herself to imagine something of the opulence of the previous evening. Her first thought was that the prince had forgotten his promise. Then again, perhaps she had not understood him correctly. As she stood in the center of the turquoise-tiled chamber, trying to think what could have happened, the prince arrived.

Dressed in flowing black robes edged with gold filigree, and wearing a turban of glistening Damascus cloth, he was the very embodiment of princely nobility. Slender and tall, his trim waist wrapped in a wide cloth belt into which had been bound a long curved dagger with a ruby handle and golden sheath, he swept across the room to her in bold, eager strides, and greeted her with a kiss on both hands.

Sensing her petulance, he smiled with wry amusement, clapped his hands and, in the manner of a sorcerer demonstrating a wonder, cried a word in Arabic which sounded like: "Haydee!"

Doors at the far end of the empty chamber were flung open and a succession of white-turbaned servants appeared. First came four men carrying iron standards, one in each hand; on each standard a candle-tree burned with ten lit candles. Hard on the heels of these first came four more men, carrying a lengthy roll of scarlet-and-blue figured carpet, which they placed at one end of the room and proceeded to unroll to the other; before they had reached the end, four more serving men appeared bearing enormous satin cushions on their heads, and a smaller carpet roll under their arms. No sooner had the first servants finished, than the second rank unrolled their rug in the center of the carpet, and placed the cushions on it.

Meanwhile, two more servants had entered carrying a low table between them, which they placed before the cushions. Scarcely had these departed when the first returned pushing gigantic pots of hammered brass containing miniature palm trees on wheeled platforms. Additional tables appeared, and more plants and live greenery in beaten brass containers, until the room began to take on the aspect of an Arabian garden. Then followed satin-covered chests and carved wooden boxes of various shapes and sizes; three flaming charcoal braziers and two cauldron-shaped copper incense burners; and a three-panel pierced screen made of rosewood, which was set up behind the bank of cushions; and an enormous brass gong.

Lastly, a canopy of blue silk was placed over the table and the candles arranged around it to bathe the diners in a golden glow of gently flickering light. Cait was captivated by the speed with which the transformation was effected, and by the wonderful result. In her excitement, she kissed the prince lightly on the cheek.

Five musicians appeared, arranged themselves and their instruments at a discreet distance from the canopy, and began to play. As the softly swaying melody filled the air, Hasan lifted his hand and declared, "This is how a true Prince of the Orient lives. Wherever he goes— whether to dine, or sleep, or," he paused, taking Cait's hand, "to receive his honored guests—the noble Arab has only to command, and his naked word is transmuted into magnificence and splendor.

"But come," he said, leading her to the bank of cushions, "let us sit and take our ease. I have arranged food and entertainment for your pleasure. Tonight, darling Ketmia, you will sample delicacies to make the angels envious."

"Will Danji be joining us?" she asked. "Or Rognvald?"

"No, not tonight." He smiled, his black eyes glinting in the candlelight. "Tonight, my love, we spend together, you and I."

Cait felt a quiver of illicit excitement at the implications of his declaration, but suddenly the skin at the nape of her neck crawled. A sensation of dread descended over her, and she felt as if she had just seen a snake. At any other time, this reaction would have warned her. Now, however, it irritated her. Where, she demanded of herself, was the danger?

She told herself that Prince Hasan was an admirable and generous host, a thoughtful and trustworthy friend; he was elegant, wealthy, and refined. He had already demonstrated his loyalty to her in his vow to save her sister, and now he spoke his love. No man, until now, had ever called her beautiful; to be thought so thrilled her in a way she could not have imagined. Who else had ever said the things to her that Hasan had said? A woman might search all her life for such a man and never find him. And here he was beside her, bidding her to take her ease and join him in a night of pleasure and delight.

And yet, the prospect, for all its seductive charm, produced not the rapturous warmth of mutual regard, but a thin, icy tingle of danger. She saw Hasan's smile, and it was the corpse-like grin of death.

Why should this be? Why should his loving declaration raise such dread?

As she walked to the table and sank down onto the satin cushions, she determined to ignore the warning sensations and enjoy the evening to the full. Firmly, and with an air of defiant indulgence, she pushed all such unpleasantness from her and willfully embraced the prince's invitation to luxuriate in the warmth of their new-kindled affection.

Folding her legs beneath her, she reclined on an elbow while the prince, taking up a leather-tipped mallet, struck the gong twice. Before the sound had faded, the door opened and serving maids appeared—two of them with trays, one bearing a jar and two gold chalices, and one a selection of silver bowls. While one of the serving maids placed the bowls on the table, the other poured the wine.

"There is good news," said the prince, watching the dark wine splash into the golden cups. "The storm abated somewhat at midday, so I was able to send Halhuli and some of my men to take word of my offer to the settlements. It will not be long, I think, before we hear word of his whereabouts."

"Oh, that is good news. Thank you, my lord. I owe you a debt of gratitude."

"It is my pleasure to serve you, my sweet Ketmia," said Hasan, passing her a cup. "Let us drink to a splendid and glorious future together."

Cait accepted the cup without hesitation and thus began a night of such intimacy and tenderness that when she finally rose to return to her quarters, she felt as if she were leaving part of herself behind.

Now, in the thin morning light, as she lay in bed still floating on the ebullient tide of emotion, she experienced the first faint twinges of regret. Outside, the storm rampaged with renewed vigor. She could hear the gale-driven sleet and snow rattling against the windows, and the wind booming and bellowing as it hurled itself against the walls in waves like a raging ocean swell.

She pushed any thoughts of reproach or misgiving firmly aside and got out of bed. Her serving maids had risen and were waiting to dress her, and adorn her hair. When they were finished, she went out to find Rognvald to tell him that he need not worry about resuming the search.

She found him, along with Svein, Dag, Yngvar and the two Spanish knights hurrying across the snowy courtyard to the stables. They were dressed in heavy skins, wool, and leather, and carried bags of provisions on their backs. At her call, the tall knight sent the others on, and returned to hear what she had to say.

"The horses are saddled. We have provisions enough for three days on the trail. With God's help we will return before then."

"But the storm still rages."

"And it may continue for several more days before it is finished. We have already lost three days, we dare not waste any more."

"There is no need," she said lightly. "The prince has already sent word to the settlements. We have only to wait and Ali Waqqar will soon bring Alethea to us."

"I beg your pardon, my lady, but I do not think it wise to abandon the search."

"Now you are just being stubborn," she told him.

"And you are being gulled by a man used to having every whim satisfied," he replied, straining to keep his tone even. "Mark me, a dalliance with a man like Hasan can only end in misery."

"How dare you come high-handed with me!" she charged, instantly furious with him. "And I will thank you not to speak of our benefactor in that coarse and insinuating way."

"Benefactor?" Rognvald dismissed the notion with a scornful laugh. "That man only thinks to benefit himself. I should have thought a woman of your discernment would recognize a poisonous snake when she saw one."

"Take that back!" she snapped. "Hasan has treated me with more respect and esteem than any man I have ever met. He is a prince in both word and deed, and a nobleman worthy of the name."

"Is he?" the knight challenged. "Is he indeed? Then consider this: do you not think it strange how this *noble* man seems to know such a great deal about the price of slaves in Tunis?"

"What of that?" Cait countered waspishly. "Even *I* know the ransom price of a pig-headed knight rescued from a Damascus prison."

Rognvald glared at her, his mouth a firm, hard line, his blue eyes bright with cold fire.

"Nothing else to say, my lord?"

"Sneering does not become a lady."

"Nor does petty spite and envy appear more seemly in a man," she retorted. "If you could keep your contemptible observations to yourself, I would count it a blessing."

Still glaring, he made a curt bow. "As you will. Pray give my regards to your prince; my men and I will resume the search for Abu and your sister."

"Then go—for all the good it will do!"

He stepped quickly to the door and paused. "I made a vow before God," he said in solemn earnest, then hurried out into the storm.

Furious still, and determined not to allow him the satisfaction of the last word, she dashed to the open door and shouted after the swiftly retreating figure. "Hasan is twice the man you are!"

Her words were lost in the rattling howl of the wind. Rognvald walked on, and the sleety snow soon took him from view. She turned to the door and, pushing with all her might, slammed it shut with a booming thump; the sound brought the two porters on the run. They admonished her in rapid Arabic, but she paid no heed and stalked off, leaving them to wipe up the puddle of melted sleet on the floor.

Seething inside, she stormed along the deserted corridors of the *al-qazr*, smacking her fist against the wall now and then, and cursing Rognvald's insufferable insolence. She swore on her soul that she had never known a more vexatious and annoying man.

She did not know which was the more irksome—the Norwegian lord himself, or the fact that, impudent as he undoubtedly was, he was also right: a dalliance with the prince could bring serious, not to say disastrous, consequences.

Not yet ready to admit as much, Cait dismissed the thought from her mind and made her way back to the women's quarters without pausing to summon Jubayar to escort her. Presently, she reached the covered courtyard and paused at the fountain to look at the water lilies and chide herself for being so angry with Rognvald.

She was gazing at her own glum reflection in the water when she heard the soft brush of a light step on the gallery above, and glanced up to see Hasan's sister Danji watching her intently. Forcing a smile, she raised her hand in greeting, and drew breath to speak. Before she could utter a word, however, the young woman silenced her with a frantic gesture, and motioned for her to come up onto the upper gallery.

Glancing around quickly to make certain they were unobserved, Cait hurried up the stairs only to find that Danji had moved on. She was standing a few paces away, and as Cait made to join her she disappeared through a door leading to one of the inner chambers. Uncertain what to do, Cait hesitated, and a moment later Danji's hand appeared, beckoning her on.

Cait hastened to the door, which was open, and stepped inside; the room was cold and dark, the only light coming from a small window covered by a heavy grill. With a look of intrigue that sent a quiver of complicity racing through Cait, the young woman pulled her into the room and closed the door behind her. She then moved to the window and motioned for Cait to follow.

"I must speak to you," Danji said. "But we must never be seen together." Her voice trembled, but whether with fright or cold, Cait could not tell. "Promise me you will tell no one."

"You can speak Latin," said Cait.

"You must promise," Danji insisted. "Now. This instant—or I will tell you nothing."

"I do promise. I will tell no one what passes between us," she agreed firmly.

"Very well. Do not think me unkind, but you must leave here at once. It is not safe." She gripped Cait's arm for emphasis. "You must believe me."

"Why? What is wrong, Danji?"

Glancing around as if she feared they would be overheard, Danji shook her head. "I can say no more."

"Why must I leave?"

"You are in danger." She edged closer to the door.

Cait held her. "Tell me why? Where is the danger?"

"Please, I can say no more. He would kill me if he found out I spoke to you." Danji moved quickly to the door.

Cait followed. "Who?" she asked, but received no reply. Clearly she would get no more from the frightened woman this way, and decided to try another approach. "No harm will come to you," she said, trying to reassure her. "I thought Hasan said you could not speak Latin."

"Hasan says many things," the young woman replied. "He said also that I was his sister."

"Are you not?"

"No." Opening the door a crack, Danji peered out to see if anyone was watching. As she stepped out onto the gallery, she looked back over her shoulder. "I am not his sister," she whispered. "I am his wife."

THIRTY-TWO

"In Anjou before the snow," muttered Renaud de Bracineaux thickly as he stared at the muddy track before him; white-topped mountains in the distance seemed to be holding up a sky like rumpled gray wool. "Winter at your estate—that is what you said." He spat into a puddle.

"I blame the emperor," the baron replied indifferently. "If we had not been made to lavish attendance on his silly cow of a niece, we would have been there and back by now."

De Bracineaux continued as if he had not heard, "Not to mention the priest disappearing."

"Ho, now! I will not have that laid at *my* feet," d'Anjou objected. "Anything might have happened to him. Wild animals might have got him for all we know."

"God's teeth," snarled the Templar, "it was that damnable woman! And that is another thing you were wrong about." He regarded the man on the horse beside him with rank disgust. "I am curious. Tell me, d'Anjou, have you ever been right about anything in your life?"

Sergeant Gislebert reined up just then. "The company is ready, commander."

De Bracineaux cast a glance at the long double rank of troops and pack animals and wagons. The knights sat hump-shouldered on their mounts; hooded, their once-white surcoats now brown with mud, they looked like the ruined remnant of a vanquished army. Turning away abruptly, the commander looked again at the low, sullen sky as rain began to spatter on the mud-slick road. "Let us make a start," he said. "God knows we will not get far today." Raising a hand, he signalled the columns to move forward, and they rode on into another day of drizzle and cold.

At midday, they stopped at the ford of a swift-running stream to rest and water the horses. While there, the scouts who had been sent out the previous day returned. The commander met them as they rode in. "Well?" he said, impatience making him sharp.

"We have found something, my lord," said one of the Templars. "We think you should take a look."

"What is it?"

"Remains of a camp," said the second knight.

"How far?"

"Not far. We can be there by nightfall."

De Bracineaux accepted this estimate without comment. He turned to Gislebert. "Get fresh mounts for these men," he ordered. "And have one of the cooks prepare them something to eat. I want to be ready to move on as soon as the horses are watered."

Until now, the trail had not been difficult to follow. The abbot of Logroño reported having spoken to a foreign knight, and having attempted to dissuade him and his party from continuing their journey. At Milagro and Carcastillo, the villagers told them that yes, of course, a party of knights passed through; they stopped and worked in exchange for bacon, flour, oats, and such. Yes, they said, there were women with them, and a priest. They stayed a few days and then departed, heading north and east along the river.

The Templars followed the river, too, and when the settlements grew so far apart and so far off the trail to be dependable sources of information, de Bracineaux took to sending out scouts. The trail was old, but the scouts were expert trackers, so the Templars slowly followed their quarry further and further into Aragon's high, empty hills.

With the approach of winter, the wind and rain and occasional frost had begun making the thieves' trail increasingly difficult to raise. For the last two days, they had journeyed on without clear indication that they were still in productive pursuit. Now, however, the scouts had turned up another clue to help them continue the search a little longer.

Even so, de Bracineaux knew not to allow himself to become too overjoyed by this development. Winter was coming to the high country, and if he did not discover where the priest was leading his band of thieves before it fell, he might never find them. The thought that they might yet escape his grasp filled him with an icy and implacable rage that drove him on.

By the time they reached the place the scouts had marked, the day had ended in a damp gloom which descended over the rain-soaked track like a curtain. "We can see nothing now," said de Bracineaux. "Set up camp down there," he pointed back down the trail to where the troops were waiting. "If there *is* anything to see, I do not want it trampled into the mud. We will give the place a thorough inspection as soon as it is light."

The tents were raised and the evening meal prepared in the rain and dark—five tents with four men each for the knights, one for the commander, and one for the baron. When space permitted, they clustered the tents around two or three large campfires which both warmed them and dried their sodden clothes. This night, however, because of the trees and thick underbrush they strung them in a line along the track, and had to rely on small campfires before each tent; there was little warmth, and no one went to sleep in a dry cloak or boots.

The next morning dawned clear and, while the sergeant oversaw the troops as they prepared to resume the journey, de Bracineaux, d'Anjou, and the two scouts rode up to the abandoned campsite. Dismounting a few score paces away, de Bracineaux walked to where the fire had burned. He squatted down and looked at the ground inside the fire ring. The ashes had been washed away by numerous rains; all that remained was a milky-gray puddle and a few unburned ends of branches, with a small pile of sticks stacked beside the ring of stone.

Rising, he turned and looked across the clearing toward the trees. A large branch lay on the ground before a rock outcropping between two trees. He went to it, lifted it, and examined the end. The cut was ragged; it looked as though the branch had been half-chopped, half-yanked from the tree. He stood fingering the cut and looking around.

"Lord commander, have you found something?" asked one of the Templar scouts.

"I cannot say," he replied. "I think there was some trouble here. You there," de Bracineaux called to the other scout, "search in those trees. And you—" he said to the other, "we know they had a wagon; see if you can find any tracks."

While the scouts carried out their orders, the commander walked back and forth slowly over the clearing. Although it was difficult to tell for certain, it did appear as if the turf was broken and churned up in several places—more than it would be by a company of travelers stopping for a night or two.

"Here, d'Anjou," called de Bracineaux, "look at this and tell me what you think."

The baron leaned low in the saddle, holding his head to one side then the other. "I think it is too wet and too damnably cold to be searching for weevils in the porridge."

"The ground, damn you," barked de Bracineaux. "Look at the ground." He paused for a moment, then demanded, "Well?"

"It looks as though they have had a falling out. A fight among thieves perhaps?"

"Not *among* thieves," the commander corrected. "*Between* thieves."

"There is a difference?"

"There is every difference, d'Anjou," replied de Bracineaux. He then declared: "They were attacked."

The baron regarded the muddy patch doubtfully. "A bit of scuffed-up turf is hardly indication of a pitched battle."

"Scout!" shouted the commander. The nearest Templar came running. "Fetch the sergeant and four more men. I want a search made of the perimeter."

The man disappeared on the run and de Bracineaux, fists on hips, head bent down, continued his close scrutiny of the soggy ground. Every now and then, he stopped to examine something that caught his eye, before moving on again.

"Lord commander! Here!" called the remaining scout.

De Bracineaux joined the man at the edge of the clearing. "What have you found?"

"It appears to be barley meal," replied the knight, stooping low over a pale heap of sodden matter.

The commander knelt, and removing a glove, picked up some of the soggy stuff. He rubbed it between his fingers, held it under his nose and sniffed. "I think you are right."

"There must be a quarter of a barrel spilled there," the knight pointed out. "Either someone was very careless—"

"Or in a very great hurry," concluded the Templar commander. "Too great a hurry to salvage what he had spilled."

"And there," said the scout, pointing to four shallow, evenly spaced indentations. "Those could be from the wagon wheels."

D'Anjou approached and sat on his horse a little distance away. "Does anyone smell what I am smelling?" he asked, lifting his beak-like nose into the air. "Something has given up the ghost."

De Bracineaux walked to where d'Anjou, head tilted back, was sifting the air for the scent. "It is somewhere off through there," he said, pointing across the clearing toward a stand of taller trees.

Sergeant Gislebert and the additional men arrived just then. De Bracineaux met them in the center of the clearing. "There is something dead in those trees just there," he said, pointing to the place d'Anjou indicated. "Start your search there. Call out if you find anything."

The Templars hastened off into the wood, and almost immediately the cry came back. "Commander! There is a grave!"

Baron D'Anjou smiled as he dismounted. "*I* may never be right, but this nose of mine is rarely wrong." He followed the commander into the wood and they quickly arrived in another small clearing to find the Templars standing beside a wide rectangle of mounded earth. A crude cross was pressed into the soft dirt, and around it were the spent stubs of burnt branches.

De Bracineaux took one look at the mound and said, "Dig it up."

The knights hesitated. One of their number made bold to reply. "My lord commander," he said, pointing to the cross, "Christians are buried here."

"Unless you wish to join them," growled the commander, "do as I say. Dig it up!"

Still the knights hesitated. "My lord," said Gislebert, speaking up, "the shovel is in the wagon back there."

"Damn the shovel, Gislebert! You have swords, do you not? Hands? Dig!"

Slowly, and with great reluctance, the Templars began to burrow into the soft wet earth with their bare hands. With every handful of dirt they removed, the stink d'Anjou had noticed grew stronger. Soon the men were holding their noses with one hand and digging half-heartedly with the other as, slowly, five human forms began to emerge.

"Dig, damn you!" cried de Bracineaux, growing impatient. The soil was less damp nearer the bodies, and the stench all the stronger. The Templars continued to scoop away the dirt, one or two with tears streaming down their beards, the rest clutching the edge of their cloaks to their faces. Slowly, individual bodies were revealed. There were five of them; two big men in dark brown cloaks laid out on either side of a slender man in black.

"Hold!" called the commander, bending near. "What have we here?" He pointed to the one in the center. "Pull the hood away from his face."

The nearest knight did as he was told, and pulled the hood of the corpse's dark robe from his face. The flesh was wan and waxy, but the cold ground had prevented the body from bloating so it still resembled the man that had been. The beard was black against the bloodless pallor of his skin, and the lips held the hint of a smile.

"It looks like a priest," said the Templar, pulling a small wooden cross from beneath a fold in the robe.

De Bracineaux nodded. "What about these others?" he said, indicating the corpses either side of the priest. Another knight pulled back a hood covering one of the faces. Here the worms were at work on the eyes; the sudden sight of squirming, half-empty sockets proved too much for the knight, who jerked back his hand as if he had been burned.

"A Spaniard," observed d'Anjou. "Judging from their clothing, so are the others." Indicating the priest, he said, "Do you think that could be Matthias?"

De Bracineaux nodded. "Five dead," he mused. "If the villagers at the last place were telling the truth, she has only six left."

"Do you want me to bring the archbishop to see the priest?" asked Gislebert.

"He insists they never laid eyes on one another," replied d'Anjou.

"Bring him anyway," the commander ordered, "for all the good it will do. By the Rood, I wish I had sent him back; the man is a very millstone." Turning to the knights standing nearby, he said, "Well? Search the rest of the area, and be quick about it."

In the end, they found nothing else—save the ragged remains of three human carcasses which had been gnawed by animals. The dead were Moorish, from what they could gather from the remains and scraps of clothing. Of the company that had been attacked, no further signs were found, so Commander de Bracineaux ordered his scouts to begin scouring the area, working out in ever-widening circles from the camp, in the hope of raising the trail again.

The day ended without success, but the next morning one of the scouts found a small heap of rocks beside a nearby stream—and an-

276

other on the opposite side, pointing the way. "They passed this way, and marked the place," the scout told them. "They seem to be heading into the mountains."

"Hear that, d'Anjou?" said the commander. "We have found the trail." Lifting his eyes to the mountains in the distance showing above the trees, he continued, "The hind is swift, but the hound is persistent. We will yet run her to the ground. And when we do, I will tear her apart."

THIRTY-THREE

Despite Danji's revelation and the urgency of her warning, Cait dined with Hasan again that night, and also the next. In any event, she had little choice. Rognvald and the knights were still away, and she could think of no reasonable apology she might offer to excuse herself without rousing unnecessary suspicion—all the more since she ardently professed to enjoy their evenings together. And she did enjoy them, albeit somewhat warily now as she tried to determine the nature of the danger Danji had intimated.

She perceived no change in Prince Hasan; he remained as charming and engaging as ever, and each evening's meal was pure enchantment from beginning to end. Still, the worm of doubt had begun to gnaw its way into her heart. Was he, or was he not, the man she thought him to be?

During the day, she pondered this question, turning it over and over in her mind. On the one hand, she could not discern anything amiss in either mood or manner: he was solicitous, thoughtful, respectful and polite in every way. On the other hand, there was Danji. If she was telling the truth—and Cait had no reason to doubt her—Hasan was not at all as he appeared.

Although she looked for any opportunity to speak to Danji alone, she did not see the slender young woman again—but she did notice that Jubayar was much more attentive and present than previously.

On the second day, the storm subsided and by dusk the sky had cleared. Cait decided to try the prince's integrity for herself. When they met for dinner that evening, she said, "The storm has abated, and that is a blessing. Therefore, I was hoping we might ride to one of the valley settlements and inquire whether anyone has word of Ali Waqqar."

"Of course, my lovely Ketmia; if that is what you wish," replied the prince smoothly. "After so many days shut inside, even the most splendid palace becomes dreary as a prison. We will ride down to the valley and see if the seeds I planted have borne fruit." He paused, as if considering the matter more thoroughly. "Although—" he began, then hesitated. "No, it is not important."

"What is it?" asked Cait, alert to even the slightest nuance of deception. "Tell me."

"Well," he said, "I do not expect we shall learn anything, for if Ali Waqqar had heard the terms of my offer, the rogue would have been here already." He smiled suddenly. "But you must not worry. No doubt the storm has prevented word from reaching him."

"Yes," Cait agreed absently, "I suppose it would be wrong to expect too much just yet."

Hasan's smile broadened; he held out his hand for hers. "Precisely, my love. Give it another day or so, and no doubt the brigand will be beating on these very doors, demanding payment."

"And then what will you do?" asked Cait sweetly.

Hasan appeared distracted by the question. "Please?"

"What will you do with Ali when you catch him?"

"Why, I shall throw him in chains and, before the sun has set, his ugly head shall adorn a pike above the gate." He pulled her to him. "But come, Ketmia, it is not seemly for a woman to discuss such unpleasant subjects. Let us talk of finer things. I have written a poem for you. Sit here, my lovely, and I shall read it out."

Nothing more was said that night, and the next morning, true to his word, the prince had horses saddled and ready for their ride. They left before the sun quartered the sky, and rode out into a bright, crisp winter day. The storm had scoured every cloud, leaving the vault of Heaven clean and polished to a brilliant crystalline clarity.

Wrapped in her fine new cloak, Cait enjoyed the stinging fresh air and the stunning views from the ridgeway high above the valley floor. The trail was steep and winding, and so they rode in single file to the valley. The prince led, followed by Halhuli; Cait came next, and then four mounted guards with banners attached to their spears.

As they neared the lower slopes, they passed through a snow-dusted forest where Hasan pointed out the delicate hoofprints of red deer, and the less dainty tracks of wild pigs in the unbroken snow. Upon reaching the valley floor, the snow vanished entirely, and the track became a road. The nearest settlement was some distance away and it was after midday by the time they reached the place: a small upland village of squat white-washed houses, forlorn amidst bare muddy fields.

At their approach, the villagers came out to watch and greet them. A gaggle of ragged children, wide-eyed and stiff-legged, pointed at the brightly colored banners and exchanged whispered observations behind their hands. While Halhuli and his men looked on, the prince dismounted and spoke to the villagers in Arabic; he passed along the line, handing out silver coins to one and all. The children danced with excitement.

Presently, a stout man with a rough beard and dirty yellow turban appeared and, with a gesture of welcome, loudly hailed the prince. Hasan turned to Cait and called, "Here is Abdullah, the head man. We will learn something now."

The two walked a little apart from the clutch of villagers. Cait watched them closely, but saw nothing to arouse her suspicion one way or another. After their conversation, the prince placed his hand on the man's shoulder, and then embraced him. They parted then, and the prince returned to his horse and climbed into the saddle.

"Abdullah says that the bandits were seen skirting the village four nights ago—before the storm."

Cait's heart leaped at this sudden revelation. "And Alethea, was she with them? Did they see her?" She looked at the man, who was now standing beside the prince's horse. "Oh, please, ask him. I must know."

"I am sorry, Ketmia. It was growing dark and they were far away." The prince spoke to the head man, who pointed across the fields to a line of trees in the distance. "He says they were riding east toward the hills. One of the boys saw them, and Abdullah went to look but could not tell how many there were—eight, ten, maybe more."

The prince thanked the villagers and moved his party on, escorted from the village by the children who ran along behind, ululating in a weird chorus of acclaim. They proceeded to the next settlement—a short ride away on the other side of the river which divided the valley in half. Here, as before, the same custom of greeting was observed, and the same discussion alone with the head man of the village—a toothless, hump-backed old man this time—who told them that two of the bandits had come to the village to buy ground meal and cured bacon.

It was almost dark when the men appeared, the chieftain reported, and the villagers were afraid of what the brigands would do if they were turned away empty-handed. So they sold the bandits meal and bacon, and some wine—and the men rode away.

On further questioning, the old chief said that although he did not see any more riders, he knew there were more waiting nearby. Was it Ali Waqqar? asked the prince. Who else? replied the toothless chieftain. It is always Ali Waqqar.

"Then you were right," said Cait, much relieved by what they had learned. "It is Ali Waqqar." Her relief was short-lived however, for in the very next breath she asked, "But now that he has provisions, what if he has moved on? What if he is riding south even now?"

"Peace, dearest Ketmia. A little faith can move great mountains—so it is written, is it not? You must trust me." He remounted his horse, cast a quick look at the sky, and said, "I think we should begin the journey home."

"So soon?" asked Cait.

"Alas, my love, even a prince cannot prevent the sun from setting." He smiled sympathetically. "Still, it has been a good day. We have learned much, and I have repeated my offer of ransom. It will not be long now, I think, before we obtain your sister's release."

Thus, they started back, reaching the steep trail to the high *al-qazr* as the sun dropped below the ridge to the west casting the valley in shadow. They were just beginning the long climb up the winding mountain track when they were hailed by riders from the south. Halhuli spoke a word of command and the prince's guards lowered their spears and took up a protective position between the oncoming riders and the prince.

"It is Lord Rognvald!" shouted Cait when the newcomers were near enough to recognize.

Hasan shouted a command to his guards, who raised their weapons and rode out to meet the knights. "Greetings, my lord knight," called the prince as the Norsemen, escorted by his guards, reined up. "Good hunting?"

"No," said Rognvald, his voice cracking with fatigue, "not as good as we had hoped."

"We saw smoke from a campfire once," offered Svein.

"But we lost it before we could find the place," concluded Dag.

"We never saw it again," added Yngvar. Too tired to speak, the two Spanish knights shook their heads in agreement.

"Most unfortunate," answered the prince. "Still, there is cause for joy. We have learned that Ali Waqqar is nearby."

"Indeed?" Rognvald looked from the prince to Cait, who confirmed Hasan's assertion with a nod.

"The bandits have been seen," she told him. "They came into the valley for provisions three or four nights ago."

"That *is* good news," agreed Rognvald. He rubbed his face wearily. "They are still in the region at least."

"Yes," said Hasan. "I think it will not be long now before our efforts are rewarded. As the poet says: 'A silken net to catch a bird; a silver net to catch a thief.' Ali Waqqar will come to us very soon."

"I pray that it is so, lord prince," replied Rognvald.

Hasan signalled to Halhuli, who began leading the way back to the palace. The prince took his place beside Caitríona and rode with her for the rest of the journey. Twilight was full about them by the time they entered the outer courtyard, the stars shone as bright needles of light in the thin cold mountain air.

They dismounted, and as the grooms came running from the stables, the knights began moving slowly and stiffly toward the palace entrance. The doors were open, and rosy light from the braziers burning in the anteroom spilled out onto the steps and into the courtyard.

"You and your men are exhausted," said the prince, falling into step beside Rognvald. "Allow me to send a hot supper to you in your quarters. That way you can use the baths and eat at your leisure."

"Well," said Rognvald, glancing back at Cait, who appeared not to have heard, "if it is no trouble."

"Not in the least," Hasan assured him. "I myself often do this when I return from a day of hunting. Otherwise, I would fall asleep at the table, and that would never do. We will talk tomorrow."

He sent them off with words of encouragement and, turning to Cait, said, "I am afraid you must endure my company once again. Your knights have chosen to take their meal in their quarters tonight. To be sure, it is for the best—they have been riding three days and are very tired."

"Oh," replied Cait, disappointment flitting across her features. "I had hoped to hear more from Rognvald about their searches."

"Tomorrow, my love," promised the prince. "We will all sit down together and tell what we have learned. And, who knows? Maybe tomorrow Ali Waqqar will join us and we can put an end to this trouble at last."

Dinner that night was as sumptuous and enjoyable as any that had gone before. Prince Hasan was charming and attentive, winsome in his manner, and subtly insinuating in his flattery. This time, however, she was able to plead weariness and leave the table with most of the night still before her. Under Jubayar's stern and silent eye, she returned to her chamber feeling more than ever as if she were playing the hapless hare to the prince's falcon.

Mahdi and Pila'i were surprised to see her so early, and took the opportunity to brush her hair and braid it in preparation for bed, chattering away to her, blithely indifferent to the fact that Cait could not understand a word they said. So absorbed were they in their talk that neither one of them heard the gong ringing at the entrance to the Ladies' Court.

"Shh!" said Cait, putting her finger to her lips. "Listen."

The gong sounded again—a low ringing tone, not loud.

Cait stood and was moving toward the door, when it burst open and Lord Rognvald entered. The two serving maids began to cry out, but Cait silenced them with a sharp slap on the arm apiece. "Hush," she said. "I will speak to my friend."

She crossed to where Rognvald was waiting by the door. "Rognvald, I was hoping to speak to you. How did you know where to find me?"

"Please, I have little time," he said. "Svein and Rodrigo will keep the guard Jubayar busy as long as they can, but he could return at any moment and I dare not let him find me here."

"Yes, go on."

"God knows it gives me no pleasure to say it."

"Pray, speak. What is it?"

"The prince is lying about the offer of ransom. He never sent his men to the settlements."

"But, just today I saw—"

"No." Rognvald shook his head firmly. "The offer was never made."

"Are you certain?"

"I know enough Arabic to discuss ransom," the knight replied. "And no one in any of the villages knew anything about Hasan's offer."

"And Ali Waqqar?"

"Him they knew about—that much was clear. But no one would talk to us. I think they are afraid."

"What should we do?"

Rognvald regarded her intently, his eyes searching, probing. "If you are with me in this—"

"I am."

"Then we must confront Hasan and make him tell us the truth."

"I agree," Cait replied. "And it must be soon."

"Tomorrow morning—when we meet to breakfast. We will take him by surprise."

Cait nodded and, suddenly very grateful for the tall knight's stalwart devotion, she gave him a quick kiss on the cheek.

Rognvald smiled suddenly. "Your change of heart is wondrous to behold. Truly, I did not think you would hear any word against the prince."

She raised an eyebrow. "Have I been so prickly of late?"

"Lady, a bramble thicket is more welcoming."

Putting her hands on his chest, she pushed him toward the door. "Go now, my lord. I fear you have outstayed your welcome."

He opened the door a crack and looked both ways along the gallery before stepping out. The door closed silently, and he was gone.

Cait turned to her two gawking handmaidens and, through a series of what she hoped were sternly pointed gestures, warned them to secrecy. In an effort to maintain the pretense that nothing unusual had taken place, she commanded them to continue brushing her hair and making ready her bed. They fell to readily enough, and were soon whittering away again like birds.

When they finally blew out the candles and settled down for the night, Cait could not rest. Sleep eluded her; she kept thinking about the lies she had been told, and tried to discern what might be behind them. Daylight found her ill-rested and in a foul humor, but all the more eager to face Prince Hasan and demand an explanation of him.

She woke her sleepy servants and dressed hurriedly, leaving the women's quarters in the company of a grimly disapproving Jubayar. She was first to arrive at the room where they most often broke fast—

a small, bright room with colored tiles of blue, green, and yellow, and a large window overlooking a garden court below. There was no one about, so she settled down to wait, and presently an old servant appeared, bowed in greeting, and began making up the fire in the hearth.

After a time, more servants came to prepare the table, spreading bright cloths on which they placed baskets of bread and cold sliced meat. One servant began cooking oat porridge in a pot on the hearth, and others brought a large bowl of hot almond milk spiced with cinnamon. Cait accepted a cup of the warming drink, and waited while more servants came and went.

Where was Rognvald, she wondered? What could be keeping him?

She went to the door and looked out into the antechamber and the corridors beyond, but aside from Jubayar, slumped asleep in a corner, there was no sign of anyone about. She waited some more, and had just decided to go in search of the knights when she heard footsteps and voices in the anteroom. She jumped up from her place at the table and ran to the door to meet Prince Hasan and his advisor, Halhuli.

"Allah, the Ever Gracious, be good to you," exclaimed Hasan. "Darling Ketmia, how lovely you look this morning. I did not know you would be waiting or I should have come sooner."

Cait greeted him pleasantly, and said, truthfully, "I did not sleep well last night, so I rose early." She looked beyond the two men. "I was hoping to speak to Rognvald, too. I wanted to hear how he fared in his search."

"But Ketmia, he is gone."

A sudden anxiety overcame her. "What do you mean? Where would he go?"

Raising a calming hand, the prince said, "Peace, my darling. I am sorry. Had I known you wished so ardently to see him, I might have prevented him from leaving."

She looked to Halhuli for confirmation; he merely shrugged, as if to say there was nothing to be done.

"But why would he go off without telling me?"

"Allah alone knows, my love. We will ask him when he returns. But, if I may speculate?"

"Please do," said Cait, her tone growing brusque.

"It seemed to me that he was disheartened by his lack of success in finding Alethea. The man is very stubborn, as you know." Hasan offered a sadly sympathetic smile and spread his hands. "I believe he could not accept his failure. He and his knights roused the stablemen and ordered fresh horses to be saddled. They compelled the porters to open the gate, and rode out just before dawn."

Cait looked at him blankly, a feeling of desperation rising up from the soles of her feet and into her belly. She knew the prince was lying, but she could not understand why, or know how to force him into an admission. "He might have left some word for me," she said darkly, as if her anger were directed at the thoughtless knight.

Hasan turned to his silent advisor. "Did he leave any word?"

Halhuli shook his head. "No, my lord."

"I am sorry, Ketmia. Now you are angry and unhappy. What shall I do to cheer you?" He tapped his chin with a finger as if in thought. "I know! The Winter Garden is ready now, and it is a rare delight. The day is fine; we will break our fast and then I shall take you for a walk in the garden."

"Later, perhaps," said Cait. "I think I would like to go back to my room. Lord Rognvald's thoughtlessness and negligence have spoiled my appetite. I pray you will excuse me."

She left then, lest the prince find some means of persuading her to stay. On the way to her quarters the realization struck her that her position had suddenly grown extremely precarious. She was all alone now, and there was no one she could trust, or turn to for help.

By the time she reached the women's quarters, however, the first fright at her predicament had passed; in its place had settled a cold determination not to allow the prince to work his devious will. The heat of righteous indignation fired her thoughts. And, by the time she reached the door to her room, she had remembered that there was someone she could trust to help her now: Danji.

THIRTY-FOUR

Cait waited through the day for Danji to appear. By way of signs and gestures, and the repetition of Danji's name, she had at last brought Mahdi to comprehend something of the urgency and apprehension she felt. The handmaid went off on her secret errand and Cait settled back to wait. Tired from her restless night, she soon closed her eyes and descended into a fitful sleep, full of fragments of images and half-remembered dreams.

She stood again on the high cliffs above the little bay south of Banvarð, alone, the sky filled with the cry of the gulls circling high overhead . . . dark stone buildings and green fields beyond, snug between heathered hills, a thin silvery thread of smoke rising to flatten on the wind from the sea . . . a tall figure dressed in black standing alone on the clifftop—Sydoni, gray hair combed by the wind, taking her by the hand and saying, "Caitríona, dear heart, it is good to see you. I was hoping you would come and bid me farewell."

Sydoni vanished, and Cait was outside the gate of the stronghold in the twilight. Abbot Emlyn was there, they were walking very quickly and he was talking to her, but she could not make out the words. And as they walked along she kept falling further and further behind. Desperate, she cried, "Wait! Abbot Emlyn, wait for me!"

The kindly old abbot did not stop, but turned his head and called over his shoulder, "*Sanctus Clarus*, Cait, remember. Sanctus Clarus—it is your birthright. One day, it will be your name." And then she was alone once more. The walled stronghold was gone and she was alone with the night and the stars . . . and Mahdi's gentle touch.

"Ketmia?" Mahdi said, touching her lightly on the arm.

She came awake at once and looked around. The room was dark; the small round windows admitted no light. She had slept longer than she knew, and as she sat up she found her mouth was dry and her face was warm, her forehead slightly damp. "Danji," she said. "Is Danji here?" She made motions with her hands to communicate her question.

The handmaiden understood and shook her head. In an effort to fight down the desperation she felt coiling like a serpent around her heart, Cait threw back the silk covering and rose from her bed. She moved to the door, opened it, and then stopped, realizing she did not know where she was going.

There was, she concluded, only one place *to* go.

Having decided, she walked quickly through the covered courtyard and out into the anteroom. Jubayar was nowhere to be seen, so she moved swiftly on lest her nerve desert her, composing her thoughts as she went. She would find Prince Hasan and confront him, demand the truth from him, and hold him to account.

By the time she reached the main corridor leading to the reception hall, she knew exactly what she wanted to say to the prince. It was Halhuli, the prince's overseer, she encountered first, however. She greeted him and asked whether he knew where Hasan might be found.

At the question, Cait saw a stiffness come into the servant's face. His eyes shifted away from her. "I do not know, lady."

"I must speak to him, Halhuli. It is important and there is no one else I can ask."

"I must beg to be excused." He turned to leave.

"No!" said Cait. "Stop." The force of her command caught and held him. "Hear me, Halhuli. There is something wrong here—something very wrong. I will do all I can to see that it is put right, but I need your help." She moved beside him. "Please, Halhuli, help me."

"I do not know what you are talking about. I am sorry."

"I think you do, Halhuli. You know exactly what I am talking about." He looked straight ahead, and said nothing. "I can see that I am right," Cait continued, softening her tone. "I think you want to help me, but your loyalty to your master prevents you. I understand."

"I am katib to the prince," Halhuli told her. "Like my father before me, and his father before him, we have served the House of Tashfin. I am my prince's to command," he paused, and added, "whether in honor, or dishonor."

288

Cait pounced on the morsel he had given her. "But if the prince is behaving dishonorably, then is it not the katib's duty to save his prince from the infamy and disgrace of his actions?"

Halhuli regarded her with deep, sad eyes, but remained silent.

"I know that if I had lost my way, I would want you to lead me back to the path of virtue." In her pleading, Cait put her hand on the katib's arm. "I do not ask you to do this for my sake, but for Hasan's. For, if the prince has strayed, who will rescue him if not his wise and loyal katib?"

Halhuli raised his eyes and regarded Cait for a long time. She could almost see the battle taking place within him. At last, he straightened, having made up his mind. "Follow me. I will take you to him."

He led her to a part of the *al-qazr* she had never seen before. The rooms were smaller, the walls thicker and far less ornate. They climbed a flight of stone steps to an upper floor where Halhuli stopped before a low wooden door. Cait put her hand to the iron ring, pulled up the latch, and would have pushed open the door, but Halhuli prevented her. "May Allah forgive me," he said, and pushed open the door himself.

There, in the center of the room, lay Danji, shoulders bared and hands tied with cords of braided leather—prostrate before an enraged Prince Hasan who was using the other end of the braided cord as a lash to raise angry red welts on the delicate skin of her back.

As the door swung open, the prince glanced around, saw Halhuli and Caitríona standing in the doorway, and halted the beating. Danji lifted her head as the prince moved quickly toward the door. "Ketmia," he said, forcing a sickly smile, "what are you doing here?"

He reached for Cait's arm, but she deftly sidestepped him, moving quickly to the injured woman. Raising her up, she tugged on the braided cord. Hasan made to take hold of her shoulder. "Ketmia, you must not—"

"Or what?" demanded Cait, whirling on him. "You will beat me, too?"

Prince Hasan started, the color bleeding from his distraught features. "You do not understand."

"This is beneath you, my lord," Cait told him, her voice shaking with fury. She bent once more to free Danji's hands. "Perhaps Moors are permitted to whip their wives, but Christians detest the practice."

"She is not my—"

"Save your lies," Cait snapped. "I know she is your wife."

Prince Hasan swallowed hard; his hands fluttered toward the kneeling Danji as if he would appeal to her. She looked up at his face and said something in Arabic, which Cait took to be confirmation.

Hasan stood caught between the two women, his expression angry, bewildered, shamed, and mortified all at once. He looked from one to the other of them, and then at Halhuli who was standing just inside the door. "Why did you not prevent this?" he snarled, his fury finding outlet at last. "Is everyone against me now?"

"Forgive me, my lord," replied the advisor with quiet resolve. "Princess Danji is also my mistress, and I could not see her treated so."

"You speak above your place," blurted the prince.

"He speaks the simple truth," Cait retorted sharply.

"Believe me, Ketmia," said Hasan, appealing to her, "it was never my intention to harm you in any way." He took her hand in both of his. "Truly, your love has enslaved me."

Cait glared at him. "You lied to me," she said. Jerking her hand from him, she moved to Danji and gently pulled her robes over her shoulders, then raised her to her feet and stood holding her.

"Since the first moment I saw you, my heart was slain by your beauty," the prince said. "I swear before the throne of Allah, I wanted only to keep you with me. I knew that once you tasted of life in the palace, you would be content to stay. I would have married you," he raised his eyes hopefully, "I would marry you still—"

"You are already married," Cait pointed out tartly.

"It is no impediment to a Moor of my rank and wealth," replied the prince, recovering something of his former composure. "We are permitted more than one wife, and I would make you very happy."

Cait turned her face away.

"I have disgraced myself in your eyes," the prince said.

"Yes," agreed Cait sharply. "We agree on that at least."

"Tell me how I can redeem myself, and it shall be done."

"Then tell me what has become of my knights," she demanded. "They did not ride out this morning. Where are they?"

Hasan hesitated. The anguish on his face appeared genuine.

"Tell her, my lord," Danji said.

The prince looked to Halhuli for help, his eyes pleading. "I will tell her, if you wish," the advisor said. Hasan nodded, and lowered his head in shame.

"Your knights are resting comfortably, my lady," said Halhuli, stepping forward. "They have been confined to the Ladies' Tower. They have not been harmed."

"You must release them at once," Cait insisted.

Prince Hasan hesitated.

"My lord prince, you profess to feelings of affection for me. If that is true, you must release my knights. I will speak to them," Cait said. "Lord Rognvald is an honorable man, and he will understand. There will be no blood shed over this—only you must set them free at once."

The prince raised his unhappy gaze to Cait. "Very well." To Halhuli he said, "See that it is done."

More relieved than angry, Cait did not have it in her to sustain her fury any longer. "All will yet be well, my lord prince," she told him. Taking Danji by the arm, she said, "Come, we will see to those bruises while we wait."

Leaving Prince Hasan to stew in his misery, the two women proceeded to the reception hall to wait for the Norsemen's release. While they waited, Danji's maidservants applied a soothing balm to the red stripes on her shoulders and back.

"You have suffered this injury for my sake," said Cait as the servants finished applying the unguent. "I am sorry, Danji. If we had left the palace when you warned me . . ."

"It is finished. We need not speak of it again." She waved the servants away and arranged her clothing once more. "Please, I would not have you think ill of my husband."

"I *do* think ill of him," Cait replied. "A man is a brute who would do a thing like this to—"

Danji shook her head. "You do not understand." She sighed and gazed at her hands which were clasped in her lap. "My husband is an honorable man. He is good and kind, but great as is the love within him, greater still is his grief."

Cait regarded the dark-eyed woman before her. "Are you telling me *sorrow* has driven him to behave this way?"

Danji nodded. "Two years ago this palace was a very different place. We were happy then. The voices of children rang in the courtyards and corridors, and the women's quarters were full of gossip and activity.

Truly, Al-Jelál was a small portion of paradise on earth." Her gaze fell to her hands once more. "Now it is a tomb."

"What happened?"

"The fever." Danji shook her head. "It was very bad. The children were taken first. I lost my baby, and Hasan's sister lost two of hers—and then Hasmidi herself was taken, and Hasan's mother also. Four of the serving maids died in one night. After that, the fever spread to the rest of the palace."

Cait was beginning to understand the enormity of the tragedy. "What did you do?"

"There was nothing to be done, but wait, and watch our people die, and bury their bodies when the fever was finished with them. The plague passed to the servants' quarters, and most of them were taken, and the stablehands and grooms—the fever even killed some of the horses. And still it had not reached its full height.

"Tughril, the old prince, Hasan's father, was taken, and his last remaining wife. Then Hasan's younger brother, Kalaat, and his wife—they had been married less than a year."

"Oh, Danji, I am sorry. I had no idea."

"In the end, Hasan lost all of his family, except me. He lost his sons and heirs." Danji raised sad eyes to Cait. "Please, the prince is not a bad man. He is desperate to make this empty shell of a palace a home once more. He has been praying every day for a way to make this happen. And then he found you."

Cait understood at last. "When he saw me in the wood, he must have thought . . ." She shook her head in wonder. "I had no idea."

"Truly, I do not believe he meant to harm anyone."

"I thank you for telling me. It is indeed a sorrowful tale, but I feel better for knowing. I will not judge your husband too harshly."

They sat together in silence for a time and then, hearing footsteps in the anteroom, turned as Lord Rognvald and two of the knights came trooping into the hall. Lord Rognvald hurried to where Cait and Danji stood waiting. "Thank God you have not been harmed," he said, taking her by the arms. "I was worried. I did not know what he might do."

"Is there anything to eat?" wondered Svein, eyeing the empty tables.

"Or drink? It is thirsty work being a hostage," said Yngvar.

"Be seated, all of you," said Danji, rising. "I will order food and drink to be brought."

"It would be a kindness," Cait told her. "Perhaps I should go with you."

"There is no need," replied the young woman. "My husband's shame is sufficient; he will not increase it with another attack."

Danji walked with slightly pained dignity from the room, and the knights took places at the empty table to wait for the food to appear.

"I did not know she could speak Latin," said Rognvald when she had gone.

"Nothing here is quite as it seems," Cait replied. "Lady Danji is not Hasan's sister; she is his wife. And, if he had won his way, *I* would have been his wife as well."

This brought a smile from Rognvald.

"What?" demanded Cait accusingly. "And is that so unlikely that you should mock?"

"It is not mockery you see, but pleasure. I confess, I much prefer the Lady Caitríona before me to the swooning, cow-eyed maid we have been seeing of late."

"Cow-eyed indeed," replied Cait with an indignant huff. "Perhaps I should have left you locked in the tower."

"That would have been a shame," replied Rognvald lightly, "for then we would never learn where Alethea has been taken."

"Hasan? You mean he knows where she is?"

"That I do believe." The tall knight nodded firmly. "In any event, I sent Dag, Rodrigo, and Paulo to fetch the prince, so we will soon discover the truth of this treacherous affair."

PART III

September 7, 1916: Edinburgh, Scotland

I read through most of the night, and all the next day. My reckoning may be faulty, for it is difficult to gauge the passage of time below ground. Without the sun to aid orientation, one loses all sense of regularity and proportion; the body quickly succumbs to its own peculiar rhythm. Hence, I ate and slept as it seemed right to me, performing any small tasks as need or whim dictated—washing, grooming, tending the fire—and the rest of the time, I read from William St. Clair's old book.

When I grew tired of sitting in bed, I sat on the stool; when the stool grew uncomfortable, I took a fleece from the bed and laid it before the hearth and read by the flickering light of the fire. Eager to finish Caitríona's tale before Evans returned for me, I read the hours away—discovering in the process that without the ordinary distractions of daily life with all its clamor and clutter, without the tyranny of petty demands and humdrum obligations, the mind soon ceases its continual fretting and gnawing over the events of the day. The spirit calms and peace descends like a balm over the soul.

Feeling very much like a monk who has devoted his life to prayer and study in quiet solitude, I read the book and the bare confines of my cell ceased to exist. I was transported across the centuries to that far-off time at the embryonic beginning of our long-lived order. In short, as my understanding grew toward completion, I envisioned the form my final initiation would take and began to prepare myself accordingly.

My time of contemplation passed so peacefully that I was actually startled when I heard the door open at the end of the passage and footsteps descend the stone steps. I was ready when Evans reappeared at the entrance to my cell. And again I started a little, for he was not wearing the scarlet of the Inner Circle, nor the ordinary gray of brotherhood; he was wearing a long white robe without emblem or insignia, but belted with a wide woven band of cloth of gold.

He carried another white robe which he held up for me, saying, "Peace and grace to you, brother." By this I knew the formal ceremony had already begun. I returned his greeting, and he said, "The Council of Brothers has gathered, and we await your presence." He glanced at the book on the table. "I trust your time here has been of profit to you."

"It has been inspirational," I replied, slipping into the offered robe, "and I am grateful for it."

"Good." He held out to me a woven belt like his own. I passed it around my waist, and he tied it for me, arranging the knot at the side. He stepped back, regarding me with a critical eye, then nodded his approval. "If you are ready, we will proceed."

I replied that I was, and taking up the candle, he led me from the cell. We did not return to the Star Chamber, as I might have expected, but continued down the passage leading deeper into the underground interior. I followed and we walked without speaking until reaching a low door at the end. Evans knocked on the door. There came the long metallic scrape of a bolt being drawn, and the door was opened from inside. Evans held the candle above the lintel and indicated that I should enter. I stooped, bent my head low, and stepped inside to see Genotti standing beside the doorway, candle in hand.

My first impression—that the room appeared to have been carved out of the living stone which formed the church's foundation—turned out to be correct. This was swiftly followed by the recognition that I had been in this room before: years ago, when I was elevated to the Seventh Degree. Then, I had been blindfolded; but there could be no mistake: this was the cavernous chamber into which I was lowered on that night, when, a blind man searching in the darkness, I had found the beginning of the path which had led me to this final revelation.

I saw, in the flickering glow of candles in tall sconces around the room, the other members of the Inner Circle—De Cardou, Zaccaria and Kutch—waiting before a stone altar; they were, like Evans and Genotti, robed in white. Behind them, to one side, was the vestibule wherein I had found the Iron Lance. The sacred relic was there; I could see its slightly bowed and crooked length resting in the shelved niche carved for it in the solid rock wall, and the sight produced a feeling of intense elation which flooded through me like a warm wave of triumph.

Opposite this vestibule, there was another. Evans, who had joined Genotti, saw my glance and knew I was curious to explore and so gave his assent with a silent nod. The others stood by and watched as I moved to the semi-chamber, ascended the single step and went in to find another carved niche. My heart quickened as I saw the dark scarred length of ancient timber and knew that I beheld the Black Rood.

The heavy-grained wood was grooved and sinuous with age, its deeply patined surface smoothed by saintly veneration to a satiny luster that shimmered dully in the gently flickering light. The truncated and much abused relic had been ornamented with simple gold bands which covered the rough-sawn ends. Humbled by its presence, I held my breath and ran my fingertips along the length of ancient wood in a caress of profound gratitude, reverence, and, yes, love.

My thoughts returned to the sunny island of Cyprus where I had encountered the tale of the relic in a copy of Duncan's handwritten manuscript in the monastery of Ayios Moni amid the pine-forested peaks of the Troodos mountains. Had it really been fifteen years since Caitlin and I had passed the winter on that sleepy island in the midst of the sun-bright sea? We had always meant to return and relive that happy time . . . now we never would.

I left the vestibule and returned to where the others were waiting for me. "There is but one more secret to be revealed," Genotti said. "Tonight there are no blindfolds; there will be no stumbling and fumbling in the darkness. Tonight we stand and move in the glory and radiance of the Sanctus Clarus."

"Are you ready, brother?" asked Evans.

"I am," I replied, little knowing how unprepared I truly was for what was about to happen.

THIRTY-FIVE

By the time they came in sight of the ridge the wind had turned raw, whipping at the horses' tails and manes, and stinging the faces of the riders. What had begun as a crisp, sun-bright day slowly sank into a dull, freezing mist, and Cait was glad of the handsome wool cloak Hasan had given her. She had offered to return it, along with the other gifts, but he would not hear of it.

"I would brave the everlasting fires of Jahennem itself," Hasan had declared boldly, "for the merest hope of your forgiveness, Ketmia. Leading your beloved sister to freedom will be but a token of my sincerity and contrition."

Cait readily accepted his pledge, but Lord Rognvald was of a less forgiving mind. Despite the apparent change in Hasan, and the prince's oft-repeated pledges of fidelity, benevolence, and selfless resolve, the wary Norwegian maintained a sceptical attitude; having been burned once, he was not inclined to wholly trust the fire again. Even so, inasmuch as Prince Hasan professed to know where the outlaw Ali Waqqar could be found, he had no choice but to swallow his misgivings and allow the contrite Moor to lead them to the bandit's refuge.

During the night the horses, supplies, and weapons had been made ready, and the company departed at dawn—led by Hasan; Rognvald, Cait, and the knights came next, followed by Halhuli and three more servants leading a train of seven pack horses. They reached the first valley, crossed it, and continued on into the ragged northern hills beyond—a rough, desolate land of tumbled rock and deeply eroded ravines inhabited only by herds of tough little mountain goats and flocks of wild sheep.

Shortly after midday the prince halted the party; while Halhuli and his men set about preparing a meal, he led Cait, Rognvald, and the knights a little further along the trail. "Observe that ridge which rises before you like a wall," he said, lifting his hand to a massive bulwark of mottled brown rock in the distance. "That is *Arsh Iblees*—or, as you would say, the Devil's Throne. Beyond it is a narrow valley, and that is where we will find Ali Waqqar."

"It will be dark before we reach the ridge," observed Rognvald.

"I think so," agreed Hasan. "I suggest making camp here and beginning again at first light."

"But the day is not so far gone," Cait pointed out a little anxiously. "We could ride a fair way yet."

"We might, it is true," allowed the prince. "We will be more comfortable here, however, and there is less chance of alerting the bandits to our presence. I would prefer to arrive unannounced."

Thus Cait was forced to endure yet another restless night on the trail. She lay sleepless in a little round tent, the front of which was open to a campfire that blazed throughout the night, and rose early and set about saddling her horse once more.

Waiting had made her sullen and surly. She begrudged the slowness of the others, and wished to high Heaven she had never embarked upon this disastrous course. She was cold and tired and aching with the knowledge of her own failure, folly, and conceit. With what arrogance had she conceived this reckless enterprise, with what sublime ignorance, what consummate vanity.

When at last they set off again, she turned tired eyes to the featureless sky above, and the bleak beginning of another dismal day in the saddle. So empty. So hopeless. And, like the revenge she sought, so endlessly, abysmally pointless.

Out on the winter trail with a fretful wind swirling about her shivering shoulders, grief enwrapped her in its cold clutch and squeezed her hard. Where before she had been able to ease her sorrow and remorse with the assurance that the reward was worth the cost, in the pale light of yet another dreary dawn that assurance foundered. Like a pack horse forced to carry a crushing burden far too long, her confidence collapsed, never to rise again.

It was all she could do to stifle the scream of desperation she felt rising up in her throat. She lashed her horse to a plodding trot and rode out ahead of the others so that they could not see the tears of frustration sliding down her frozen cheeks.

They spent the morning fighting a wet and gusty wind which threatened to sweep them off the trail. By the time they gained the top of the ridge and began their descent, Cait had determined to abandon the search for the Holy Cup. Her ill-advised pursuit of the relic had so far brought nothing but death and misery. It was time—and long past time—to renounce her ambition.

While sojourning in Hasan's palace, she had been able to hold off the decision she had known all along was coming. Now, as she sat freezing in the saddle, all she wanted was to win her sister's freedom, and return to Bilbao and her waiting ship while she, and those with her, still had life and breath to do so.

De Bracineaux would win; he had killed her father, and he would gain the Mystic Rose, too. There was nothing she could do about that. She would walk away empty-handed, but at least, she told herself, she would still be alive. That would have to be enough.

In a little while, they came to a wide place halfway along the downward trail. Here, sheltered by the ridge wall behind them, they stopped to rest and warm themselves. The riders dismounted and the prince summoned Cait and Rognvald to join him.

"I do not see any settlements," Cait informed him glumly, gazing down into the pinched ravine of a valley—little more than a deep, crinkled gash with a rock-filled stream at the bottom.

"No," Hasan said, "there are neither settlements nor holdings in this wilderness. The land is not good for farming."

"Then where will we find the bandits?"

"The hillsides below are seamed with a great many caves," Prince Hasan told them. "This is where Ali Waqqar hides. As to that, I think it would be best if you and your men were to wait here and allow me to go on ahead alone."

Rognvald frowned, and Cait shook her head.

"Please, Ketmia, what I propose is wisdom itself. Ali and I have had dealings in the past, you see. If I go to him alone, he will allow me to come near and speak to him. Surprise him with an army, however, and he could easily disappear into his labyrinth of caves where we could never find him."

Cait resisted the idea. Alethea and Abu were somewhere down there and she meant to get them out.

"Truly, it is for the best," insisted Hasan.

"Oh, very well!" She nearly screamed with exasperation. "Go on then!"

"Yngvar, Svein and the others will wait here with you," Rognvald told her. "But I will go with the prince." He turned to regard Hasan with quietly stubborn defiance.

Seeing the knight was adamant, the prince reluctantly agreed and commanded Halhuli to find a turban for Rognvald and exchange cloaks with him. As soon as Rognvald was suitably disguised, they remounted and Hasan cautioned the tall knight to sit low in the saddle and avoid drawing attention to himself. "Pray that Ali Waqqar is of a mood to receive visitors today," he said, then raised his hand in farewell.

Cait watched the riders disappearing down the side of the hill and changed her mind. Crossing quickly to her mount, she climbed into the saddle, and was off before anyone could stop her. Dag and Rodrigo ran a few steps and called for her to come back, but she ignored them and rode on. The riders heard the commotion, turned, saw Cait, and halted on the trail.

"Say what you like, I will not go back," she told them in a tone suggesting that Heaven and earth could pass away long before she would be persuaded. "I have not come this far to stand aside and wait."

"Yu'allah," sighed Hasan; he glanced at Rognvald, who made no move to intervene, then relented. "So be it."

"Whatever happens, stay close to me, my lady," Rognvald instructed. "Keep your blade ready to hand."

"See you keep your head covered with the hood of your cloak," added Hasan. "It may be they will think you are Danji, and take no notice."

Having won her way, Cait became compliant; she did as she was told and fell in behind Lord Rognvald. They moved on, reaching the floor of the valley a short time later, where Cait saw that it was as Hasan had said; as she gazed at the broken, boulder-strewn slopes all around she could see the entrances of small caves as dark holes in the sides of the hills.

Leaving the ridge trail, they rode out into the narrow valley, passing among fallen rocks the size of houses. Hasan found his way to the stream and they followed the path beside it. Owing to the high, protecting walls on every side, the air was calm and silent on the valley floor; the only sound to be heard was the rippling splash of the water as it coursed along its stony bed. In a little while, it became clear that the prince knew exactly where he was going.

They came to a place where the stream pooled as it passed around the base of an enormous, mound-like boulder, providing a good fording place. They paused to allow the horses to drink, then crossed the stream and turned toward the towering eastern slope. A few hundred paces from the ford a great stone slab lay like a toppled pillar on its side; the trail passed between two of the shattered sections. They rode through a gap wide enough for horses to go two abreast and continued on toward the slope, picking their way among the chunks of stone fallen from the heights which lay scattered over the rising ground, and in a little while arrived at the entrance to a cave.

Potsherds and the droppings of sheep and horses covered the flat area at the base of the slope which served the cave as a yard. Aside from that, and a faint whiff of smoke adrift in the still air, there was no sign that anyone had ever been near the place. Rognvald halted a little way off, and Cait behind him; Hasan rode to the cave entrance and shouted, "Ali Waqqar!"

He waited a moment and shouted again, adding a few words in Arabic. The call had scarcely died in the air when a figure emerged out of the darkness of the cave mouth. The man was a dark-skinned Moor, shabbily dressed, his clothes stiff with grease and dirt, his beard matted and long, his hair unkempt. His fat belly hung over his drooping belt, and the sleeves of his cloak flapped in rags about his hands as he stared warily out at the three visitors.

He spat into the dirt at his feet before making bold to answer. Prince Hasan addressed the man sharply, and to Cait's surprise the burly fellow straightened and made a curt bow. Hasan spoke again, whereupon the man disappeared.

"He is one of Ali's men," Hasan explained. "He is meant to be on watch, but—" he lifted a hand equivocally, "you can see how it is."

"Is Thea here? Did you ask if—" Cait began, but the prince cut her off.

"Hush, Ketmia," he warned quietly. "All in good time."

They waited in silence for the guard to return. When he did, it was with three other men, one of whom, taller than the others, appeared slightly better dressed and reasonably more alert. He bowed and addressed the prince politely, moving out from the mouth of the cave for a closer look at the visitors. Prince Hasan spoke to him the while, raising his voice in demand when the guard appeared to take an interest in the two accompanying the prince. A few paces from Cait, he swung around sharply and moved to Hasan's side, offered another bow and hurried into the cave once more, leaving the others behind to stare dully at the visitors until their leader returned; appearing at the cavern entrance, he motioned the newcomers to follow him.

"The danger is past," said Hasan, visibly relieved. "It appears Ali Waqqar will be pleased to receive us in his lair. Do you wish to accompany me, or would you rather wait here?"

"We will attend," said Rognvald.

"Very well." Prince Hasan swung down from the saddle. "Follow me. But see you keep your wits about you."

Cait dismounted and followed the men into the cave, regretting her decision at once. The entrance opened onto a high-ceilinged chamber, the walls of which were streaked gray with bat dung; a fair few of the grotesque creatures hung in wriggling clusters from the rocks overhead. On one side of the chamber, a winding passage led deeper into the heart of the mountain. The lower walls of the passage were damp and reeked with the sour stench of stale urine. Nor was that all. As they moved further into the cave, she encountered other odors too—the acrid tang of horse sweat, the earthy ripeness of manure and human dung, and the putrid stink of rotting meat—all of them so rank and malignant as to make her eyes water. Pressing a hand to her mouth, she hunched her shoulders and hurried on. Ahead of her she heard Rognvald mutter something under his breath as they passed by one particularly malodorous heap of refuse.

The passage ended in another doorway carved in the rock. Bending almost double, they stooped beneath the grimy lintel and stepped into a large dome-like room which was lit by the blaze of a log fire barely contained within a crude hearth in the center of the cavern. Haunches of meat were sizzling on wooden spits placed around the perimeter of the hearth, filling the air with oily smoke. Water trickled down one wall to fill a small pool made of rocks and mud. Beside the pool were a half-dozen enormous earthenware jars; several large grass baskets were stacked here and there along the wall, with a few well-made wooden caskets among them—containing plunder, no doubt, from raids or other nefarious doings.

At first glance the room appeared to be deserted, but as Cait looked around she began to see human forms in the quivering shadows along the arching walls and upper ledges; what she had first taken for lumps of stone were in fact men, wrapped in cloaks and turbans and sound asleep. There were others sitting quietly slumped in attitudes of drunken stupor, oblivious to events around them.

In all, she estimated there were perhaps twenty or so, and the sight of them infuriated her: to think that these indolent sots were the brigands who had killed five good men and carried off her sister. Now that she saw them again at last, she fairly squirmed with the urge to draw her sword and separate their odious bodies from their worthless souls. It took all her strength of will to keep her hand from the blade at her side and walk on by with averted eyes. For Alethea's sake, she did just that.

The visitors were led to a place on one side of the hearth where skinned pine logs formed benches of sorts near a slab of rock upon which had been spread a fine rug and a satin cushion—this, Cait guessed, was where the outlaw chieftain held court. They sat down, and after a short wait three more bandits entered the chamber. One of them cried out as he entered: "Hasan!" It was, Cait thought, a greeting of particular intimacy.

The guests turned to see Ali Waqqar step quickly around the hearth fire and approach the prince with open arms. Cait regarded the bandit with keen interest, and felt unexpected relief in the certainty that she had never seen the man before; he was not among those who attacked her camp that day.

A man of imposing height—made more so by the elaborate turban of gleaming blue satin on his head—he walked with the eager, rolling gait of a man hurrying from one dissipation to another. Closer, Cait could see the tell-tale signs of long and habitual overindulgence: a muscular frame now thick and flabby, loose wattles about the neck, dirt ingrained in the lines of his face and beneath fingernails; once-handsome features bloated. His clothes were of good quality, but filthy, and the cuffs of his sleeves and the hem of his mantle were threadbare. In all, his appearance proclaimed a man much come down in the world—and yet, he still possessed the arrogant confidence of a warrior.

306

The prince rose to receive the homage of the bandit and it was then that Cait realized the dealings the prince admitted to having with Ali Waqqar were of a more familiar kind than he had led her to believe. The recognition produced a perverse sort of hope that the apparent amity between the two men would lead to release for her sister and Abu.

What was more, she could see from his expression that Rognvald discerned this, too, for his eyes narrowed and his nostrils flared with suppressed anger. Cait quickly averted her gaze lest he see that she did not share his indignation at being deceived.

Hasan and the outlaw leader stood gripping each other's arms for a moment and exchanged a few pleasant words. Then the prince turned and said, "Allow me to present my friends: Lord Rognvald of Haukeland, and Lady Caitríona of Caithness."

Ali Waqqar stepped before them; Rognvald rose as he was introduced, his face impassive—magnificently so, Cait thought, considering what she had seen only a moment before. Whatever he felt at the sight of the marauding brigand, there was now no visible sign at all.

And then it was her turn. She made no move as the bandit chief turned from Rognvald and made a slight bow before her. To her horror, he reached down and took up her hand. She writhed inwardly from his touch but, emboldened by Rognvald's poised example, forced a thin smile and lowered her head demurely.

Prince Hasan spoke a few words to the bandit, who nodded his head in assent, and then, in the manner of a hosting lord, clapped his hands. A dirty boy appeared, bearing a battered silver tray containing an ill-matched assortment of small golden cups. The bandit took up one and indicated that the others should do likewise. Raising his cup, Ali exclaimed, "My friends, though my cave is a stinking hovel unfit for nobles of your obvious rank and refinement, you are welcome here. I drink to your health."

To Cait's surprise, his Latin was polished and smoothly spoken. She wondered whether he had stolen it along with everything else he possessed. She put the cup to her lips and sipped daintily, unwilling to taste even the smallest morsel of the brigand's rude hospitality.

They were invited to sit once more, and resumed their seats on the log benches, while Ali took his place on the rug-covered slab, adopting the manner of a potentate enthroned. Hasan and Ali exchanged idle pleasantries until the cups were drained, and then the bandit called for meat to be brought.

One of the roasting joints was pulled off a nearby spit and brought dripping to the bandit leader. He pulled off a strip of flesh and stuffed it in his mouth and, licking his fingers loudly, indicated that the others should likewise enjoy a succulent bite.

"Now then," said Ali, chewing thoughtfully, "pleased as I am to entertain noble guests . . ." He lifted an ambivalent hand in their direction, "in my experience, people do not seek out Ali Waqqar unless they desire something of him. So, tell me, if you please, what is it that you wish of Ali?"

"Most astute," replied the prince affably. "As always, you have discerned the heart of the matter. The day is speeding from us, and we have a long ride awaiting, so I will be brief. It has come to my attention that you may have a slave to sell. We have come to buy."

"I see." The bandit nodded, looking from one to the other of his guests. "Although it grieves me to say it, I fear you have had a long cold ride for nothing. I have no slaves at this time." He took another draft from his cup. "None."

"We seem to have been misinformed," replied the prince. "Forgive me, but I was certain they said you possessed a young female slave."

"Truly," said Ali placidly, "I wish I had such a slave to sell, for she would be yours this instant. Alas, my friends, I have no slaves at all of any description. Business this year has been very poor, owing to the prohibition on travel between cities. You must have heard of this."

"To be sure," said the prince. "Even so, it is a very great pity to have come all this way to no purpose. Perhaps I might be so bold as to suggest that I would be willing to pay seventy-five thousand dirhams for a likely young woman," he paused, "*if* you should happen to hear of anyone who has such a slave to sell."

"I will bear it in mind," agreed Ali Waqqar. "Now, I beg you to excuse me, but you have had the misfortune to find me in the midst of a particularly busy day." He rose from his cushioned slab. "Accept my apologies. Duty, you know, is a harsh task master, and never satisfied."

"Of course. As it happens, our return cannot be delayed any longer." Hasan stood slowly. "Until we meet again, Ali Waqqar." The prince made a flourish with his hand.

The outlaw chieftain made a cursory bow and the visitors were escorted back through the cave and returned to their waiting horses. Cait watched the prince climb into the saddle; she strode to his mount and took hold of the bridle. "Is that it?" she demanded. "Is that the end of it?"

"Ketmia, hush!" he cautioned. "They will hear you."

"He was lying! He has Alethea. I know it."

The prince glanced toward the cave entrance where the guards were watching them with dull interest. "He does not have her," he said in low tones. "Believe me, he would never have allowed seventy-five thousand dirhams to slip through his fingers. If he had even the slightest hope of producing her, we would be haggling over the price even now."

"If he does not have her, then he knows what happened to her," Cait countered. "He *knows*, and you must make him tell us."

"Ketmia, please, this is not the way." He looked to Rognvald for help. "We must leave at once."

"I think the bandit was lying, too," Rognvald said. "He may not have Alethea now, but I believe he knows what happened to her."

Cait held tight to the bridle. "I am not leaving until I learn what happened to my sister."

"And I am telling you that if we do not depart at once, we will join her in her fate."

"You seem very well acquainted with these brigands. It seems to me you know them better than you led us to believe."

"It is because I know them that I say we must go," growled the prince, losing patience. "If you do not believe me, then believe your own eyes." He indicated the cave entrance where three more of Ali's men, carrying swords and lances, had joined the first two; behind them, others could be seen moving in the dark interior of the cave.

Frustrated beyond words, Cait gave out a strangled shriek and stormed to her horse. She mounted quickly, and started away. Rognvald waited until she had passed him, then fell in behind her. They had ridden only a few hundred paces when there came a cry from the cave.

"*Sharifah!*"

Cait heard it and glanced back. Over her shoulder, she saw a slender, dark-haired figure racing toward them. The cry sounded again, and she swung around for a better look. Her heart clutched in her breast.

"Abu!"

Instinctively, she jerked hard on the reins; her horse halted and reared. "Rognvald!" she shouted. "It is Abu!"

THIRTY-SIX

Rognvald's sword was in his hand before her cry had ceased. He flew past her, shouting, "Ride on, Cait!"

Ali Waqqar appeared at the mouth of the cave, saw Abu darting away, and roared a command at his men, who stood looking on in flat-footed indecision. He roared again and started shoving men right and left, knocking two or three over; those still on their feet leaped after the fleeing youth.

Abu put his head down and ran as if all the hounds of hell were snarling at his heels.

Rognvald, naked blade high in the air, raised himself in the saddle; he swept by the young man and made instead for his pursuers, closing on them with blinding swiftness. With a rattling battle cry, he drove headlong into them, scattering attackers in all directions. Wheeling his horse and making long, looping slashes with his sword, he kept the wary bandits at bay.

More brigands boiled out of the cave. Ali Waqqar stood in the center of a confused knot of men, shouting and shoving. And then, even as Cait looked on, the chaos suddenly resolved into an attacking force. They came forth in an angry rush, shouting, swords flailing.

Heedless of Rognvald's command, Cait hastened to Abu's rescue, galloping across the rough, rocky ground, reining up hard as she reached him. With a tremendous bound, the young man flung himself onto the back of her horse, shouting, "Fly! Fly!"

She turned her mount and felt one bony arm encircle her waist. "Fly! Fly!" Abu screamed. Away they flew: Cait, head down, lashing with the reins, and her passenger bouncing like a sack of meal and clinging on for dear life. She found the path by which they had come and headed out across the narrow valley.

Prince Hasan sped past them, racing to Rognvald's aid. "Make for the ridge!" he cried as he thundered by. "Summon the knights! We will hold them at the ford."

His shout dissolved into a whirring sound—like the sizzling buzz of an angry hornet—and suddenly the prince jolted upright in the saddle as an arrow instantly appeared in his upper chest. Grasping the shaft with his free hand, he wrenched it out and threw it carelessly aside, continuing his headlong plunge into the fight. Another vicious *whirr* sounded in the air, ending with a meaty thud. Abu gave a startled cry. "Go, sharifah! Fly!" Cait urged her horse to greater speed, streaking away over the rocky ground.

Two more arrows fizzed past before she was out of range. She struck the path and raced to the broken stone slab, passed through the gap, and splashed across the ford, speeding along the stream to the base of the ridge where she was met by the knights who had seen her approach in haste and had come down armed and ready for battle.

As soon as she was near enough, she shouted, "Go! Rognvald and Hasan need you!"

Yngvar was the first to reach her. "Where are they, my lady?"

"Follow the stream," she gasped, breathless from her ride. "You will find them beyond the ford. They are attacked. For God's sake, hurry!"

Yngvar turned to the others. "Ready arms!" he cried. "Follow me!"

With a shout, the knights clattered off. The last was Dag, who paused long enough to ask, "Would you have me stay to protect you, my lady?"

"No. We will be safe here. Go!"

The knight bounded away. Cait watched as the warriors raced out along the stream; in the near distance, she could see the pool which marked the fording place and, beyond it, the divided slab. Yngvar and Rodrigo reached the tumbled stone, and disappeared through the gap. The others pounded through one after another and were gone. "They will return soon," she said with more hope than conviction. "You will need a mount, Abu."

When he did not answer, she swivelled in the saddle to look behind her. Abu, one hand still holding to her cloak, sat with his head down as if contemplating the tip of the arrow which had passed through his upper back and now protruded between the bloody fingers of his other hand.

Cait slid from the saddle and caught the wounded youth as he toppled to the ground. She laid him down as gently as she could; forcing calm to her shaking hands, she rolled him onto his side.

The arrow had found its mark in his back just below the shoulder to emerge on the other side between two upper ribs. The iron arrowhead was small, but it was barbed; pulling it out the way it had gone in would do far worse damage, so she thought it best to break off the fletched end and remove it from the front. Grasping the slender wooden shaft in her hand, she tried to break it; the movement brought a groan of pain from Abu, so she decided to leave it for the moment.

"Ahh, God forgive," he gasped, his voice thin and brittle. "I am sorry, sharifah. You were proud of me once. I wanted you to be proud of me again. I failed. I am sorry."

"Never say it." Removing her cloak, she shook it out and draped it over him. "I *am* proud of you, Abu. If not for your markers, we would never have found our way. Rest here a little while I go and fetch Halhuli. The arrow must come out."

She made to move away, but his hand snaked out and snatched hold of her sleeve.

"You need help, Abu. I will go and quickly return. I will—"

Abu threw aside the cloak and struggled onto an elbow; the effort sent blood spilling from the wound in a scarlet rush. His face contorted with pain. "Thea," he said, squeezing his eyes shut. "I must tell you about Thea."

"I am listening." She lowered him back to the ground and replaced the cloak.

"Thea is not here," he said, gasping. "She escaped . . . ran away. I helped her." He opened his eyes, imploring her to understand.

"Where, Abu? Where did she go?"

Before he could answer he was taken with a fit of coughing which left him panting for breath and unable to speak. "Rest easy," she told him. "I will get some water."

She dashed to her mount and untied the small waterskin from beside the saddle, and brought it to him. Kneeling down, she drew the stopper and allowed a little water to flow out onto his lips. "Here," she said, lifting his head, "drink."

He sipped a mouthful of water and then looked at her, his eyes big and bright with pain. "Listen, sharifah, there is a lake . . . and a village beside the lake. I learned of it from shepherds. She is there."

He drank again, swallowing hard, and then laid his head on his arm and closed his eyes.

"Where is the lake?" Cait asked.

When he did not reply, she put her lips close to his ear. "Please, Abu, tell me. Where is the lake? I must know if I am to find Thea."

His eyelids fluttered open. His dark eyes were no longer as bright as they had been only a moment before. "The lake . . ."

"Yes, Abu, where? Where is it?"

"There . . ." he said, his voice a breathless whisper. "The mount of gold . . ."

"The Mount of Gold? Abu, I do not understand. Tell me, what is the Mount of Gold? Where is it?"

His mouth opened and a small gurgling sound came from his throat as he tried to make the words. "*There . . .*" he gasped at last, staring straight out across the crooked valley. Cait saw the tawny glint of reflected light in his eyes and followed his gaze to a snow-topped peak rising in the near distance; bathed in the light of the westering sun, it glowed with a rich golden hue.

"Is that the mountain?" asked Cait. "Abu, is that the one you mean?"

She turned and saw that although the reflection of the mountain still filled his eyes with light, sight was already fading. "Oh, Abu," she said, her voice cracking. She bent her head and placed her hand on his cheek, her tears falling onto his still face. "Go with God, my friend," she whispered, then gathered him in her arms and held him as deep silence descended over them.

Halhuli found her that way—crouched beside the trail, shivering with cold, still holding the young man's corpse. "Lady Ketmia," he said, hastening to her side. "May I assist?"

Without waiting for an answer, he lifted the young man from Cait's grasp and lowered him gently to the ground. He removed the cloak from Abu's body and put it over Cait's shoulders, then, taking hold of the arrow below the head, gave a solid tug and pulled it through the wound. He laid the arrow on the ground, and set about straightening Abu's limbs, placing the knees and feet together and folding the hands over his chest. He closed the young man's eyes and mouth, and as he worked, Cait became aware that he was praying over the body—his low, murmuring chant had not ceased since he began tending Abu's ragged corpse.

Next, he poured some water from the waterskin and washed the young man's hands, feet, and face. He then washed his own hands, dried them, and kneeling beside the body raised his hands and face to heaven and intoned a prayer in Arabic. When he finished, he bowed and touched his forehead to the ground.

"Thank you, Halhuli," said Cait.

"He will commence his journey with an easier spirit now," replied the prince's overseer.

At that moment a raw, wordless cry sounded across the valley; it was followed by the savage rattle and clash of weapons. Cait and Halhuli rose and stood gazing toward the gap in the broken slab as the sounds of battle waxed and waned, much as the sound of sea waves tumbling rocks on a pebbled shore.

And then the clamor stopped. Cait held her breath.

She balled the fabric of her cloak in her fists and watched the gap for warriors to appear. "Lord save us," she prayed through clenched teeth.

An instant later, Prince Hasan rode through the cleft. He paused at the ford, and was soon joined by Dag and Svein; Rodrigo was next, carrying Paulo with him across the back of his horse, followed by Yngvar and, lastly, Rognvald.

They rode to the foot of the ridge trail where Cait and Halhuli waited. The knights, breathing hard from the exertion of their brief but fearsome toil, wiped sweat from their faces, and extolled one another's skill and bravery.

"The dogs have abandoned the chase," Rognvald informed her. "Paulo and Hasan have been wounded. We must get them back to camp at once."

"My injury is not so bad," Hasan said, shaking his head. "But we must not linger here lest Ali Waqqar dares to tempt fate again."

Rognvald signalled the knights to ride on. As they clattered past, Cait reached out and put her hand to his knee. "What about Abu?" she asked.

Rognvald heard the sorrow in her voice, looked past her and saw the body of the young man lying still on the ground, the fatal arrow beside him. He rubbed a hand over his face and shook his head. "Did he say anything before he died?"

"He told me Alethea escaped," Cait replied.

"That is something, at least."

"And I think I know where she may be found." She quickly explained what Abu had told her, then looked back over her shoulder at his body. "I do not want him left here."

"Nor do I." Rognvald dismounted, crossed quickly to the corpse, lifted it in his strong arms and carried it back to his mount. Cait held the horse while Rognvald secured the body, and then they rode silently back to camp.

The sun was dropping below the mountains to the west by the time they reached the top of the ridge; the encircling wall cast the valley into shadow. There were no bandits following them, so they hurried on, making their way along the switchback trail leading down the other side of the ridge. The sun fired the mountain tops, causing the snow-topped peaks to glow like red-hot brands, and Cait watched the colors slowly fade as the short winter day gave way to a misty dusk.

They halted at the edge of the clearing, and Rognvald lifted Abu's body down from the horse and laid it on the ground. He straightened, crossed himself, then turned to find Cait watching him. "We will bury him soon," he told her.

"You are wounded," she said, regarding the ragged rent in his sleeve above the elbow.

He saw her glance and said, "A small cut. It is nothing."

She reached out to take his arm for a better look, but he held it away from her grasp. "A scratch only," he insisted. "Leave it be."

They walked to the camp to find the knights standing around the outstretched body of Paulo while Halhuli examined his wound and the prince's servants scurried for supplies. Cait pushed in beside Svein and watched as Halhuli probed the unconscious Spanish knight's wound, then looked up. "The cut is deep," he said, "but clean. With rest and care, I think he may recover."

Satisfied, the knights nodded and moved off to other tasks. While Rognvald and Halhuli made Paulo comfortable in one of the tents, Dag, Svein, and Yngvar found a place at the edge of the camp and dug a deep grave. Then, as the first stars began burning in the east, the knights buried the Syrian servant. While Cait and the wounded Hasan stood looking on, they pressed crude wooden crosses into the mound of soft earth, and prayed over the grave, commending the soul of the slender youth to the Almighty Giver and Receiver of Life.

By the time they finished, the prince's servants had a hot supper prepared, so they all sat down around the fire to warm themselves and eat a simple meal. Cait related what Abu had told her about Alethea's escape and where to look for her. "Then something good has come of this, at least," Hasan observed. "Allah is wise and merciful."

They finished their supper in silence, each wrapped in private thoughts which none cared to disturb. When they had finished, Hasan, his face pale with fatigue, rose. "The excitement of the day has given me a headache," he said, "and I am tired. May Allah grant you a peaceful repose." He bade them a good night and retreated to his tent.

After he had gone, Rognvald called the knights to attend him; they moved a few paces away from the fire. "It may be that darkness will inspire the thieves to boldness," he said.

"Let them come," said Yngvar. "We will make the wolves a feast they will not soon forget."

"Nevertheless," said Rognvald, "we will take no risks. Rodrigo and Dag will take the first watch. Yngvar, you and Svein take the second watch, and I will take the third."

Thus prepared for the night, the rest of the party retired to their tents to sleep—except Cait, who noticed the way the tall knight had begun favoring his arm as he ate his supper. "A moment, my lord," she said as he came into the light of the fire, "I would examine your wound."

"A scratch," he insisted, "is scarcely a wound."

Not to be put off, she stepped before him. "Then it will scarcely matter if I have a look at it." She took his arm, and led him to the fire where she had prepared a bowl of hot water and some strips of clean cloth. "Sit you down, and remove your shirt."

"Lady, it is cold. I will certainly freeze."

"Listen to you now," she chided, undoing the laces at his throat. "And you, a True Son of the North, crying about a little cold."

"God preserve us," he sighed. Shrugging off his cloak, he pulled open his shirt, and drew it over his head.

It was the first time she had seen him without his shirt and the broad sweep of his muscled shoulders and the pale curly hair on his chest pleased her. She found herself gazing raptly at him in the wavering glow of the fire.

"Well?" he said, stirring her to action. "Get on with it then."

Kneeling beside Rognvald, Cait took his arm, lifted it and stretched it out. The errant blade had caught him on the back of the arm, poked a hole through his shirt and produced a small ragged-looking gash. The edges of the cut were puckered and inflamed; there had not been much bleeding, but some of the fabric of the shirt had been driven into the wound. She could see several discolored threads sticking out, but all in all, it was as Rognvald maintained, little more than a nasty scratch.

Cait set to work, dampening a square of cloth in the bowl and applying it to the wound. She put the hot cloth against the cut and held it there to soften the dried blood. Rognvald, adopting the pained expression of a man who is being made to endure humiliation at the hands of an inscrutable higher power, stared at the fire, avoiding Cait's eyes.

After a while, she asked, "How long do you think Alethea could survive out here—alone in the cold?"

"It is difficult to say," Rognvald replied. "Water is good and abundant. The days are not so cold in the valleys, and there is shelter to be found. If she kept her wits about her, she would not be much worse off than she was before."

"What about the wolves?"

He shook his head. "Yngvar thinks *every* forest abounds with wolves. Have you heard any wolves since coming to these mountains? Have you seen even so much as a wolfish footprint in the mud or snow?"

"No, but—"

"If there were any wolves hereabouts, we would have known about them long since."

She accepted his judgment, and continued dabbing at the cut, washing it gently. When she had cleaned it, she turned his arm toward the firelight, and proceeded to pull the embedded shreds of his shirt from the wound. The first threads came free dragging clots of blood, and drawing a wince from Rognvald.

"Am I hurting you?"

"No," he said. "It is just a little cold, that's all."

"Here." She picked up his cloak and made to pull it up around his shoulders. As she did so she saw that his back was a lumpen mass of welted scars, poorly healed, and livid still. The sight caught her by surprise. "Your back!" she gasped. "What happened to you?"

"The Saracens," he muttered.

"In battle?"

"After," he told her, pulling the cloak around him. "They thought I might tell them the strength of the garrison at Tripoli—" he paused, "— among other things."

"But you refused to tell them so they tortured you," she guessed.

He looked at her sideways, and then shook his head with reluctant resignation.

"You *told* them?" said Cait, mildly appalled by this revelation.

"Aye," he confessed, "I told them. I am not proud of it, mind. But it was no secret anyway. The city was not under siege; travelers came and went as freely as birds. The next merchant through the gates would have told them if I did not—they had only to ask."

"Then why did they torture you?"

"Because," he replied, as if the subject wearied him, "Prince Mujir ed-Din had just come to the throne, and the wazir hoped to impress him with his skill in dealing with Christian prisoners. When I answered him outright, I made the wazir look foolish. So, he had me beaten in revenge."

"I see," replied Cait. Pulling two more scraps of cloth from the wound, she flipped the bloody threads into the fire, then washed the cut again before binding it with strips of clean linen cloth. "Had I a little unguent," she said when she finished, "it would heal more quickly."

"All the same, I am much obliged, my lady," Rognvald said, flexing his bandaged arm. "I thank you."

He drew his shirt back on and sat for a moment, regarding her in the firelight. He lifted his hand as if to touch her, hesitated, then stood abruptly. "If you have no further need of me, I will sleep a little before I take my watch."

Cait bade him good night and watched him walk away, then went to her own tent, but found she could not sleep for thinking about Alethea. The thought of the young woman—unprepared in so many ways—wandering lost and alone in the high mountain wilderness kept her awake long into the night. She kept seeing her sister struggling through the snow, shivering, freezing, gasping out her last breath on a lonely mountainside, her pitiful cries for help unheard and unheeded.

Pangs of guilty remorse assailed her. She stared into the dwindling fire and heard again her father's dying words: *Promise you will not avenge me . . . Let it end here.*

THIRTY-SEVEN

The sun rose as a pale red blot in a darkly ominous sky, and Cait rose, too. A servant brought her a bowl of warm water, and she washed, then held the basin for a time letting the heat seep into her fingers. The rest of the camp was stirring and she heard the voices of the knights as they commenced the morning ritual of feeding, watering, and grooming the horses.

She sat clutching the bowl and listening to the knights, and her heart quailed within her. Dread, thick as the wintry mist shrouding the mountainside, swept over her. Closing her eyes, she bit her lip to keep from crying out, all the while telling herself that her distress was born of agitation and frustration, and that her spirits would improve as soon as they were on the trail once more. But, as her thoughts turned to renewing the search, she remembered those they would be leaving behind, and the stifling black desolation of the previous day descended upon her once more.

This day, she thought hopelessly, would be no different from any that had gone before: beginning in futility, ending in despair, with nothing but bone-cold monotony in between. She held little confidence that they would be able to find the place Abu had tried to describe, and even if they did, it would not make the slightest difference: Alethea would not be found and the search would go on. Indeed, the search would go on—and on and on and on forever more without end.

She dragged herself from her tent and stood for a moment, looking up at the dark, unsettled sky. Clouds swirled on a swift east wind, but the tall pines around the camp remained untouched. The air was heavy. There would be rain or snow before day's end; she could already feel the relentless numbing cold of the trail and her sense of aching dread increased.

Rognvald appeared silently beside her. "Caitríona." She jumped as he spoke. "I did not mean to startle you. I was just telling the men we should strike camp and move on. We can breakfast on the trail, but I fear it would be unwise to remain at Ali Waqqar's doorstep any longer."

"What about Paulo? Is it safe to move him?"

"Perhaps not," allowed the lord, "but we cannot leave him here."

"Very well."

He heard the defeat in her voice and said, "Come, my lady, we must appear confident for the men."

She looked at him and wondered at the source of his fortitude. "Why?"

"Because," he told her, "they are trusting in us."

He moved away; as she made to follow, Halhuli called to her from across the camp. He was standing before Prince Hasan's tent wearing an expression she had not seen before. She hurried to him. "What is wrong, Halhuli?"

"The prince is not well," he replied. "When he did not rise this morning, I went in to wake him. I roused him with the greatest difficulty, and gave him a drink. I thought he would get up, but I went in just now to find he has fallen asleep again."

Cait frowned. "That is worrying." She stooped to the entrance of the low, round tent. "Fetch Lord Rognvald."

The overseer hurried away, and Cait pulled back the tent flap, tied it, and stepped in. The prince was lying on his back with his head on a cushion, one arm across his chest, the other outflung. He was dressed in a loose robe, and his turban lay to one side, a small heap of winding cloth. His mouth was open, his breathing rapid and shallow.

She knelt beside him and touched her hand to his forehead—the skin was hot with fever. She took him by the shoulder and shook him gently. There was no response. She shook him again, harder this time, and called his name. The prince slept on.

She was shaking him a third time, and calling his name, when Rognvald arrived. He ducked in, regarded the sleeping prince, and said, "Here, let us carry him outside where we can look at him properly."

"A moment, my lord," suggested Halhuli. He gestured to the two servants standing with him. Taking the lower edge of the tent, they unfastened the stays from the pegs and peeled back the heavy fabric, rolling it up and over the hoops. When they had finished, he ordered them to make up the fire so the prince would not grow cold.

"Open his robe," said Cait.

Rognvald knelt beside Cait and parted the prince's robe to reveal a small red puncture in the fleshy part of the upper chest. The skin was raised and discolored around the cut. "He was struck by an arrow," she said. "I saw him brush it off."

Rognvald pressed his fingers lightly to the wound and examined it closely. "There was little issue of blood," he said, sitting back on his heels. "I have seen men endure much more and fight all the harder the next day."

"Do you think the arrow was poisoned?" said Yngvar. He and the other knights had gathered around the stricken prince.

"Do they do such things?" wondered Cait.

"We have seen it at Bosra," Svein assured her. "In Homs they did this also."

"The dogs," spat Dag.

"Alas," confirmed Halhuli, "it has been known." He placed a hand on the prince's chest. "The skin is hot and inflamed. I think we must suspect poison."

"The wound is not so deep," Rognvald pointed out. "Perhaps the poison is not of sufficient strength to kill. Could we get him back to the palace, do you think?"

Halhuli, worried, his face ashen, gazed at his lord. "It is as Allah wills. If he is to die, then it will be. If he is to recover, then that, also, will be. Allah, the Merciful, bends all purposes to his own."

"What do you want to do, Halhuli?" asked Cait. "Do you want us to take him home?"

He nodded. "I should like to try."

"We can make a litter for him," volunteered Yngvar.

"And drag the poor man over mountain and valley?" said Svein, outraged at the idea.

"It might be carried between two horses," suggested Dag, "but a sling would be better."

"Aye," said Svein, "a sling would be better." He turned up his nose at Yngvar. "A litter! Tch!"

"Cut two stout branches," Rognvald ordered, "and lash them to the cantles of the saddles. We will fashion a sling."

The knights attended to this, and the others set about striking camp. In the midst of their activity, Prince Hasan awoke. Cait turned her back on him for a moment, and when she turned around he was sitting up, taking in the bustle around him with a slightly bewildered expression. "Are we attacked?" he asked.

"No," replied Cait. "You have been asleep. We could not wake you, so we are preparing to return to Al-Jelál."

"There is no need," replied Hasan. "I am perfectly able to ride. We must not abandon the search on my account."

Cait regarded him doubtfully. "You have been wounded," she explained. "I do think it best to return to the palace."

"Nonsense!" he scoffed, and made to rise.

The effort made him dizzy; he lurched forward and Caitríona caught him. "Sit down," she told him. "Rest a moment."

The prince collapsed on his bed once more. "Ah, perhaps you are right," he said. He closed his eyes, pressing a hand to the side of his head.

"Here, drink a little," she said, pouring water into his horn cup; his hand shook so much as he lifted it to his mouth, that she had to steady his arm.

"Allah, the Merciful, be praised!" exclaimed Halhuli, rushing up. "You are awake, my lord."

"Bring me my clothes. We are going home."

"At once, my lord," he said, and hurried away.

Cait called for Rognvald, who returned a moment later to find Prince Hasan drawing on the clothes Halhuli held out for him. "He tells us he feels well enough to ride," Cait said. "Do you think it wise?"

Rognvald squatted down and regarded the prince. "I have no wisdom in the matter," he answered at last. "If a man feels he is able to ride, who can say otherwise?"

"Precisely," agreed the prince. Indicating the wounded Paulo's tent, he said, "Your man needs warmth and care, which he will not receive on the trail. If we leave now, we can reach the palace before dark."

"That would be best in any case," Rognvald conceded. "We will make the journey as easy as possible." He stood and called to the knights to prepare the sling for Paulo and ready the prince's horse. "Those of us who are ready will leave at once—the rest can come after and catch up on the way."

"No, my friend," Hasan objected. "Your destination is within sight. I will not allow you to abandon the search now. Halhuli and my servants will attend me. The rest of you must go on."

Cait hesitated. While she had no great hankering to resume the search, the thought of going back to Al-Jelál only to take up the trail another day filled her with an even greater dread. "But what if something should happen on the way?" she protested mildly.

"Listen to me, Ketmia," the prince replied. "At all events, we would be forced to return to the palace in a day or two for supplies. Take the provisions and go on ahead."

"He is right," Rognvald concluded. "If Abu was not mistaken, we are closer now than ever before. We dare not allow this chance to slip away—we may not get another."

"Paulo and I will rejoin you in a few days when we have rested and our wounds have healed."

"Unless we find Alethea first," Rognvald put in.

"Of course!" declared Hasan. "You see? Find Alethea and bring her to the palace."

"Very well," Cait relented.

Thus it was agreed. The final preparations were quickly made; despite his feeble protests, Paulo was placed in the sling, and the prince, holding himself like a man who feared one false step would shatter his legs, walked to his mount. With Rognvald on one side and his faithful katib on the other, Hasan climbed into the saddle. "I will see you in a few days," he called as they started off. "Farewell, my friends."

Cait and the others watched until the prince and his entourage were out of sight. "Do not worry, my lady," said Yngvar, trying to comfort her. "They will reach the palace, never fear."

"Aye," said Svein, "providing they do not meet up with any of your wolves."

The wind grew colder as the day wore on. They spent much of the morning skirting Ali Waqqar's valley lair, and stopped to breakfast once they had put the valley behind them. While they were eating, it began to snow. The mountain Abu had indicated lay directly ahead—no more than a half-day's ride by their best estimation—so they pressed on.

The snow persisted through the day, drifting down through the tall pines in great, silent feathery clumps, concealing both the path and the mountain before them in a soft layer of white, and covering the heads and shoulders of the knights, and the rumps of their horses. But they rode on, climbing higher and higher into the gently swirling curtain of flakes.

Yngvar was leading the way when Cait saw him stop at the crest of the hill. She lifted the reins and urged her mount to a trot, and came abreast of him. The slope of the hill dropped away to form the rim of a bowl-shaped valley. There below them, in the center of the bowl, lay a lake, its surface smooth and dark as polished jet. At the far side of the valley rose the mountain, not golden now, but brooding and dark, its top obscured by the clouds, its lower slopes covered with a dense forest of pine—each bough of every tree now bending beneath the heavy weight of snow.

"This is the place," said Cait, hardly daring to speak aloud for fear that it would vanish mysteriously, leaving them no closer than before.

"Maybe we will not have to sleep in tents tonight," Yngvar said, pointing away across the valley to the far side of the lake.

Cait looked where he indicated and saw a cluster of buildings and a few enclosures for cattle—little more than a smoke-gray smudge in a field of white. She turned and called behind her to Rognvald and the others who were just coming up to the crest of the hill. "There is a settlement!"

Without waiting for the others, Cait started down into the valley, keeping her eye on the tiny village which was already fading into the gloom of twilight. She had reached the side of the lake and started around when Rognvald caught her. "Do you think Alethea is there?"

"I pray she is," Cait replied. "But I hardly dare believe it might be true."

"Then I will believe it for both of us," replied Rognvald.

"Do you never grow tired?" she asked.

"Tired of the trail?"

"Tired of the search—the endless riding and riding, always searching, never finding. The futility of it all . . . I am weary to the bone with

324

it and I would to God it were over. One way or another, I wish it would just end." She looked at his face, a pale softness in the winter gloaming, unmoved by her sudden outpouring of despair. "I suppose now you despise me for being a weak and flighty woman."

"My lady," he said, his voice low. He did not turn his eyes from the snow-covered trail ahead. "You are the most stalwart woman I know."

That was all he said, and they spoke no more. But it gave Cait a warm feeling that lasted long into the night.

THIRTY-EIGHT

It was dark and the snow was deep by the time they reached the settlement. If not for the faint glow of light from the windows of several of the houses, they would have been lost in the snowy void of night. Rognvald halted a few dozen paces from the nearest dwelling: a low hovel built of turf and timber and thatched with tight-bundled reeds from the lake.

There was a small window covered with oiled sheepskin and set deep under the drooping eaves. A fine ruddy glow showed in the window and under the edge of the rough door. "It is a cow-byre," said Dag, regarding the rustic house. "But there is a fire, at least." The others remarked that they did not care if it was a hole in the ground so long as it was a dry hole.

"Let us see if they are of a mind to receive us," said Cait, and Rognvald dismounted and walked to the house. He stooped to the door and rapped on the planking. He waited, rapped again, and called out.

When nothing happened, he pulled the leather strap which lifted the wooden latch, pushed open the door, and looked inside. Warm golden light spilled out onto the snow, making the new whiteness glisten like fine samite.

"There is no one here," he reported to the others who sat looking on.

"Do you think they saw us coming and have gone into hiding?" said Yngvar.

"He would be a blind man who saw *you* coming and did not hide," replied Svein.

"Listen," said Rognvald, holding up his hand for silence.

From somewhere in the village there came the distant, bell-like sound of voices lifted in song. The words seemed to come drifting down out of the sky with the falling snow—as if angels were singing, the notes clear and ringing in the softly silent air. Cait listened to the slow, majestic strains and her breath caught in her throat: it was a song she had sung at home in Caithness every Yuletide since she was old enough to remember the words.

The realization brought tears to her eyes; before she knew it they were running freely down her cheeks. *Here,* she thought, *in this place. How could it be?* Quickly, lest the others see her, she rubbed them away with the backs of her hands.

"Do you hear?" said Rognvald.

"It cannot be Latin," said Svein. "Or Arabic."

"And it is not Danish or Norwegian," added Yngvar.

"Nor Spanish, I think," offered Dag, none too certain. Rodrigo shook his head.

"No," Cait told them, "it is Gaelic."

"You know it, my lady?" asked Svein.

"I know it well." She raised her face to the falling snow and sang:

Iompaím siar go dtí Goiroias,
an Chathair Tintrí,
Dún an tSolais,
Dún Gleadhrach Glóir,
Dún Feasa,
Baile don Tiarna Ioldánach . . .

Her voice, gentle and melodious in the snow-smothered silence, wrought a magical change in the knights. They stared at Cait with rapt, almost ecstatic expressions of amazement—as if she had suddenly sprouted wings.

"What does it mean?" asked Rognvald when she finished.

"It is an old invocation," she replied. "It means:

I am turning toward the West,
toward Goirais, the Fiery City,
Fortress of Light,
Fortress of Blazing Glory,
Fortress of Wisdom,
Home of the Many-Gifted Lord . . ."

She broke off suddenly, aware of the wondering stares of the knights. "It is part of a Yuletide ritual performed by the Célé Dé," she explained.

"Yuletide," remarked Svein. "Can it be the Christ Mass?"

"This way," Dag said, starting off along the path leading into the settlement. The others followed, and they shortly arrived at a small village green. At the end of the green was an odd round building of rough mountain stone. Larger than any of the surrounding houses and barns, it was roofed with turf, and topped by a wooden cross. A round window above the chapel door allowed light to stream out into the darkness—along with the clear, poignant strains of the song the congregation was singing.

The knights, so rapt in their fascination with the song, remained motionless in their saddles, listening as the last notes of the graceful melody faded away.

"If it is the Christ Mass," said Yngvar, breaking the silence at last. "Let us go in and join the celebration."

Svein and Dag were out of the saddle and hurrying toward the door before he finished speaking. Rodrigo and Yngvar followed. "Lady," said Rognvald, "it seems we are going to church."

"So it seems, my lord, and not before time."

As they dismounted, the congregation inside the chapel began singing again. Recognition caused Cait's heart to beat faster; she halted in midstep to listen.

"*A Fionnghil,*

A Lonraigh,

A Feasaigh . . . Tíana anocht . . . Tíana, Naofa Leanbh, anocht . . ."

Seeing Cait had stopped, Rognvald turned and heard her repeating the words of the song. "O Bright One, O Radiant One, O Knowing One . . . Come tonight . . . Come, Holy Child, tonight . . ." she said, translating the words for him.

The tall knight smiled with genuine pleasure then nodded to Dag to proceed.

Dag pushed open the door of the chapel and stepped inside, with Yngvar, Rodrigo and Svein close on his heels. The singing stopped instantly. Cait and Rognvald entered to find the villagers gaping in amazement at the snow-covered, half-frozen knights—as if at the Wise Kings appearing fresh from the Judaean hills on their fateful journey.

The chapel blazed with the light of hundreds of candles, and, in the center of the timber floor, a large bronze bowl filled with glowing embers. Before this glowing bowl stood a priest in robes of undyed wool, his hands still raised in supplication, his mouth open, the song fresh on his lips.

At Cait's appearance, the priest lowered his hands. He spoke a few words in a language Cait did not know. "*Pax vobiscum,*" she offered by way of reply. Stepping forward, she quickly searched the congregation for her sister, but did not see her and realized, with a pang of disappointment, that if Alethea were here, she would have made herself known by now.

"*Pax vobiscum,*" the priest answered excitedly. "*Pax vobiscum! Gloria in excelsis Deo!*" He moved quickly around the burning bowl and came to stand before Cait. "Lady of the Blessed Night," he said in curiously accented Latin, "I greet you with a holy kiss." Seizing both her hands in his, he raised them to his lips and kissed them, then led her by the hand into the center of the round chapel.

This caused a hushed sensation among the villagers—a group of fewer than seventy souls, young and old; the people gawked and murmured over their priest and the strange woman. Cait glanced around at the ring of watching faces once more in the forlorn hope that Alethea might yet be found among them—perhaps overcome by the sudden appearance of her sister and unable to step forward.

Meanwhile, the priest turned to the knights. "Welcome, friends," he exclaimed, pulling Cait with him to the bright burning bowl. "Come in! Come in! Close the door and warm yourselves by the fire."

"Please," Cait said, turning to the priest at last, "we had no wish to disturb your service. We heard the singing, and thought merely to join you in your observance."

"But you *have* disturbed us," replied the priest. "Even so, we welcome the disturbance, for it is an honor to entertain visitors on this most holy of all nights."

"Is it the Christ Mass?"

"It is, daughter," answered the priest. He regarded her with a bemused expression. Now that she saw him better, Cait decided the priest was not so young as she had first thought him. Indeed, he was, she surmised, as old as Abbot Padraig—if not older. Yet his deportment and demeanor were those of a man half his age.

"Then, by all means, continue with your songs and prayers," she said. "We would be pleased to listen."

The priest assented, and turning to his congregation, raised his hands once more. He called them to attention, and began singing again; gradually, the people resumed their songs and prayers—if somewhat self-consciously now for the presence of the strangers in their midst.

They were, Cait observed, a small, sturdy people, short-limbed and thick-set, with broad, handsome faces. It was the eyes, she decided, that gave them such an unusual appearance—large and dark, set deep above prominent cheekbones either side of their fine straight noses, and each and every one gleaming with quick curiosity and humor. The old Orkneyingar told of the little dark people who had inhabited the islands long before the coming of the tall-folk. She wondered if the people of this strange, hidden place could belong to a similar race.

As the Christ Mass followed its hallowed sequence, Cait was moved by the extraordinary peculiarity of what she was hearing—to be so far from home, yet listening to people sing the old familiar songs in the same familiar accents. She closed her eyes; with the voices filling her ears, she was once again back in Caithness—as she remembered it a long time ago. She was sitting in her grandmother Ragna's lap in the church her grandfather Murdo had built, surrounded by men and women of the settlement, and important guests and visitors. The monks of the nearby monastery were singing, their voices creating dizzying patterns as they rose, swirling and soaring up to the cold, clear star-dusted heaven on the holiest night of the year.

Before the gathered listeners stood her Uncle Eirik; only, tonight he was not her special friend, he was the abbot, straight and tall in his fine robes as he led the good brothers in their song. And beside her, his rough hand gently patting out the rhythm of the music on his knee, her dear old grandfather Murdo, his hair white as the snow on the hills and rooftops of Banvarð, his beard a grizzled frost on his cheeks and chin.

She saw it all so clearly, and the memory made her heart catch in her throat. The most potent yearning she had ever known rushed over her in a flood of longing so powerful it took her breath away. She had no doubt this was the *hiraeth* old Padraig had often spoken of: the home-yearning—an affliction of the traveler which produces a craving of such unrivalled magnitude that some poor wayfarers had been known to waste away in hopeless pining for their far-off home.

Cait bore the ache of the *hiraeth* even as she exulted in the memory of that Christ Mass long ago, and gradually the conflicting emotions produced in her a pleasurable calm. As the voices announced the age-old gospel of the Blessed Messiah's birth, she felt a peaceful acceptance of all that had been and would be—an inexplicable recognition that somehow she was where she was meant to be; however she had come, whatever trials she had faced, she belonged here, her presence was or-dained by forces beyond her imagining.

At last the service finished; the priest blessed his congregation, and then turned to his visitors. "My friends, we would be honored to have you stay with us and share our hospitality. Humble as it is, I daresay you will not find better tonight, nor, I think, a more heartfelt welcome anywhere."

"Your offer is most kind, brother—" began Rognvald.

"Forgive me, I am Brother Timotheus," the priest said quickly, "known to one and all as Timo."

"If, as you have proclaimed tonight," Rognvald continued, "a simple barn was good enough for the Holy Child, it will be good enough for us."

"Well said, brother," replied the priest. "But we can do better than that." He turned and called several of the villagers from among those who were timidly eyeing the large, fierce-looking newcomers. The knights were surrounded by a knot of boys who showed a lively inter-est in the swords hanging from their belts.

"Dominico," the priest said, laying his hand on the shoulder of one of the men, "is head man of this village, and these two fine young men are his sons. I will instruct them to find places for you among the peo-ple, if that is acceptable. We are but a small village, as you will have no-ticed, and there is not a house large enough to hold you all. Nevertheless, I can assure you of a warm dry place among kindly folk. Many a king could wish for as much, yes, and full many the—" Timo-theus broke off suddenly. "Ah, forgive me, I am preaching again." He smiled meekly. "I seem to do that more and more these days. I cannot say why."

"We would be pleased to accept your kind invitation," Cait told him, "so long as it does not overtax the charity of the people."

"Heaven forbid!" sniffed the priest. "It will be good for them." He turned and spoke quickly to the village chief who, with much nodding and smiling, hurried away with his sons, taking a fair portion of the population with him. Rognvald commanded the knights to go along and see that the horses were cared for. They all clumped out into the snowy darkness.

"What is the name of this place?" asked Cait, smiling at two little girls hiding behind their inquisitive elders.

"It is called *Pronakaelit*," the priest said. "It means Hidden Valley."

Cait repeated the word, and asked, "What language is spoken here?"

"Ah, yes," replied Timotheus. "Despite my best efforts, they speak but little Latin, as you have astutely observed. The tongue they prefer is their own. Their name for it is *Euskari*."

"But the songs," Cait pointed out, "were Gaelic."

Brother Timotheus smiled proudly. "I know. I taught them."

"As it happens," said Rognvald, "we have come in search of a young woman—tall and with long dark hair. Her name is Alethea, we were hoping to find her here."

"Were you indeed!" replied the priest with some surprise. "She has been here, I can tell you that."

"Truly?" Cait clasped her hands together and raised them to her chin, hoping against hope that she had heard the priest correctly. Rognvald reached out and put his hand on her arm in anticipation of the news.

Before either of them could ask what he knew, the priest asked, "Who is she that you should seek her so ardently?"

"She is my sister," Cait said. "Is she well? Do you know where she has gone?"

"Please," said the priest, holding up his hands to stem the flood of questions he feared were forthcoming. "I can tell you she is well, and she is nearby."

"God be praised," breathed Rognvald, his voice a slow sigh of relief.

"Where?" demanded Cait, excitedly. "Can we go there now?"

"Peace, my lady," the priest protested gently. "I dare not say more."

"Alethea was abducted by bandits," Rognvald explained. "They carried her into these mountains, and we have been searching for her since she was taken."

Brother Timotheus nodded as if he suspected that this had been the way of things all along. "I believe you, my friends. I assure you, I do believe you. And if it were up to me, I would send for the girl at once and happily preside over your joyful reunion." He spread his hands apologetically. "Be that as it may, however, it is not so easy as that, nor can I say more."

Cait, mystified by this irrational reluctance, stared at the monk in bewilderment. "But why?"

"I promised Annora that I would say nothing."

Rognvald, seeing the clouds gathering on Cait's furrowed brow, moved to avert the storm. "Who is Annora? Could you tell her that we have come for Alethea?"

"Annora is abbess of the Order of the *Klais Mairís*. The good sisters maintain an abbey near here."

"Klais Mairís," said Cait, repeating the words. The name was, so far as she could tell, quite similar to the Gaelic she knew; it meant the Gray Marys. "Is it far, this abbey? Can we go there?"

"Alas, no—at least, not tonight," said the priest, "but tomorrow I can send word to the abbey that you are here."

Cait shook her head in dismay. The kindly priest frowned with sympathy. "I am sorry, daughter," he said. "This is how it must be. But be of good cheer, for she is safe and well cared for, and I have no doubt that in a day or two you will be reunited with your sister."

Rognvald thanked the good brother for this assurance and Cait, forcing a smile, thanked him too, and said with as good a grace as she could muster: "We have waited this long, I suppose a day or two longer will make no difference. In any event, it is good to know that she is safe and well—wherever she may be."

"Yes, that is the spirit." Timo rubbed his hands. "Now then, you must be hungry and thirsty from your journey. Would you and your men care to join me in a simple repast? It is only beans and bread, mind, for tomorrow is the first of many feast days."

"We would be most happy to break bread with you," replied Cait, overcoming her disappointment. "But nothing would please me more than to hear how one of the Célé Dé came to be living in this remote fastness."

Brother Timotheus' eyebrows arched high in surprise. "*Deus meus!*" he exclaimed. "You know of the Célé Dé?"

"Oh, I know enough to recognize them when I see them," Cait assured him. Rognvald regarded her curiously, but said nothing. "You see, my family has long supported a Célé Dé monastery on our lands."

"Come along then, daughter," he said, taking her hand excitedly. "You must come and sit with me and tell me everything."

The priest busied himself with snuffing the candles, beginning with those on the altar—pausing before each one and bowing three times before lowering the crook-shaped snuffer over the flame. He moved around the room with a sprightly step, humming to himself and glancing every now and then at his visitors as if to reassure himself that they had not vanished as suddenly and inexplicably as they had arrived.

Then, taking up a lantern from beside the door, Timotheus led them out and around to the back of the chapel to a cell built against the church wall. Darting inside, he collected his staff and hooded cloak, and then led his guests across the village square to the settlement's largest house. The door was open and there was music coming from inside. "This is Dominico's house," he told them. "That is his baptism name, mind. I cannot pronounce his birth name."

Inside, they found the knights huddled together beside a generous hearth, their feet stretched before a log fire while they listened to a pair of lively young men play music on a pipe and drum while womenfolk of various ages darted here and there with platters, bowls, and cups. Dominico stood in the middle of the room, welcoming his guests, singing loudly, and calling orders to all the others in their incomprehensible tongue, while his wife, a small, round woman called Elantra, directed the preparations with quiet efficiency.

"Glad Yule, my lady!" called Yngvar as Cait and Rognvald entered. "They have already fed our horses and now they are going to feed us."

"Glad Yule!" added Svein, lofting the cup in his hand. "They have ale, too!"

"And black bread like home!" said Dag, waving half a loaf at them.

"It seems the Yuletide celebrations have begun after all," remarked Rognvald.

"The people here are like children in many ways," sighed Brother Timotheus, "they can never wait for anything."

Dominico, chattering excitedly, gathered the late arrivals and herded them to a bench opposite the hearth. He dashed away, returning a moment later with two overflowing ale cups and a young girl bearing a tray of bread. The dark-eyed girl, grave with the weight of her responsibility, stood straight and, looking neither left nor right, offered the noble guests loaves of black bread from her tray. While Rognvald took charge of the cups, Cait accepted one of the loaves, smiled pleasantly, and thanked the girl, whose stoic solemnity wilted at their exchange. The household honor satisfied, she turned and scampered away, calling loudly for her mother.

The musicians, meanwhile, finished their song to the noisy acclaim of the knights, who began stamping their feet and slapping their knees and clamoring for more. The two boys grinned and quickly commenced another, yet more spirited tune. Dominico, clapping his hands and calling like a bird, began whirling around; spinning this way and that, his feet beating time to the music, he rounded on Cait, scooped her up and spun her onto the floor. The next thing she knew, she was caught up in the dance to the dizzy delight of one and all.

More and more villagers were crowding into the house by the moment, some bringing jars of wine and ale, and others bearing festive foods: boiled eggs, smoked meat and fish, flat bread flavored with anise. When there was no more room in the house, the merrymaking spilled out into the snow and then the neighboring houses. More musical instruments appeared: tabors and shakers, pipes made of gourds and clay, wooden flutes of several sizes, and an oddly shaped lyre with four strings.

They drank and sang and danced, and then drank some more. Cait quickly became the most sought-after partner, as one after another of the male villagers, young and old, seized the opportunity to dance with their noble visitor. Once, presented with two obstinate partners who asked at the same time, she averted hurt feelings by taking on both at once—to the exuberant approval of the women looking on.

Amidst the singing and dancing, the food came and went, and the night with it. One night's revelry spilled over into the next day's celebration. The light of a Yuletide dawn was showing when Cait finally found a chance to creep away. She went into her host's chamber, loosed her swordbelt and put the weapon aside, before sinking into a bed piled high with furs. She closed her eyes and slept only to be awakened a short time later by the clanging of a bell outside the house.

THIRTY-NINE

Cait sat up in bed; so strong was the sense of familiarity, she imagined she was home again in Caithness. The priests at Banvarð rang the bells to signal the beginning of the Yuletide celebrations; she wondered if Brother Timotheus did the same.

When the music began again, she relinquished any expectation of sleep, rose from her bed, and made her way outside to a world of sparkling white made brilliant by the light of the rising sun. The sky was clear and heart-breakingly blue, and the high, encircling mountain peaks burned with a rosy glow like fired bronze.

The villagers were making their way in procession to the chapel, led by Brother Timotheus exuberantly swinging an oversize bell. The air was biting cold, and the pealing of the bell piercing in its clarity. Yngvar, Dag and Rodrigo were in the forefront of the parade, trampling triumphantly through the snow as if to make a path for those behind; they were followed by Dominico and his sons, and all the rest. Neither Rognvald nor Svein was to be seen, but Cait fell into line behind the others and proceeded to the church.

The service was blessedly short. Brother Timotheus simply read out a Psalm and led his faithful flock in a few prayers; the congregation sang a song, and then they all trooped back outside where everyone hailed everyone else with an enthusiastic Yuletide greeting. Cait was swept up in wave upon wave of hugging and kissing, as one after another of the villagers embraced her. Then they all went off to resume the celebration.

As the last released her and hurried away, she looked up to find Rognvald standing before her. "Glad Yule, Lady Caitríona," he said. "It seems I am too late for prayers, but not, I hope, for a greeting." With that, he opened his arms and folded her into a warm embrace and gave her a kiss that left her blinking at its sudden, virile intensity.

"Glad Yule, my lord," she said, gazing up into his face.

He smiled, his blue eyes keen and clear as the skies high overhead. "Will you breakfast with me?"

"It would be a pleasure," she replied, taking Rognvald's arm. They walked slowly, enjoying one another's company and the fine, sparkling day. The sound of the snow squeaking beneath her feet filled Cait with a youthful joy she had not known for years. "It seems our search is soon concluded," she said after a time.

When Rognvald did not answer, she glanced sideways at his face and saw that he was gazing at the mountains towering above the village, their smooth, snow-dusted slopes gleaming in the new day's light. They appeared to Cait like stately monarchs robed in winter furs and enthroned around the bowl of the valley, gazing at their own splendor in the bright mirror of its lake.

"Tell me about the Célé Dé," he said. "Who are they?"

"There is little enough to tell," she began. "They are priests of an order that holds itself apart from Rome—a small order, but tenacious, and fiercely loyal to its calling."

"What is that?"

"To preserve the True Path and guard the Holy Light."

Rognvald nodded. "They are heretics then."

"Not in the least," Cait protested. "They simply embrace an older tradition than Rome. There were Christians in the West *before* Rome, you know. The church of the Celts is older by far than the one decreed by Emperor Constantine, and—"

Rognvald chuckled.

"Are you laughing at me?" she said defensively.

"You sound like a priest now," he replied, "trying to convert the unbeliever."

"I suppose I am," she allowed, accepting his chiding. "The Célé Dé are a small and much maligned sect, and we grow protective."

"Are *you* one of these Célé Dé?"

She nodded. "All of my family belong to the sect—ever since my grandfather went on the Great Pilgrimage to Jerusalem."

"He discovered them in Jerusalem?"

"No, he met some priests aboard the ship that carried him to the Holy Land. He would not have survived the journey without them. When he returned he rewarded them with lands, and money to build a monastery. And," she added with quiet defiance, "no matter what anyone says, they are the kindliest, most compassionate, and thoughtful people you will ever meet."

"If that is true, why are they so reviled?"

"But they are not reviled!" protested Cait.

"You said they were maligned," he pointed out. "It is the same thing."

"No it is not!" she snapped. "There is a world of difference. The Célé Dé are never reviled."

"No?" He looked at her askance. "If they were not, would you defend them so heartily?" Before she could challenge this observation, he said, "What is this True Path that they follow?"

"I am not going to tell you," she replied crisply. "You will only make sport of it, and—" Rognvald stopped walking. He was looking straight along the path beaten through the snow by the villagers. "What is it? Why have you stopped?"

"More visitors."

"Bandits?" Cait looked around quickly, but could not see anyone. "Where?"

"Just there." He indicated a clump of villagers a few dozen paces before them. Cait had been looking for horses and riders, and missed the two pale, slender figures standing directly in her path. Like Brother Timotheus, they were dressed in hooded robes of undyed wool and, judging from the enthusiastic welcome they were receiving from the villagers, they were well known and well liked.

"They arrived last night—burst in on us during the service," the priest was saying. "Ah, here are two of them now!" He motioned Cait and Rognvald to join them. "Here, I was just telling Sister Efa about you. And this," he said, indicating the woman next to her, "is Sister Siâran."

"God's peace to you, sisters," Cait said. "I am pleased to meet you. I am Caitríona, and this is Lord Rognvald of Haukeland in Norway."

Both nuns pressed their hands together and inclined their heads politely. "God bless you and keep you," they intoned together.

When everyone had become a little better acquainted, Brother Timotheus said, "I believe these good people have business with Abbess Annora. I was going to send word to you today, although now, as you are here, I will let them speak for themselves." Before Cait could open her mouth, however, the priest said, "But come, it is cold and they will have made a warming drink for us. Let us discuss matters over our cups before the fire."

They proceeded to Dominico's house where, as Timotheus had predicted, a cauldron of hot, spiced ale was just being poured into jars—much to the noisy delight of the knights, who extolled the virtues of their host with rousing cheers as they drank his health, and that of his sons, and wife, and daughters.

Cait, Rognvald and the two sisters settled on benches in a corner of the room and the priest went to fetch the ale. "It is such a beautiful morning," said Cait, easing her way into the conversation. "Have you traveled far?"

The sister called Efa replied, "A small distance, my lady."

That was all she said, and when it appeared there was no more forthcoming, Rognvald spoke up. "Your robes are very like Brother Timo's here. Are you of the same order?"

"Yes, my lord," she said, and looked down at her hands folded tightly in her lap.

"I see," he said. "Then you are Célé Dé, too."

The two glanced quickly at one another in nervous amazement. "You know of the Célé Dé?" asked the one called Siâran.

"I know all about them," he said confidently. "Lady Caitríona here is a stalwart defender of the order. Her family's lands support a monastery in the far north—a place called Caithness. Have you ever heard of it?"

The nuns shook their heads. "It is true, my lady?" asked a wide-eyed Sister Efa. "Your family maintains a monastery?"

"Yes," Cait assured them. "And my uncle is abbot of the order."

"Truly?" wondered Brother Timotheus, returning just then. "Celebrations came between us somewhat last night, but I still want to hear all about this haven in the north."

"You must be Alethea's sister," volunteered Sister Siâran.

"She is that," said Rognvald, beaming with the pleasure of making these small revelations.

"We have been searching for her," explained Cait quickly. "Brother

Timo told us she was with you." Cait smiled, trying to put the timid sisters at their ease. "I understand she is well."

"Yes, my lady," replied Efa, then lapsed into silence once more.

"Where is she? I want to see her at once. Is it far?"

The two sisters exchanged an uncertain glance, but said nothing.

"Is there something which prevents me from bringing her home?" asked Cait, growing frustrated with their reticence.

"Allow me, my lady," said Timotheus. Addressing the two young nuns, he said, "If I am not mistaken, you have been instructed not to speak of this matter—am I right?"

Sister Siâran, looking at her hands in her lap, nodded.

"There! You see?" cried Timotheus, as if this were the answer to all their troubles.

"But why should they refuse to speak about it? I am her sister," Cait said, "we have been searching for her a very long time. I want to see her, and—"

"Please, please," said Timotheus quickly, "all in good time. I imagine the abbess will have her reasons."

"Then I will not press you," Cait replied, trying to remain calm and reasonable. "But you must take me to her. Please, I need to see her— you must understand."

"But my lady—" protested Efa, looking to Brother Timotheus for help.

"It may not be convenient—" the priest began.

"I want to go to my sister," she insisted, her tone growing sharp. "I do not care if it is convenient or not. We have traveled a very long way and . . . people have died." Her voice broke and hot tears came to her eyes. "I have to see and know she is well."

Rognvald put his hand on her shoulder and she allowed herself to be drawn close. "It is true," he said to Timotheus. "We have endured many hardships in the search. It seems a needless cruelty to deny us when we are so close."

"Forgive me, my friends," said Timotheus soothingly. "I have spoken without sufficient forethought." He gave Cait's hand a fatherly pat. "You shall see your sister, of course you shall. This very day."

"We will leave at once," Rognvald said, "and go as swiftly as horses can carry us."

"Oh, no!" said the priest shaking his head in dismay. "It is not permitted."

"What?" said the knight. "Are you saying horses are not permitted?"

"Men are not permitted!" replied Timotheus. "Nor weapons, either. The abbey contains women only. You must stay behind, my friend. The abbess is most strict about this. In all my years I have never known an exception."

"Perhaps I may be allowed to escort the women part way," suggested Rognvald. "Would there be any objection to that, do you think?"

"Providing you left your weapons behind," the priest agreed, "I suppose it would be allowed."

"Thank you, brother," Cait said, "I am much obliged." She stood quickly. "I will gather my things and make ready to go."

"I would still prefer to announce your arrival," Timotheus answered, "but in light of your feelings, I see no reason why we cannot forgo that formality. Yes, why not? When the sisters have concluded their visit, you shall return to the abbey with them."

Cait hurried away, leaving the others to finish their festive ale. When she returned a short while later, she was dressed in her best clothes and her hair had been brushed and her face washed until the skin glowed. She fairly hummed with happy anticipation as she hurried outside where Rognvald had brought horses for Cait and himself, and one for the two nuns, dubious riders at best, to share.

Brother Timotheus and some of the villagers accompanied them to the edge of the settlement, and bade them farewell. The nuns pointed out the path, and they quickly found themselves on a steeply rising trail leading into the mountains which towered above the village. They rode in silence, enjoying the crisp, crystalline beauty of the day, listening to the birds in the snow-laden branches of the tall pines growing alongside the trail. After a time, they left the trees behind; the track became more narrow and winding as it snaked up and up into a sky of blazing blue.

The snow-covered path bent inward, following a fold in the mountainside. The sides of the trail rose high and sheer as the walls of a fortress, and when the riders emerged once more, they could see the little village far, far below, snug in its hollow, as if nestled in the palm of a gigantic hand, the surrounding peaks like fingers.

Another bend removed the village from sight, and they came to a chasm dividing two peaks. The gorge was deep and narrow, spanned by a simple bridge made of rope and wood. Rognvald reined in and dismounted; he examined the bridge and concluded that he dare not risk taking horses across. "The abbey is not far," Sister Efa told them. "We will walk from here."

"Then this is where I leave you," the knight said to the women as he dismounted. He helped the nuns down from the saddle, and then watched as they tripped lightly across the fragile-looking bridge. Then it was Cait's turn. Rognvald wished her God's own speed, and said, "I pray you find all is well, and eagerly await your return."

Cait, watching the swaying bridge with mounting apprehension, nodded; gripping the side ropes in either hand she took a deep breath and started across, her eyes fixed firmly on the waiting figure of Sister Efa. Rognvald watched until she had safely reached the other side where she turned and waved him farewell, then he gathered up the reins, turned the horses, and returned to the settlement.

Beyond the chasm, the trail passed between two steep bare rock slopes before arriving at a low tunnel which had been chiselled out of the mountain stone. Although the tunnel was dark and damp, it was not long, and Cait emerged on the other side to find the trail winding gently down beside a racing mountain stream. The three women walked along, quiet in one another's company, and soon arrived at a stand of tall thin birch trees.

They walked through the wood, which ended shortly, and Cait stepped out from among the trees into a high mountain glade. At the far end of the snow-drifted meadow, she could see a cramped huddle of buildings which, she assumed, formed the Abbey of the Gray Marys.

They followed the trail beside the stream, and soon came to the first of the outbuildings: two simple barns with adjoining stone enclosures for sheep and goats, and four modest but well-thatched storehouses, solid-looking on their stone foundations. Next they passed the square expanse of a field, its rippling ridges visible beneath thick snow. At one end of the field was an orchard of small, well-tended trees; on one side of the grove stood a fine tall stack of chopped wood, and on the other side was a triple row of beehives; the familiar sight of their high-mounded white humps sent a pang of homely longing through Cait and her heart quickened.

Even from a distance she could tell that this was a place of order and peace, of humble industry and dutiful purpose. Closer, she saw the tidy yard, its smooth-cobbled paving swept clean of snow. On opposite sides of the yard were long rows of individual cells, each with a single tiny window and a low wooden door; on the third side of the yard stood a large, amply proportioned house of two floors with shuttered windows and, rising sharply behind this larger structure, a rugged tawny shoulder of the mountain whose sheltering peak soared high above the neat little abbey.

There was no church or chapel that she could see, but the abbey's unadorned, uncluttered simplicity appealed to Cait; she warmed to the place even before she heard the singing—which stopped her in her tracks with its clear, angelic mellifluence.

"What is that?" she said, her breath catching in her throat.

The two sisters glanced at one another. "It is the prayer before the midday meal, my lady," answered Siâran.

"It is beautiful," Cait replied, and was instantly reminded of Abbot Emlyn's strong melodious voice as he stood before the festal table in Murdo's hall, head back, arms spread wide, a song of blessing bubbling up from his throat as from a deep sweet spring. It was, she realized, the second time in as many days that she had been brought up short by singing—once in the village and now here. "It reminded me of something," she said, as a pang of yearning pierced her heart. *It reminded me of home.*

"Alethea will be there," she said, stirring herself once more. "Let us go and join them."

The three hurried on, quickly crossing the yard and coming to the door of the refectory. The singing had stopped and Cait could hear the low murmur of voices from within. She paused at the door and allowed Sister Efa to open it and beckon her inside.

Trembling with anticipation, she stepped lightly across the threshold. The large room was dim, but warm; a single wide table occupied the center of the room with benches on either side for the thirty or so nuns who had gathered for their meal. Talk ceased as Cait stepped into the room, and every face turned toward her. She glanced the length of the table for Alethea, but did not see her.

"Welcome," said a kindly voice, and Cait turned to see a trim elderly woman hastening toward her. She was dressed as the others in a long robe of undyed wool and, like old Abbot Emlyn back home, wore a large wooden cross on a leather loop around her neck. Her hair was white, and the bones stood out on her wrists and hands, but her step was quick and her dark eyes keen. "I am Abbess Annora. We are just beginning our meal. Please, join us."

"God be good to you. I am looking for my sister," said Cait, scanning the table once more. "Brother Timotheus told me she would be here."

The older woman smiled. "You must be Caitríona. Alethea has told us about you." Addressing the nuns at table, the abbess announced the identity of their visitor, and bade the sisters make her welcome. Cait offered them a hurried greeting, then once more turned to the abbess, who said, "Alethea has been praying for you."

"Then she *is* here," said Cait, hope flickering bright once more. "Where is she? Can you tell her I am here? She will want to know I have found her at last."

"Are you hungry?" asked the abbess. "Would you like something to eat after your long walk?"

"Thank you, no," said Cait, frustration sharpening her tone. "Please, I want to see my sister."

"Come with me." She took Cait by the elbow and led her through a door at the far end of the refectory. The room they entered was small, containing only a simple straw pallet bed in a raised box, a chair, and a table. In one corner a fire cracked brightly on a tiny stone hearth.

"Your sister is well," said Abbess Annora, closing the door behind them. "Moreover, she is happy. But you cannot see her just now."

"Why?" demanded Cait, feeling the heat of frustration leap up within her. Forcing down her anger, she said, "Please—you must tell me. I have come a very long way, and—"

"Caitríona," said the elderly nun, her voice soft and caressing as a mother's. "Your sister is in preparation for a special ceremony which will take place tonight."

"A ceremony . . ." repeated Cait. Would she never see her sister again? "I do not understand. What kind of ceremony?"

"Alethea has been called to join our order. Tonight she will take the first step toward becoming one of us."

FORTY

"Alethea—" Cait stared in disbelief at the kindly abbess "— to become a nun."

"That is her dearest wish."

The strength seemed to flow from Cait's legs; she sat down on the edge of the box bed. "But how can that be?"

"Although she has not been with us long, Alethea has changed. The change is profound and it is genuine. She is as astonished by this as anyone." Annora smiled. "She has embraced the order with a zeal which gladdens the hearts of all who see her."

Cait shook her head from side to side, trying to take it in. "But we've come all this way," she said, fighting to keep her voice steady against the emotions boiling within her. "Are you telling me that she will not be coming back with us?"

"Caitríona," the abbess said gently, "try to understand. Alethea has heard the call of God, and she has answered. Her place is here."

"I want to see her," Cait said bluntly. "I want to see her now."

"Rest assured, you will see her—all in good time. Alethea is alone with God and cannot be disturbed."

"In good time?" Cait snapped, unable to hold back her frustration any longer. "Is she a prisoner here?" She stood abruptly, fists tight, arms stiff at her sides. "I have endured hardships beyond sufferance. I have spent day after day after day in the saddle—cold and hungry and often wet, but what of that? Four warriors, a priest and one brave servant have forfeited their lives in pursuit of her freedom—they lie cold in their graves beside the trail and," her voice faltered, "— and Alethea is not to be *disturbed*?"

Cait stared at the woman in a misery of disbelief as bitter tears came to her eyes. Through every trial she had persevered, hoping against hope that Thea would be found; she had faced death, destruction, and discomfort of every kind only to be told her sister wished to be alone with God. It was beyond her ability to comprehend.

"If you will not help me," declared Cait, "I will find her myself!" Turning on her heel, she moved swiftly toward the door.

"Caitríona!" said the abbess sternly. "Stop!"

To her own amazement she halted, her hand on the latch.

"Think what you are doing," said Annora. "If you ever had any feeling for your sister, then I ask you to honor her wishes. She did not enter into this decision lightly, and she will not thank you for interfering now."

Cait could feel the icy center of her resolve melting away.

Annora softened. "Alethea is coming to the end of a period of prayer and fasting in preparation for the ceremony which will take place tonight. Tomorrow, when the ritual is finished, you will be together."

Unable to make herself reply, Cait merely nodded. The abbess took her hand. "Come, it is a splendid day. Why not spend it with us? Share our meal, and then I will show you something of our work here, and you will come to know us better."

Although Cait no longer felt hungry, she allowed herself to be led back into the refectory where she ate a few bites and then gave up as black melancholy overcame her. When the abbess offered to show her the rest of the abbey, she complained of fatigue and asked instead to be shown where she might lie down and rest. The abbess summoned one of the sisters, a woman of similar age and appearance to Cait. "This is Sister Besa—she will take you to the guest lodge."

Cait thanked her and followed the sister out across the cobbled yard to one of the cells. "We have few guests," the nun told her, "but we keep a room ready for anyone the Good Lord sends our way. It is this one on the end." The sister lifted the wooden latch, pushed the door open, and stepped in. "Oh, it is cold in here, but I will make up the fire and it will soon be warm enough."

The sister hurried away, leaving Cait to stare at the bleakly simple room: a table large enough to hold a candle, a three-legged stool and neatly stacked logs beside the tiny half-circle hearth, and a straw pallet topped with a rough woollen coverlet. The room's sole adornment was a wooden cross which had obviously been made by one of the nuns; it was fashioned from two bent pine branches, smoothed and bound together with a strap of braided leather, and hung below the tiny round window.

Cait was still standing in the center of the room when Besa returned with an armful of kindling and some live embers in a small pan. "I suppose Alethea stayed here," she said absently.

"Why, yes. For a time." The sister placed the wood beside the hearth and gently shook the embers from the bowl. "She has her own cell now."

Cait waited for her to say more, but the nun proceeded to arrange the wood around the little heap of glowing coals. After a moment, Cait said, "How long have you been here?"

Besa glanced at her and then quickly away again, as if the question was distracting. "All my life," she answered after a moment. "Or, very nearly."

"But you are not from Aragon," Cait suggested.

The sister lowered her face to the heap of kindling and blew on the embers. "No," she replied, sitting back on her heels. "I am not from Aragon. I was born on the other side of the mountains." She leaned forward and blew on the embers once more. Thin threads of smoke were soon curling up from the hearth as a cluster of yellow flames bloomed among the twigs. "But this has been my home so long I do not remember any other."

"You never visit your family?"

"I did once," replied Sister Besa, rising to her feet. "But no more." She smiled wanly, and moved to the door. "I will leave you in peace now, but if you need anything, my room is next to this one."

She closed the door quickly behind her and was gone. Cait sat on the stool, watching the flames catch and burn more brightly. When the fire appeared hearty enough, she added several larger chunks of wood from the stack, and then retreated to the bed where she stretched herself out. After gazing petulantly at the age-darkened pine roof beams, she eventually drifted into an uneasy sleep.

She dreamed of hoofprints and felt herself once again on horseback, riding through deep-drifted snow. In her dream she seemed to be fleeing someone—although she twisted in the saddle and craned her neck from time to time, she could not see who it might be. Still, she could feel a disturbing presence gaining ground behind her, and the dull malevolence mounted until she grew afraid to look around anymore.

And then, just as she knew she must confront the swiftly approaching evil, there came the slow tolling of a distant bell. Instantly, she felt the unseen wickedness falter in its onrushing flight. She turned in the saddle, lashed her mount, and raced up the steep mountain trail leading to the abbey. Above the wild drumming of her heart she could hear the rhythmic ringing of the bell.

The sound grew, and seemed to take on a more urgent note and she awoke. It took Cait some time to realize that it was a real bell she had been hearing. As the last sonorous stroke faded into the air she rose and stepped to the window. The fire on the hearth had burned out and the short winter day had ended; it was growing dark outside. She crept to the door, opened it and looked quickly out. There was no one to be seen, but she assumed the bell summoned the sisters to prayer, and so went out—realizing halfway across the yard that she did not know where the chapel might be. She had seen none when coming to the abbey, nor had the abbess mentioned it.

She paused for a moment, looking around. The sky yet held a blush of fading sunset, but the first stars were glowing high overhead. A light wind was blowing down from the surrounding flame-touched peaks, and it made her cold. As she turned to retreat into her cell, she heard the bell again, and decided to follow the sound—which seemed to come from behind the nearby refectory.

She flitted quickly to the end of the building and saw, in the rock curtain rising sheer from the ground, a wide, low entrance cut into the living stone of the mountain. The snow was tracked with dozens of footprints leading into a cave; as Cait followed them to the dark entrance, she heard singing from within.

After the first few paces, the darkness was all but complete. With one hand to the wall beside her, and the other outstretched and waving before her, she edged slowly on, guided by the singing of the nuns. The texture of the wall beneath her fingertips as she felt her way along suggested that the tunnel had been carved into the rock; both the wall and the floor were smooth and fairly even.

The wall ended abruptly and the air suddenly became warmer, and held the slightly musty smell of damp rock. Taking a hesitant step, she entered a larger chamber; a gentle, almost imperceptible breeze blew over her face from left to right. Instinctively, she turned in the direction of the airflow and saw the pale glimmer of candlelight on the rim of another tunnel opening a dozen paces to her left. She reached the tunnel doorway just as the glint of light faded, leaving her in darkness once more.

More confident now, she proceeded down the corridor as before, keeping her hand to the wall beside her. The floor slanted downward; she could feel it tilting away, and the slight cant quickened her step as if in anticipation of what she would find when she reached the end. The singing grew louder.

And then the tunnel opened out wide and she was standing in the high-arched entrance of an enormous chamber. In the near distance Cait saw, as through a gloom-wrapped forest of limbless trees, the shimmering of ghostly lights. The trees, she realized, were the tapering, slightly misshapen shafts of great stone pillars rising from the cavern floor to the unseen roof high above. The light came from candles in the hands of the nuns, whose voices set the vast empty spaces of the chamber reverberating with the rippling music of their song.

Stepping cautiously forward into this peculiar, frozen forest, Cait moved silently from tree to tree, pausing at each trunk to look and listen before moving on again—fearful of being discovered, yet desiring above all else to be allowed to stay and observe.

Closer, she caught a whiff of incense—a cloying sweet vapor that filled her head with the essence of lavender. She felt her empty stomach squirm at the heavy scent, and paused to swallow before moving on.

The singing stopped, and so Cait halted, too. She heard someone speaking, but was too far away to make out the words. Presently the address finished, and there followed a lengthy silence which was broken at last by the ringing of a bell. The nuns began singing again and, flitting from one column to the next, Cait crept carefully, cautiously nearer.

When the music ceased, Cait peered discreetly from her hiding place behind the last rank of pillars, now but a few paces from the first of three low, wide steps which rose from the level floor to make a platform on which the Gray Marys had assembled before an altar adorned with a great golden cross with two lamps burning on either side; in their gently wavering light the ornately patterned gold of the cross seemed to melt and move.

Abbess Annora stood motionless before the altar with hands raised shoulder-high, palms upward, as if expecting to receive a gift. On the floor between the abbess and the waiting sisters, two richly embroidered lengths of cloth were spread; on each a young woman knelt in an attitude of prayer. Dressed in the same drab gray robes as the others, they were set apart only by the long crimson hoods that covered their heads. Both supplicants were bent over their clasped hands, and both were trembling slightly. Although she could not see their faces, Cait easily recognized the slender, willowy form of her sister, Alethea.

At long last . . . Alethea! Cait's heart leaped in her breast, and she pressed the back of her hand to her mouth to keep from crying out. Closing her eyes, she slumped against the pillar and felt the cool stone bear her up as relief rolled over her in waves.

I believe, O God of all gods,
  that Thou art the eternal Father of Light.

The voice was that of Abbess Annora, and she was immediately joined by a chorus of sisters who repeated the phrase three times with but slight variation.

I believe, O God of all gods,
  that Thou art the eternal Father of Life.
I believe, O God of all gods,
  that Thou art the eternal Father of All Creation.

The ceremony was in Gaelic. Although the inflection was odd, and some of the words seemed curiously old-fashioned, Cait understood it readily enough, for the chant had the same qualities she had heard since she was old enough to sit upright in church and listen to Abbot Emlyn's bold, handsome voice declaring the high holiness of the God of Love and Light and his Conquering Son.

Oh, Thea, she thought, *that you, of all people, should strike such a bargain.* She wondered what her father would make of it, and then remembered that he was dead and would never know. Well, better this, she supposed, than an unsuitable marriage. And where Alethea was concerned that had always been a live possibility; the young woman's gift for making the most ludicrous and improper alliances had long been a worry to almost all who knew her—save Duncan alone. Now, it appeared that his long-suffering faith was about to be repaid.

When she had better control of herself, Cait once again edged from behind the column. After the recitation, there followed another song, which afforded Cait the opportunity to steal to another pillar for a better view. When the song finished two of the sisters approached the kneeling figures with long, tapering unlit candles. Addressing the novices, the abbess spoke in a low voice to each in turn and was answered, whereupon the candle was offered. The two women rose and approached the altar to light their tapers from the lamps burning there.

Returning to their places, both young women knelt once more, set the lit candles in golden sconces which had been provided, and then stretched themselves full-length face down on the embroidered rugs and extended their arms to either side in emulation of the cross.

The abbess took her place before them, her hands outspread above their heads, and she began to pray. When she finished, the two novices rose and, resuming their kneeling posture, began to pray aloud, saying:

Thanks to Thee, Great of Light, that I have risen today,
  to the rising of my life;
May it be to Thy glory, All-Wise Creator,
  and to the glory of my own dear soul.
O Great King, aid Thou my soul,
  with the aiding of Thy mercy,
  with the aiding of Thy love,
  with the aiding of Thy compassion;
Even as I clothe my body with this wool,
  cover Thou my soul with Thy Swift Sure Hand.
Help me to avoid every sin,
  and the source of every sin forsake;
As the mist scatters on the face of the mountains,
  may each ill thought and deed vanish from my heart.

There were more prayers, and when these finished the novices rose and one of the sisters came forward bearing a jar of consecrated oil with which she anointed them, dipping her finger and signing them with the cross on their foreheads. Then each of the novices pledged her life to the service of the community, taking a holy vow which the abbess administered with solemn approval.

After the vows, the nuns began singing again. This time, as they sang, they arranged themselves in two concentric rings around the altar holding their candles before them. Cait took advantage of the movement and edged closer for a better look. From behind her pillar she now viewed the hooded figures from the side; Alethea was nearest her, though Cait could not see her face.

Returning to the altar, the abbess picked up a small wooden cross on a leather loop. Stepping before Alethea, the older woman held out the cross for the younger to kiss. Alethea leaned forward slightly, reached out, took hold of the cross and brought it to her lips. As she did so, Cait felt a pang of yearning pierce her heart. This took her by surprise. She had not thought to be moved by the ceremony in this way. What did it mean?

She had little time to wonder about this, however, for Abbess Annora nodded, and Alethea reached up, pulled back the hood and lowered it to rest on her shoulders. It was then Cait saw that her sister's head was completely shaved. The sight made Cait's breath catch in her throat—all that lovely long dark hair . . . gone. Strangely, the sight of her sister this way, on her knees, denuded head bent in prayer, awakened Cait to the solemn seriousness of her sister's decision. *Oh, Thea,* she thought, *dear, dear Thea, for once in your life I hope you know what you are doing.*

The abbess moved to the other young woman and repeated the conferral of the cross. Then one of the sisters stepped forward, holding two lengths of dove-gray cloth across her outstretched palms. Taking one of the cloths, the abbess draped it around Alethea's shoulders like a shawl; leaning close she kissed the younger woman lightly on the forehead, then raised her to her feet. The procedure was repeated for the second novice, whereupon the two newest members of the abbey were embraced by the abbess and each of the other sisters in turn; thus were they welcomed into the intimate fellowship of the Order.

Cait thought the ceremony would end now, and the Gray Marys would leave, but as soon as the new sisters had received their welcome, the nuns reformed their circle. The abbess turned once more to the altar. Crossing her hands over her breast, she bent her head, and called out, "In the meeting of our hearts and minds: Thou. In the calling of our souls, dear lord: Thou. In the weaving of life below with life above: Thou, savior lord, and Thou only."

So saying, she stepped to the altar, pressed her hands together, and then placed her palms flat on either side of the huge golden cross as if she would remove it—an unusual gesture, and unexpected, which drew Cait's attention. As she watched, the abbess withdrew her hands, and Cait saw that a door had opened in the base of the cross, revealing a hollow place. Reaching in, the abbess brought forth a footed cup.

Cait could not see it clearly from where she stood, but it seemed an ordinary drinking cup of wood, perhaps, or pottery. A glint of candlelight traced the rim as the abbess turned and presented the cup to Alethea, who, gazing steadily at the vessel, extended her neck slightly as the abbess brought the cup to her mouth to drink. No sooner had the cup touched her lips, than the young woman gave out a loud cry. She raised her head and in the candlelight Cait saw her younger sister's face aglow with a strange light that seemed to dance over her features. Alethea cried out again and swooned, crumpling slowly onto her side.

It was all Cait could do to keep from rushing to her sister's aid. Instead, she bit the back of her hand and forced herself to stay behind her pillar. The cup was offered to the second novice, who likewise accepted a drink and promptly sank to the floor, a smile of ecstasy on her fresh young face. At the same time, Cait became aware of a sweetening of the air, as if a blossom-scented breeze had suddenly wafted into the cave.

The two young women lay before the altar for a long, silent moment. The sight of them sleeping so peacefully, their features suffused with such rapturous abandon, produced in Cait a longing she had not felt for a very long time. *Oh, to know such peace,* she thought.

After a while, the abbess returned the cup to its hidden nook, and then stood over the stricken novices; stretching her hands above them, she intoned:

Now art thou the beloved of God.
Receive these gifts from the Gifting Giver:
The grace of form,
The grace of voice,
The grace of good fortune in all things,
The grace of kindness,

The grace of wisdom,
The grace of charity,
The grace of modesty and fair virtue,
The grace of whole-souled loveliness,
The grace of pleasing speech.

So saying, Abbess Annora stooped and placed a hand on each young woman's head. Then, resuming her place once more, she said, "As you abide in Christ, He abides in you. Therefore, through all things whatsoever shall befall you, remember:

Thou art the joy of all joyous things,
Thou art the light of the sun's glorious beaming,
Thou art the door of generous hospitality,
Thou art the shining star of guidance,
Thou art the amity of the deer on the hill,
Thou art the comeliness of the swan on the lake,
Thou art the strength of the steed on the plain,
Thou art the beauty of all lovely desires,
Henceforth and forever more.
Amen.

The abbess placed her hand on the novices' heads once more and said, "Arise to life renewed." With these words, both young women rose and stood smiling, looking slightly bewildered—as if they were indeed seeing the world for the first time. Abbess Annora blessed the newest members of her order, and the nuns re-formed their ranks and began withdrawing from the rock-cut sanctuary, singing as they went. Taking up their candles once more, the two young nuns fell into place behind them, leaving the abbess alone for a moment.

After the others had gone, Abbess Annora made reverence herself before the altar, and then knelt, head lifted high, gazing up into the darkness of the cavern, arms outstretched as if to receive a gift from her unseen lord. Cait watched, and something about the simple devotion touched her, and she wondered how long it had been since she had knelt like that and experienced the tranquillity of a free and open heart. Instantly, she was seized by ferocious yearning to be at peace within herself once more.

When Annora's prayers were finished, Cait waited until she could no longer hear her footsteps and then crept out from her hiding place behind the pillar. She thought to take a candle from the altar so that she might find her way back through the tunnelled passages.

Stepping quickly to the altar, she reached for one of the candles and paused to look at the handsome golden cross. What from a distance appeared a work of solid metal, closer observation revealed to be carved wood overlaid with sheets of beaten gold. At the base of the cross she saw the thin vertical crack which defined the door of the niche containing the communion cup.

Moving closer, she placed her hands on either side of the base in imitation of the abbess. Although she felt nothing save the cool smoothness of the metal, the pressure of her palms caused the thin covering of gold to bulge slightly beneath her right hand. She pressed the bulge with her palm; there was a click, the little door opened in the base of the cross, and there was the cup.

Thinking only to admire its simple, uncomplicated shape she reached in and brought it out. It was, as she had guessed, a simple footed bowl of pale, deeply grained wood, to which had been added a golden rim, and the foot gilded. In the gentle light of the candles, the wooden bowl shone with a fine luster where the touch of many hands had polished it over the years.

She tilted the cup and looked inside. It was empty; more than that, it was dry—which she thought odd, for she had seen Alethea and the other novice drink from the cup. Even if they had drained it there would still remain some residue of the wine they had tasted. But there was none.

Raising the vessel, she put her nose into the bowl and sniffed. The faintly sweet aroma she had smelled at the offering of the cup during the ceremony still lingered there. The scent reminded her of beeswax and rose blossom, but lighter, and somehow fresher.

Then, more in imitation than expectation, she touched her lip to the golden rim and tilted the cup. A warm fluid met her tongue.

She gave a squeak of surprise and jumped back, almost dropping the cup. She steadied her hand and looked into the bowl which was now filled with a darkly gleaming crimson liquid.

FORTY-ONE

Trembling, Cait closed her eyes and brought the cup to her lips. The dark liquid seemed to flow of itself over the rim of the cup and into her mouth. It bathed her tongue with a heavy sweetness like that of honeyed wine.

The taste so surprised her that she jerked the cup away. What was it the nuns had prayed, she wondered. The words came at once to her lips and she spoke them out:

> *I believe, O God of all gods, that Thou art the eternal Father*
> *of All Creation. O Great King, aid Thou my soul,*
> *with the aiding of Thy mercy,*
> *with the aiding of Thy love,*
> *with the aiding of Thy compassion;*
> *Cover Thou my soul with Thy Swift Sure Hand.*

Raising the cup, she drank deep of the sweet, dark liquid. A quick warmth spread from her throat; it coursed through her body, flowing through her limbs to the tips of her fingers and toes. Her heart beat faster.

Cait looked again into the cup to see that it now contained more of the liquid than it had when she had first drunk. Her breath came faster and her temples throbbed. A strange distress crept over her; unseen needles pricked her throat and breast. *What have I done?* she thought.

Her breath came now in quick bursts and gasps. Fearing she might drop the sacred vessel, she carefully replaced the cup on the altar, and made to step away. Remembering the candle, she reached for it, and saw that her hand was marked by a delicate tracery of tiny lines that seemed to glow from beneath her skin—as if instead of blood her veins now pulsed with living light.

Thrusting her hand behind her, as if hiding it from sight would conceal what she had done, she closed her eyes, but—wonder of wonders!—she could now see through her eyelids. The world was vastly altered: for instead of a mountain cavern and rough stone altar, she stood alone in the center of a low-ceilinged room. A single large window opened onto an early twilight sky where a solitary star was shining.

The objects in the room, and the room itself, possessed the distinctive clarity of a dream. All the same, she did not feel as if she was asleep; all her senses were keen and sharp—never had she been so aware, so alert, so alive.

The room in which she stood was large, and before her a low table was prepared for a meal. It was surrounded by rugs and cushions in the Eastern manner, and spread with a fine blue cloth; there were bowls of various sizes, and jars of several shapes and kinds, but there was no food.

Through the open window a soft breeze was blowing, and she could hear the dull clinking of a cattle bell outside. The soft evening air held the scent of the East, of sun-baked earth, of sandalwood and jasmine.

Stepping around the table, she moved to the window and peered out. The room overlooked the rooftops of the surrounding buildings, some of which had small palm trees in pots, or booths of striped cloth stretched over wooden frames. She heard the bell again and looked down into the narrow street below, where a shepherd in a ragged cloak herded a small flock of sheep led by a shaggy, long-necked goat.

From further up the street came the sound of laughter. A group of men entered the street—six or eight of them together—dark-haired, bearded, all dressed in loose, belted robes, and each carrying a cloak of light material rolled upon his shoulder. They walked with the easy familiarity of brothers, or soldiers; full of bluster and confidence, jostling one another good-naturedly; one or two had their arms around the shoulders of their fellows. They were happy, laughing, talking loudly, luxuriating in the exuberance of their companionship.

Cait envied their enthusiasm—so light, so effusive. Men and sheep met in the middle of the street, and there was a momentary impasse, before one of the men gave out a shout and stamped his feet, which sent the sheep leaping over one another in a frantic effort to get by. The shepherd cried out in alarm, and shaking his staff at the raucous youths he ran after his flock. The men bleated like sheep, and continued on up the street, arriving beneath Cait's window, where they stopped.

Not wishing to be seen, she backed away, and a moment later heard voices in the house in the room below her. Then she heard feet on wooden steps and the voices grew louder. They were coming up!

She spun around, searching for a place to hide, and saw, at the far end of the room, one of two wooden pillars which supported the central roof beam; beside one of the pillars stood a large woven reed basket containing rolled-up rugs. Moving to the pillar, she slipped behind it, as the company trooped into the room, talking all the while in a language Cait could not understand.

They were dark-skinned young men, most with short dark beards and long hair, which some of them wore neatly plaited with curled sidelocks at either temple, and others loose in a shaggy mane. Some of them, she saw, carried cloth bags which they proceeded to empty onto the table: bread in large, flat rounds, dried fish, and grapes. More voices sounded from the street. One of the men leaned out of the window and shouted down to those below as feet pounded on the stairs, and more men burst happily into the room to be welcomed by their fellows.

Sacks of food were produced, and jars of oil in carriers of knotted grass. Cait became aware of the smell of roasting meat, and two men appeared, carrying a whole spitted lamb on an enormous wooden platter. They had no sooner set down the roast lamb when three more men came in bearing a huge open jug of wine, into which the jars on the table were immediately plunged. Several women arrived, dressed in similar fashion to the men; the cloth of their garments was finer stuff, however, and more brightly colored, and they wore flowers in their long, black hair. Some brought bowls heaped high with blue-black olives, and others bowls of dates stuffed with almonds.

The room was soon full of people, and still more were crowding in. With everyone talking at once the sound was a noisy babble, but the commotion served to lessen Cait's fear of discovery. Plucking up her courage, she moved to stand beside the pillar as the festivities commenced. Everywhere men and women were talking, quickly, excitedly, eyes and teeth glinting with laughter. Suddenly one of the young men approached Cait's pillar and pulled a rolled-up rug from the basket. She made to step behind the pillar once more, but the fellow merely smiled at her and hurried away.

The talking and laughter continued unabated, but Cait sensed a change in the room. Like an eddy in a swift-running stream, the happy commotion suddenly swirled with new intensity and depth, and the room suddenly seemed brighter. She felt a shiver of excitement course through the gathering—as when the king arrives in a Yuletide hall, or the bride appears at a wedding party.

She searched for the source of the commotion, and saw that more celebrants had entered and were clustered in a tight knot by the door. She strained for a glimpse of who it might be; then the crowd parted and *he* stepped into the room.

He wore a simple belted mantle, the sleeves of which were rolled up to the elbows. Like the other young men, his cloak was folded on his shoulder, but where the others favored the brighter colors, his was the pale, unassuming gray of day-laborers and the poor. His beard was dark and curly, his brow even, his swarthy skin darkened by long days in the sun. His eyes were large and deep-set, his glance quick and keen.

"Master! Yeshua!" called one of the young men. "How do you like the room we have found for you?"

"You have done well, Nathanael," replied the master.

"It was just as you said it would be."

"Yeshua . . ." Cait whispered the name under her breath.

If, in appearance, he was a simple laborer, in bearing he was an emperor: head erect, shoulders straight, confidence and nobility flowed from every movement. Even from across the room, Cait could tell from his winsome smile that he was the source of the exuberance she and all the others felt. He was the sun whose presence warmed all who stood within the circle of his bright radiance.

He was smiling and laughing with the others, and as Cait watched he removed his cloak and laid it aside. He took up an empty bowl from the table and filled it with water from one of the jugs. Taking a cloth, he wrapped it around his waist and began moving among the crowd of friends. He stopped near to Cait's corner where two burly young men were talking; he knelt down and without a word began washing the feet of one of the fellows. The man laughed and stepped back, cheerfully declining the service, but Yeshua persisted, and so the fellow relented and allowed water to be poured over his dusty feet.

When he finished, he turned to the second man—a stocky, rough-handed fellow—who remonstrated more forcefully. They were near enough for Cait to hear what was said, and as they spoke, intelligible words gradually emerged from the welter of speech that filled the room. "Master!" cried the man. "What are you doing? Get up from there. Heaven forbid you should wash my feet."

"Peace, brother," Yeshua said. "Let me do this."

"Never!" protested the young man; his arms were big, and his shoulders massive. He stood a head taller than anyone around him and his voice boomed out with the force of a man who has lived his life in wide open places. At his objection, others standing nearby turned to see what was happening. "Rather it is I who should wash you."

"Hardheaded Kepha," replied Yeshua, "do you not understand? Unless I wash you now, you can have no part of my kingdom later."

"Very well," said the big fisherman, thrusting out his arms, "then wash my hands and head as well."

"Take a bath if you must, Shimeon," answered Yeshua, resuming his duty. "Your big feet are labor enough for me."

The onlookers laughed at this, and Shimeon, with much huffing and puffing, suffered the humiliation of having his feet washed by his Master. Yeshua continued on, making a circuit of the room. Cait watched him as he went here and there, pausing to wash his followers' feet in his lap and dry them with the cloth he had tied around his waist. Some laughed at the novelty of the situation, others grew quiet and submitted with solemn formality.

When he finished, Yeshua returned to the table and put on his cloak once more. Then, addressing the gathering, he spread his arms wide and said, "Beloved friends, the Passover feast is ready. Come, let us sit and enjoy it together. For I tell you the truth, I shall not eat it again until the kingdom is fulfilled."

Cait could see that some wondered at the meaning of this invitation, but their questions were swept away in the general rush to find places at the table. Clearly, there were many more people present than would fit around the single table, and some would have to make their places on rugs spread about the room.

As the genial crowd pushed forward, two of the younger members jostled one another for a seat. One bumped the other in his haste to claim a place. His friend shoved him aside saying, "Leave the table for the elders. Children sit over there."

Yeshua heard them. "What is this?" he chided gently. "Are we now become like Roman kings who lord it over the people and claim every high place as their right?" Having drawn the attention of the Master, the two grew embarrassed and shrank back. "May it never be. Instead, let the greatest among you be like the least. For in the kingdom to come, you will eat and drink at my table and each and every one of you will sit on thrones, judging the Twelve Tribes of Israel."

This brought a delighted laugh from those around him. One at the end of the table called out, "I will be King Shimeon!" To which someone else added, "Ruler of the Fishes and Turtles in the sea!"

"Kings will you be," affirmed the Master. "But in the kingdom to come, the one who would rule must be as the lowliest servant in his house."

The two slunk away, ashamed; their places were quickly taken by others and everyone settled down, some reclining on cushions, others sitting cross-legged on their rugs. When all was quiet, Yeshua blessed the food and the festal meal commenced. Soon they were all eating and talking—laughter gusted in quick bursts, most of which, Cait noticed, originated at Yeshua's side of the table.

Loath to take her eyes from him, Cait drank in each small gesture, each smile and nod, the lift of an eyebrow, the knowing glance as, like a good shepherd, he gathered his flock about him for a last meal.

How is this possible? she wondered. *How is it happening?* Then, fearful that her questioning might somehow destroy the vision, she silenced her doubts and gave herself wholly to the moment.

One of the women of the group rose from her place and picked up a pitcher. She passed along the table, filling cups with wine, and came to where Yeshua was sitting. She filled his cup also, and as she made to move on he reached out and took her hand in his, pulled her to him and kissed her lightly on the cheek. No one else saw this small intimacy which passed between the two; or if they did, accepted it as a commonplace unworthy of comment. But Cait felt a warmth rise within her, and felt her face grow flushed—as if it had been herself the Master had honored in this way.

He is a man, after all, she thought.

The dark-haired woman smiled, touched his cheek, and moved on. Yeshua stood and raised his cup as if he would drink the health of his followers. Instead, he tilted back his head and said, "Father of Lights, I give you thanks that you always hear me. Let this cup be to your honor and glory."

Then, taking up a round flat loaf from one of the baskets, he blessed it likewise, and said, "I am the living bread which has come down from Heaven. Anyone who eats of this bread, shall have eternal life." With that, he ripped the loaf in half, and held out the two halves to those on either side of him. "The bread which I give you is my flesh. Take it and divide it among you. From now on, when you gather to break bread, remember how my body was broken for you, and for the sins of the world."

At these words, a hush descended like a heavy curtain over the room. Cait sensed a quickening in her spirit, and felt a thrill of excitement ripple through the room. Some understood, but others did not. "What is he saying?" someone whispered. "What is this?" asked another. "He thinks the bread is his flesh?"

Taking up the cup once more, he held it out before him and said, "This is my blood which is shed for you, my beloved friends. Henceforth, let all who drink from this cup, do so in memory of me until I return."

A dissenting voice called out from among those at the table. It was Shimeon. "Lord and Master! This is a hard thing you are saying; who can understand it? Tell us that you speak in jest."

"I tell you the truth, anyone who will not eat the flesh of the Son of Man, nor drink his blood, shall not see the Kingdom of God. But anyone who eats my flesh, and drinks my blood will have life everlasting, for I will live in him and he will live in me."

So saying, He passed the cup to the young man sitting at his right hand. The man accepted it, but did not raise it to his lips. Yeshua saw his reluctance. "Do not be afraid, Yochanan. It is for you. Drink."

At this, the man drank from the cup, and hurriedly passed it back. "I wish you would not talk so, Master," he said. "You know the Temple priests are like hounds baying for your blood."

Yeshua, his face alight with the glory to come, placed his hand over the top of the cup. "Behold, I am making a new covenant in my blood. Rejoice! Again I say, rejoice! For the Kingdom of Heaven is at hand."

A few of his followers cheered, but most remained silent as the veiled meaning of the Master's words awakened a dark apprehension. Taking the cup, Yeshua began to move among the groups of people; he served them all, men and women alike from the same cup, and then, as he passed by the place where Caitríona was standing, he paused, and turned. "There you are," he said, as if he had been searching for her. "Why hide in the shadows when you could rejoice in the light?"

Cait's breath caught in her throat. She was discovered. She gazed at him, her heart pounding in her ears, unable to speak.

"O, small of faith," he chided gently, "the bridegroom himself summons you to his feast. Put aside your doubts and fears and enter into the celebration."

Unable to bear his scrutiny, she bent her head and looked away. Someone called out from the other side of the room, but Cait could not make out the words. Then she felt the Master's touch as he put his hand beneath her chin and turned her face to his.

"Woman, why do you hide?"

"Please, Master, I do not belong here," Cait said, scarcely aware that she had spoken. The words seemed to come of themselves. "I am not worthy of your regard."

"Daughter," he said gently, "my own dear child, do you not know that the day of salvation is near? Behold, the Lord has prepared a banquet; he has consecrated those he has invited." He offered her the cup; when she hesitated, he placed it in her grasp and covered her hand with his own saying, "This is my blood which is shed for you. Drink all of it."

Cait raised the cup and drank the wine. It was raw in her mouth, but she drained all that remained. Yeshua smiled; removing his dove-gray cloak, He placed it on her shoulders. "Blessed are you, beloved, for though you were barren, yet would your children be more numerous than stars."

He raised his hand to her cheek, smiled, and kissed her on the forehead. Just then, one of the men who had been sitting at the table rose and hurried out. Yeshua turned. "Go your way, Y'hudah," he called as swift footsteps descended the stair. "Do what you must, but do it quickly!"

Cait heard a door bang shut in the room below, and then footsteps outside in the street. Shimeon was on his feet. "Yochanan! Ya'akov! Come with me, we will go and bring him back."

"No, stay," said Yeshua. "Stay. I will be with you only a little longer. Let us rejoice while it is light, for the darkness is coming when no man can rejoice."

These words were spoken to a stunned silence. Yeshua returned to his place at the table amidst a low rumble of murmuring which grew to fill the room as questions gave way to anxious shouting, and calling on the Master to explain the meaning of his worrying remarks.

The sound filled her ears as a meaningless babble, and Cait looked down at the cup in her hand, and clutched it to her breast. *This I will keep and treasure to the end of my life,* she thought. She pulled the dove-gray cloak around her shoulders, and gazed with bittersweet longing at the Master, now surrounded by his closest followers who were demanding to know what he meant. She closed her eyes again, and clung to her blessing:

Children more numerous than stars.

FORTY-TWO

Cait slowly became aware that she was lying on the floor before the altar, her cheek cradled on her arm. The cavern sanctuary was silent save for the faint *plip . . . plip . . . plip* which sounded nearby. She raised her head. One of the altar candles had gone out; the other was burning low, and molten wax was splashed steadily onto the bare stone. She rose and glanced around guiltily, as if afraid she had been observed and would now be punished for her presumption. The sanctuary was empty. She was alone.

Then she saw the cup, and the memory of her vision struck her with a force that rocked her back on her heels. She swayed on her feet and clutched the side of the altar to steady herself.

She had been there. She had seen the Savior. She, Cait, had touched him, and he had touched her. She lifted her fingertips to her forehead where he had kissed her—the place now burned with a tingling sensation as though flames of fire danced there. Inside, she was filled with a strange quivery airiness, as if she had been scoured hollow, poured out, and the newly emptied void filled with effervescent light.

"Lord and Master," she whispered to herself. "I want to walk in the True Path once more. Guide me with your Holy Light."

She stood before the altar, gazing at the cup. Her search for the relic had ended; she had found the Mystic Rose. What is more, having experienced something of the vessel's sacred and mystic power, she knew she stood in the presence of true holiness and was far from worthy. Her hard-hearted, unthinking pursuit of the Mystic Rose was corrupted by ambition and unholy revenge, and she felt the weight of her sin clinging to her, dragging her down like a filthy, bedraggled garment. All she wanted was to be free of it and clean once more.

"Forgive me, Lord," she sighed, and bent her head. Breathing out a prayer of humble confession, and breathing in the Master's forgiveness, she picked up the Holy Relic and carefully, and with all reverence, replaced it in the hollow at the base of the cross. Closing the little door, she took up the remaining candle and, with a last look around, hurried from the rock-cut sanctuary, through the connecting corridor and the outer passage, quickly retracing her steps from the cave.

The courtyard was dark still, although the cloud-filled sky was blushing pink in the east and all but the brightest stars had faded away. Flitting out from behind the refectory like a shadow, she made her way to the guest lodge and slipped back into her room. With a last look behind her, she closed the door quietly and, removing her boots, crept back into bed, pulling the bedclothes around her to take away the chill.

She lay in bed and shivered—half with the cold, and half with the excitement still tingling through her. She had drunk from the Holy Chalice and a mystical communion had taken place. She had met with God.

This knowledge produced an almost frightening ferment in her soul. It filled her to bursting with an elation that fizzed and burned and threatened to overflow at any moment in wild laughter, or wilder song, or dazzling miracles. Her heart raced; the palms of her hands were hot and dry; her fingers tingled.

Squeezing her eyes shut, she relived the vision of the upper room, remembering the touch of the Lord Jesu as he placed the cup in her hands. It was all she could do to keep from crying out with the ferocious exuberance of her joy.

In a little while, the bell rang and presently she heard the sisters stirring in the yard outside. There came a soft rapping at her door and Sister Besa entered. "My lady, it is time for morning prayers," she said. "If you would like to join us, you would be most welcome."

"Thank you," said Cait. "Of course I will join you. I would like nothing better." Throwing back the bedclothes, she quickly slipped her feet back into her boots, and followed the nun out into the courtyard where they fell into place behind the other sisters making their way to the refectory.

During the winter, morning prayers were held in the long, oven-warmed hall. As Cait entered she heard a shrill squeal and was instantly enfolded in a fierce embrace. "Thea!" she gasped before the air was squeezed from her lungs.

"Oh, Cait!" Alethea clasped her tightly, as if she would obliterate the days of their separation through physical force. "The abbess told me you were here. I wanted to see you right away." She thrust Cait at arm's length. "You look well, Cait. You do."

"And you, Thea," replied Cait. Her eyes traveled to her sister's shaven pate.

Suddenly mindful of her shorn locks, Thea released her sister and raised a hand to her head. "I am a nun now," she said, smiling self-consciously. She paused, reflecting on the wonder of it, and then raced on once more. "But Cait, there is so much to tell you. There was a ceremony last night. I wish you had been there. It was wonderful. I wish you could have seen it."

"She did." Abbess Annora was standing not two paces away, regarding Cait with a stern expression. "Did you not?"

"Truly?" asked Alethea. "You saw the ceremony?"

"It is true," Cait admitted with genuine contrition. "I heard the bell and followed the sisters into the cavern. I saw it all."

"And you have drunk from the Holy Cup," the abbess said, stepping close.

"Cait!" gasped Thea, her dark eyes growing wide.

"It is true," Cait admitted. To the abbess she said, "I meant no disrespect. Indeed, I did not know it was against the rule of the order. I merely thought to—"

The abbess cut short her explanation. "It is nothing so simple as a rule of the order. There are far more serious implications."

"I am sorry," she said. "Truly, I am. But how did you know?"

"Do you think someone so long in the service of the chalice would not know in the instant I saw you?" The abbess frowned with sharp displeasure. "Come with me—both of you. Sister Besa, you come, too."

Leaving one of the other nuns to lead prayers, Sister Annora led them to her room at the end of the hall, sat them down on the bed, and closed the door. Sister Besa, uncertain about what had happened, took her place before the door.

"Please," began Cait, "you have every right to be angry. I do not blame you in the least. I would not have interfered in the ceremony—

only, I was that desperate to see Alethea at long last. I beg your forgiveness. I meant no harm."

"That is a matter of small consequence." The abbess crossed her arms over her narrow chest, and regarded Cait with a hawk-like stare. "Tell me, did you see anything when you drank from the cup?"

"I did, abbess," answered Cait.

"What did you see?"

Cait lowered her eyes. The vision was so perfect, so beautiful, she did not want to spoil it by putting inferior words to it.

"The truth now," demanded the abbess. "What did you see?"

"Tell her, Cait," urged Alethea. "Abbess Annora is very fair; the punishment will not be harsh."

Cait shook her head. "If I hesitate it is not for fear of punishment. It is because I do not trust myself to speak of wonders beyond my understanding."

At these words, the abbess softened. "Tell me. Perhaps I can help you."

"I had a vision," Cait began. "I have never known anything like it, for it seemed as if everything was happening all around me and I was there."

"Where were you?" asked the abbess.

"I was in the upper room with Jesu and his disciples. It was the night of the Passover feast."

At this revelation the abbess's face blanched pale. Both Thea and Cait saw the blood drain from her features. "Abbess?" said Thea, rising to offer her seat on the edge of the bed. "Are you well?"

"Sit you down, Abbess," said Besa, moving to her superior's aid. She took her elbow. "Rest a little, and I will fetch you some water."

Annora waved her aside; holding up a hand to forestall any more offers of aid, she gazed at Caitríona for a long moment as she struggled to regain her composure. Slowly, her expression of startled distress gave way to acceptance. "So," she said softly, "it has happened at last."

Cait and Alethea stared at the abbess, but said nothing. A long moment passed. Annora drew a breath and motioned Cait to stand. "Daughter, give me your hands."

Cait stretched out her hands. The abbess took them and turned them over, pushing up the sleeves. To Cait's amazement there appeared deep red welts on both wrists. She stared in disbelief at the blood-red marks.

"Holy Jesu be praised," gasped Sister Besa, turning wide eyes to the abbess. She made the sign of the cross, and folded her hands beneath her chin and began to pray.

Bending down, the abbess lifted Cait's gown away from her feet. "Remove your shoes," she said.

Cait did as she was told, withdrawing first one foot and then the other. Each instep was marked by welts similar to those on her wrists. Rising, the abbess said, "Now your mantle."

Cait hesitated.

"There will be another mark on your side," Annora told her, "in imitation of the spear wound Christ suffered on the cross. I must see it to be certain. Please."

Untying the laces at her neck, Cait removed her cloak and loosened the top of her mantle; she pulled her arms from the sleeves, and pushed the mantle down over her breasts to her waist. She glanced down her torso, hardly daring to look.

There below her ribs on the right side was another ugly blood-red welt, larger than the others; shaped like a ragged gash, it did appear as if she had been stabbed and the blade had left a thin oblong slash in her flesh. She touched it gingerly, but though the skin was raised she felt no discomfort, only the slightest tenderness.

"There is no mistake," concluded the abbess.

"Oh, Cait," whispered Alethea, "what have you done?"

"Nothing." A quiver of astonishment touched her voice.

"Does it hurt?"

"Not in the least," answered Cait in a daze of wonder. "I feel nothing." She pulled her mantle up over her shoulders once more. "What has happened to me?" she asked, retying the laces.

"They are the Stigmata of Christ," the abbess told her. "See here," she held out her arm and drew the long sleeve of her robe away from her wrists. The blotches were faded to a pale pink hue, and looked like scars from old wounds. "Behold," she said, "the Mark of the Rose."

It was true, the marks did look something like miniature roses—especially compared to Cait's, which looked like fresh lacerations. Cait shook her head in disbelief. "What does it mean?"

The elderly abbess traced the marks lightly with a thin fingertip. "It means, dear child," she replied, lifting a hand to Cait's face, "that you are to be the next Guardian of the Chalice."

FORTY-THREE

"Chosen," the abbess was saying. Her voice seemed to come from very far away and Cait was having difficulty making herself understand the words. "You have been chosen, Caitríona." She paused, regarding the young woman before her with sympathy. "And now *you* have a choice."

"You must decide whether to answer the call," volunteered Sister Besa.

"Do you understand?" asked the abbess.

Cait stared at the livid marks of the stigmata on her wrists and shook her head. "No."

"In this way the succession is ensured," Abbess Annora explained. "Whenever a new guardian is required, someone is chosen. The stigmata are the visible signs that the choice has been made. However, no one can force you to serve. That is your decision and you must make it on your own." She smiled. "The Lord has called you, Caitríona, and now you must decide how you will answer."

"Will you help me, Abbess Annora?"

"Of course, my dear, I will help you in any way I can."

"Oh, Cait, this is wonderful," said Thea, putting her arms around her sister's neck. "God has marked you for his own. Think of it!"

Cait smiled doubtfully; already she could feel the unwieldy bulk of responsibility beginning to settle upon her. From the other room came the sound of a benediction spoken aloud, and then the scraping of benches on the stone floor as the sisters began to breakfast.

"Do you want me to tell the sisters?" asked Besa.

"Not yet," replied the abbess. "I think it would be best for Caitríona to have a little time to herself just now. I will call a special chapter meeting tonight and we can tell the others then."

She turned toward the door. "Now we will eat, and then you can have the remainder of the day to pray and ponder how you will answer." To Thea, she said, "I know you are anxious to be with your sister, and there is much you have to tell one another; but, in the circumstances, I wonder if that could wait a little while. I think Caitríona would like to be alone for a time, and you have new duties to perform."

"Of course," replied Alethea somewhat reluctantly. "I understand."

"Thank you, Thea."

"We will talk later." She kissed Cait on the cheek and went out. Besa followed, closing the door behind her.

"Will you stay with me?" asked Cait. "I have so many questions and I would rather not be alone with them just now."

"If that is what you wish," replied Annora. "In the end, however, it is to God you must go for guidance. I can only tell you the way it has been for me."

"That," said Cait, "is what I want to hear."

"Come, let us walk. The day is bright and the cold will clear your head."

They passed through the busy refectory. A few of the nuns raised their heads from their meals as they passed; both Besa and Thea glanced up briefly, and then looked away again lest either by expression or sign, they should draw attention to her. For that, Cait was grateful.

The abbess led Cait out into the yard, then along the path leading to the barns and outbuildings. They walked in silence; Cait took deep breaths of the cold mountain air and found it helped banish the fevered thoughts from her mind.

At the first barn they stopped to put some fodder into the crib for the animals. The barn was warm, and heavy with the sharp smell of sheep and their oily wool. The abbess left the door open to allow the fresh air inside. Several of the ewes were already round-bellied with lambs, including one poor old ewe which appeared ready to burst. "We call that one Sara," the abbess told her. "She was barren once, but no more. Every year she has triplets or twins." She reached out and stroked the animal's woolly head. "But this lambing will be her last. Sara is getting too old. Like me." She looked at Cait. "It is time for someone younger to take my place."

"Abbess Annora," began Cait, "surely I cannot—"

"Hush, daughter, I did not mean you—at least not yet. As I said, the choice is yours. I merely meant that I have been feeling my age of late. I know the time is coming when I must lay my burden down and step aside."

"I see." Cait nodded, brow puckered in thought.

"All in God's good time, child." The abbess regarded Cait in the dim light of the barn's open door. "But there is something else, I think."

"I have a confession," Cait said. "Once you have heard it, you may change your mind about me."

Abbess Annora laughed. "Do you know how many confessions I have heard over the years?"

"I doubt you will have heard this," Cait replied, frowning. There was nothing for it but to name the black deed and face her judgment. She drew a deep breath and blurted, "The cup—the Mystic Rose—I came here to steal it."

An expression of wonder rearranged the elderly abbess's features. "Well, you are right. In all my years I never have heard *that*. And now that I hear it, I am not at all certain that I believe it."

"Oh, I assure you it is true. Sadly, I am no better than the worst thief who ever lived."

"Neither do I believe that. Still, I suspect there is a tale here, and I would hear it. Come, you can tell me while we see to the pigs."

They walked to the next barn to refresh the water in the pigs' trough, and while they went about this homely duty, the abbess scratched the old boar behind his large ragged ears and listened to Cait's long and rambling explanation of the events that had brought her to the abbey and to this decisive moment.

She told it all—about her father's murder, how she had gone to confront the murderer, to hold him to justice, but had been thwarted by the appearance of the White Priest, and had stolen the precious letter instead. The letter, she explained, described a great treasure. She went on to tell how, upon discovering the prize to be won, she had raised a company of knights, and traveled to Aragon with the intent of claiming the Holy Cup of Christ for herself. She told about the attack on the trail, and how Thea had been abducted by bandits, how they had searched and searched for her, and how they had at last been found by Prince Hasan Al-Nizar and taken to his palace in the mountains, the resulting skirmish with Ali Waqqar, and how Abu's dying words had led them to the village by the lake.

She finished, saying, "I prayed to be God's instrument of justice. I thought to use the Mystic Rose to lure my father's killer to his doom. For that, I needed the Holy Chalice, and I came here to take it." Overwhelmed by the enormity of her crimes, Cait lowered her head, awaiting the abbess's censure. "You must think me a most brazen and contemptible sinner. The audacity of my deeds amazes even me."

"Aye," agreed Annora, observing Cait with a shrewd appraising eye. "In truth, it does amaze me also. But I do not know what amazes the more—that you should hold yourself so low, or that you should fail to see the Swift Sure Hand at work in these dark deeds to bring about his glorious purpose."

Cait made to object, but the abbess asked, "Did you know that the Sacred Chalice was here?"

"Why, no," replied Cait after a moment. "When Brother Matthias was killed all knowledge of the cup was lost, and we gave up any hope of finding it. Also, Alethea and Abu were missing so we abandoned the search in order to rescue them."

"You did not know the Holy Cup was here until you drank from it, and then its true nature was revealed to you."

"Yes," replied Cait. "That is the way of it."

"Why did you do that, do you suppose?"

Cait recalled the ceremony in the cave. "I saw Alethea and the other nun drink from the cup, and it produced such rapture that it roused me to envy."

"It is not envy to see the joy of the Lord manifest and want it for yourself. Rather, it is the voice of the Good Shepherd, calling you to himself." She allowed Cait to think about that for a moment, and then said, "Let us walk some more."

Cait followed the abbess out into the bright sunlight and crisp cold air once more. Across the field, some nuns were taking firewood from the pile and carrying it to the abbey yard. "We drink but twice from the Holy Cup," Annora told her. "Once when we begin our life in the abbey, and once when death's dark angel approaches to gather us to our rest. That is the same for all of us.

"But not everyone enjoys the same experience of the cup. Some see visions, it is true, but visions are very rare, and even more rarely the same. As each soul is different, each encounter with the Holy Cup is different, too. Neither Alethea nor Sister Lora saw what you and I have seen. And, of course, neither of them received the stigmata."

Abbess Annora stopped walking, turned and took Cait by the shoulders. "Do you not see that you have been led here? All that has happened is according to His purpose."

"Perhaps," allowed Cait doubtfully.

"Not perhaps. Not maybe. It is as certain as sunrise." Taking Cait's hand in hers, she laid her fingertips lightly on Cait's wrist and the livid marks now hidden beneath the cloth of her sleeve. "Tell me you cannot see that even now."

Cait gazed at Annora, desperately wanting to believe what the abbess said might be true.

"Daughter, I said you were *chosen*." She squeezed Cait for emphasis. "From the beginning your feet have been directed on the path which has led you here."

"All is as it must be," Cait murmured to herself. At the abbess's questioning look, she said, "It is something Abbot Emlyn used to say." Recalling that old scrap from her childhood comforted her a little; she clutched at it and held on tight.

The abbess released her and stepped away. "It is a beautiful day, but my old bones do not like the cold. I will leave you to think on this a while. We will talk again in the evening."

The elderly woman walked back along the path, and Cait watched her until she disappeared behind one of the buildings. So wise, she thought, so patient and understanding. Could I be like that? she wondered. Perhaps, as an abbess, one might, given sufficient time, grow into such goodness.

She turned her face to the clear, bright, sun-washed sky. The blue was a pale and delicate bird-egg blue, and the snow-covered peaks of the mountains round about shone with an almost aching brilliance. Pulling her cloak more tightly around her neck and shoulders, she wrapped her arms around her chest and walked on. Lost in thought, she did not heed where she was going, but simply walked until the path ended and the trail leading down into the valley began. Although she could not see the village, she knew that the Yuletide festivities were continuing apace. And Rognvald was waiting for her.

The thought of him down there, waiting, knowing nothing of the extraordinary changes she was facing, produced a restlessness in her. Rognvald and the knights, her stalwart protectors and faithful companions—she had promised to lead them home . . .

Home—the thought of Caithness far away brought a confused welter of images before her eyes: the churchyard where her mother was buried, and where she had vowed to bury the heart of her father . . . the lands and fields and the wide, restless bay . . . the slate-colored sea beneath storm clouds . . . the copper-colored hills when the heather was red . . . Suddenly the idea of remaining forever within the close confines of the abbey seemed abhorrent to her. It was astonishing enough that Alethea should choose this life; for herself it was inconceivable.

Raising her hand, she held her wrist before her face, and was again awed by the deep red mark emblazoned on her flesh. There, for all the world to see, was the indisputable sign of her calling.

The vision still burned in her mind with all the heat and force of a bonfire. There was no denying what she had seen—any more than she could deny the visible signs it had left in her flesh. But neither could she deny who she was—a proud, sometimes arrogant, often stubborn woman—yes, and vengeful—used to thinking her own thoughts, speaking her own mind, and having her own way. Her tolerance for fools, incompetents, and miscreants could be measured in the speed with which she dismembered them with a cutting remark or slashing reply. Anyone who knew her at all, knew the sharp edge of Cait's tongue was a cruel and ready weapon.

How, then, in the name of God's Sweet Son, could she endure the endless cycle of confession and forgiveness of weak-willed, selfish and unthinking offenders? The notion of shepherding a flock of nattering women, and officiating over the mundane concerns and petty grievances of an all-female fellowship left her cold as the snow-topped mountain peaks towering aloof and frozen in the distance.

And yet, she reasoned, perhaps this was precisely what it meant to be chosen. Perhaps God was calling her to a life of sacrifice: never to know the love of a man, never to hold a child of her own in her arms, never to see her dear ones again, to surrender her considerable will and live in continual, everlasting submission to the One Great Will, and never allow herself to *be* herself ever again.

Thus, she had come to an impasse. She stood gazing at the trail as it passed between the towering shoulders of the mountains, and it was as if the steep and rocky descent signified her dilemma. To answer the call was to go down into the valley of despair, from which there was no return.

God in Heaven, she thought miserably, *it is a fate worse than death. What should I do?*

The soughing of the wind in the high rocks made a distant whispery sound, as if their ancient voices would speak to her.

And they did speak. For, as she listened, she heard the sound of storm-roused waves on the rough shingle of the bay below Banvarð. She heard the rustle of bracken on the low sun-splashed hills; she heard the driven rain rippling through the dry stubble of the grain fields. As a child she had roamed the green wilderness of Caithness; in the long years of her father's absence, she had come to love the land and the people who lived in it.

Caithness was the place that stirred her heart, even now, and nothing—not even the Stigmata of Christ—could ever change that. To live and die in a land not her own and never to see the high wild skies of Caithness again—the thought was almost crushing.

I cannot do it, she concluded. *The abbess said I have a choice. God help me, I cannot do it.*

Cait was all too aware of her many failings, but self-deception was not one of them. She knew herself. She knew her mind. And where some women might cheerfully resign themselves to serving the simple needs of their sisters and the people of the village, Cait knew she would quickly tire of the tedium, the dull routine of the daily round, the endless repetition, the deadening sameness. Life in the abbey would begin to chafe. Sooner or later she would begin to resent the choice. Resentment would harden into loathing, and loathing into hate. She would end up hating the abbey and, in time, that hatred would come to poison and pervert the very thing she was honor bound to uphold and protect.

No, it was impossible; she knew it in her heart and soul—not that knowing would make the telling any easier. She drew a deep breath and made up her mind to tell Abbess Annora at once. Better by far to end it now, before things went any further.

Cait turned and started back along the trail to the abbey, intent on relating her decision. She had taken but a few steps, however, when she heard someone calling from the valley trail behind her. She stopped, looking back, and saw a small figure toiling up the last incline to reach the abbey path.

It was a young girl; she had begun shouting as soon as she saw Cait on the path. Cait quickly retraced her steps, reaching the girl as she collapsed at the end of the trail to lie gasping in the snow. That she was from the village, there was no doubt. Cait thought she recognized the young girl as the eldest of Dominico's daughters.

Her lips, fingertips, and cheeks were blue from the cold. In her haste, she had come away without her cloak, or had lost it along the way. Her hands were scraped raw, and through the holes in her mantle Cait could see that her knees and shins were bloody where she had fallen and skinned herself on the rocks.

Cait rushed to the child and flung her cloak over the trembling body, gathering her up as she tried to rise. "What is it? What has happened?"

The child, gasping, clutched at her and jabbered in her incomprehensible tongue. Cait could neither understand the girl, nor make herself understood. Taking the child's hands in her own, she rubbed them and blew on them to warm the thin, freezing fingers. "Come," she said when the girl had calmed somewhat, "I will take you to the abbess. She will know what to do."

Cait helped her to her feet and together they moved off along the path. Upon reaching the second barn, the nuns who had been carrying firewood heard Cait's call and came running to her aid. At sight of the nuns, the girl started babbling excitedly again. "I found her on the path," Cait told them. "Can any of you make out what has happened?"

One of the nuns knelt down in the snow in front of the child, and took her hands; another stepped close and put her arm around the slender little shoulders. The first nun spoke quietly and, as Cait watched, the sister's expression of concern deepened. "Brother Timo says to come quickly," the nun explained. "A great many soldiers have arrived in the village; they have put all the people in the church, and the priest says the abbess is needed at once."

"What do the soldiers look like?" said Cait. "Ask her."

The nun holding the girl's hands asked and listened to the answer, then raised her eyes to Cait. "She says they are very big, and ride horses."

"What about their clothing?" demanded Cait impatiently. "What are they wearing?"

Again the nun asked and received the answer. "They are wearing cloaks." The child interrupted to add another detail to her description. "The cloaks are white, she says, and have a cross in red just here." The nun touched the place over her heart. "And on the back."

The other sisters regarded one another in bewilderment. "Who can it be?" they asked one another.

"I know them," Cait replied, fighting down the fear spreading like a sickness through her gut. "The Templars are here."

FORTY-FOUR

"Templars?" Abbess Annora repeated the word uncertainly. "Is that what you called them? But who are they?"

"They are priested knights," Cait answered, realizing how little the Gray Marys knew of the events beyond the protecting mountain walls. "They belong to a special order called the Poor Soldiers of Christ and the Temple of Solomon, but they are known as the Templars, and they are dedicated to the protection of pilgrims and travelers in the Holy Land, and the defense of Jerusalem."

"They are renowned warriors," Alethea added.

"Fighting priests," mused the abbess, shaking her head at the strangeness of it. "Whatever can they want with me?"

"They have come for the Sacred Cup," Cait told her.

"Have they indeed?"

"It is true," replied Cait. "I am sorry."

This admission caused a sensation among the gathered nuns. They all began talking and crying out at once. "Silence!" commanded the abbess. "Silence—all of you. Return to your duties. Those of you who have finished may go to the chapel and pray." The sisters did as they were told, leaving Cait, Alethea and the abbess alone. "What else do you know about this?" asked Abbess Annora when the others had gone. She regarded Cait sternly. "And I think I had better hear it all this time."

"You led them here," declared Alethea accusingly. "They followed you."

"So it would appear," admitted Cait unhappily. To the abbess she said, "I should have told you everything from the beginning. But yes, I knew about the Templars. Their leader is a man called Renaud de Bracineaux; he was the one who murdered my father in Constantinople."

"The letter," replied the abbess, adding this information to that which Cait had already told her. "It belonged to him."

"Yes," Cait admitted. "It belonged to him." She looked to the wise abbess with pleading in her eyes, begging for her understanding. "I knew he wanted the Holy Cup, and I thought if I could get to it first, I could use it to bring de Bracineaux to justice."

"And you would not shrink from carrying out that justice yourself, I suppose?"

"No," confessed Cait. "I would not."

"I see." The abbess nodded, her mouth pressed into a thin, firm line.

"What are you thinking, abbess?" asked Alethea after a moment.

"I think I must go and speak to these Soldiers of Christ and learn how the matter is to be resolved."

"I will go with you," said Cait. "I may be able to help."

"Cait, no," objected Alethea. "They will recognize you."

"Not if I go in habit," she replied.

"Hurry then," Annora said. "Alethea, go to the chapel and wait there with the sisters, and tell them to pray for God's will to be revealed to us. Caitríona, you come with me, we will find you a mantle and robe, and then we will go down to the village—*and*," she added pointedly, "you can tell me anything else I ought to know along the way."

Two nuns arrived in the village a little before sunset; the sky was livid, staining the undersides of the clouds violet and muddy orange. The two lone figures made their way through the deserted village to the church where a number of white-cloaked men were gathered around a fire they had made outside the door of the timber building. The abbess and her companion marched directly to the knight standing guard at the door, and said, "I am Abbess Annora. I was told someone wanted to see me."

The Templar regarded the two women without expression. Both were dressed in the gray robes of their order, hooded against the cold.

"I will tell the commander you are here," said the soldier, and disappeared inside, reappearing a moment later. "Please come in, abbess. Grand Commander de Bracineaux will receive you now."

The abbess and her companion stepped through the door and into the dim interior of the church. Brother Timotheus met them just inside the door. "Abbess Annora," he said, rushing up, "thank God you have come. I have been telling these men that there is no need to hold everyone like this. I am certain matters can be settled peaceably to the satisfaction of all concerned."

Cait looked past the village priest and saw de Bracineaux sitting in one of Dominico's chairs before the altar. His white hair was matted and damp, clinging to his head like wet leaves; his face was red from the cold and wind, but his eyes were keen as blades. Beside the Templar sat Archbishop Bertrano; Gislebert stood behind his commander's chair, and the fair-haired man named d'Anjou was pacing in the shadows behind the altar. The villagers were sitting on the floor in family groups—silent, watching, waiting. She searched among them for her own knights, but Rognvald and the others were not there. She wondered where they might be hiding.

The priest, seeing Cait, opened his mouth to greet her, but the abbess cut him off saying, "I came as soon as I received your message. Tell me, what is the urgency? And why are all the people here? Are they being held captive?"

"They are here to help us keep things from becoming, shall we say, needlessly complicated. Also, to pay their respects," said de Bracineaux, rising slowly from his chair. "After all, it is not every day an archbishop comes to call."

At this, Bertrano also rose. "God be good to you, abbess." He introduced himself to her, and said, "I think you will find that we are both serving at the pleasure of the pope and his Templars in this matter."

"So it would appear," answered the abbess. "But perhaps someone could be so kind as to explain what it is that requires my most urgent attention."

"It is very simple," began the archbishop. "Some little time ago, I received word that the Holy Cup of Christ was preserved in this village. Naturally, I was intrigued, and inasmuch as the stability of the region has lately come under threat due to the continuing reclamation of Christian lands from the Moors, I decided to seek advisement in th—"

"Enough!" said de Bracineaux sharply. He stepped forward, pushing past the archbishop. "Thank you, Bertrano, for airing your explanation, but if we stay to hear you finish it, we will be here all night." He took his place before the two nuns, arms folded over his broad chest. "Just tell me this," he said, gazing sternly at the abbess, "do you have the cup?"

"Yes," answered Annora. "The holy relic of which you speak resides at the convent."

The commander's smile was greedy and wide. "Good. His Holiness the pope has determined that the cup is to be delivered into my hands for safekeeping."

"That I will not do," answered Annora, "until I know the reason. The Holy Cup has been in our possession since the Blessed Apostle himself came to Iberia. You cannot expect me to give it up without good reason."

De Bracineaux's gaze grew fierce. "Yet, I say you *will* give it up."

"Allow me to speak," put in the archbishop, interposing himself between them. "This is my doing, for it was my letter which alerted the pope to the danger of losing the cup to the Moors."

"Very well," de Bracineaux growled. "If it will help bring the matter to a close. We have wasted too much time here already."

"Dear abbess," said Bertrano, stepping close, "the region is in turmoil; war and strife are rampant throughout all the land. It is the wish of His Holiness, the Patriarch of Rome, that the cup should be removed to a place where it can be guarded in all safety. You and the sisters of your order have performed your duty admirably well—indeed, I have nothing but the highest praise for your faithfulness and care, and I will see to it that the pope learns of your long obedience—but you must see that the time has come to make better arrangements for the safekeeping of what is certainly Christendom's single most valuable object. It simply cannot reside here any longer—that much, at least, must be clear to you."

Annora's face hardened. "It is clear to me that you have created a problem where none existed. Certainly, now that the world knows about the Holy Chalice its continued safety is compromised." Her thin lips pressed themselves into a line of harsh disapproval.

"Just so," conceded Bertrano. "I am sorry." His remorseful gaze drifted to the Templar commander, and he added, "You will never know the depth of my regret."

"There!" said de Bracineaux, impatience pinching his tone. "You have heard the reason. Will you now give us the cup?"

382

"We may be secluded here in the mountains, but we are not blind to the dangers you mention," the abbess replied crisply. "It would seem the time has come to make better arrangements for the cup's safe-keeping."

"Then you will give us the cup?" said de Bracineaux, his tone rising to a demand.

"If the archbishop assures me in the name of his holy and sacred office that all he has told me is true, and that this has been ordained by his superiors in the faith," Annora regarded Bertrano closely, "then, yes, I will deliver the Sacred Cup of Christ to you."

"Abbess, no—" objected Cait, dismayed by what she was hearing. She reached out to take Annora's arm, as if to protest the decision. De Bracineaux saw the movement, and his hand snaked out, seizing her by the wrist.

"I think," he said, "the abbess has made a wise decision."

Revolted by the touch, Cait jerked her hand free from his grasp. As she did so, the hood slipped back on her head and the side of her face came into view. She quickly replaced it, but de Bracineaux continued to stare at her.

The archbishop also saw, and opened his mouth to speak, but the abbess took Cait by the shoulder and turned her toward the door. "Wait for me outside, sister." As Cait moved away, the abbess turned to face the archbishop. "Well? What is your answer?"

"Good abbess," said Bertrano, watching as Cait departed, "I am Archbishop of Santiago de Compostela, and however much I might wish it was otherwise at this moment, all I have said of this matter is true. However loathsome it is to find myself in agreement with the commander, nevertheless, on my holy and sacred office, I do assure you of my veracity. But know that it is with a heavy and contrite heart that I do so."

"Satisfied?" demanded de Bracineaux.

"You shall have the cup," Annora repeated. "I will deliver it to you following our last Holy Communion. You understand, I must allow the sisters of my order a chance to say farewell to the Sacred Vessel. The service will be held tonight at the convent, and we will bring the Holy Chalice tomorrow morning."

"Splendid," sighed the archbishop, much relieved. "We will await this historic occasion with God's own patience."

"Better still," countered de Bracineaux, "we will come and retrieve the relic, and save you the trouble of bringing it to us."

"Thank you, but that will not be necessary," the abbess declined. "Instead, I will insist that you respect the hallowed tradition of our order which does not allow men to set foot within the boundaries of the convent."

Cait glanced back as she opened the door to step outside. She heard Archbishop Bertrano say, "Let it be as you say. Until tomorrow then." And then she was through the door and away.

They were silent on the way back to the abbey. The short winter day ended, and picking their way along the trail in the deepening twilight was difficult work, so it was not until the moon rose and the stars came out that the way grew easier. Upon reaching the upper path, the abbess turned and waited for Cait to join her. "You do not agree with my decision."

"I did not say that," Cait replied.

"No," allowed Annora, "but your silence is most eloquent. You think I am wrong to give it to them."

"I do, yes."

"Do you also see that I have no choice in the matter?" When Cait did not respond the abbess stopped walking. "Listen to me, Caitríona; it is ordained. Oh, yes, I do believe so. Despite whatever you may think of the instruments God has chosen to perform this work, the fact remains: Archbishop Bertrano wrote a letter to the pope, who has entrusted the Templars to carry out his wishes." She softened, placing a hand on the younger woman's shoulder. "They would have come for the cup in any event." Cait made to protest, but the abbess raised a hand in admonition. "The pope is my superior before God. I must obey."

"Regardless of the consequences?" Cait asked bitterly. "I thought God had chosen me to be the next guardian of the cup." She thrust her hands out to show the red welts on her wrists. "I was chosen. That is what you said."

"Caitríona, the ways of God are beyond reckoning. Even so, I know he is at work in this. We come to him with the shattered remains of our best intentions, and he gathers all the broken pieces, reforms and reshapes them, and makes them new according to his purposes. He is able to achieve his will in the world, never doubt it."

There was nothing more to be said, so they continued in silence. The abbess knew the last stretch of the path along the fields, and moved quickly; Cait followed, her spirit in turmoil. True, she had already decided that she could not become the next Guardian of the Chalice; yet she was far from prepared to see de Bracineaux get his profaning hands on the sacred object. She did not see how she could prevent that now. The abbess had spoken and that was that.

Although night was hurrying on, and they were cold, hungry, and exhausted from their long climb, upon their return to the abbey the abbess bade Cait to sound the bell to gather the sisters. When they were all assembled in the refectory, Annora announced, "Tonight a strange and portentous thing has happened. The Archbishop of Santiago de Compostela has arrived in the village with a charge from His Holiness the Pope to take possession of our Blessed Cup." A fretful murmur coursed through the assembled nuns. "As abbess of this order, I am sworn to obey, and have pledged my assent to the pope's wishes."

Some of the sisters took this hard. They raised their voices and stretched out their hands, pleading to know if there was not some other way. The abbess turned a deaf ear to their cries. "Peace, dear sisters," Annora continued. "Cease your pleading and have faith. All shall be well. I have requested a last communion with the cup, and it has been granted. Each sister will partake of the cup this night. Now, I want all of you to go and wash, and put on your best habits; let us pay a reverent and joyful farewell to the Holy Cup we have protected so long."

The sisters did as they were told, and were soon gathering in the yard outside the refectory, each with a candle to light the way to the chapel. The gently flickering gleam on the snow mirrored the heavens as the nuns stood waiting. One of the sisters began to sing, and all quickly joined in, their voices ringing in the crisp, cold air. They sounded like a heavenly choir, Cait thought, as the angelic sound swirled up and up into the moon-bright sky.

When all were assembled, the abbess led them to the chapel cut into the rock of the mountain. They processed along the deep-shadowed passages, the song echoing down unseen corridors and walls round about, until they entered the cavernous sanctuary where they silently formed a wide circle around the altar.

After lighting the altar candles, the abbess turned to the nuns and said, "Beloved Sisters in Christ, for generations beyond counting our order has remained faithful to its calling. Tonight, our long vigil of obedience is at an end. Tomorrow we will deliver Our Lord's Sacred Chalice to the agents of the pope, and a new day of God's grace will dawn."

These words brought tears to the eyes of many of the older nuns, and a gentle sniffling could be heard around the candlelit ring.

"Though the cup shall no longer form the center point of our life here in the abbey, nevertheless life will go on. What our duty shall be, we cannot yet tell. But I know that whatever is given us, we will strive to serve God with the same humility and faith that have distinguished our order from its beginning to this day.

"My dear sisters, your tears show that you have borne your duty with loving hearts, and this is right and good. But do not give in to sorrow; rather let your hearts be glad. For surely, this is the long-awaited sign that the Day of the Lord is upon us; our redemption is drawing near."

Here the old abbess turned to face the altar; she knelt briefly, and then approached the great golden cross which occupied the altar top. Placing her hands on either side of the cross, she gently pressed the hidden catch and the door opened in the base. Making the sign of the cross—once, twice, three times, while saying a simple prayer for purity—she then withdrew the holy relic from its hiding place in the base of the cross. Turning to the sisters, she raised the chalice high and said, "This will be the last time we partake of the Blessed Cup together. Let us do so with the love of Our Lord in our hearts, and the prayer on our lips that God's mighty purpose shall achieve its fulfillment in our sight."

Taking the cup, she bowed her head over it and stood for a long time in silent prayer; then, eyes closed, she raised her face toward Heaven and said, "Father of Lights, in whom there is no darkness at all, nor shadow of turning: we, the humblest of your many servants, greet you with gladness, and glory in the greatness of your holy name even as we remember the countless blessings you have showered upon us throughout these many years. Tonight, according to your will which has been revealed to us through your emissary on earth, we lay down our duty of care and relinquish the charge we have long maintained. Know that we have only ever sought the pleasure of your service, O

Lord, and we ask you to look kindly on the work of your servants, for the sake of your Son, Our Savior."

Then, beginning with the oldest member of the order, Abbess Annora took the cup to the sisters and gave them to drink, lingering before each one, speaking softly, offering words of comfort and hope. Cait, standing next to Alethea, watched as the Holy Vessel made its slow way around the circle and wondered if she, along with her sister, would be included in the sacred rite.

As the cup came nearer, she heard Alethea praying to herself, and so bent her head as well. But what to say? Her thoughts and feelings were in such a ferment of confusion she did not know how to pray. To honor the abbess, she must go against her call by the White Priest; yet, to obey the White Priest, she must betray the abbess. In the end, she fell back on her first, and most heartfelt desire. *Lord of Hosts, and Ruler of Destinies,* she prayed, *a great injustice has taken place; the blood of my father, your servant, cries out to be avenged. You, whose judgment against the wicked is everlasting, make me the instrument of your vengeance. Lord, hear my prayer.*

Voices sounded in the passageway. There was a shout. She looked up and saw men with torches swarming into the sanctuary. In the wildly flickering light, she caught a glimpse of a red cross on a white cloak and knew the Templars had come to take their prize.

FORTY-FIVE

The rock-cut sanctuary was suddenly filled with Templar knights. Swords drawn, they rushed for the altar. The circle of nuns collapsed into a tightly huddled knot around the abbess and the Holy Cup. Within moments they were surrounded by the white-cloaked knights. Some of the frightened sisters cried out in terror, others fell to their knees, hands clasped in desperate prayer, as the naked blades encircled them.

From the center of the close-crowded mass, Cait observed the nearest knights. Faces tight in the lurid light, they stared with oddly hesitant severity at the quaking nuns. Young men for the most part, they were not yet jaded by the constant warring of their order, and unused to attacking women—much less nuns. They glanced guiltily at one another, growing more uncertain of their duty with every passing moment. Someone called a calming order from across the sanctuary; Cait looked out and saw Sergeant Gislebert approach, a torchbearer on either side.

As he drew near, the abbess pressed the Holy Cup into Cait's hands, saying, "I will speak to him."

Taking the chalice, she felt a mild burning sensation in the marks of her stigmata, as if the sympathetic wounds in her hands and feet and side were aroused by the nearness of the Holy Vessel. The abbess turned and pushed through the protective cluster of distraught sisters to address the sergeant. "What is this?" she demanded angrily. Before he could reply, she said, "You invade sanctified ground like brigands and violate the custom of our order to interrupt a sacred and holy sacrament by force of arms." She stepped before him, pushing the point of his sword aside with a bare hand. "By what authority do you perpetrate this sacrilege?"

Abbess Annora stood defiant before him, holding her frail body erect, her whole being ablaze with holy anger. The sergeant was taken aback by the force of her outrage. He looked around as if seeking the aid of his absent superior.

"I demand an answer!" said the abbess, her voice sharp as a slap. Some of the Templars shifted uneasily in their places.

"By the authority of the Master of Jerusalem," replied Gislebert unhappily, "and under his command, we have come for the Sacred Cup."

"I agreed with your commander that we would bring it in the morning," said the abbess. "We are not finished with our observance."

"He wants it now," muttered the sergeant dully. "Where is it?"

"The Blessed Cup is in my keeping until I place it in the hands of the archbishop," Annora said. "And *I* say when that will be. Until then, you shall not touch it."

Gislebert, out of his depth with this spirited woman, seemed at a loss to know how to proceed in this confrontation. He looked across at the trembling nuns and came to a decision at last. "You can take up the matter with the Master." Turning away, he called a command to his knights. "Bring them," he shouted. "Bring them all!"

The entire order, with the abbess at its head, was driven out into the frigid night and made to toil down the steep mountain pathways by the fitful light of the Templar torches. The knights, embarrassed to be riding while the nuns were made to walk, offered their mounts to the oldest captives, and the rest dismounted at intervals and took up places along the way in the more perilous steeps where, due to ice, or loose rock, the path had become unsound. Thus, they lit the way for the order as, silent but full of reproachful glances, the Gray Marys made their slow way down to the village.

Night was far gone when they reached the valley. Sergeant Gislebert marched his straggling charges through the silent village to the church. By the light of low-burning candles on the altar, Cait could see that the people were still there—most of them asleep in heaps on the floor. Grand Commander de Bracineaux dozed in his chair, and Archbishop Bertrano was stretched out on the low platform beneath the altar. Baron D'Anjou came awake as the door opened; he stood and nudged the Templar commander, saying, "Wake up, de Bracineaux. The sergeant has returned with your lady friend."

"At last," said the commander, sitting up as the nuns entered, limping and staggering from their enforced ordeal in the dead of night. He took one look at the line of exhausted women, and cried, "What have you done, Gislebert? I send you for the relic and you bring the entire convent."

"Just so," mused d'Anjou, a perverse smile playing on his lips. "This affair ripens most deliciously."

The entrance of the sisters wakened the sleeping archbishop and townsfolk. They roused themselves and stood. Some of the villagers, seeing the distress of the sisters, all of whom they knew and loved, ran to their aid; they sat the women down, wrapped them in cloaks and mantles and chafed their hands to warm them. Cait and Alethea found places at the back of the assembly near the door. *Where are they?* Cait wondered, quickly surveying the dim interior for any sign of her knights. *What has happened to them?*

Despite her fatigue, the abbess strode to where de Bracineaux sat, and said, "We agreed that I would deliver the cup tomorrow in my own good time. Why have you violated our agreement?"

The archbishop, alarmed by this unexpected development, rushed to intercede. "What has happened? Dear sister abbess, come, sit you down." To de Bracineaux, he said, "What is this, commander? What have you done to these poor women?"

"He ordered his soldiers to storm the convent," the abbess declared loudly, "and bear the Blessed Cup away by force."

"Is this true?" demanded the archbishop, aghast at the accusation.

"Be quiet," snapped de Bracineaux irritably.

Undeterred, the abbess said, "You would take by force that which was to be freely given? What manner of man are you, Commander de Bracineaux?"

"An impatient man." He glared at the abbess. "I might have granted you the condition we agreed upon if you had not dealt falsely with me."

"Preposterous!" said the abbess.

"Oh?" sneered the commander. "Do you deny that you shelter a known enemy beneath the cloak of your order?" He thrust an accusing finger at Cait. "That one—bring her here."

As a nearby Templar worked his way toward them, Cait removed the cup from inside her robe, where she had carried it lest she stumble and drop it while on the trail. "Keep this out of sight," she whispered, passing the Sacred Vessel to Alethea. She stepped out from among the sisters at the rear of the church and took her place beside the abbess. "So, you thought I would not recognize you a second time," de Bracineaux said. "Most unwise, lady. Most unwise."

Levelling his malignant gaze at Cait, he said, "See here, archbishop, this is the woman who stole your letter. You know her, I think."

"I have seen her before, yes," the archbishop confessed. To Cait, he said, "Lady, is it true? Did you steal the letter?"

"Why ask *her*?" demanded de Bracineaux angrily. "You know the truth of it—how else could she have cozened you with lies about my death?"

"Let her speak," said Bertrano. "I would hear it from her own lips." Turning once more to Caitríona, he said, "Is it true, lady? Did you steal the letter from Commander de Bracineaux?"

"I did," answered Cait simply. "And I would do it again."

"Why?"

"What difference does it make?" charged de Bracineaux, rounding on her again. "She has admitted the theft, and stands condemned out of her own mouth. She must be punished for her crime—and all who aided her in this deception shall be punished as well." He glared around the church as if he meant to begin seizing villagers then and there.

Brother Timotheus pushed his way forward. "Heaven forbid!" he cried. "We know nothing of any crime. This lady has shown us only kindness and respect. She is a true noblewoman in every way."

"No doubt she can appear so when it suits her," said de Bracineaux smugly. "The archbishop and I know otherwise."

Archbishop Bertrano turned sorrowful eyes on Cait and asked again, "Why did you take the letter? Was it to steal the Holy Cup for yourself?"

"I did take the letter," she replied. "I went to the commander's room that night to avenge the murder of my father, Lord Duncan of Caithness. Renaud de Bracineaux killed him in Constantinople," she said evenly, pointing to the commander. "I wanted to find a way to hurt him, and I allowed myself to imagine the Blessed Cup would help me to do that." She paused and looked to Abbess Annora. "I was wrong."

"Yes, of course," said de Bracineaux as the last details of the explanation fell into place, "you were with him in the church that day." His face twisted in a paroxysm of hate and gloating triumph. "So, Duncan had a daughter. I imagined he was alone, otherwise I would have finished you, too."

The archbishop turned astonished eyes on the Grand Commander of Jerusalem. "Is this true? You murdered her father?"

"I settled an old debt, yes," replied de Bracineaux carelessly. "As Defender of Jerusalem, it is my right to vanquish the enemies of the Holy Land—wherever I encounter them."

"Very messy, my friend," said d'Anjou, shaking his head slowly. He regarded Cait with an expression of delight that made her skin crawl. "It seems you've made an extremely resourceful enemy. You want to be more careful."

"Archbishop Bertrano," said the abbess, "I refuse to deliver the Sacred Chalice of Our Savior into the hands of a self-confessed murderer. If we are to surrender the holy relic, I demand that it be given to Pope Adrian himself, and no one else."

"From your hands to his, abbess," answered Bertrano. "In view of all that has come to light, I agree that would be best."

"No!" roared de Bracineaux. "That we will *not* do. It has been entrusted to me, and I will fulfill my duty." He stepped nearer so that he towered over the abbess. "I want the cup. Now. Give it over."

"I will not."

De Bracineaux's hand whipped out and caught the old woman on the cheek. The force of the blow snapped her head sideways and she staggered backward. Cait caught her as she fell and bore her up.

"I will not ask you again, old woman." De Bracineaux stood over the half-kneeling abbess. "Bring me the cup."

Brother Timotheus rushed to interpose himself between the Templar and the abbess. He raised his hands before the commander's face, crying "Peace! Peace!"

"Fool, get out of my way." De Bracineaux shoved the priest violently aside. The cleric fell, striking his head on the stone-flagged floor. He groaned and lay still.

All at once the villagers rose up with a shout. They had watched the conversations in bewildered silence, but an attack on their beloved priest was something they understood. They rushed forward in a mass, swarming over the commander, lashing at him with fists and feet.

"Sergeant!" roared de Bracineaux as he fell.

D'Anjou and Gislebert, swords in hand, leaped to defend the fallen commander. Two of the Templars near the door sprang forth, wading into the clot of people. Cait, still holding the abbess, moved back through the surging crowd, pulling the elderly woman back from the fray.

It was over in a moment. When the shouting and chaos subsided, three lay unconscious and four more were wounded. Gislebert, d'Anjou, and the two Templars stood over the commander with bloody swords, defying anyone else to come near. De Bracineaux climbed to his feet; he was bleeding from a split lip, and sputtering with rage. "Get these people out of here!" he shouted, swinging his arm wildly in the direction of the cowering congregation. "This outrage will be avenged. Get them out!"

The Templars started forward, but before they could lay hands on any of the offending villagers the church door burst open. "Master!" shouted the Templar soldier who entered. "You are needed at once."

From outside someone shouted, "Moors!"

De Bracineaux whirled toward the open door. "What?"

"Hurry, my lord. We are attacked."

FORTY-SIX

Commander de Bracineaux glared at the messenger. "How many?"

"Thirty, my lord. Maybe more."

The Templar commander turned and called, "D'Anjou, keep everyone in here." Then, shouting for the sergeant to fetch his sword and shield, he strode from the church and out into a raw red dawn.

As soon as he had gone, the townsfolk rushed to the bodies of their wounded. Archbishop Bertrano moved to the stricken priest and the nuns hastened to the aid of their injured abbess. Annora waved them off, saying, "I am not hurt. Go and help the others."

"Stay where you are, all of you," shouted d'Anjou, but no one paid any attention to him. Within moments, the door of the church was open and villagers were crowding the entrance.

Cait motioned Alethea to join her. "Wait here with the abbess."

"Where are you going?" she asked, but Cait was already dashing away.

She pushed through the press at the door and looked out. High clouds were coming in from the north, drawing a veil across the pale dawn sky. The Templars were racing to their mounts as de Bracineaux called them to arms. Above the shouting and clamor of men and horses could be heard the rhythmic drumming of hooves, and through a gap between the nearer houses came the attacking riders as they rounded the lake and rode for the village. A moment later, the first rank came into view at the end of the wide expanse which served the town for a street.

Even in the pale light of dawn Cait could see from the turbans and battledress that the riders were, indeed, Moors—and they were coming fast. *Ali Waqqar!* she gasped. The bandits had found them and now joined the fray. Hands clenched in helpless desperation, she watched as they drew swiftly closer. Now she could pick out individuals from among the dark mass of advancing riders. There, in the center of the front rank, was the bandit leader. She recognized the imposing, arrogant bulk, and her heart sank.

But then a movement in the ranks caught her eye. The riders parted and Prince Hasan appeared in the gap, astride his black stallion, his warriors at his back. Beside him rode Halhuli; like those with them, they carried small round black shields and long, slender-bladed lances.

The Templars were quickly armed and mounted. The speed with which they had prepared themselves to meet the enemy was remarkable and, Cait thought, demonstrated their renowned and formidable discipline. They had met Arabs before, and were not afraid.

With a single word from their commander, they formed the battle line and rode out to meet the attack. Cait, watching from the church door, heard a movement behind her, and someone grabbed hold of her arm to pull her back. "Please," she said, "I have to see."

"De Bracineaux misjudged you," said Baron d'Anjou. "But I will not. We cannot have you running loose out there, can we? That would not do at all. Who knows the trouble you might make?"

Contempt and revulsion roiled within her as she looked into the baron's dead eyes. "I beg you," she said, swallowing down her loathing. "Let me stay."

"Very well, if only because I want to see it, too. We will stay here together, you and I." D'Anjou moved close beside her, maintaining his tight grip on her arm. Others were pushing in around them now—villagers eager to witness the clash, and nuns praying for deliverance. The crowd gave a push, and Cait and d'Anjou were carried out into the yard. Soon almost everyone from inside the church had joined them, including Archbishop Bertrano and a very dazed and bewildered Brother Timotheus pressing a hand to his injured head.

The Templars urged their horses to speed. Levelling their lances, they prepared to meet the onrushing Moors. Up from their throats arose a cry: "For God and Jerusalem!"

The battle cry of the Templars was met and drowned by a mighty shout from the Arabs: "*Allahu akbar!*" they cried, spurring their mounts to a gallop. Over the snow they came, the horses' legs lost in a blurring cloud churned up by their swift hooves so that the riders seemed to glide like avenging angels flying to the fight.

"Now we see whether the Moors have mettle enough to stand to a real fight," observed d'Anjou.

"The Templars are outnumbered," Cait pointed out.

"Dear, deluded lady," replied the baron, "the Templars are forever outnumbered. That is how they prefer it."

The two lines closed with heart-stopping speed and Cait, unable to look away, held her breath. At the last instant, the Moors split their line, dividing neatly in two. The main body of the Templars found themselves carried into the midst of a fast-scattering enemy and suddenly exposed on either flank.

This brought a cry from the watchers at the church. Some of the nuns sank to their knees, clasping their hands and crying to Heaven; others stood and gaped in open-mouthed amazement. All around her, Cait heard the quick babble of voices as the villagers discussed the maneuver excitedly, and the nuns prayed with increasing fervor.

De Bracineaux, a bold and decisive commander, realized the danger and signalled the retreat at once. Rather than allow his force to become surrounded, he chose flight. In an instant, the Templars wheeled their horses. Back they came, the Moors in close pursuit.

Halfway to the church, however, there came a rattling movement and out from among the houses of the villages another mounted force appeared. At its head was Rognvald, leading a score of Arab warriors with Dag and Yngvar beside him, and Svein and Rodrigo right behind.

The sudden and unexpected appearance of the knights sent the villagers into a rapture of delight. D'Anjou tried to shout them down, but to no avail. There was nothing he could do to make himself understood. He appealed to the priest. "Tell them to be quiet!" he shouted at Brother Timotheus. "Shut them up!"

"If they do not speak," replied the priest neatly, "surely the stones themselves will cry out."

Rognvald's troops rounded on the retreating Templars, who now discovered themselves caught between two swiftly closing forces.

Surrounded, their retreat cut off, the Templars halted and de Bracineaux formed his soldiers into a tight defensive circle. Shoulder to shoulder, they took shelter behind a ring of stout shields and a lethal array of razor-keen lance blades. The Moors whirled around the circle, shrieking with exultation. Not a blow had been struck and already the foe was forced into its final stand from which there would be no retreat.

Around and around they flew, the swift Arabian horses spinning like black leaves in a whirlpool of white. The Templars remained unmoved as a boulder surrounded by surging rapids.

The battle began in earnest.

At first the great revolving wheel of warriors appeared content simply to surround the Templars, screaming, whistling, jeering and taunting as they spun around and around. Then suddenly one of the Moors broke from the swiftly circling pack and drove in to strike a glancing blow at one of the Templars—a quick darting chop of the sword and away again before the knight could react. No sooner had he returned to his place than another Moor repeated the slashing lunge, and then another, and another. Soon the Moors were striking at will—but to no avail, since the Templars refused to break ranks and attack. Despite their superior numbers, the Moors gained no advantage.

The diving feints continued for a time and d'Anjou, thoroughly fed up with the lack of Moorish courage in meeting the Templar challenge head-on, vented his frustration. "Cowardly bastards," he sneered with profound distaste. "They refuse to stand and fight, the craven dogs."

The Moors circled, the great wheel slowly revolving while those on the inner rim performed their wary darting sallies. Cait felt her heart, buoyed by hope, begin to sink. The Templars would not be drawn into a fight they could not win, and Hasan's troops appeared unable, or unwilling, to force the confrontation.

She watched, hands clenched beneath her chin, as her own frustration grew. A few more lunges, a few more wild sweeping chops, and suddenly a cry went up from the Moorish ranks. In the same instant, Cait saw the head of a Templar lance spinning into the snow. A moment later, another lance head was carried off.

D'Anjou saw it too, and knew what it meant. "Filthy devils!" he spat. "Stand and fight!" he cried.

Three more Templars lost their lances in rapid succession. The knights did not move. They sat firmly in the saddle as if anchored there, faces hard, staring grimly ahead at the whooping, gyrating foe. Now and again, Cait caught sight of Rognvald, Yngvar, Dag, or Svein, or one of the Spanish knights as they careered around and around in the ever-revolving dance.

The slashing attacks continued with increasing ferocity and speed. The villagers gathered outside the church watched with dread fascination as one by one the lance blades fell to the reckless Moorish swords. Still the Templars held their ground. Indeed, the first indication they gave that the attack was wearing on them came when one of their number threw down his headless, battered lance and drew his sword. De Bracineaux steadied his men with a command; the ring tightened further on itself, and they held on.

It was not until fully half of the lance-heads had been hacked off that the Templars broke from their rock-like stance. When it came, the charge was quick and savage. Cait did not discern any signal; it seemed to her that one moment they were inert and resolute as when the battle began, and the next instant all were in motion. Down went the ruined lances and out flashed the swords even as they spurred their mounts into the rotating wall of foemen.

They hit hard and fast—twenty Templars striking as one. The sound of the clash was like the crack of a gigantic tree the instant before it falls.

The force of the charge carried the Templars deep into the revolving ranks of the Moors. Those nearest the charge could not swerve out of the way in time and were simply struck broadside. Men and horses went down. More than one Arab was crushed beneath the weight of his mount.

The rearward ranks gave way to allow their comrades to escape the onslaught and all at once the Moors were thrown into confusion. Suddenly all was rearing horses and flailing hooves. The ferocity of the assault was devastating. Again and again the Templars charged, driving into their evasive enemy, their swords rising and falling in deadly harmony.

Surprised, their formation broken, the Moors gave way before the assault. The swirling Arab ranks thinned at the point of attack and the Templars seized the first opportunity they had been offered. They drove into the weakened line and a small gap opened. For the briefest of instants the way was clear. By twos and threes, the Christian knights sped through the breach, smashing through the terrible whirling wheel.

By the time the gap closed once more, a dozen Moors lay dead in the snow, and not one of the Templars was unhorsed. Cait counted the fallen from Hasan's force, and then counted them again just to make certain. But there was no mistake: the prince's advantage in numbers had shrunk.

The Moors made an attempt to regain control of the field. Separating quickly into two divisions—one under Rognvald and the other under Hasan—they threw out two wings, one to either side of the Templars as the Christian knights reformed their ranks. But de Bracineaux was not about to allow his troops to become surrounded and trapped again. As the two wings closed on the Templars, the commander directed the whole of his force to meet the line of assault at its nearest leading edge.

Once again, the Templars' heavier horses and armor proved sufficient not only to blunt the attack, but to drive through the more lightly armed Moors. The Arab wing scattered, leaving four more dead or wounded behind, and the Christian knights quickly turned to face an onslaught of the combined enemy wings. Again Cait counted the remaining combatants—Hasan's troops, including Rognvald and her knights, numbered thirty to the Templars' original twenty. What was more, the Templars now had the houses of the village at their backs; unless they were drawn into the open, they could not be surrounded again.

"Now the field is even," remarked d'Anjou with evident satisfaction. "Let the slaughter commence."

Cait bit her lip and did not dignify the comment with a reply. The archbishop, meanwhile, gathered the nuns around him and led the sisters in a prayer for a swift end to the battle and a peaceful resolution.

Thus, the two opposing forces faced one another across a narrow space—fewer than a hundred paces separating one from the other. And here they paused. The horses were growing tired. Steam rose from their nostrils and from their rumps and flanks.

For a brief moment all was silent, save for the murmured prayers of the sisters and archbishop kneeling in the snow. Then there came a movement from the Moorish line, and Cait saw Rognvald ride out a few paces into the open alone. "Renaud de Bracineaux," he called, his voice loud in the hush, "for the sake of your men, I ask you to surrender."

This brought a laugh from the Templar commander, who moved out a few paces to meet the Norseman halfway. "Surrender?" he laughed. "To you? Your confidence is commendable, sir, but it is misplaced. We are winning this battle."

"You have fought well," Rognvald acknowledged. "It would be a wicked waste to lead such good soldiers to their deaths. Lay down your arms, and the killing can stop."

De Bracineaux laughed again. "The killing has not yet begun." He turned then, and rode back to his waiting ranks.

"I give you one last chance," Rognvald called after him. "By the God who made me, Templar, unless you forsake the fight, I swear you will not walk from this battleground."

The commander's reply came by way of a sudden charge. Even before de Bracineaux reached the line, his men were in motion, spurring their horses forward. Rognvald raised himself in the saddle and, with a sharp chop of his hand, signalled Hasan's troops to meet the sortie. The Moors swept across the narrow space dividing the two forces.

It was only as the combatants closed on one another that Cait realized that something had changed within the Moorish ranks: they now carried lances. While Rognvald was exchanging words with the Templar commander, the Moors had replaced their swords with stout, long-shafted spears, which they now levelled upon the onrushing Templar knights.

The two forces collided with a crash like thunder. The clash shook snow from the nearby rooftops and shuddered the frozen ground. Seven Templars were unhorsed, and two of those did not rise; they lay in the snow with broken lance-shafts protruding from pierced ribs.

The force of the charge carried each side through and beyond the line of the other. As soon as they broke free, both sides turned and readied themselves for another foray. Again came the command, again they spurred their mounts to speed. Again the clash shivered the frigid air. Cait looked away at the last moment, and when she looked back four more Templars lay in the snow. Only nine were left to stand against Hasan's thirty.

De Bracineaux knew he could not risk another attack so this time, as soon as they passed, the Templars reined up, wheeled their horses, and flew at the backs of the retreating Moors. They succeeded in cutting down three of Hasan's troops, but the rest quickly surrounded the nine Templars. Lances were no use in close fighting, so they were abandoned in favor of the sword. This was the fight de Bracineaux wanted, and once again the heavier armor and skill of his men began to tell against the more lightly protected Moors.

One after another, the Moors fell to the Templar blades—three fell at once, followed by three more, and then two more in quick succession. Cait watched with growing apprehension as the Templars slowly cut their way through the Moorish ranks.

"De Bracineaux will have their hearts for supper," said d'Anjou, almost glowing with exaltation at the splendid spectacle of carnage. "Perhaps I should start the cooking fire now."

Cait tried to pull away from him, but he tightened his grip and held her to her place. "You wanted to watch, my lady," he gloated. "You *will* watch!"

There came a movement from within the Moorish ranks, and Cait saw her knights moving through the press to join battle with the Templars, who had been forced once more into a tight defensive circle. Rognvald, with Yngvar at his left hand, pushed in on one side of the ring, and Dag, Svein, and Rodrigo forced their way in from the other. The Norsemen—larger than their Moorish comrades, and used to fighting with heavy weapons—shouldered the brunt of the offensive, driving in with relentless ferocity.

Rognvald, his arm rising and falling in deadly rhythm, rained devastating blows on the Templars before him. Shields, helmets, and swords were battered and broken before the Norsemen's onslaught. The sound of their terrible hammering blows resounded across the battleground: *Crack!* Now a shield was riven. *Crack!* Now a helm split asunder. *Crack!* A blade shattered. Disarmed, the unlucky Templar left the saddle, diving for the ground rather than face Rognvald's killing stroke. Whirling with dread purpose, the Norse lord singled out another foe.

Slowly the balance of battle swayed once more.

Yngvar and Svein each succeeded in unhorsing an opponent, leaving only six Templars in action. Seeing they were at last beginning to overcome the stubbornly valiant Templars, Hasan's troops redoubled their efforts. A great shout of triumph arose from the Moors as they swarmed in for the final assault.

Cait was watching Prince Hasan as he forced his way to Rognvald's side and did not see the deadly struggle taking place at the far side of the dwindling band of Templars. But just as another Templar knight fell before the Norsemen's blades, a lone rider broke free from the mass and galloped toward them with Yngvar and Svein in pursuit.

The fleeing Templar reached the church, reining up a few paces from where Cait and d'Anjou were standing; he was out of the saddle before his horse had come to a halt. Throwing off his battered helm, he lurched toward them. It was de Bracineaux. "You!" he said, reaching for Cait. "You are coming with me."

FORTY-SEVEN

Bleeding from a deep cut to his forehead, his face ashen with fatigue, de Bracineaux snatched Cait from d'Anjou's grasp. Cait screamed and clawed at him, but he grabbed her arm with his free hand and, still clutching his sword, threw his arm around her waist. He lifted her off her feet and dragged her out from among the crowd gathered in front of the church.

"Here!" cried the archbishop, rising from his prayers in the snow. "Let her go! This is not the way, de Bracineaux."

"Stay back, priest," said d'Anjou, shoving him down once more. "This is none of your concern."

"In God's name," Bertrano cried, "I beg you: let her go. End the bloodshed." Struggling to his feet, he started after the Templar commander. "De Bracineaux!" he called. "Stop!"

"Keep him away!" shouted the Templar over his shoulder.

Baron d'Anjou moved to head off the interfering cleric. "I told you to stay back, priest." He grabbed the archbishop by the arm and pulled him around. "Bother God with your prayers, and leave the rest to us."

"Release me, sir!" Bertrano shrugged off d'Anjou's hold. "You will not presume to tell me what to do." He turned and started after the commander and his captive once more, calling for Caitríona's release, and an end to the fighting.

The baron grabbed Bertrano's arm and tried to pull him back, but the big man shook off his assailant, and bulled ahead. He reached de Bracineaux and put his hands on the Templar. "Put down your sword, commander," the archbishop called. "Sue for peace. I will speak to them." He took hold of the Templar's sword hand and tried to break his grip. "Let the woman go."

"Get back!" snarled de Bracineaux, elbowing the cleric aside. "D'Anjou! Keep him away from me!"

D'Anjou seized the archbishop by the belt of his robe and pulled him back a few paces. The churchman made a wild swing with his arm, knocking the baron aside; he turned and started once more for the Templar. D'Anjou lunged after him. "Stay back," he growled.

Bertrano shook him off and turned. D'Anjou darted after him, appeared to make a grab, but missed. The archbishop took another step, then stumbled and went down.

He writhed in the snow, pressing a hand to his side. Several of the nuns hurried to his aid. One of them screamed when she took hold of Bertrano's hand. Her own hand came away wet and red; there was blood in the snow, spilling from a gash in his side. "I warned you," Baron d'Anjou said, wiping the blade of his dagger with a handful of snow. "You should have listened."

Kicking and scratching, Cait succeeded in squirming free, but de Bracineaux got his fingers in her hair and dragged her with him. "You have cost me dearly," he wheezed, his breath coming in ragged gasps. "Now you are going to repay me in full."

Cait lashed out at him with her fists, swinging hard, the blows muted by the mail and padding. Wrapping his hand securely in her hair, he hauled her to her knees and pressed the ragged edge of his sword to her throat. She felt the cold steel bite into the soft flesh of her neck, and stopped struggling. From the corner of her eye she saw two Norse knights approaching.

"That is close enough!" de Bracineaux shouted as Svein and Yngvar came running up. "Any closer and the lady will lose her head." As if to demonstrate the veracity of this threat, he tightened his grip in her hair and jerked her head up, pressing the sharp blade harder against the base of her throat. She felt something digging into her shoulder and realized it was the golden pommel of de Bracineaux's dagger which was hanging from his belt. If she could get her hands on it, she might have a chance to defend herself.

"Let her go, Templar," said Yngvar. "We mean to treat you fairly."

"Do you think I would trust any of your promises?" replied the commander. "No, I have a better idea. Throw down your weapons and she may yet live."

Cait edged sideways slightly, freeing the dagger from behind her shoulder. De Bracineaux punished her for the movement by jerking her head higher and pressing the blade harder still. She heard a horse galloping swiftly nearer. "Release her, de Bracineaux," called the rider. She heard the voice and took hope: it was Rognvald. "Let her go, and we will settle terms of peace."

"I will give you my terms!" roared the commander. "This woman dies unless you give me the cup." When no one moved to respond, de Bracineaux forced Cait's head down and started to draw the blade across her throat; she felt the skin break and blood begin to ooze.

Rognvald made to dismount, but the Templar commander shouted, "Stay back!" He pulled Cait's head up and back, stretching her throat to show the cut he'd made. "Bring me the cup!" he screamed. "Now!"

Turning to those standing outside the door of the church, Rognvald called for the cup to be brought out. "You should think about your men," Rognvald told him. "There are nine Templars still drawing breath. Their lives, and yours, are forfeit if you harm this woman."

"The Devil take them," de Bracineaux replied. "Devil take you all." He turned his head toward the church. "D'Anjou! Where is that cup?"

Alethea appeared at the door of the church just then. "It is here," she said.

"Bring it to me!" shouted de Bracineaux. "Bring it here to me!"

Holding the Sacred Vessel in both hands, Alethea stepped forward. A way parted through the crowd as she moved, walking slowly, and with grave deliberation as if in a holy procession. She held the cup high for all to see, and the morning light glinted off the gilded rim, creating a glowing halo of gold which hovered above her hands.

The commander saw the precious relic and his face twisted in an ugly gloating grin. Still he held his hostage firmly, the swordblade hard against her throat. Cait could feel the warm blood trickling down her neck and soaking into her clothing. She heard Rognvald say something; he was trying to dissuade the Templar from carrying his scheme any further. Some of the nuns and villagers huddled outside the church began to weep and cry out in their anguish. Cait heard it all, but the sounds meant nothing to her; she could only watch with mounting dread as Alethea drew step-by-slow-deliberate-step closer with the Sacred Chalice in her hands.

When Alethea had come within three paces she stopped. "Here, girl!" de Bracineaux snarled. "Give it to me!"

Alethea looked steadily at him, her features expressionless, and slowly knelt in the snow.

"Here!" said de Bracineaux angrily. "Here to me!"

She made no move to come nearer. Instead, Alethea stretched out her hands and raised the Holy Cup above her head as if in offering.

The Templar commander shouted again for her to deliver the cup into his hands, but Alethea, kneeling meekly in the snow, remained unmoved, holding the cup just out of his reach.

De Bracineaux gave a grunt of impatience. Releasing his grip on Cait's hair, but still holding the sword to her neck, he reached out for the cup with his free hand. Leaning far forward, he took a half-step toward the cup. Arm extended, fingers stretching, he grasped the golden rim and plucked the Holy Chalice from between Alethea's hands. As he reached out, the dagger at his belt swung free.

Alethea rose with catlike quickness. Her long fingers closed on the weapon as she came up. With a single, smooth stroke she drew the knife from the sheath and drove the point of the blade up under de Bracineaux's chin.

With a startled cry, he dropped the cup and the sword. Cait fell forward onto her hands, then collapsed face down in the snow.

De Bracineaux seized Alethea's wrist and tried to pull the dagger away. Wrapping her other hand around the Templar's, Alethea stepped nearer and, with all her strength, drove the knife blade to the hilt. The two stood for a moment in a weird and deadly embrace; and then, with a muffled cry of rage and pain, de Bracineaux pulled his hand free. He made a sweep with his arm and knocked the girl aside.

Alethea fell back in the snow. De Bracineaux pulled the blade from his neck and turned on her. He lurched forward, slashing wildly with the dagger as blood coursed freely from the hole in his throat.

Rognvald rushed in, sword ready.

Alethea lay where she had fallen, gazing up at him—neither trembling, nor cowering in fear, but with calm defiance. Commander de Bracineaux took one step and then another. Blood cascaded from his wound, staining his beard and soaking into his tunic. He reached for her, the knife gleaming red in the sun. But as he made to strike, de Bracineaux's legs buckled beneath him. He fell on his side, blood spewing a bright crimson arc in the snow.

Rognvald, crouching behind his sword, put himself between Alethea and the Templar. De Bracineaux hauled himself onto his knees, regarding Alethea dully, as if trying to understand how a nun could have done such a contemptible thing to him. He opened his mouth to speak, but the words came out in a dark, bloody bubbling which gushed over his teeth and chin, and splashed down his white surcoat, blotting out the red Templar cross on his chest.

Alethea rose to her feet, pushed past Rognvald and stood over de Bracineaux, gazing down with pitiless indifference at her stricken enemy. Unable to speak, he lifted uncomprehending eyes to her impassive face; his jaw worked, forming a single word: *why?*

"Because," she said, as the wounded Templar slumped lower in the snow, "Lord Duncan had *two* daughters."

FORTY-EIGHT

Rognvald rushed to Cait's side and knelt beside her in the snow. Alethea took a quick step and kicked the dagger from de Bracineaux's slack grasp. She stooped and retrieved the Blessed Cup, backing away as the Templar made a last scrabbling grab for it.

"My lady," said Rognvald, "you are hurt."

"No," replied Cait as she tried to get up. "I—" The pain made her gasp.

Rognvald eased her down once more. "Rest a moment. Let me look at the wound." Dropping his sword, he shook the glove from his hand and pressed his fingertips to the side of Cait's neck just below the jaw where blood was oozing in a thin crimson sheet down her throat. "It is a nasty cut," he observed, "but not deep, I think."

"Help me to my feet."

He was just gathering her into his arms to lift her, when there came a sudden rush from behind. Rognvald glanced back to see Baron d'Anjou bearing down on them—a savage leer on his face and a knife in his hand. He ran with surprising quickness, closing the distance in an instant. Rognvald spun around; knowing, even as he reached for his blade, that he would be too late, he placed himself between d'Anjou and Caitríona, shielding her with his body.

Yngvar darted in from the side, flailing with his sword as d'Anjou passed. The blade slashed, went wide. D'Anjou dodged the blow easily. Closing on them, he prepared to strike. Cait saw the baron's arm draw back, and then halt, its forward progress abruptly halted. The baron spun around and into Svein's fierce, bone-bending embrace. D'Anjou gave a little cry of surprise and Cait saw his spine stiffen as the Norseman's blade slid in beneath his ribs. The baron roared in anger and pushed himself away, slashing wildly with the knife. Rognvald snatched up his sword, stepped in behind, and with the action of a man putting a mad dog out of its misery, made a quick chop at the base of the baron's neck. D'Anjou staggered, the dagger spinning from his hand. As his knees gave way beneath him, he looked up at Cait with an expression of mild reproach. "Damn it all," he sighed, then pitched forward onto the ground beside the dying Templar.

Then everything became confused for Cait. It seemed as if a dense cloud descended over her, muffling sight and sound. She felt Rognvald's strong arms beneath her, sensed movement, and guessed that he carried her to the church. Alethea was there, holding the Holy Chalice, and several nuns flew around her, fussing and clucking while they cleaned and bandaged the wound at her neck.

Prince Hasan was there, too, and some others, including Brother Timotheus. There were voices, movement, and then she felt fresh air on her face once more, and saw the mountains gleaming in the sun . . . dead bodies in the trampled bloody snow . . . wounded men holding their seeping wounds . . . nuns with white hands binding brown Moorish limbs . . . horses, long winter coats lathered and wet, heads down, noses to the ground in exhaustion, their flanks steaming in the cold sunlight . . . And then it grew dark and when she awoke she was no longer in the church; she had somehow been transported to Dominico's house, and there were people talking somewhere nearby but she could not see them.

She raised a hand to her injured throat and felt the cloth of her bandage. She made to rise and the movement started a fierce pain throbbing in her neck. She lay back down and waited for the pain to subside, and listened to the voices in the next room—somber, subdued, earnest.

After a time, the throbbing eased to a raw ache; she tried again to rise, more carefully this time, and succeeded in holding her head in a way that did not aggravate the wound again. She was light-headed, and slightly wobbly on her feet, but she steadied herself by the bed and then walked slowly to the next room. Rognvald was there, together with Prince Hasan and Brother Timotheus, while Dominico and his family flitted around them preparing a meal. Yngvar and Svein sat on a bench against the far wall, their long legs stretched out in front of them. Dag and Rodrigo sat on stools nearby, jars in hand, drinking in great thirsty drafts until the ale ran down their beards.

To a man, all were so preoccupied that no one saw her standing in the doorway. She took a step forward, and Elantra, Dominico's wife, glanced up and ran to her side. The others noticed the sudden movement and looked around to see Cait walking gingerly, aided by the diminutive woman. "My lady," said Rognvald; he was on his feet and beside her in an instant. "Come, sit down." He took her elbow and led her to the table as Elantra scurried back to the hearth. "How do you feel?"

"Well enough," replied Cait, scarcely recognizing her own voice. She sounded as if she had been swallowing chips of flint, and it hurt to speak; but, aside from the ache in her throat and a brace of bruises on her arm, she felt tolerably hale and whole. "It seems you shall not be rid of me just yet."

"Nor, I hope, for a very long time to come," he said, his voice low so that the others did not hear. She glanced up and saw in his eyes a warmth of regard she had not seen before.

"I am sorry, Ketmia," said Prince Hasan, rising from his place as they arrived at the table. "We came as soon as Lord Rognvald reached us with news of the Templars' arrival, but if we had been here sooner . . ."

Cait did not let him finish. "It is *I* who should thank *you*, my lord." Taking his hands in hers, she kissed him lightly on the cheek. "That is small thanks, but it carries all my heart. My debt to you is great, and grows ever greater."

Turning to Rognvald, she said, "I owe you more than I can say. Thank you, good friend. One day, perhaps, I will find a way to repay you." She kissed him, too, and then sat down in the offered seat. "Where is Alethea?"

"She is helping the sisters who are caring for Archbishop Bertrano," replied Brother Timotheus, his tone grave. He paused to swallow down his emotion. "They are doing all they can, but . . ." His voice faltered and he left the rest unsaid.

"It is not good, Ketmia," Hasan told her. "Halhuli is with them. Whatever can be done for the priest, will be done. Yet I fear there is little anyone can do but pray."

"We were just discussing it when you joined us," Rognvald said. "His death will—"

"Heaven forbid it!" Timotheus put in. "We must not give up hope."

"Should the archbishop fail to recover," Rognvald said, amending his words, "his death would place both Hasan and the village in peril."

"Blame would inevitably fall upon the Moors," the prince explained. "There would be reprisals. The Spanish kings would insist."

Cait nodded. "I see."

"And then there is the question of what to do with the surviving Templars," said Rognvald. "There are nine altogether—de Bracineaux's sergeant among them."

"They cannot have been privy to their commander's wicked schemes," Brother Timotheus pointed out. "We must show clemency."

"But we cannot allow them to simply ride away as if nothing happened," said Hasan.

"Would you imprison them?" said the priest.

Seeing a tedious discussion stretching ahead of them, Cait stood. "Please, excuse me. I want to see Bertrano. Where is he?"

"He is in the church," Timotheus said. "We thought it best not to move him just yet."

"Allow me to attend you," Rognvald said; rising, he took her arm. Cait covered his hand with hers and let the touch linger for a moment. Then, giving his hand a gentle squeeze, she removed it, saying, "I am well enough, my lord. Stay and finish your talk. I will return when I have seen how the good bishop fares."

She moved to the entrance where Elantra opened the door for her, then walked with her out into a fresh, crisp day. The sun was high; it had passed midday and the sky was clear and bright and blue. The dead had been removed from the battleground, and were now placed in orderly rows beside the church where Prince Hasan's men and most of the villagers were working over them, removing armor, weapons, clothing, and boots—anything that could be of use to the living.

As she drew near the church, she saw that someone had tried to dig a grave; a long, narrow rectangle had been scraped in the snow, and the green turf beneath was cut. But the ground was too hard, so the work had been abandoned. Down by the lake, she saw men working to erect a wooden pyre; the corpses would be burned.

Upon entering the church, she stood for a moment to allow her eyes to adjust to the dim interior. Then she saw, against the south wall, a heap of wadded cloaks; around it huddled three or four nuns, and Halhuli, sitting on his heels, his hands resting idly in his lap. They turned to look as Cait entered, then returned to their vigil as Alethea rose to greet her sister. The two met and embraced without speaking; they simply stood and held one another. After a time, Cait whispered, "Thank you, Thea."

They held one another for a little longer, and then Alethea said, "They were going to burn the village and the abbey. Once they got hold of the Blessed Cup, they were going to destroy everything."

"How do you know?"

"The Templars confessed it. Dag and Svein and the others were securing the prisoners, and they told them de Bracineaux had ordered them to destroy everything and kill everyone because he did not want anyone left alive to tell what had happened."

Cait shook her head in bewilderment and started the pain clawing at her throat again.

Alethea saw her wince, and raised a hand to Cait's neck, touching the bandage gently. "I think it will leave a scar."

"I will recover; they say Bertrano may not."

Alethea nodded. "His wound is very bad, but it does not seem to pain him overmuch."

They walked together to the makeshift bed where the archbishop lay. Halhuli rose and said, "I have made him comfortable. Now we can but wait, and pray the Great Healer to perform a wonder." Cait thanked him, whereupon he inclined his head in a bow and departed.

The nuns made room for Cait and Alethea as they took their places beside the bishop. Bertrano lay quietly, hands folded over his stomach as if in peaceful meditation. Cait thought he was asleep, but when she had, with Alethea's help, knelt down beside him, Bertrano opened his eyes and smiled weakly. "You still have your head, my dear," he said. "That is good."

"And we still have the Holy Chalice," she replied, returning his smile. "I must ask your forgiveness, archbishop. None of this would have happened if not for me. I am sorry."

"If not for you and your dauntless sister, dear lady, de Bracineaux would be halfway to Jerusalem with the cup by now. Even so, I do forgive you. Lying to an archbishop is a sin—only a very minor sin, mind, for everyone does it. Still, I would not recommend making a practice of it." He raised his hand and traced the sign of the cross. "In the name of the Father, the Son, and the Holy Spirit, I absolve you."

Cait leaned over and kissed him lightly on the cheek. "Thank you, my lord archbishop."

"And you, dear girl," he said to Alethea, "are a very brave and intrepid adversary. I absolve you, too. Any ill the commander suffered, he brought upon himself. He alone was the author of his demise."

"My only thought was for my sister," Alethea replied, "and for the Blessed Cup."

"He would have kept it, you know," Bertrano told them. "Once de Bracineaux had it, he would never have given it up."

"Well, it is safe now," said Alethea.

"No," the archbishop shook his head weakly. "The Holy Cup will never be safe here again. Sooner or later, others will come and it will be taken."

Abbess Annora appeared just then, holding a steaming bowl on a tray; Sister Besa was with her, carrying a pile of clean, folded cloths. She acknowledged Cait's presence with a kindly nod, and placed the tray beside the bed. "We must change the bandage," she said as, with Alethea's ready help, she knelt down beside Cait.

"In a moment," said the archbishop. To Cait he said, "Annora has been telling me that you have been chosen to become the next Guardian of the Sacred Chalice."

"So it would seem," Cait answered.

"Show him," whispered Alethea.

Cait stretched out her hands, palms up, and drew back the sleeves of her robe so that the churchman could see the marks of the stigmata on her wrists.

Archbishop Bertrano placed a finger lightly on the livid mark. "The foolishness of God is wiser than the wisdom of men. It is a heavy charge that is laid upon you, daughter. Still, your only freedom lies there—if you will accept it. That I do believe."

"So do I," replied Cait, realizing as she spoke the affirmation that she had decided to answer the call.

"Good." He smiled, and a spasm of pain passed over his face. He closed his eyes and held his breath. When it was over, he opened his eyes again; they were a little duller this time, his gaze slightly less intense.

"Perhaps you should rest now," suggested Thea.

"Soon I shall have all the rest I need," Archbishop Bertrano replied.

"Let us change your bandage now," said Annora. "You will feel better."

"A moment longer, and then you can have me," he replied. "I told Caitríona that the Blessed Cup will not be safe here any longer. Because of my infernal meddling, too many people know about it now. If it remains here, it will only bring trouble to the village; they would never know a moment's peace again." He reached out and took Cait's hand. "But it has pleased God to choose you. Therefore, I bid you take it. Take it far from here, and hide it well. One day the time will come when it can be revealed once more. Keep it safe until then."

Cait lifted his hand and brought it to her lips. "By the strength and wisdom of God, I will, my lord archbishop."

"There now. That is settled." Bertrano smiled again. "Now, if I might make one last request of you, dear abbess."

"Certainly," Annora replied. "Anything."

"I should like to receive the Holy Sacrament of the Cup once before I die."

"Of course, archbishop."

"Could we do it now, do you think? I do not wish to keep the ferryman waiting."

"At once, my lord." The abbess retrieved the Holy Chalice from its place on the altar, and Cait and Alethea watched as she proceeded to administer the holy rite to the dying man. Kneeling at his bedside, she spoke so softly to him that none in the room heard what passed between them, but in the end, when Bertrano drank from the cup, a smile of such serenity and pleasure lit his features that each one present felt as if they had seen a little of Heaven's bright glory reflected on his face.

When the sacrament was finished, the abbess returned the cup to the altar. Cait and Alethea drew near the bed once more and bade the dying cleric farewell. Bertrano blessed them and then lay back; he allowed the nuns to care for his wound then, and while the abbess and Sister Besa changed his bandage Cait and Alethea crept away quietly together. They paused briefly at the side of the church to view de Bracineaux's blood-stained corpse.

The Templar commander seemed smaller now and older: death had diminished him. He gazed with unseeing eyes to the boundless heav-

414

ens, the scar puckering his brow in a doleful expression. Cait looked at him and felt neither hate nor exultation at his defeat—only sorrow at the lives his reckless pursuit had wasted.

After a moment, they turned without a word, and proceeded to Dominico's house where the meal Elantra had been preparing was now being served. The Norsemen were there, too—all eating hungrily, their bowls to their mouths, sopping gravy with chunks of bread. Brother Timotheus called for Cait and Alethea to join him at table with the others; Cait sent Alethea ahead saying, "Tell him I will join them in a moment. I would speak to my knights first."

With that, Cait walked to where Yngvar was sitting; the Norseman stopped eating and raised his face to her as, without a word, she bent and kissed him lightly on the cheek. She then did the same with Svein, Dag, and Rodrigo in turn.

"Your courage is matched only by your loyalty and skill," she told them. The knights looked with pleasure at their lady. "You have my admiration and my gratitude. And," she added, "as soon as we return home, you shall have your reward."

"My lady," said Yngvar, glancing at Svein and Dag beside him, "it would be no small reward to be allowed to continue in your service."

"We have been talking," said Dag. "And you will be needing good men-at-arms when you return home. This is what we think."

"And what does Lord Rognvald think?"

"He has given us leave to follow our own minds in this matter," answered Svein, adding, "He is making plans of his own, I think."

"I see." Cait nodded. "Very well. Then hear me, all of you. I will not say you no, but neither will I agree just yet. It is a long way to Caithness, and much can happen before we arrive; you may change your minds. If you do, you will not be bound."

"That is fair," Svein agreed for all of them, "and we will abide. Only, tell us if you view our offer in a kindly light."

"Dear Svein, and all of you," Cait said, "I look upon your offer with nothing but the highest esteem. I will never forget what you have done for me and Alethea."

Svein reached out, took her hand, and pressed it to his lips. "Your servant, my lady."

She turned to the Spanish knight who sat looking on. "And you, Rodrigo? Have you decided also?"

"My lady, nothing would give me more pleasure than to remain in your service. These men have become my friends, and I would not hesitate to cast my lot with them. But I promised Paulo I would wait for him. He is improving, but is still too weak to ride. With your permission, my lady, I will wait as I have promised."

"As to that," said Yngvar, "the prince has said we can winter with him at the palace."

"He has sworn on the beard of the prophet that he will not break faith with us again," added Svein. "And after what I have seen today, I believe him."

"It is a generous offer," allowed Cait. "We shall see."

She left them to their meal, and joined the others at table; she tried to eat a little, but it hurt her throat to swallow, so she gave up and just sat listening to their talk. The day faded and as twilight stole into the valley, deepening the shadows and turning the sky to inky violet, one of Prince Hasan's men came to the house to say that the funeral pyre was ready. They went out to the lakeside where a great tower of timber had been erected. The Moorish troops had formed a wide circle around the pyre, and the villagers and some of the nuns had assembled on the slope of the shore to watch.

At the prince's command, Halhuli stepped forward and, taking up the torch, raised it three times, calling out in Arabic each time. He then passed the fire-brand to the warrior next to him; the man did likewise, raising it to the chanted exhortation and then passing it onto the next in line, and so on until all the surviving warriors had performed the rite.

At last, the torch came to the prince; he received it, stepped forward, and upon completing the third exhortation, lowered the torch and touched it to the tinder which had been prepared. Flames licked out and up, bright yellow in the blue dusk.

He moved to the next side of the four-sided pyre and lit the tinder there, too, then proceeded to the remaining sides, lighting each in turn. When he had completed the circuit, the flames were rising through the latticework of the pyre, skipping from branch to branch, leaping higher and higher into the darkening sky. The shadows of the watchers flickered and danced in the orange glare of the fire on the snow. Inside the tower-like structure, the corpses had been neatly wrapped in their cloaks and stacked on a stout platform, and this caught fire, giving off a silvery smoke as the bodies began to smolder.

When the flames had caught hold and begun their work in earnest, Brother Timotheus moved out from the circle and approached the burning tower. Raising his hands, he called out in a loud voice to be heard above the crack and roar of the inferno. He said:

Thou goest home in this night in the depth of winter;
To thy eternal and perpetual home, thou goest.
Sleep, friends, sleep—and away with sorrow;
Sleep, friends, sleep—in the absence of fear;
Sleep, friends, sleep—in the Rock of All Forgiving.

The black wrath of the God of life
Is upon the dank gloom of death as thou goest.
The white wrath of the Lord of the Stars
Is upon the dark path that leads beyond this worlds-realm.
Thou Great God of Salvation,
Pour out thy healing grace on these souls
As the fire pours out its bright and eager heat,
And gather them into your wide and loving embrace.
Forever, and forever, always and forever. Amen.

When he finished, he stepped back into the circle, and the company watched in silence until the towering pyre began to collapse, sending bright sparks spinning up into the night-dark sky.

So that the brave Moorish dead would not have to suffer the ignominy of sharing a funeral fire with the enemy who had slain them, Prince Hasan had commanded a separate, smaller pyre to be made for the slain Templars and their disgraced leader. As the watchers began making their way slowly back to the village, this second pyre was fired, too. But, aside from Timotheus who paused to offer up a prayer for mercy on behalf of the misled Templars, no one stayed to watch.

Upon their return, Abbess Annora met them outside Dominico's house with word that Archbishop Bertrano was dead. "He was at peace to the end," she told them, "and passed away lightly as a sigh."

"I am sorry to hear it," said Rognvald. "He was a good man." Turning to Prince Hasan, he said, "I am sorry, too, that your fears have been realized."

"More blood will flow from this," replied Hasan ruefully. "Such is the will of Allah. So be it."

"There will be no more bloodshed," declared Cait firmly. "We will take the archbishop's body back to Santiago for burial, and we will tell them that he died at the hands of the Templars. Blame for his death will not be laid upon you or the people hereabouts. I will see to that."

"I am grateful, Ketmia. Unfortunately, it is a far distance"; the prince pointed out, "by the time you reached Santiago there would be little worth burying."

"In summer perhaps," remarked Alethea. "But it is winter now, and if we do not tarry along the way the cold will keep his body from corruption."

"Such things are known in Norway," offered Rognvald. "It may work here."

"Even if it did not," offered Cait, "we would be no worse off than before. But, Alethea is right; if we are to have any chance at all we must leave without delay." To Hasan, she said, "I am sorry, but it appears we will not be able to take advantage of your kind offer to winter at Al-Jelál."

"Alas," replied Hasan, "it would have been a rare and special pleasure. Nevertheless, I understand. Still," he added quickly, "perhaps you would not object if I see you safely on your way?"

"Not in the least," Cait replied. "I can think of nothing I would like better." She glanced up and saw the shadow of disappointment flit across Rognvald's features. As he turned away, she slipped her hand through his arm. "Well, there is perhaps just one other thing," she confided, adding, "Have you ever been to Caithness, my lord?"

By the end of the next day, all was ready. At dawn the following morning the company bade farewell to Brother Timotheus and his faithful village flock and set off, leading a wagon packed with snow and ice in which the archbishop's body was preserved. With them went Prince Hasan and a company of his Moorish soldiers, who would accompany them as far as Palencia where Gislebert and the nine surviving Templars would be turned over to Governor Carlo—with a request that they be detained long enough to allow a specially prepared report of their actions on behalf of the apostate Commander De Bracineaux to reach the pope, and for Cait and her company to reach the ship at Bilbao.

At Al-Jelál they stopped long enough to pick up a second wagon to follow the first. In this wagon were Paulo—who insisted he was well enough to face the rigors of the road—and three nuns of the Abbey of Klais Mairís, chosen by Abbess Annora to begin a new Order of the Gray Marys in Caithness: Sister Siâran, Sister Besa, and the newest member of the order, Sister Alethea. Accompanying the sisters, as a gift to the new order, was a large gilded cross—and, snug in its hiding place in the base of the cross, the Most Holy and Sacred Chalice, the Mystic Rose.

EPILOGUE

The memory of that night remains as vivid and vital as this morning's sunrise. I have merely to bring the image before my mind—the rock-cut sanctuary, the altar dressed in white, the great gilt wooden cross shimmering in the candlelight, the Inner Circle robed in white standing in attendance—and I am there again, on my knees, the Blessed Cup cradled in my hands.

It is empty as I look inside. But as I raise it to my lips the bowl is suddenly filled with crimson liquid. I take it into my mouth and taste the heavy sweetness—of life, of hope, of the everlasting joy of serving the Eternal One. With each remembrance, I drink again from the Holy Chalice and my vow, like the quickening liquid it contains, is renewed.

To remember, for me, is to enter again the vision I was granted on that night. "Not everyone sees a vision," Zaccaria told me then. "And not everyone who sees a vision sees the same thing. You have been richly blessed, brother."

True enough, but as it is written: from those to whom much has been given, much shall be required. My joy comes at a price which none but those who have likewise borne that heavy cost can ever know.

Caitríona knew. Pemberton also.

That night, as I took the sweet, life-changing liquid into my mouth and felt the holy fire spread through my dull limbs, the cavernous room, altar, and men who presided over the sacrament—everything!—vanished. I raised my eyes from the cup to see that I was kneeling before a man dressed in the robes of a simple priest—a young man, his hair dark and curly, his beard a thick black mass of tight curls through which his quick smile broke like a flash of light from a cloud-troubled sky. "Greetings, friend," he said, "I have been waiting for you."

"Brother Andrew." I had no need to ask—knowing it was he. "How may I serve you, lord?"

"I am not a lord that you should kneel to me." He reached down, took my elbow. "Does one servant kneel to another? Stand on your feet, brother, and let us speak to one another as servants together of the Great King."

He took my hand and turned it over, exposing the wrist. And there, imprinted on my flesh, was the livid red wound-like stigma: the Mark of the Rose. The other wrist bore the sign, too, and I gazed upon the blood-red marks in wonder.

"As you have been chosen," Brother Andrew said, "so you must choose."

I plucked up my courage to reply, but before I could speak he raised a hand in warning, saying, "But I would not have you choose in ignorance. For you must know that to be a guardian is both blessing and burden, and I would have you count the cost."

"Tell me, then."

"Any who take up the service of the cup will extend their lives in the world—far beyond the age reached by other men and women of mortal birth. You will neither age, nor experience frailty, infirmity, or decrepitude. Your allotted span will be measured in scores, not years, and you will grow great in wisdom."

I was just thinking that the burden did not seem overwhelming, when he said, "Know also that you will live to see your friends grow old and die, your children, too, and their children after them. Not only this, you will watch many whom you would befriend drown beneath the tides of illness, insanity, and evil which sweep restlessly over the world. You will see dear friends suffer and succumb; you will see good men stumble and fall by the wayside through weakness, and your heart will break—not once, but a thousand times."

I looked upon the wound-like marks on my wrists, and at last began to understand what it meant to be a guardian and what was being asked of me. *Could I shoulder such a burden,* I wondered, *could I watch those I loved fall one by one into the sleep of death? Could I stand aside and watch the sufferings of the world, and not yield to the crushing pain?*

"It is a hard thing you ask of me," I told him.

"It is a hard thing, yes," he agreed. "As it is written: many are called, but few are chosen. But if it helps to make the choice any easier, hear me when I say there will be no more guardians after you, my friend. You will be the last. You will live to see the glory of the Great King acknowledged throughout the world when the treasure so faithfully preserved by the Célé Dé is at last revealed. In you, the long obedience of these loyal Servants of Christ will be rewarded, and it will be the glory of the ages."

It was then I realized what Pemberton had been trying to tell me. *The pain is swallowed in peace, and grief in glory.*

He had been a guardian. He had known the pain and grief that now stood before me, and he wanted me to know that it would be all right. That, in the end, the pain of my guardianship would be redeemed, any grief I suffered would be swallowed in the glory to come. Ultimately, the blessing would be far greater than the burden.

"The time has come to decide, brother," said the White Priest. "What will you choose?"

"It is an honor to be chosen," I replied. "And I will do my best to prove myself worthy. Yes, I will serve."

Brother Andrew smiled and offered me a blessing. He then told me of the trials to come, and how I must prepare myself to meet them. We talked of this, and of other things before he went away and I awoke from the vision with the burning certainty that the course before me had been established long, long ago.

I was the last in a line that stretched back to a young man in the Orkney Isles—to Murdo, who was not willing to stand by and see his birthright stolen. Foolish, reckless, headstrong, and impetuous, Murdo, and Duncan, and Caitríona in their turn, remained true to the vision they were granted, to make of their place in the world a haven "far, far from the ambitions of small-souled men and their ceaseless striving." Together they made a place where the most precious and sacred objects under Heaven could reside undisturbed until the day of their unveiling, when the world should again see, and remember, and believe.